I Love
Bad Boys

I Love Bad Boys

Lori Foster
Janelle Denison
Donna Kauffman

BRAVA

KENSINGTON PUBLISHING CORP.

http://www.kensingtonbooks.com

BRAVA BOOKS are published by

Kensington Publishing Corp.
850 Third Avenue
New York, NY 10022

All Kensington titles, imprints and distributed lines are available at special quantity discounts for bulk purchases for sales promotion, premiums, fund-raising, educational or institutional use.

Special book excerpts or customized printings can also be created to fit specific needs. For details, write or phone the office of the Kensington Special Sales Manager: Kensington Publishing Corp., 850 Third Avenue, New York, NY, 10022. Attn. Special Sales Department. Phone: 1-800-221-2647.

Brava and the B logo Reg. U.S. Pat. & TM Off.

ISBN 0-7582-0134-6

First Kensington Trade Paperback Printing: August 2002
10 9 8 7 6 5 4 3 2 1

Printed in the United States of America

CONTENTS

Indulge Me
by Lori Foster
1

Naughty By Night
by Janelle Denison
91

. . . And When They Were Bad
by Donna Kauffman
189

Indulge Me

Lori Foster

To Jackie Floyd,
Thanks for providing the fun background information.
I know your night out was much more fun than mine!

Chapter One

Becky Harte inched through the doorway of the risqué sex shop, Wild Honey, with a great deal of trepidation. Warmth and the subtle scent of incense greeted her. She knew her eyes were huge, but she couldn't manage a single blink.

It was still something of a shock that the small, conservative town of Cuther, Indiana had such a shop in its midst.

It was doubly shocking that small town, conservative Becky would be visiting that shop.

Her heart pounded, her face was hot, and her hands shook. Never ever in her life had she expected to do such a thing. Yet here she was, not only inside Wild Honey, but on a sexual mission. A mission designed by her two well-meaning friends, Asia and Erica. Becky knew they were both watching her progress from the company lounge across the street, in the toiletries factory where they all three worked.

Before the door closed behind Becky, she peeked over her shoulder and sure enough she could see the twin pale faces of Erica and Asia pressed to the window on the second floor of the factory. She couldn't back out because they'd both know and she liked them too much to want them to consider her a coward.

The three of them had made a pact, and by gosh, she'd keep to her end of the deal.

Drawing a steadying breath, Becky released the door and it swung shut with a tinkling of chimes and a sense of finality that made her jump. Becky held her coat tightly closed at her throat and looked around. What she saw was . . . unexpected.

Wild Honey was actually pretty elegant. It was clean and neatly organized and colorful. There were display tables laden with books and tapes, every wall lined with shelves of more books, magazines, and some boxed items. Biting her lip, Becky forced herself to take a few steps. A woman behind the counter greeted her. "Hi. Can I help you find something?"

Good Lord! Surely the saleslady didn't expect her to discuss such things. Numb, Becky shook her head and turned away, hurrying to the back of the large room. An open door that led into another room offered her a place to hide. She ducked inside.

And immediately stalled.

Mouth falling open, Becky stared about in mingled horror and fascination at the items hung from the walls. Why, there were things that looked like . . . like *penises*. Enormously large penises. Blue, white, and black penises. Penises in every color of the rainbow. Two-foot long penises, for crying out loud. *Double-headed penises.*

Without realizing it, Becky drifted closer, mouth still gaping, eyes so wide it was a wonder her eyeballs didn't fall out. This had to be a joke. Sure, she wasn't experienced, but she wasn't an idiot either, and there was no way all those penises could be . . . functional. No way. It was impossible.

She looked away from the display of artificial penises with a disbelieving shake of her head and a barely audible snort. They were probably gag items, used for bachelor parties and such. That made more sense than anything else.

Her attention got snagged on a new contraption and she studied it. She had no idea what it might be, but there were boxes stacked beneath the one on display, with instructions printed on the back. Made of what looked to be hard plastic, the device had several elastic straps and little pointy rubber things sticking out here and there, and a place for batteries. Becky studied it, then picked up the box to read the description.

Gasping, she dropped the box, jerked around—and ran full tilt into a tall, hard male body.

She would have screamed if she had any breath. As it was, she staggered back from the bruising impact and almost fell over the stacked boxes. At the last second, the man caught her and held her upright.

"Hey, easy now."

Becky froze. Dear God, she recognized the voice that had haunted her most carnal dreams for two years now.

Big hands settled on her shoulders, steadying her, and with a wince of dread, Becky slowly looked up—into familiar mocking black eyes.

Oh no. *No, no, no*. Not someone she knew. Not this particular male someone.

He bent to meet her eye level, one glossy black brow raised, one side of his sensual mouth tilted up in a smile. "You okay, Ms. Harte?"

Becky squeezed her eyes shut, praying that not seeing him might help. It didn't. She was oh so aware of him standing there.

"Becky?" His voice was gentle, insistent, rough, and masculine. Her skin tingled from his touch and her heart lodged in her throat.

Using the edge of his fist, he tipped up her chin, which effectively closed her mouth, too. After a second, he chuckled. "You know, you're so damn red you're going to catch the place on fire."

Becky swallowed hard and rallied her scattered wits. In a whisper, she admitted, "I'm mortified."

"Yeah? How come?"

She tucked in her chin, refusing to look at him again.

George Westin was the man of her dreams, the epitome of everything dark and erotic and forbidden. Whenever she thought of how sex should be, she thought of George.

He had the most compelling eyes—dark, daring, filled with carnal knowledge and challenge. He looked at a woman, and she felt his attention like a physical stroke.

He was looking at her now. Becky gulped.

All the women at the factory adored George, and they all whispered about him. Becky had heard the rumors about his astounding reputation and the validations by a couple of the women he'd dated. By all accounts, George had . . . *a lot,* and knew how to use it. Becky wasn't entirely certain what *a lot* meant, except that he could make a woman very, very happy in bed.

For the two years that she'd known him, she'd done her best to hide her own reaction to him. She hadn't wanted him to see her as just one more woman who lusted after his gorgeous body and his sexual knowledge. She'd pretended an indifference to him, pretended to see him only as a supervisor, not as a man.

In truth, being anywhere near him made her tongue-tied.

Now here she was, not a foot away from him, his hot hands touching her, standing in the middle of a *porn* shop with pleasure probes behind her.

Becky groaned.

Apparently amused, George released her, only to throw a heavy arm around her shoulders. He led her a few feet away, his hold easy but secure. "Take deep breaths, Becky. It'll be all right."

At his casual familiarity, Becky peeked up at him again. His neatly trimmed, silky black hair was disheveled by the blustery wind outside, and his cheeks were ruddy with the cold. He must have just come inside. And of course, she had to literally run into him.

He leaned around to see her face. "I can call you Becky,

right? I mean, the situation lends a certain intimacy, don't you think?"

Think? She was supposed to think? He had to be kidding.

"Becky?"

He was incredibly tall. And he smelled incredibly good. She wanted to lean into him and inhale his wonderful scent.

At work she always made sure they stayed on a professional footing. George had often tried joking with her; he'd tried flirting with her a little, too, teasing her. But she'd known there was no future in it, that she couldn't get involved with him. She'd kept things friendly, because she'd rather have at least that much with him, than nothing at all. If she'd encouraged him, he was the type of man who would have wanted sex.

Incredible sex.

Naked, sweaty sex.

And she couldn't do that.

So he'd backed off. Not completely, because he still chatted with her and he sought her out more than most of the men she worked with. But he seemed to have accepted her unspoken decision—to be friendly associates, but nothing more.

The poor man had no idea she lusted after him every single night.

After clearing her throat—twice—Becky managed to say, "We're not at work, Mr. Westin, so sure, you may call me Becky. There's no reason to be formal . . ." She strangled on the word, *here*.

"Exactly." George gave her an approving smile, likely because she'd succeeded in stringing more than two words together. "And do call me George."

Like a sleepwalker, Becky allowed herself to be led through the shop. When she'd agreed to this daring scheme with Erica and Asia, she had envisioned running into some unknown, never-to-be-heard-from-again man and getting through the whole ordeal with a modicum of remote familiarity. Not once had she envisioned running into George.

Tomorrow, she'd see him at work, probably several times. He was a supervisor, not over her floor, but they had contact on and off throughout the day. He'd look at her, and he'd know she'd been here, checking out . . . penises and pleasure probes and God only knew what else.

She'd never survive the embarrassment.

George halted them next to a very small curtained booth well away from the wall displays. "Better?"

Becky drew a breath and forced herself to stop behaving like the backward and inexperienced hick she actually was. "I'm sorry. I'm just . . . well, I'm obviously not used to being in places like this."

"Obviously." George released her and shoved his hands deep into his pants pockets. His coat and suit coat parted over his middle, showing a flat abdomen, a wide chest. His hands pulled his slacks taut, and she noticed other, more interesting things.

He cleared his throat, and Becky jerked her gaze away from his belt buckle and the heavy weight of his sex beneath. Being in a porn shop must have muddled her senses to have her staring at him *there* like a lecher.

At his leisure, George lounged back against the wall, next to that dark curtain. *He* wasn't embarrassed. In fact, he still looked amused as he studied her face in that scrutinizing way of his. "Looking for something in particular, are you?"

At first, she thought he was referring to where she'd just been staring—at his crotch—and her mouth fell open in shock. Then she realized he meant his comment in a more general term, concerning her visit to the porn shop. Her reaction to that wasn't much better. Only sheer force of will kept her from running away. "I was just . . . curious," she lied.

She wasn't about to tell him the truth, that she was here to meet a man.

A specific man.

A man with precise sexual predilections, which would finally enable her to get rid of her virginity without distress.

"Uh-huh." George grinned, showing white teeth and a dimple in his cheek.

To Becky's mind, George was already too handsome for his own good. The dimple was overkill.

Even Erica had made note of him several times, and Becky trusted her opinion since Erica knew a whole lot more about men than she ever would. But Erica had also called George a rogue, a womanizer, even a sex addict.

Becky remembered that Erica had smiled when she'd made those accusations.

Asia, now madly in love with Cameron, had commented on George, too. In fact, Asia had commented on him several times recently, as if she'd been determined to make sure Becky noticed him. Becky shook her head. It wasn't likely any woman could not notice George, considering he stood so tall and was so dark and emanated such raw sex appeal.

She figured him to be in his late thirties, and judging by his reputation, he'd lived those thirty-odd years to the fullest.

"Cat got your tongue?" George cocked his head to the side. "Or are you considering buying one of those pleasure probes?"

Becky reeled back, scandalized, horrified, embarrassed beyond belief at the mere suggestion. "Of course not!"

George chuckled, but his chuckle dwindled into a warm smile when he looked at her mouth. He kept looking, his expression so fixed Becky began to fidget. "Calm down, Becky. I was just teasing."

The front door chimed and several more men from her workplace wandered in. Becky blanched at the thought of being recognized yet again. "Oh good Lord."

George glanced at the men. "Don't want to be seen here, huh?"

Panicked, Becky searched around for a place to hide. "I'd rather not, no."

"Then I'll be your white knight." So saying, George took her upper arm and moved the curtain aside. He stepped into the booth, dragging Becky with him. "We can hide in here until they're gone."

The curtain dropped back into place, leaving them in darkness. Becky went utterly still, more aware of George as a man than she'd ever been of any man in her life. Of course, she was sequestered with him in a tiny booth, in the darkness, in a porn shop.

How in the world had she gotten into this predicament?

She and her friends had made the deal—they'd each go to Wild Honey, find a man who shared an interest in her fantasy, and approach him.

The idea had been to get back into the sexual swing of things. Not that Becky had ever been in the swing. She was twenty-five and a blasted virgin, as innocent as a child, without a single speck of experience.

But not for the reasons her friends assumed. Yes, she was shy. Yes, she was moral and believed in love and marriage. But that had nothing to do with why she'd avoided any intimate contact with a man.

The real reason was a shame that ran bone-deep, an . . . affliction she'd dealt with using avoidance.

Until now.

Her proclaimed fantasy, that of bondage, had everything to do with it. If a man was tied up, well then he couldn't control anything. Like the lights. She could keep the room black as pitch. She could even blindfold him and there'd be nothing he could do about it. He'd probably even like it.

She'd be able to find out what all the hoopla was about sex, without worrying that he'd see her, or touch her. She'd be able to look at him, to sate herself on his body, to touch him and taste him and yet she'd keep her own appearance, her body, *her flaws,* private.

He'd never know.

Asia had gone first, and for her things had worked out perfectly, to the point where she was due to marry Cameron soon. Not that Becky expected to get married, not now, not ever. But she was so lonely, so hungry. She wanted to share lovemaking. She wanted to experience mind-blowing sex. She craved so, so much.

All she needed was the right man to indulge her.

Becky drew a breath, trying to reassure herself. Instead she breathed in George's scent again. It turned her insides to mush.

George moved beside her in the cramped space, and she heard a clink, like the dropping of change, then a small hum. Two seconds later, the booth lit up and a film played on the wall in front of them.

Becky stared. "This is a movie booth?"

"A place to see previews of the different videos before buying one." George studied her, strangely alert, as he waited for her reaction. "You pop in a quarter, pick the number of the film you're interested in, and you get to see a few minutes of it."

"My, um . . . what a good idea."

Becky turned away from George's scrutiny to watch the movie, and felt the increased acceleration of her heart. Fascination gripped her as the lights flickered and shifted. She saw a well-built man, dressed only in worn jeans, wander into a darkly lit room. The film was poor quality, gritty. But it still held her enthralled.

Beside her, George shifted again, moving behind her, watching the show over her head. He seemed to take up too much space in the small room, with his shoulders that were twice as wide as hers, his body big and solid and hard.

Tension tightened all her muscles, from the movie, from George's nearness, from the rapid way things were progressing. Becky could smell him again, the delicious scent of cologne and hot male flesh.

The man on-screen moved into a room—where a woman was tied to a bed. Becky started in surprise. Why, this movie was about *bondage*. Had George chosen it on purpose?

The woman was atop the covers, completely naked. Her legs were held wide apart, secured to the foot posts on the bed with black cords. Her arms stretched out over her head and were also tied. She was vulnerable, fully exposed. She wore a blindfold and as she sensed the man's approach, she moaned softly.

Unable to look away, Becky drew a strangled breath—and felt her back touch George's chest. She started to jerk forward again, but he settled his hands at either side of her throat, keeping her in place.

"Shhh. If you make too much noise," he said close to her ear, "they'll know we're in here."

Shaken by the touch of his warm breath in her ear, Becky whispered, "Who?"

"The guys from the factory."

"Oh." That's right. The reason he'd led her into this booth in the first place was to avoid detection by others. "Thank you."

The man in the movie knelt on the bed beside the naked woman. She squirmed, a little frantic, her bare breasts jiggling with her efforts, rising and falling, but the ropes held her tightly. She couldn't move more than an inch.

She couldn't move away from him.

The man trailed his fingertips over her arm, up and down, over her ribs, making the woman twist and moan some more. Slowly, very slowly, he cupped her breast and gently squeezed. Becky's own breasts tingled, her nipples pulled tight.

George leaned down and this time his warm breath teased her temple. He spoke in a drawing whisper that made her eyelids feel heavy, her insides warm and liquid. "You ever watch a dirty movie, Becky?"

She could barely speak, didn't dare blink. She shook her head, her gaze fixed on the movie so she wouldn't miss a thing.

George's fingers caressed her shoulders, subtly, with encouragement. "I know women," he whispered, "and you, Becky Harte, like this particular film."

Was she really so obvious? Did she even care? "I . . ." *I want to do that to you.* Becky knew she couldn't say that, so she said nothing.

"Some people are turned on by dominating, some by being dominated."

Becky swallowed hard. "He won't hurt her?"

"Of course not. That has nothing to do with bondage, or with pleasure."

George spoke with confidence, making Becky wonder if he had firsthand knowledge of this. "I . . . I see."

The man began kissing the woman. His mouth touched her nipples, first softly, then sucking until she cried out. He rasped her with his thumbs, and laughed when she tried to escape him. He kissed her again, licking everywhere, her throat, over her breasts, down her stomach . . . *between her legs.*

The woman jumped.

So did Becky.

"Shhh," George murmured, making Becky shiver in reaction.

The woman arched, but her movements were limited because of her restraints. She cried out, bucked, and bowed but the man stayed with her, his mouth on her, against her sex, his hands holding her hips steady, and seconds later she found her release in a long raw groan that had Becky catching her breath and shaking uncontrollably.

"Becky?"

Feeling almost feverish, Becky wavered, and found herself flush against George's body.

George had an erection.

On-screen, the woman moaned in soft acceptance. Inside the booth, Becky did the same. She could feel George, long and hard, firmly pressed against her behind. It was a first for her.

Everything today was a first.

"Watch," George insisted, and Becky could have sworn she felt his mouth touch the rim of her ear. She all but melted into a puddle.

Since she couldn't seem to draw her attention away from the film, George's instruction was unnecessary.

From one frame to the next, the setting of the film changed, and now the woman sat astride the man, while it was his arms stretched high and tight, tied to the bedposts. His head was tipped back, his chest muscles starkly defined as the woman rode him hard and fast.

Becky breathed too hard in reaction. This was what she wanted. Oh, she wanted it so much. The man in the movie wasn't blindfolded, and he wasn't nearly as appealing as George. But Becky could pretend he was. She could pretend that he'd take his pleasure with her, and not be able to see her, not be able to touch her.

Suddenly the woman's mouth opened on a scream and Becky knew it was a scream of pure excitement. The woman shuddered, climaxed . . . and Becky felt George's hand slip around her to settle beneath her left breast. His fingers were hot, long, curving on her rib cage. His hair brushed her cheek, cool and silky. His heart rapped against her back.

Awareness and need held Becky perfectly still so George wouldn't stop touching her.

"Your heart is racing, Becky."

This time she knew for certain his mouth touched her. He placed a gentle kiss on her temple—and the film died.

Neither of them moved. The sound of her breathing filled the small booth. Becky had no idea what to do or what to say, so she did nothing. George's big hand was still on her, beneath her coat, right below her breast, not moving, just resting there, warm and sure and confident.

"I think I know what section you were looking for, Becky."

In that moment, more than anything, Becky wanted him to touch her breast. It was insane, but she craved his touch. "You . . . you do?"

"Oh yeah. You want some restraints, don't you, sweetheart?"

He'd called her sweetheart. "Um . . ." Should she just blurt it out? How did a woman go about telling a man she'd like to tie him to her bed? And she did want to do that.

With George.

Becky was now very glad she'd run into him, and not some other man. This small incident felt right in a way she knew it wouldn't have been with anyone else. She'd been wanting George for a long time, so now was her chance.

It was possible that he'd chosen that particular film because he was into bondage, and wanted her to know it. Becky found it hard to imagine that George—sexy, gorgeous, experienced George—would be willing to leave himself at her mercy. But the idea was a very tempting one.

The pros and cons of having sex with a man she worked with winged through her head in rapid order. But before she could find the right thing to say, George moved the curtain aside. "C'mon. I'll help you."

Again, Becky found herself being led by him. He drew her to the back of the store toward another isolated room. Along the way, Becky looked around at all the amazing contraptions. One particular item caught her interest and she turned her head to stare.

Beside her, George paused. With his dark gaze on her face, he said, "It's for female pleasure. Most of the stuff in here is geared for women."

"Really?"

At her surprise, George narrowed his eyes. "It's not always as easy for a woman to climax as it is for a man."

He spoke so casually that Becky blinked, still looking at the small contraption and trying to figure it out. There were so many things in the shop that seemed to require an instruction manual. "I see."

"Do you?" When she didn't answer, he expounded on his explanations. "Just having a man inside a woman doesn't always do it for her. She needs to be touched other ways, other places."

Becky opened her mouth, but nothing came out. She tilted her head, studying the ridiculous device, but still it didn't quite make sense how it would work.

George made an impatient sound. "You can't be that naive."

Becky turned to stare up at him.

He ran a hand over his head, further mussing his hair. Then, to her horror, he snatched up the device and held it in front of her. "See this opening? It fits over a man's cock. When he rides a woman, this part right here strokes her where she's most sensitive. Because it vibrates, if he goes deep inside and just holds still, it'll work too."

Becky was floored by this outpouring of sexual instruction. George didn't seem the least bit shy about discussing things with her. It was astonishing and embarrassing and very educational.

She wasn't sure if she should thank him or not.

When she remained silent, he frowned. "Becky, do you understand?"

"Yes, I think so."

"You *think* so?"

Her curiosity overrode her shyness. "Have you ever . . . ? You know."

"What?" He waved the thing under her nose, then tossed it back on the shelf. "Worn one of those? No way. I don't need them." He looked at her mouth and his dark eyes glittered. "Any man worth his salt knows how to make a woman come without all these gizmos."

Ohmigosh, ohmigosh. Becky gulped. Would he illustrate that for her, too? She sort of hoped so.

His gaze moved down her body, to her lap. "Remember the guy in the video? There are better ways to ensure a woman's satisfaction."

There it was, his explanation and that look that felt like a physical touch, given with his blatant suggestion that he enjoyed kissing a woman . . . *there,* and Becky's knees went weak. She caught the shelf for support, refusing to crumble in front of him, even over the idea of oral sex.

Trying to sound as cavalier as George, she changed the subject. "It was designed by a doctor."

He smiled. "Yeah."

"Wouldn't you think most doctors had medical emergencies or something to occupy their time?"

This time George laughed outright. "Amazing."

"What's amazing?"

He didn't explain, he just took her hand and finished leading her to the other room. Becky looked around in awe. Velvet-lined handcuffs, dark blindfolds, satin ropes and restraints of every style and extreme decorated the walls, some even hanging from the ceiling. "Oh my."

George crossed his arms over his chest. "Did you bring your charge card?"

"No." She didn't want any legal documentation from her trip here. "But I brought plenty of cash."

Looking very pleased, George said, "Then allow me to guide you through a few purchases. And, Becky?"

"Hmm?"

"When we're through, we'll set a date to get together."

Becky whipped around to face him. "A date?"

"Oh yeah." He touched her cheek and tucked her hair behind her ear. "You see, Becky, we're of a similar mind. And I think we'll get along real well, don't you?"

Chapter Two

George watched that intriguing color darken Becky Harte's soft cheeks again. God, but he loved the way the woman blushed. Since he was still touching her, he even felt the heat. Would she flush all over like that when he had her securely bound to his bed, naked and hungry and waiting for him to give her a screaming orgasm?

He had a feeling she would, and he could hardly wait.

What a little fraud she was.

He'd worked at the factory as a supervisor for two years now. In that time, he'd gotten to know Becky well. Or so he'd thought. She was very young—too young he'd sometimes thought. And though at twenty-five she should have had her share of experience, Becky still had "sweet and innocent" stamped all over her in a way that made a man's primal instincts go on red-hot alert.

From her big blue eyes, to her bouncing blond curls, to her sweet small-town accent, she exuded artless naïveté. She was the type of woman who—he'd thought—would want to get married if she got intimate with a man.

Still, he thought of her nearly every day, and wanted her more often than that. At work, he couldn't help stopping to chat with her whenever possible. She was so sweet, so open, damn near every man at the factory felt drawn to her, himself included. But Becky never seemed to notice.

And she never seemed to want male attention.

She'd certainly turned him down. She hadn't been rude or inconsiderate about it, but rather she'd feigned misunderstanding. He'd tease, and she'd give him a blank look, then call him *Mr.* Westin in a way that made it clear she considered him a supervisor, a casual work friend, and nothing more.

In many ways, her youth, her fresh-faced candor, and her disinterest had made her more appealing, to the point he nearly felt obsessed with her. Of course, her body had helped in that, too.

He absolutely burned with the need to see beneath her conservative clothes.

Her long skirts and buttoned-up blouses couldn't quite disguise a sweetly rounded figure ripe with curves. The way she tried to conceal herself only made his imagination go wild. More often than was wise, he'd fantasized about getting her into bed.

And now he knew the truth. Sweet, innocent Becky wasn't into marriage. No, she was into bondage. She wanted to be tied down, she wanted to be vulnerable. She wanted to be at a man's mercy.

Yet she still blushed, and she honestly seemed to be clueless about things sexual in nature.

What an intriguing conflict.

Becky Harte wanted to be dominated—and George was just the man to accommodate her. He sure as hell wasn't going to let any other guy do it.

With her bottom lip caught between her teeth, Becky turned away from him to study the wall of blindfolds. George studied her ass.

He could hardly wait to get his hands on her.

Today she wore a beige denim skirt that hung clear to her ankles, but he could see that her feet were small, her ankles trim. Her bulky coat over a loose thick sweater hid her waistline, but couldn't hide the thrust of her full breasts.

George's palm tingled as he remembered slipping his hand beneath her coat to feel her heartbeat. She'd trembled gently, her heart thumping hard and fast, her breast a warm firm weight against the back of his hand.

He'd wanted to slide his fingers higher and cup her breast. He'd wanted to stroke her nipple until he felt it puckering tight.

She'd wanted the same.

But not teasing her now would get him further later, so George had controlled himself, and in the process, he'd controlled her, though she might not have realized it. All in all, sexual preferences aside, he was experienced enough to know that she *was* innocent, and that delightful mix of timidity and hot sensuality had him hard and more than ready.

And here he'd considered Cuther, Indiana a dull place. He grinned. With Becky Harte wandering loose, there was nothing dull about it. Since first meeting her, he'd wanted her. Against his better judgment and her apparent disinterest, he'd wanted her.

Now he'd finally have her.

George watched her pick up and examine a black velvet blindfold with shaking fingers. She peeked at him out of the corner of her eye, then lifted her chin, tucked the box under her arm, and moved on to the handcuffs.

His thoughts mired in carnal speculation, George followed.

If she wanted to wear a blindfold, that was fine and dandy with him. He liked her big blue eyes, but it was her body he was dying to see.

Maybe it would help her to hide, to not see what he was seeing. He realized now that much of her past reticence was due to inexperience. Her shock at the items sold in Wild Honey had proven that.

Or maybe she liked the idea of being blindfolded because she thought it would heighten the sense of touch and anticipation. Maybe it would feed her need to be controlled. George shrugged. He would happily oblige her.

He'd leave her wanting more.

When Cameron, another supervisor at the factory, had first approached him with this bizarre plan, George had been skeptical. He assumed Cameron had seen his lust for Becky, and was pulling a joke on him.

Cameron was due to marry Becky's friend, Asia, and he'd claimed the women had some goofy dare going that was centered around the porn shop. Cameron had refused to reveal the details behind his and Asia's circumstances, but he had explained that it was Becky's turn, and Asia wanted to make sure Becky wasn't hurt.

George wanted to make sure, too.

Both Cameron and Asia thought that by ensuring Becky's partner—him—they could protect her from other, more unscrupulous men. Smart. The thought of Becky going off with anyone else set George on edge.

She'd been unattainable, a fantasy, for too long. Now that he was part of this plan, he'd already begun to think of her in *his* bed, already begun to imagine all the carnal fun *he'd* give her. Until she indulged his craving for her, he damn sure didn't want any other man touching her.

After they were through . . . well, he just didn't know, didn't want to think about that right now. The idea of Becky getting down and dirty with anyone else felt repugnant.

Cameron had told George that if he was willing—*ha* — he was to meet Becky at the shop and show an interest in bondage wares. That had nearly floored him, but Cameron, damn him, had been so blasé about the whole thing, George had refused to show his shock.

Becky Harte and bondage—a combination guaranteed to give any guy a steel boner.

Now he was beyond glad he'd taken up the challenge. Bondage wasn't something he'd explored much in the past, but hey, if that's what it took to finally get Becky into bed, he was willing, able, and ready. Actually, now that he'd thought about it—and he hadn't been able to think about much else—having Becky tied to his bed appealed to him in a dozen different ways.

"There's so much to choose from."

George watched the expressions flicker across her face when he asked, "Do you want it rough or gentle?"

Her eyes widened comically before she gathered herself. She cleared her throat and made a point of not looking at him. "I don't think the idea is for anyone to be roughed up, do you?"

That was a relief. He wasn't into manhandling women at all. Just the opposite. Once he had Becky bound, he'd worship her body until she cried with the pleasure of it. He could hardly wait.

"How about the velvet cuffs? They close with Velcro, so they'll be quick and easy to use." And he'd have her snared before she even knew what he was doing.

His cock throbbed with that thought and the accompanying image of Becky spread-eagle, naked atop his mattress, taut, trembling, waiting for what he'd do to her.

Her chin lifted. "Good idea." She snagged up the box and held it.

"Why don't you let me carry those for you?"

Face averted, Becky thrust her packages at him. "Thank you."

With every second that passed, George got more turned on, more eager. He rubbed his chin and thought about everything he wanted to do to her. He eyed her legs, then made another suggestion. "There are ankle cuffs too."

She wore a considering frown. "Do you think they're necessary?"

Oh yeah. "That's up to you."

"Yes, of course." She bit her lip, snagged up the package, and tossed it at him.

"Anything else?"

"Like what?"

Her determination was adorable. "I don't know. It's your show, Becky. You tell me."

That startled her, then she beamed. "Yes, it is, isn't it?" She looked around, her brow puckered in a frown, then shook her head. "No, I think that's it for now."

"Becky?"

She peeked up at him.

"Do you want me to pay for these?"

Her shoulders slumped in relief. "Would you?" She dug in her purse and pulled out several bills. "I have to admit, the idea of getting caught at the register doesn't exactly thrill me."

George didn't take the money. She'd be fulfilling a two-year long fantasy for him, so letting her pay didn't seem right. "This'll be my treat."

His offer stiffened her spine. "Oh no, it's my expense."

Seeing that she wouldn't change her mind, George shrugged. "All right then."

"But aren't you going to buy anything?"

He'd already given due thought to his own purchase. "Yeah, I think I'll get the video we watched. We only saw a small portion of it. Wouldn't you like to see the rest?"

Becky flushed. "If you'll watch it with me."

"Absolutely." He'd watch her watching it. Seeing the fascination on her face was better than anything on-screen.

Her breath came fast. "When?"

George could see she was anxious, which fed his own urgency. "Friday night?"

It took her a moment before she screwed up her courage. "All right, yes. You can come to my place. I'll order a pizza if that's okay."

He'd rather have her in his house, on his ground. But it wasn't worth debating the issue. "Do you have a VCR?"

She bobbed her head. "Yes."

They'd watch the movie, then get those restraints out of the box and break them in proper. God, he could hardly wait. Though today was Thursday, it felt like Friday was more than a month away.

George forced a smile. "Six o'clock?" They both got off work at five, so that'd give her an hour to get home and get ready for him.

"All right."

By silent agreement, they started making their way to the register. Becky kept watch for other customers, and when they neared the front of the store, George took pity on her and told her to wait out front for him. She smiled and quickly ducked through the door.

When he joined her minutes later, he caught her waving to the factory. He looked up, but saw no one. "Your friends?"

She yelped and whirled to face him. "What? Oh, yes. I think I saw . . . uh . . . Erica."

"Erica Lee?"

"Yes." Becky frowned in suspicion. "Do you know her?"

He knew both Erica and Asia, mostly because Becky hung out with them every day during breaks and lunch. "Just in passing."

"Erica's dated nearly every guy at the factory." She glanced up at him, then away. "You've never been out with her though."

"Nope." Erica Lee was a pushy broad, demanding and too damn independent. She epitomized what many men termed a ball buster. She was sexy, no doubt about that, but he liked gentler women.

He liked Becky.

They walked across the street to the parking lot for the factory. When they reached Becky's car, George handed her the bag. She took it, smiled up at him, and said, "Thank you."

His gaze settled on her mouth. Damn it, he couldn't wait another second. For two years he'd wondered what it would be like to kiss her, how she'd taste, how she'd fit against his body. "Friday is too damn many hours away."

Becky gave him a look of confusion.

"I'm going to kiss you, Becky."

Her eyes widened and she stumbled back a step. "You are?"

"It'll be all right," he murmured, leaning down slowly so he wouldn't startle her. "Consider it a small prelude to tomorrow night, all right?"

Her lips parted. "But . . ."

He cupped her nape, turned her face up to his. Her blond hair was as soft as he'd always imagined. It felt warm against the back of his hand. "Just one kiss, Becky."

Her eyes drifted shut. "Yes."

She had one of the prettiest mouths George had ever seen, soft and full, always ready to smile. She never wore lipstick, but that was fine by him. He loved the way her naked mouth looked.

The moment his mouth settled on hers, he realized she tasted wonderful as well. She was breathing too hard and fast, as if she'd never been kissed before, but George decided it was anticipation that had her nearly panting. He understood that, because he wanted her so badly right now, he felt near to exploding.

Her bag dropped to the ground with a thump.

One of her hands touched his chest, fisted in his coat. The other curled over his biceps.

George slipped an arm around her waist, pulled her up close against his body, and sank his tongue deep with a groan. Her mouth wasn't only pretty, it was delicious, too. Sweet.

And damn, she was hot.

She went on tiptoe and kissed him back, awkwardly at first, but with enthusiasm. She stroked his tongue with her own, even sucked at his tongue a bit.

It was a caress guaranteed to make him nuts.

He wasn't just kissing a woman, he was kissing Becky. And she was wild for him.

Finding himself overwhelmed with rioting sensation for the first time in ages, George hugged Becky closer until their bodies pressed from knees to chest, until he could feel the wild beat of her heart and the gentle cushion of her belly. He wanted to absorb her. He wanted to take her right here, right now.

Lost in the sensuality of the moment, he drifted his hand down to that curving bottom of hers. She was a sexy handful and Friday night she'd be his.

Her ragged moan brought him to his senses. George lifted his head and looked around. Thankfully the lot was empty, but it was still a public lot, still out in the open and visible to anyone driving by or coming in or out of the building. Cold wind blasted his face and tossed Becky's hair, but it had little effect on his lust. He teetered on the ragged edge and knew it. "Jesus."

Becky, still clinging to him, still burning hot, stared up at him with vague eyes and a damp mouth and rosy cheeks. "George?"

He wanted to drag her behind a parked car, lift her long skirt, open his pants, and sink into her. He just knew she'd be wet. And tight. And she'd groan. . . .

He had to stop. Now.

Damn it, he wasn't a man who went crazy with lust. He wasn't a man who took women in parking lots in the middle of cold fall weather. He was a man used to control, and

Becky, more than most women, wanted his control. She wanted him to restrain her with velvet bonds.

He shook with that thought and the resultant carnal images.

"I'm sorry." He drew a ragged breath and tried for a smile. "We're out in the open, baby."

Her eyes were large and dark and hungry.

George muttered another curse. "Look, Becky, maybe you should just come home with me now. We're both free tonight, right?"

"Oh." Becky stiffened, looked around in appalled awareness of their surroundings. The warm flush of excitement was replaced by the hot wash of embarrassment. "Oh no, I can't. Not yet."

"Why?" George was so tense he'd never live till Friday. He wasn't sure he'd survive another two minutes.

"I'm not . . . ready."

Not ready? The hell she wasn't. She'd been clinging to him, all over him, with him every step of the way.

George drew himself up on an ugly suspicion. Did she have another date for tonight? Had he just warmed her up for another man? No way in hell was she going to crawl into bed with another guy who'd get to tie her up and watch her burn.

The mere thought had George outraged, and that bothered him, too. What she did away from him shouldn't concern him—but damn it, it did. He frowned. Maybe they should get a few things straight right now.

But Becky was back to blushing and she turned to fumble with her car door. The second she had it open, she slid into her seat and stuck the key in the ignition.

George picked up the bag she'd dropped and handed it to her. Leaning down into the car, eyes narrowed, he said, "Listen, Becky . . ."

She locked her hands on the steering wheel. "I have to hurry. Asia and Erica are, um, coming over tonight."

Asia and Erica? Well, that was different. She could visit with all the women she wanted to. Then it occurred to George how close the three women were. They spent every break, every lunch hour together at work. Would Becky tell them everything? Would she share every intimate detail? Would they know he intended to restrain her with hand- and foot-cuffs?

Women could be so damn gossipy. George wasn't sure he wanted his private affairs discussed—especially before he'd even *had* the private affair. He frowned and rubbed his jaw. "Erica and Asia, huh?"

Becky nodded so hard, her curls bounced wildly. "Yes. But I'll be ready Friday. I promise."

She looked eager to escape him. George gave up. "All right." But he added, his tone tinged with warning, "I'll see you at work tomorrow."

That idea seemed to horrify her. She gave him a sickly smile, slammed her door, and started the car. George stepped back and Becky, with an airy wave and unnecessary haste, drove away.

Friday. About twenty-four hours. He could wait, just barely.

But no way would he allow her to avoid him at work. Regardless of her kinky preference for bonds, Becky was naive so she probably didn't understand what they'd started. He'd have to let her know that they were now on new footing. They had something going, and he expected to reap the benefits of their new association for as long as it lasted.

In fact, the sooner they got that straightened out, the better.

Becky barely got to the top of the stairs leading to her second-floor apartment when she felt the stairs shaking. She knew even before she turned back to look that it was Asia and Erica thundering up the steps after her. She unlocked her apartment door and waited.

Asia and Erica burst onto the landing. Asia looked ripe with curiosity, and Erica was grinning like a loon. They both saw her, grabbed her, and screamed together, "You did it!"

Becky couldn't help but laugh. They knew how shy she was, knew that she never dated. For her to have actually gone through with her end of the pact was nothing short of a miracle. "Shhh. Come inside before my neighbors call the police. They'll think you're both accosting me."

The women moved inside, still huddled together, and shut the door. The second they all had their coats off, Asia enfolded Becky in a tight hug. "Becky, *that kiss*. Oh man. We watched from the window, and *shew*. Talk about a scorcher. Even Erica was impressed. That man's ears were steaming."

Erica snatched her up for a hug, too. "And you were in the shop for so long." She held Becky back and teased, "Had to check it all out, huh?"

"No! Of course not. It's just that . . . well, George and I got to talking . . ."

"And?" Erica squeezed her. "Did you buy any bondage stuff?"

Blushing, Becky gestured toward the bag. "Actually, George went through the checkout for me. Wasn't that sweet of him?"

Both women went mute. Asia rolled her lips in and stared at Erica with a worried frown.

Erica finally laughed. "George Westin, sweet? Now, Becky, honey, don't get disillusioned. He's a wolf, a hunk, the baddest of the bad boys and sexy as they come, but no way in hell would any sane woman call him sweet."

Becky thought he was very sweet. And very sexy.

"Becky," Asia cautioned, "he'll eat you for dessert if you're not careful."

Becky's face flamed at that unintentional double entendre. If they only knew how partial George had seemed to that idea. She remembered the way he'd stared at her lap while claiming he knew exactly how to make a woman happy in the sack.

She lifted her chin, not about to let them talk her out of her decision. She wanted George, and he was willing. That was good enough for her. "He's the one."

Asia surprised her by nodding in satisfaction. "I just knew it."

Erica frowned at her. "What do you mean, you just knew it?"

"I, ah, well, I could tell he was a bit kinky and because he obviously knows women, he'll be the perfect man for Becky. That's all I meant."

Becky wasn't quite convinced, but then Erica dumped out her bag. "Oh my. Look at this stuff."

Being fair-skinned was a curse, Becky thought, as she felt her face turn hot yet again. At this rate, she was going to give herself a sunburn.

Planning to handcuff a big muscular man to her bed for sexual purposes, and actually discussing it with her friends, were two different things. Normally she told them everything, but now, because it was George—her secret fantasy man—the idea of discussing him made her feel disloyal.

Erica, correctly reading her hesitation, looked at her with a wide smile. She pulled the velvet-lined handcuffs out of the box and let them dangle from her finger. "I can just see Geoge now, all stretched out and naked, straining, sweaty, sexy . . ."

Becky snatched the cuffs from her and stuffed them back into the bag. "Are you two staying around awhile?"

Erica folded her arms and looked at Asia. "Is she trying to get rid of us?"

Asia lifted one brow. "Probably wanting to moon over George."

"She can moon with us, right?"

"We'll give her pointers."

Erica laughed. "Have you ever tied up a man, Asia?"

"Well . . . no."

"That's what I thought."

Asia flipped her long brown hair over her shoulders. "I have a good imagination though."

"You'd have to, because I can't see Cameron letting you tie him down any time in the near future." She heaved a sigh. "Looks like it's up to me to instruct her."

"And I suppose you have experience in bondage?"

"Why certainly." Erica winked. "Men are most enjoyable when controlled, you know."

Becky ignored her friends and headed for the kitchen. She tied on a starched white apron over her denim skirt. "I'll put on some coffee," she called to Erica and Asia, "to go with the cookies I made this morning."

While her two friends continued to debate sexual experiences, Becky pondered the wonders of experiences to come. Though she was nervous, she could hardly wait. *Stretched out naked, straining, sweaty and sexy* . . . Oh yeah, she could hardly wait to see George that way.

In between conjuring up images of George naked, George touching her, George kissing her again, Becky remained aware of Asia and Erica sitting at her small kitchen table. They blustered back and forth, teasing and joking. Erica claimed to have a lot of sexual experience, and neither Becky nor Asia disbelieved her. She was a strong, confident woman, and she knew what she wanted where men were concerned. But they still liked to tease her about her hard-nosed ways with the guys.

Asia on the other hand had gotten involved with Cameron during her foray into the porn shop. In whirlwind fashion, they'd both fallen hard, and subsequently gotten engaged on Valentine's Day, a mere month ago. The wedding would follow just as soon as they could get everything arranged.

As Becky measured coffee, she considered Asia and Cameron. Unlike Erica, Becky didn't doubt for a minute that Cameron would let Asia do whatever made her happy, even if it meant tying him up.

"When's the big date, hon?" Erica asked.

Drawn from her thoughts, feeling the tiniest bit melancholy because Asia had found something so special, Becky shrugged. "Tomorrow. After work."

Asia flopped back in her seat. "So soon?"

Erica snickered. "I don't remember you and Cameron waiting. And why should Becky wait anyway? If George is willing, and it looks like he is, why then, I say go for it."

The coffee machine began spitting and Becky got out three cups. She set them on the table near the matching sugar bowl, then filled the small creamer. "If I wait, I'm liable to chicken out."

Erica looked at the cloth napkins and silver spoons Becky arranged on the table. "You're such a Suzy Homemaker. It's a wonder some guy hasn't talked you into marrying him yet. Men adore the domestic types. Makes them secure."

Without meaning to, Becky heard herself say, "George is already secure."

"Oh Lord." Erica tangled her hands in her blue-black hair and groaned. "She's singing his praises and the man hasn't even made it to her mattress yet."

Becky frowned. "Well he is."

"And she's defensive of him too!"

Asia shook her head. "Erica, not all men are weak asses."

"No, only most of them."

Asia threw her spoon at her. "You, lady, are a sad cynic."

Erica merely laughed. Trying to ignore them both, Becky

got up to pour the coffee. She'd just finished filling all three cups when her doorbell rang.

She froze. Somehow, with absolute conviction, she knew who was at her door.

Asia and Erica stared at her, then Asia took the coffeepot from her and set it on the hot pad. "Expecting company?"

"No."

Erica rolled her eyes. "Well, do you suppose you ought to see who it is?"

"Uh . . ." Becky wrung her hands together. She knew who it was, she just didn't know what he wanted.

Asia pushed back from the table. "I'll get it."

"Wait." Becky hustled after Asia, and Erica fell into a hurried trot behind her. En masse, in parade fashion, they quick-stepped it to the door. Asia turned the doorknob just as Becky reached her.

Provocative as the original sin, George lounged in the door frame with a devil's smile. His long-lashed, black eyes were glittering with intent.

At the sight of him, Becky drew up short. Erica plowed into her. They both knocked into Asia.

"Hey, easy now." George, somewhat startled by the un-expected greeting, reached out and kept them all three from toppling. He ended up with his arms full of females—and to Becky's eye, he didn't seem to mind in the least.

Chapter Three

George chuckled as the women began righting themselves. He didn't exactly hurry to get them out of his arms, but then, hey, he liked holding women. "Helluva greeting, ladies. Thanks."

Erica, the black-haired witch, managed to send her elbow into his middle before pulling away. George grunted, but refused to give her the satisfaction of rubbing at it.

Asia gave him a chiding look and muttered in all seriousness, "*Behave.*"

Becky just stared up at him with that adorable look of innocent shock that seemed to melt his heart, his common sense, and his touted self-control. She didn't move away, and he damn sure wasn't going to insist. They stared at each other, and finally she blinked her way into speech. "George. What are you doing here?"

Her blond curls were mussed—a typical state for Becky, he was beginning to realize—and he went about smoothing them back into place. As badly as he wanted her naked and under him, he enjoyed simply touching her, too.

He ignored Erica, and only winked at Asia to reassure her, then said to Becky, "You forgot your change."

"My change?"

"From your . . . purchases?" George wasn't sure if she'd

told her two coconspirators about the bondage stuff yet, so he didn't want to let the cat out of the bag. All in all, it was a weak-ass excuse to be calling on her now, but it was all he could come up with.

Erica rolled her green eyes and drawled, "He means the cuffs and the blindfold, Becky."

Predictably enough, Becky gasped, embarrassed by the mere mention of the items.

George wanted to smack Erica, but Asia saved him the trouble. She shouldered the other woman and frowned fiercely. Erica gave her a "what?" look that wasn't the least convincing.

George decided to continue ignoring that one. "Remember, I paid with your money. You had change coming." He pulled out the bills and coins and put them into Becky's hand.

She stared at the money. "Thanks."

Asia shoved her way between them. She caught George's arm and pulled him through the doorway, then pushed the door shut. "We were just having coffee, George. Why don't you join us?"

"Yeah." Erica grinned. "Join us. Becky even made cookies."

George eyed Becky in the frilly little apron, and all sorts of fetish images flooded through his already taxed brain. Hell, it was only an apron, and if he remembered right, his grandmother used to wear one.

But damn, it sure looked different on Becky than it had on Gram.

Sandwiched between Asia and Erica, he allowed them to drag him to the kitchen. They seemed awfully eager to keep him around, but then, it had been Asia's idea, according to Cameron, that he should be the man to hook up with Becky.

He owed her big-time, he decided, then he noticed how the apron tied snug at Becky's waist emphasized the flare of her hips. Usually her clothes were concealing. He cleared his throat and sought casual conversation.

"You bake, Becky?" Somehow, that fit. He wouldn't be at all surprised to find out she knit and canned, too.

"They're just chocolate chip cookies," she mumbled. "No big deal."

"My favorite." Along the way to the kitchen, George took in the sight of her apartment. It was small, a little crowded with knickknacks and photos. Her sofa was floral, her curtains frilly, everything spotlessly clean. It was so like Becky that he liked it instantly. Her home felt warm and cozy and comfortable.

It felt like a . . . home.

They stepped into the small kitchen and George held out a chair for Asia, who was charmed, then Erica, who was sardonic.

Becky bustled about, looking like a very sexy Martha Stewart clone, getting out another cup and saucer, arranging the cookies on an ornate plate—studiously avoiding eye contact with him. George decided to let her get away with that for now. Once he had her alone, he'd show her there was no reason to be shy with him.

"Asia," he asked, again seeking mundane conversation to ease the tension, "how's Cameron doing?"

"He's great."

"He's exhausted," Erica corrected. "Wedding plans and all that, you know."

George set his teeth and smiled at Asia. "Things moving right along?"

"A few glitches. Nothing major." She snatched up a cookie as soon as Becky put the plate on the table. "That's typical of every wedding, I suppose."

Erica snorted. "Every marriage, too."

"Someday," Asia told her, "some guy is going to make you eat those words."

"Right. Don't hold your breath."

George picked up a cookie, handed it to Erica, and said, "Here. Something useful for your mouth."

She grinned shamelessly. "Honey, my mouth can be used for a lot of things more interesting than eating . . . cookies."

She'd used just the right amount of hesitation so George couldn't miss her meaning. He raised a brow. "At the kitchen table?"

"Why not?" She popped the cookie in her mouth and eyed him up and down. "You a prude?"

Despite himself, George laughed. "Okay, let me rephrase that—at the kitchen table with *two* women present?"

Erica held up her hands. "I concede. A woman has to draw the line somewhere."

"Indeed." George glanced up and saw that Becky was disgruntled by the sexual banter. Damn, he hoped she didn't think he was flirting with Erica.

He had been, he supposed, but not out of interest. He'd merely felt compelled to hold his own against her, sort of a male against female thing. Dumb.

He wondered how Becky could stay such close friends with Erica. Their personalities were so different. He took a bite of cookie, and groaned in appreciation. "Damn, Becky, that's good. You even put walnuts in them."

Becky stopped dumping sugar in her coffee and gave him a stony stare. "Thank you. I'm so glad you like them."

Her words sounded anything but pleased. Was she jealous? Normally that would annoy the hell out of him, because grasping women drove him nuts. But this time George found himself fighting a grin. He kind of liked the idea of Becky being jealous. After putting him off for two years, she deserved it.

Becky sat opposite him at the small table, with Asia and Erica at his sides. He wanted to touch her, to reassure her, but the other women were watching him like they expected him to sprout horns at any moment.

Moving slowly so they wouldn't notice, George stretched

out his legs. His feet bumped Becky's. Before she could withdraw, he caged her legs with his own. Beneath the table their knees touched, his outside hers. He watched her over his coffee cup and saw her go still, then draw in a deep breath. Her gaze lifted and locked with his.

For long moments, they stared at each other.

Erica chuckled. "You two are embarrassing me. I think it's time Asia and I hit the road."

Asia agreed, but Becky jumped to her feet. "No. I mean, you haven't finished your coffee."

"Caffeine keeps me awake." Erica drew her close and hugged her, then said in a stage whisper that the birds in the trees outside could hear, "If we don't go now, George is liable to self-combust. The man is all but salivating and it isn't over the cookies, no matter what he tells you."

George continued to watch Becky when he replied to Erica. "How astute of you."

Erica flapped her hand at him in dismissal. "Nah. Men are just so easy to read."

"More infamous words," Asia complained. She grabbed Erica and towed her away. "Bye, Becky. Behave. And call me later."

"Call us both! But do *not* behave."

Seconds later, George heard the front door close with a quiet click. He set his coffee aside and came to his feet. Becky backed up.

He rounded the table.

She bumped into the counter.

"Are you afraid of me?" He wasn't worried about it, because he'd come to the conclusion that Becky's decision to incorporate a little bondage into her lovemaking was based on sheer curiosity and daring. No way did she have enough sexual experience to be bored and looking for a new kick. Under the circumstances, he expected her to be a bit nervous. Beyond being a real turn-on, it was sort of endearing.

She flattened her hands on the counter at either side of

her hips, bracing herself. Standing there in the frilly apron, eyes wide, lips parted, she made a very tempting picture. "No, I'm not afraid of you."

"Good." George advanced on her until his legs were on either side of hers, his cock pushed up snug against her soft belly, and his hands over her hands on the counter, effectively holding her captive.

Damn, he liked this game. He liked it a lot.

He stared at Becky's mouth. "No matter what we do," he told her, thinking of how she might feel when he had her tightly bound on the bed, legs open, unable to move, "no matter what I say, you don't ever have to fear me. All right?"

Becky frowned.

"Believe me, Becky."

She nodded slowly. "Yes, all right."

He let out his breath in relief. "I need another kiss."

"All right." She closed her eyes, turned her face up, and pursed her lips.

Grinning, George smoothed a finger over that delectable mouth. Patience, he told himself. She might be ready to try new things, *kinky things,* but she lacked any real experience. It was up to him, regardless of his urgency, to guide her gently.

The idea of tutoring her gave him another rush. "I want to taste you, babe. I want you to suck on my tongue again."

Her eyes popped open and she blinked. "You do?"

"Mmmm. Becky, open your mouth for me."

Her lips parted the tiniest bit, more out of surprise than because of his instruction, but it was enough. George groaned and took her mouth.

The second he tasted her, his intentions regarding gentle guidance went straight out the window. He licked his way inside, tasting her deeply, eating at her mouth, pushing her lips farther apart with a hunger that quickly shot out of control.

After a small, shocked sound, Becky struggled to free her hands. Frustrated, George released her and lifted his head, ready to apologize.

She launched herself at him.

Her hands were frantic on his chest and shoulders, his neck, his face. She seemed to enjoy touching him, and she definitely enjoyed kissing him. Her mouth landed on his with inept exuberance until George helped by turning his head and adjusting the fit. Becky made a hungry sound and gave him her tongue.

Now, without their coats between them, he could feel her nipples stiffened against his chest. He wedged a hand between their bodies and cuddled her lush breast in his palm.

They both groaned in raw appreciation. Becky was full and firm and so soft, her heartbeat galloping madly. He was pretty much in the zone of no return when he stroked his other hand down her narrow back and gripped her rounded behind. He lifted her into his groin and pressed against her in a tantalizing rhythm that mimicked sex but wasn't nearly as satisfying. She felt good, smelled good, tasted good.

Against her mouth, he whispered, "God, Becky, you are so beautiful."

And like a wet cat, Becky screeched and thrust him away.

Dumbfounded, all his wits now gathered below his belt, George stared at her and tried to figure out what the hell had just happened. One minute she'd been attacking him, and the next she acted like she'd been attacked.

Even now, she appeared panicked, while George simply struggled to catch his breath. They were still pressed tightly together, his cock still throbbed, and his body still thought sex was the best solution.

Becky disabused him of that notion when she flattened her hands on his chest and tried to push him away. He regretted her change of heart, but no way in hell was he going to let her put any major distance between them. Not yet. Not until he figured out what was wrong.

He caught her shoulders and held her still. "Becky?"

She turned her face away, her voice trembling, her eyes closed. "Let me go."

He hesitated, unsure about what to do. "All right. But can you tell me why?"

She wouldn't look at him. "I . . . I'm not ready yet."

What was the big deal about getting ready? He tried to sound reasonable. "Ready for what?"

"For . . . whatever you were trying to do."

"What exactly do you think I was trying to do?"

"I don't know!" She glared up at him, defiant and shaken. "You were grabbing my . . . my . . ."

"Your ass?" His voice dropped and he said with great and inadequate sincerity, "Becky, honey, you have a fantastic ass. A premier ass. A world-class ass."

She appeared startled, then laughed and covered her face with her hands. George relaxed a bit; that was more like it.

Gently, he eased her against him and began rubbing her back, not in a sexual way, but in a soothing way. She was trembling—and still snickering. His chest felt tight with an emotion that definitely wasn't sexual in nature.

He kissed her temple. "Becky? If I promise not to do any more ass grabbing, can I kiss you again?"

Her words were muffled against his chest. "That . . . that wasn't the problem."

Hmmm. Not exactly the answer he'd expected, but at least now she wasn't pushing him away. In fact, she leaned on him in a way he chose to call trusting. What a mix she was, buying handcuffs, going wild when he kissed her, then freaking out for reasons he couldn't begin to fathom.

Despite his current frustrated state, figuring her out would be a treat.

"How about we sit down and finish our coffee and cookies?"

Her forehead dropped to his sternum. "You don't mind?"

Teasing her had worked, so he tried it again. In a low sexy rumble, George said, "You've got great cookies, too, Becky."

She actually giggled, then groaned. "I'm embarrassed again."

"Why?"

"Because I acted like an idiot."

"Oh, I dunno." He nuzzled against her hair, breathing in her soft, baby-fine scent, loving the feel of her silky curls. "If some guy grabbed my ass like that, I'd probably act the same way."

She slugged him, and now she shook with laughter. George smiled, too. It amazed him, but despite a raging hard-on that by all accounts wouldn't be appeased any time soon, he was actually enjoying himself.

He kissed her hair again and moments later felt her shoulders stiffening, felt her bracing herself. Becky was shy, but she wasn't a coward. When she raised her face, he saw the determination in her gaze. "I didn't know you were so funny, George."

Cautiously, because he didn't want her to go hiding against his chest again, he said, "I didn't know you were into bondage. I suppose there's a lot we can learn about each other."

She didn't look away, but she did bite her lip.

"C'mere, Becky." George led her to her chair and seated her. Startled amazement crossed her face when he knelt down in front of her, but he wanted to see her eye to eye, to read her reactions and make sure she understood. "I'm dying to make love to you. Don't ever doubt that. But I'm not a pig. If you want to wait a bit, it doesn't have to be tomorrow. We can just . . . I don't know, go out if you want."

Amazement turned to disbelief.

George frowned at her. "I don't want you to feel rushed."

She covered her mouth with her hand.

"And as for all this bondage stuff, hey, it's fine by me, but only if you're into it, okay?" Her hair had gotten tangled by his hands when they'd kissed and now he smoothed it, tucking it behind her ears. He adored her hair and couldn't wait to feel those soft curls drifting over his chest, maybe down his abdomen when they made love. . . .

"I . . . I'm new to this."

Her admission brought him out of his sensual revelry. "I figured that out." *How new* was what he really wanted to know. But then he assumed he'd find out soon enough.

"I want it to be tomorrow, I really do."

Thank God. "Okay, if you're sure that's what you want."

"It is. It's just that I want everything to be . . . right." She looked down at her hands, then back up. "And I want . . . I want the bondage stuff. I want to use the handcuffs and . . . the blindfold. Okay?"

It was a wonder he didn't come in his pants. As it was, George had to take two deep breaths, close his eyes, and count to ten. And still he hurt.

"All right." It sounded like he was strangling.

Becky smiled and touched his jaw. "You're pretty terrific, George, you know that?"

At the moment, he felt pretty damn terrific, like friggin' Superman, with superhuman patience. Only a real hero could take this kind of temptation and still survive. The inquisition could have made use of little Becky Harte.

"Cookies." He straightened, grimaced at the discomfort from a straining boner, and moved to his seat. "I'm going to eat my cookies, drink my coffee, then go home before I insist on kissing you again." He raised his cup to her in a salute. "You, babe, are pure fire."

Becky looked down at her hands folded on the tabletop.

"But I'm not." And then, in a whisper so low he could barely hear her, "I'm not beautiful either."

George stared at her in surprise. So that's what had bothered her—a compliment. Judging by the seriousness of her expression, she really believed what she said. She also looked more vulnerable than any woman should ever look.

Trying to lighten her mood, he raised his hands and studied them.

That got her attention. "What are you doing?"

George lifted one shoulder. "I'm looking to see if I've got any visible burns so I can prove to you how wrong you are."

"Burns?"

"You *are* hot, lady. Believe me, I know. So hot, in fact, I would've sworn my fingertips were singed from touching you."

It was so ridiculous, but so sweet, Becky couldn't help but smile. George blew on his fingers and she laughed out loud. He was an incredible man.

"That's better," he told her, and he snagged another cookie.

Becky looked at him sitting across the table from her—a place she'd never, ever expected to see George sitting. Because it was getting to be late in the day, he had a dark beard shadow. She'd felt it when he kissed her, knew she had a few slight burns on her throat, her cheeks. Amazing. She'd never had whisker burn before. In many ways, it felt as though she'd been initiated.

George caught her staring and grinned. "What?"

Her smile lingered. "I was just . . . wondering about you."

He leaned back in his seat, a cookie in his hand. "Yeah? Like what?"

Becky shrugged. "I don't want to pry."

"No, it's okay. We might as well use this time to get to know each other better, right?"

She loved that idea, but having a personal relationship with a man was new to her. Having a relationship with George defied all her expectations. "You're sure?"

"Well hell, you're making me curious with all this hesitation. What are you going to ask me anyway? My social security number? How much money I make?"

"Of course not." She was insulted that he'd suggest such a thing. "I don't care about that."

His eyes narrowed a bit, making his dark gaze sharper. "Some women do, you know. What a man makes ranks right up there with the size of his cock."

Becky sputtered on the drink of coffee she'd just swallowed. He kept taking her by surprise with the things he said, his unregulated speech.

"You okay, honey?" He made to stand and Becky waved him back into his seat. If he touched her now, she was liable to attack him and then everything would be ruined. Twice now, she'd lost her head with him, in the parking lot, in her own kitchen. He was under the ridiculous assumption she was beautiful, and she didn't particularly want to dissuade him of that notion. If any of this was to go right, it had to be as she'd planned, with the bondage.

And with the blindfold.

George stared at her, must have decided she wouldn't choke to death, and shrugged. "Sorry. I didn't mean to shock you."

Becky didn't believe that for a second. It seemed to her that he took maniacal delight in shocking her. Besides, she'd already heard plenty about his dimensions. Women would whisper about him, pretend to swoon, and get all flushed.

Becky had always found it all rather silly.

And intriguing.

She cleared her throat. "Let me reassure you, I don't care . . . about what you make."

His grin was slow and suggestive, wicked. "But you do care about the size of my cock, huh?"

Deciding to face him down, to give him a little of his own, she lifted her chin and nodded. "The thought has occurred to me a few times. Especially since you're supposed to be . . . impressive."

"Yeah?" He took a bite of the last remaining cookie, for all appearances unconcerned with the idea that his private male parts had been discussed around the break room. "When have you thought about it?"

Good grief, he wanted details? Becky sought words that would explain, but wouldn't be too graphic. "Like when you were . . . you know, against me."

"Mmm." He gave her a sage nod. "Go on."

"And with all the . . . well, the talk." She shrugged. "I suppose it was natural for me to be curious about it, don't you think?"

He stared at her for a moment, then burst out laughing. He grabbed his coffee to wash down the cookie, and nodded. His eyes were still twinkling and his words were broken with chuckles. "I hate to break it to you, Becky, but truth is, I'm really quite average."

That stunned her. "No way. I *felt* you." Her brows puckered. "Surely that's not . . . not average."

His laughter dwindled, then died. Suspicion made him frown. "Becky, exactly how much experience do you have?"

She wasn't about to admit her experience was zilch. *Nada.* That other than the video he'd shown her earlier, she'd never seen a naked man.

"That's a personal question," she replied, trying to sound prim rather than evasive.

George barked a disbelieving laugh. "And the size of my dick isn't?"

That stumped her. "Well you're the one who told me to ask my questions."

"But it doesn't go both ways, huh? I'm to bare my soul and my manly measurements, but you get to keep private?"

She felt guilty, darn it. "On some things." As if to appease him, she said, "I'll tell you my bra size."

He looked at her breasts. "I'd say a thirty-six C. Right?"

Darn. That was right on the money—the man knew women much too well. She frowned, but didn't reply.

"We'll never get to know each other better unless we share, now will we?"

He had a point. "I suppose not." Then, "Do you want to . . . you know, get that familiar? I mean, you don't just want to do . . . what we planned to do . . . tomorrow night?"

That idea seemed to ignite his temper. "One night? Oh no, Becky, you can forget that right now. It'll take a damn month at least for me to even get close to getting enough of you."

"Oh." A whole month of having sex with George? The idea made her giddy. But would he continue to let her restrain him that long?

George's scowl grew darker. "Okay, this is how it's going to be. An even exchange. You can ask me a question, but for every one you ask, you have to answer one. Deal?"

She blanched at that suggestion. "I refuse to discuss past lovers." She couldn't discuss something that didn't exist. If he found out he was a guinea pig of sorts, he might lose interest or back out.

His eyes narrowed in annoyance. "Fair enough. That question is taboo—for both of us."

Well, darn. Becky sat back in a huff. There were at least three women at work who claimed to have been intimate with him. She wanted to know if there were others, if half the women there had carnal knowledge of him, and what exactly he'd done with them. The curiosity was killing her. But now she'd seem really petty if she pushed the issue. "All right," she muttered. "It's a deal."

He sat back with a satisfied nod. "Good."

Becky waited. And waited some more. "Well?"

"Well what?"

"How big is your . . . you know."

Being a complete cad, George asked with false confusion, "My what?"

Exasperated, Becky pointed.

"My waist? Thirty-four."

"No, not your waist."

His gaze was intent, taunting. Sexy. "Say it, Becky."

"Why?"

His voice changed, went husky. "Because I love it when a woman talks dirty."

Huh. She'd gotten that bit of information for free. Would she have the courage to talk dirty to him tomorrow? What kind of language qualified as dirty? With what he considered appropriate table conversation, it'd have to be pretty explicit to be dirty to him. She'd have to think about it. Or maybe ask Erica.

No, she couldn't do that. He and Erica seemed to get along a little too well to suit her.

She drew a steadying breath. "How big is your . . . penis?"

That slow grin reappeared. "Penis?" He laughed. "What a spoilsport you are. My cock is about seven and a half inches. Erect. And that's length by the way, not circumference."

"I know that!"

He laughed and finished off the last cookie.

Becky tried to picture a seven-and-a-half-inch penis—which was much smaller than the rubber penises she'd seen on the wall at the porn shop. But since she'd never seen a real one up close and personal, she decided she'd have to get a ruler out later to get a good visual. "Thank you. And you say that's average?"

"Close enough."

"Then why do they make the fake ones so big?"

George rubbed his face, and Becky suspected he was laughing. "I'll explain that to you after."

"After?"

He dropped his hands. Nope, there was no sign of amusement in his expression. "After we've had sex."

"Oh." That shut her up. She couldn't think of another single thing to say.

George leaned forward and propped his elbows on the table. "My turn."

Becky braced herself.

"Have you ever thought about having sex with me? I mean, before now. Anytime over the last two years?"

Oh, unfair! How did he come up with such a question? The last thing she wanted to do was admit that she'd fantasized over him a *lot*.

She frowned, and he just waited. She had agreed, so she met his gaze and nodded.

"Yeah?" His eyes turned hot with her confession, and he leaned closer still. "How often."

"That's another question."

"So I'm one ahead. Answer it."

Deciding a good offense was her best defense, Becky stood to pace. "You're an incredibly attractive man, George."

"Thanks. How often, Becky?"

She glanced at him, but saw no irony in his watchful gaze. She continued her pacing. "You're also very nicely built."

"Is that right?"

Becky bobbed her head. "Sure. You're tall and lean and muscular." She peeked at him. "Women like that."

"Like men like great asses and big breasts?"

Every feminine bone in her body was offended by such a cavalier, sexist comment. But once again, he'd gotten her. She'd started this stupid conversation, after all. Eyeing him, she muttered, "I suppose."

"Go on."

"You also have an astounding reputation."

To her surprise, George shook his head. "Women and their damn gossip. Believe me, I've heard some of it, and only half of it is true."

"Really? Which half?"

George settled back with an aggrieved sigh. "Is that your question? Because I have to tell you, it seems like a round-about way of questioning me on that taboo topic we agreed to avoid."

Flustered because he was right, Becky busied herself with refilling his coffee cup. When she started to move away, he caught her wrist. "Besides, Becky, you still haven't an-swered my question."

"Oh?"

"Yeah." He took the coffeepot from her, set it on the table, and tugged her into his lap. With his arm locked around her, she knew she couldn't escape, so she just held herself erect. "Now, let's talk about these fantasies of yours. Particularly how often I played a part in them."

With the back of his finger, he teased her cheek, the side of her neck. Becky gulped. "All right." She glanced at him, then away. "If I have to be truthful, then I've thought about you often."

That teasing finger went still. "How often?"

Every day. "Often enough. I'm glad you were there today, and that we seem to have a similar interest."

His hand dropped to her waist. He squeezed, caressed. "In bondage?"

"Yes." Becky felt him shift and came to a startling real-ization—he still had an erection. And he felt bigger than seven and a half inches to her.

Eyes agog, she said, "You're still hard."

He looked pained. "Yeah. Believe me, I know. And as long as you're talking about bondage, or sitting in my lap, or . . . hell, just breathing, I'm probably going to stay hard."

Fascinating. "Will you stay like that for long?"

His mouth curled with suggestion. "As long as I need to."

"Oh." She shivered at that dark promise. "Oh no, I meant tonight, after you leave here." And then a horrible, awful thought occurred to her and she frowned at him, outraged. "You're not going to be with another woman tonight, are you?"

George pulled her down for a ravenous kiss. When he lifted his head, his voice was raspy and deep. "I want you, Becky, not anyone else. Until we're through with each other, we'll both keep it exclusive, agreed?"

Relief washed over her. "Yes."

He dropped his head to her chest. "Thank God. Now, I have to go because if I don't I'm going to lose control." He lifted his face to smile at her. Becky, taking the hint, scrambled off his lap and stood in front of him. He came to his feet as well.

He cupped her head between his big hands and kissed her nose, her chin. Against her lips, he asked, "Will you think about me again tonight, babe? About what we'll do?"

"Yes." She'd think and dream and fantazise and plan.

George stepped away. "Until tomorrow, then."

It was raining when he left, a cold miserable rain, but inside her lonely apartment, Becky burned. She went to the couch, picked up the handcuffs, and began figuring out how she'd get them on him.

At least she had a four-poster bed, just like in the video. She was certain that was going to be a big help.

Chapter Four

George waited outside the women's rest room for Becky to emerge. He'd been so damn busy all day in meetings he'd scarcely seen her at all. But this was her last break of the day, and they'd both be getting off work in two hours.

He was so keyed up, so tense and impatient, he'd had to fight to concentrate on his work instead of on sexual thoughts. But always there in the back of his mind was the tempting picture of Becky submitting to his will, bound for his pleasure—and hers.

George locked his knees and concentrated on not getting hard. Damn, he couldn't wait to explore her body, to sate himself on her. He felt like a kid again, ready to get laid for the first time.

But it was more than that, too. He'd really enjoyed himself yesterday; chatting with her was always a pleasure because Becky was so unique, so different from most of the women he knew. But getting to know her more intimately, getting a few clues to her secrets, had been exciting in a way he hadn't expected.

The door swung open and Becky, Asia, and Erica walked out. Becky was carrying a wooden ruler, of all things, and Erica was laughing, Asia shaking her head. Becky fell silent when she saw him, and she nearly tripped over her own feet. Not so with Erica.

She moseyed right up to him, patted his chest, and said, "You stud, you! I'm so impressed."

George had no idea what had brought that on, but obviously whatever professionalism had existed between them on the job was now gone. He pushed away from the wall and grinned. "That's Supervisor Stud to you, Ms. Lee."

In the next instant, Becky swept past them, nearly knocking him down in her haste. Erica leaned forward and said, "Now you did it."

"What did I do?" He watched Becky's fast retreat.

Asia scowled at both of them. "You know she's shy. You should quit baiting her by flirting."

Erica shrugged. "If I wasn't flirting, what would I do?"

George saluted them both and took off after Becky. He caught her at the soda machine. She'd just popped the top on a Coke when he rounded the corner. She didn't know he was watching and she tipped up the can and guzzled it all in nearly one long gulp. Afterward she fell back against the machine, put the back of her hand to her mouth, and burped.

George laughed. He had a feeling the way she'd guzzled that Coke was her rendition of tying one on. "Have I driven you to drink already?"

Becky slanted him a narrow-eyed look. "What do you want?"

"You."

Her mouth opened, then closed. Her eyes glittered in her pique. "Oh. And here I thought you might want Erica instead."

He'd never heard that particular nasty tone from Becky before. It was all he could do to hold back his grin. "No way. Erica scares me." He inched closer.

"Yeah, I can see you shaking."

"I'm a man. Men don't shake no matter how terrified we are."

Becky rolled her eyes. "Yeah, well, Erica might be scary, but she's also plenty knowledgeable about men." She smacked him in the chest with the wooden ruler. "She said seven and a half inches is *not* average. You lied to me."

George rocked back on his heels, and to his chagrin, he felt himself going hot. Jesus, he hadn't blushed since he'd been a green teenager. "You told her what I said?"

"Well yeah. I mean, look at that!" She held up the ruler, marked by her thumb at exactly seven and a half inches. "I was . . . worried."

George looked around, and thankfully, the hall was empty. "Worried about what, damn it?"

"Fit."

"Fit?"

Looking equally embarrassed and mulish, Becky said, "I don't think you'll fit."

George no longer cared if anyone was around. He caught her shoulders and backed her into the machine. Against her mouth, he said, "I'll fit, Becky, believe me. I'll make sure you're nice and wet first, so no matter how snug it is, it'll feel great for both of us." He kissed her open mouth before she could say anything. "Two more hours, Becky. Two hours that'll feel like a week. Don't back out on me now."

Her eyes glazed over. He loved how quickly she reacted to him. Taking advantage of that, George cupped her breast, teased her nipple. It stiffened against his thumb. "Tell me you want me there, Becky. Tell me you haven't changed your mind."

"I want you there." The words were whispered and then she was kissing him, holding him tight, accidentally prodding him in the back with the stupid ruler still held in her fist.

Luckily George wasn't so far gone that he'd totally lost

track of their surroundings. He stepped away from her just as two other employees started around the corner. He caught Becky's hand and dragged her along in his wake. "Six o'clock, Becky. Be ready for me."

"George."

"What?" He kept walking, refusing to let her back down on him now because of some ridiculous anxiety over his size. Hell, he'd thought she'd be turned on, as most women were, or he never would have told her a damn thing. At thirty-seven, he felt no need to brag about his endowments.

He shook his head. When Becky found out he was actually bigger than that, that he'd shortened the dimension out of modesty, well, he could only imagine her reaction.

He wondered again at her lack of experience, but it was far too late for him to change his mind.

"You're dragging me in the wrong direction."

George stopped and struggled for breath. It was unheard of, the way she affected him. "Right." He looked up and down the deserted hall. "Give me another kiss to tide me over then, and I'll let you get back to your work."

Becky grinned. She went on tiptoe, kissed his chin, his jaw, and finally his mouth. "Six o'clock." And teasing him as Erica had, she added, "Stud," and tapped his chest with the damned ruler.

George watched the sexy sway of her backside as she walked away from him. Before his very eyes, Becky's inhibitions were wearing away. He'd done that to her, he realized, and she was sexier for it. Very sexy.

He had to stake a claim before every cursed male in the factory noticed. When the night was over, Becky wouldn't have a shy bone left in her sumptuous little body.

And *she'd* be telling *him* that they were a perfect fit.

In more ways than one.

He showed up twenty minutes early. Becky was in the process of attaching the hand and footcuffs to the bedposts,

thinking that it would be less awkward that way than trying to set things up once they were . . . in business. She hid
the handcuffs with the bed pillows, the footcuffs with the
turned-down sheet. Her hands shook, her heart pounded,
and her stomach felt very funny, sort of fluttery and tight
and tingly.

She was going to have sex. And not with just any guy,
but with George.

She closed her eyes and held her hands to her belly, trying to calm the stirring there.

The bed was all prepared, she decided. She'd drawn the
drapes to leave the room dark. And on the nightstand—on
her nightstand—was a condom and the blindfold. She felt
faint with expectation.

When the knock sounded on her front door, she actually
jumped and let out a small screech. Heavens, she was nervous. And eager. And excited.

She rushed from the room, but forced herself to slow, to
take two deep breaths so George wouldn't know how anxious she was. She'd dressed in a button-down sweater and a
long casual corduroy skirt. The sweater would be easy to
remove, the skirt easy to lift. She'd left off pantyhose and
instead wore lacy ankle socks—again, because they'd be
easy to take off.

Her door rattled with another heavy knock and Becky
peered through the peephole. George stood there, tall and
dark and so handsome her toes curled inside her slip-on
shoes.

She turned the locks, braced herself, and opened the
door.

Trying to sound calm and cavalier when she was anything but, she said, "Hello, George—umpf!"

In one movement, he stepped in and scooped her up,
then kicked the door shut. Held high against his chest,
Becky had no choice but to grab hold of his shoulders and
hang on. "George!"

His arms were trembling, his dark eyes piercing and hot. He leaned forward, nuzzled her hair, kissed her ear, gently bit her neck.

Becky jumped again, unprepared for such an onslaught of sensual attention. She had thought they'd . . . talk. That they'd . . .

"Where's your bedroom?" His voice was an aching rasp that curled through her on a wave of heat. Urgency beat inside her, matching the tempo of her suddenly racing pulse.

"My bedroom?"

"God almighty, Becky, I can't wait another single second." He strode forward though he obviously had no idea which room was hers. "Forget the movie. Forget the damn pizza." He peered into her bathroom and kept going, peered into the small guest room she used as a den. "*Where is your bedroom?*"

Becky lifted one limp arm and pointed to the last door in her small hall. Two seconds later George stepped into the room. This door he left open, which allowed the hall light to spill in. Becky wanted to protest but when he reached the bed, he dropped her. Her shoes fell off and tumbled to the floor.

Trying to ground herself, to get her bearings, Becky started to rise up on one elbow. She never made it. George threw off his coat, came down on top of her and started kissing her again, touching her, moving against her.

It was something of a shock, feeling a man lying on top of her, all heavy and hot, hard and lean. It took her a single heartbeat to realize it was also wonderful and Becky squirmed, better aligning their bodies. He caught her hips and held her still. His mouth traveled from hers to her throat to her chest.

She yelped when he nuzzled her breast through her sweater.

"*George.*" She didn't mean to, but her body arched in reaction.

He grappled with her buttons, finally just shoving the sweater down so it caught beneath her breasts. With an expert hand, he released the front catch on her bra and the cups parted.

Breathing hard, George reared back to look at her. His cheekbones were dark with color, his eyes glittering and intent. "Damn." He cupped her breasts in both hands, stroked her nipples with his thumbs, caught and held them, tugged. Her nipples felt achingly sensitive, and his touch jolted through her.

Never in her life had Becky expected so much sensation from such a simple caress. A raw moan escaped her, and then another when he bent and sucked her right nipple deep into his mouth. She clasped his head and held him to her.

Wonderful. Beyond wonderful. She was lost in feelings too exquisite to describe when his hand went beneath her skirt, up the outside of her left thigh.

Becky panicked. *"No."*

George stilled. He lifted his head to look at her. Confusion warred with the lust and other emotions that Becky couldn't decipher.

She tried a smile, tried to remember everything she'd planned. Voice shaking, she touched his chest and said, "This is my show, George, remember? You were going to . . . indulge me."

His gaze went from her face to her naked breasts. He breathed hard, closed his eyes for a long moment. When he opened them again, some of that devastating emotion was banked. "Right."

Gently, Becky pressed against his chest until he fell to his back. Still struggling for breath, he put one arm over his eyes.

Becky slid on top of him, liking that position almost as much as being beneath him. A distraction was in order, so before he could cool down and start questioning her, she kissed him.

His hands went to her back, keeping her close as she tasted his throat, the side of his neck. "I love how you taste, George."

His fingers contracted on her in reaction. Encouraged, Becky kissed his ear and breathed, "I want to see you, George. All of you. I've been fantasizing over your body for a long time."

He groaned.

Slipping to the side, Becky touched his chest, light and curious and teasing, through the open collar of his shirt. "Will you get naked for me?" Her face heated as she made that request, both with a tinge of shyness and with anticipation.

His mesmerizing gaze locked on hers. "Oh yeah. Whatever you want, Becky." Without further instruction, he started on his buttons.

It was a slow striptease and she loved it. Having George remove his clothes for her delectation was a dream come true. Becky didn't want to miss a single thing.

As he worked the buttons free, she saw the dark hair on his broad chest, the way it narrowed down his trim abdomen and curled around his navel. The sight of the downy hair below his navel, leading to his sex, made her heart race. He was full and hard, and she could hardly wait to see that part of him.

He pulled his shirttails free of his slacks, and with a taunting smile, opened the button on his pants and cautiously slid the zipper down.

He smiled at her wide-eyed fascination. "You, too, honey."

"Oh." She glanced down at her still-exposed breasts. Her nipples were puckered, darkly flushed, still sensitive. Yes, she could do that. If he enjoyed seeing her upper body, that was fine. If he wanted to touch her there again, or suck on her again, even better. "Okay."

Becky watched him watching her. Her fingers seemed far

clumsier than his had been, but he didn't rush her. Instead, still glued to the sight of her breasts, he curled forward, raising his back from the bed. Using his fist, he reached back and grabbed a handful of his open shirt, then yanked it off over his head and down his long arms. He balled it up and tossed it over the side of the bed to the floor. Becky paused in the middle of her stripping.

Wow, he looked good. His shoulders were hard and sleek and muscled, his chest hairy but not too much so. He looked so . . . manly, so edible, beyond mere sexy.

Becky accidentally popped the last button on her sweater, then just stared at him.

"Take it off." George leaned back on his elbows. "The bra too." As he waited for her to comply, he toed off his shoes and let them fall over the end of the bed. They hit her carpeted floor with a soft thunk.

There was no embarrassment, not yet, not with the hungry way George watched her. Using the excuse of putting her sweater and bra on a chair, she crossed the room to the door and shut it. Shadows enveloped them.

George asked, "Where's the light?"

"We don't need the light." Becky peeled off her sweater and bra and strode back to him.

There were two heartbeats of silence. "Now, sweetheart, how can I see you without a light?"

He spoke so gently, his tone cajoling, that Becky wished she could relent. But she couldn't, so she teased as she slipped back into the bed with him. "And here I was under the impression you already knew where everything was." She reached out, felt his chest, and pushed him flat. "Isn't that right?"

"Becky . . ."

She trailed her hands down his body to the top of his slacks, effectively cutting off his protest. He drew in a sharp breath and his hands caught hers.

"Let me," she said.

His hands dropped to his sides. "You're pushing me, babe. And I'm already on the edge."

"Good." She loved the idea that she, Becky Harte, could drive a man to the edge.

"Not good. I want you with me."

"I'm right here." She shoved the material over his hips. "Lift up."

He lifted, but said, "No way, Becky. You're eons behind me."

She got his slacks all the way to his ankles and pulled them off with his socks. Taking a deep breath for courage, she explained, "I've thought about how I want to do this at least a hundred times, George. And that's just since yesterday. Please, just lay back and let me have my fun, okay?"

His hesitation was thick and unnerving. Then with a growl, he dropped back. "Somehow, I just know I'm going to regret this."

His legs were so long, she wondered briefly if he'd overreach the length of the footcuffs. As she touched his legs, she felt how his muscles had tensed, his thighs hard as steel. She glanced up at his face, but all she could really see was the glitter of his eyes. "Relax, George."

"Ain't gonna happen, babe."

She stroked the inside of his thigh. "Try." Becky cleared her throat, then touched his erection through the soft cotton of his boxers.

They both flinched, then both groaned.

"Damn."

Becky said, "Yeah." She touched him again, explored his length. "You feel even bigger than I remembered."

"A figment of your imagination." He sounded suspiciously anxious to convince her of that.

Before she could chicken out, Becky caught the elastic waistband of his underwear and dragged them off him. George shifted his legs to help, and again reached for her.

Becky decided it was past time she got him contained before she forgot herself and everything got ruined.

She fell on top of him, kissed him wildly to divert his attention. He went still for a moment in surprise before his big hands closed over her naked back and hugged the breath right out of her. The feel of his chest hair against her nipples was incredible. Becky closed her eyes and absorbed the tantalizing stimulation.

"Becky." He started to stroke his way down her back. "You're still wearing your skirt."

"Mmmm." Becky shifted to kiss his chest, to lick her way up to his shoulder, to his biceps. She loved his various textures—crisp hair, sleek warm skin, bulging muscles. His arms went slack and she trailed her fingertips to his wrists, then stretched his arms up over his head. The position had her hovering over him, her breast near his mouth.

"Lean down a tiny bit, babe."

She did, at the same time he lifted his head. His mouth closed over her nipple hungrily. It was enough to leave Becky witless with pleasure.

It wasn't easy, but she forced herself to remember the plan. She pushed his right arm higher, fumbled for the cuff, and closed it around his wrist.

George went still. He released her breast.

Quickly, before he could get cold feet, Becky did the same with his right arm. She pulled the Velcro tight but his wrists were so thick, there was barely enough length to the cuff to wrap around and hook.

"Uh, Becky . . ." He sounded bewildered, and Becky felt him tug experimentally against the restraints.

Thank God they held. Her hands had been shaking so badly, she wasn't sure she'd fastened them right.

She sat back, which meant she literally sat on his abdomen. "Can . . . can you see me, George?"

Again his arms strained. "Damn right I can see you! What the hell are you doing?"

Uh-oh. Becky leaned over him and felt on the nightstand for the blindfold. "Here, let's get this on you."

"No! Damn it, wait a minute . . ." He twisted, but Becky easily got the elasticized band hooked across his eyes. "Becky." There was a wealth of warning in his tone.

Becky bit her lip. She wasn't quite sure what to make of his new attitude. "You promised, George."

"Like hell I did!" He jerked hard, making the bed shake and almost tumbling Becky from her perch on top of him. "You're the one who wants to be restrained, not me."

Becky gasped. "That's not true! You said you understood, that you'd indulge me. You said we were in agreement."

"We agreed I'd tie your sexy little ass down. I didn't say jack-shit about this being done to me." He yanked hard again and Becky thought it was a wonder the bedposts didn't crack. "Now unfasten the damn things."

Her heart beat too fast and her face burned. Becky moved off him so she was no longer astride him. "Oh no. This is just awful."

"It's going to get a lot more awful if you don't undo these damn things *right—now.*"

He sounded so outraged, Becky wasn't sure it would be wise to let him loose. "George, please calm down." She sounded near tears and hated herself. "It's a misunderstanding, that's all. And I'm sorry. I'll unfasten you if you promise to just go."

"Go?"

"I don't want to argue about this and I don't want a huge confrontation. I'm embarrassed enough as it is . . ."

He'd stopped struggling halfway through her diatribe. "What the hell are you talking about? I'm not going anywhere." His voice dropped to a growl. "We're going to make love."

Becky stared through the darkness at him. "Oh no. We can't now."

He practically vibrated with tension, with anger, then burst out, "Fuck. Fuck, fuck, *fuck* . . ."

"George!"

He groaned, he cursed again. Finally, he took a deep breath. "You're saying you won't have sex with me unless I let you keep me this way?"

Becky bit her lip. He was definitely outraged. She nodded her head, realized he couldn't see her, and said, "I'm sorry."

"Why?"

"Because I didn't mean to mislead you."

"No, I mean why do I have to be restrained. Did some asshole hurt you? Are you afraid *I'd* hurt you?"

"What? No!" His misconceptions further flustered her. "It's nothing like that." She leaned over him and cupped his face. "I trust you, George. And I want you. I want you so much, it's killing me. But it'd have to be this way or . . . or not at all."

She felt him breathing, felt the rise and fall of his chest beneath her. Then he spoke, his voice husky, his words enticing. "Are you wet, Becky?"

Oh, she knew this new tone. He was interested again, rethinking things. Becky touched his mouth with her fingertips and answered in a barely there whisper. "I don't know."

"Take the rest of your clothes off, okay, sweetheart?"

She was almost afraid to hope. "You've changed your mind? You're going to make love to me after all?"

"Yeah, I'm going to make love to you." He laughed, a sound of irony and frustration. "Or rather, you're going to have to make love to me, all things considered."

Becky kissed him very gently. "I'd like that."

His voice deepened even more. "Then finish taking your clothes off."

"Is it okay if I fasten your ankles first?"

He groaned. "Yeah, what the hell. If that's what it takes."

To Becky, he sounded in pain. She twisted around and

quickly caught each ankle to a bedpost so that his long strong legs were held open. Curiosity got her, and she trailed her fingertips up his thighs until she located his erection. "Is it okay if I do this too?"

"God yes."

His hips lifted with her first tentative touch. She lightly wrapped her fingers around him, amazed at how big he was, how he filled her hand.

"Harder."

Thrilled with the instruction, Becky used both hands to hold him, and stroked. Now he definitely sounded in pain, but she wasn't so innocent that she misunderstood. He was painfully aroused, and he was enormous.

"I'm going to take my panties off, George."

She could hear his labored breathing in the otherwise quiet room. His head turned toward her, but Becky knew he couldn't see her. The room was dark enough without lights; under the blindfold, he wouldn't be able to distinguish a single thing, much less her scarred leg.

Still, she left her skirt on. It wouldn't hinder their love-making in any way.

"Becky?"

"Yes?"

"If you're going to touch my cock, then I want you to sit on my stomach, with your back to me."

Naked beneath her skirt, shivering at his sexy suggestion, Becky climbed back into the bed. "How come?"

"I want to feel you, wet and hot, on my belly."

Her muscles all clenched at the provocative way he said that. He was pretty good at this business of talking dirty. She liked it.

Breathless, she said, "Okay," and again straddled him, this time as per his instructions. Slowly, her breath held, she lowered herself until she was flush against him, her thighs around his waist. His skin was hot, slightly hairy. She braced her shaky hands on his hipbones. "Like this?"

"Mmmm. Oh yeah. You are wet, Becky, and so hot. You want me, don't you?"

Somehow, this wasn't how Becky had imagined it, with him still controlling things. "I want you a lot. I always have."

"That's a good thing since I'm not at all sure how much control I have left."

Becky began touching him, and he muttered in a rush, "None. I don't have any control left."

"Just give me a few minutes." His penis was hard, throbbing with life. The velvety texture amazed her. She didn't know what she had expected, but this was much more exciting than any fake rubber penis could ever be.

"Becky . . ."

She cupped his testicles, now drawn tight, and cradled them gently in her palm. They felt so different from his penis, she couldn't help but explore them.

George's legs shifted against the bonds. He groaned.

His scent was strong, that of musk and male and sex. Adding that to the combined influences of his size, his heat, his body, and his understanding, and Becky felt swollen with need. She'd had no idea that it would be like this, so personal, so hot and still so tender. She wanted to experience everything and wallow in this opportunity to be with him.

"I love how you smell, George." She bent low to inhale deeply. His abdomen contracted against her mound, he lifted just a bit, pressing closer. She rubbed her nose against him, brushed him with her cheek.

"Becky," he warned again.

She stroked the head of his erection with her thumb, and felt him flex in her hand. "I still don't know how this is going to fit inside me."

"Oh God." He trembled, then growled. "That's it. Turn around, Becky."

She looked over her shoulder. "Why?"

"Because I'm going to come." His voice was low with

desperation, urgent. "You have to take me now, babe, or I'm going to embarrass myself."

Becky hesitated only a second before scurrying around on him. He wanted her, needed her, and she was more than ready herself. "Let me grab the condom."

He gave another pained laugh. "Lord help me."

"It'll be okay," she promised.

"Have you ever put a rubber on a guy before?"

"No. But I read the instructions, and I practiced on a banana."

The bed shook with his startled laugh, and his raging lust. "I think I've just been insulted."

"Not at all. It was a big banana." Because she'd already gone through about half a dozen condoms from the box during her practice, she ripped the package open like a professional. She was rather proud of herself. "I also bought the large-sized ones, so at least I know the condom ought to fit."

"You'll fit me too, sweetheart. I promise."

"I need a light so I can see you. Just a sec." She'd thought that out, too, and flipped on a very dim night light. "Can you see?"

He sighed. "Not a damn thing, but I imagine you're getting an eyeful."

Becky stared at his naked body, spread-eagle and bound. There were thick shadows, but they only enhanced the clench of muscles, the length of bones, the texture of hair.

The throbbing of his cock.

"Oh yes." She laid the condom on his thigh and began running her hands all over him, absorbing him, relishing him. "George, you are so incredible."

"*Becky.*" Her name emerged as a raw groan. "You're killing me, sweetheart."

"Could I . . . kiss you?"

He held his breath. "Where?"

"Here." Becky gently pressed her mouth to his erection.

He strained against her and for a startling moment, she thought he might break free. Better not to try that again.

She moved over his thighs, held him steady, and rolled on the condom. "Does that feel right?"

"Fine. Great. Now ride me. Right now."

Ride him? The things he said were guaranteed to make her melt. Shoving her skirt out of the way, Becky poised over him. "Tell me if I do this wrong."

She clasped his penis in one hand, braced herself with the other, and lowered onto him. The broad head nudged against her and she gasped. George trembled, every muscle in his body stark and delineated. *"More."*

Becky bit her lip and forced herself to settle down onto him. He was barely inside her, and already he felt much too big.

"I don't know about this, George."

His arms were pulled tight against the bonds, his body slightly arched. "You need to . . ." He swallowed hard. "You need to get yourself wetter. Move the head of my dick around, yeah, like that. Oh God . . ."

Becky closed her eyes, liking how that felt.

His teeth clenched. "Now try again, babe."

She did, and this time the head pushed inside her. Becky froze at the discomfort of it. Her muscles clamped down on him, squeezing.

George moaned, "Ah, damn . . . *Becky.*"

She stared at his face, felt him jerk, shiver, and then she knew he was coming. His body bowed hard, lifting her, inadvertently driving him deeper. Becky flattened her hands on his chest and braced herself. He went deeper still, not all the way, but it was too much. It hurt.

One of the cuffs gave way and he grabbed the back of her neck, brought her head down to him and ground his mouth against hers. Becky was too astonished by it all to consider the ramifications of his freed arm.

He kissed her and held her and groaned, and then he was

finally motionless, still inside her, his hand still tangled in her hair, his chest rising and falling like a bellows. A little in awe of his fierce reaction, Becky rested her face on his shoulder. He tasted a bit salty against her lips, and he smelled divine. She could have spent the night like that, and probably would have if she hadn't felt him stiffen.

"George?" She started to move.

His arm tightened across her, keeping her close, and then he jerked his other hand free.

With a yelp, Becky realized exactly what was happening and tried to escape, but it was too late. Using only one arm, his strength far greater than she'd suspected, he kept her gently locked to him while he jerked the blindfold away. He looked . . . well, she wasn't sure. There was determination in spades, but also a lingering of lust.

And what looked like tenderness. Maybe even regret.

Refusing to become fanciful, she shook her head to clear it. "George?"

He kissed her lightly on the mouth. "I'm sorry, sweetheart."

"For what?" Did he mean to apologize for losing control? She kind of liked it that he had.

Incredibly, his gaze darkened even more. "For this." In the next instant, Becky found herself on her back. George twisted awkwardly over her, considering his feet were still fastened, but it took him mere seconds to strap the handcuffs around her own wrists, and because she was small boned, they overlapped, holding her tight and secure.

"George, no!" A very real panic set in and Becky struggled wildly.

"Shhh. Easy, sweetheart." He bent and removed his ankle cuffs, only to catch each of her flailing legs in turn. With a smile in his tone, he said, "Ankle socks. I think I'll leave them on. They look sexy." She kicked and fought but again, he was too strong for her. With seemingly no real effort, he wrapped the restraint around each ankle and Becky found herself spread out, wide open. Vulnerable.

Her skirt covered her, but for how long?

Her heart thundered in her ears and her vision blurred. "No."

"Turnabout is fair play, babe." He tickled his fingers over the arch of her foot. "I think I have an affinity for this. 'Course, thinking about doing this to you for so long already had me in a lather."

A sob rose in her throat.

George lowered himself over her and held her face. "Becky, shhh, don't cry, honey. Becky, listen to me."

She didn't want to listen. She wanted to escape, to run away. "Please, George, please don't do this."

He looked very solemn, very resolved, as he kissed her mouth. "Do what? What you did to me?"

"George . . ."

"Right now, all we're going to do is talk."

Becky tried to calm herself, tried to think of how to reason with him. "And then?"

"And then I'm going to do everything to you I've been thinking about for two long years."

"No."

"Oh yeah. *Everything*. And, Becky, I can promise you're going to love it."

Chapter Five

He could almost see the thoughts scrambling through her mind. She was afraid, mad, embarrassed . . . It was the fear that ate at him.

As if she'd read his thoughts, she said, "You told me I didn't have to be afraid of you."

George stared at the tears glistening in her beautiful blue eyes and felt his heart breaking. Damn, somehow his good old-fashioned, straightforward lust had morphed into something much more complicated. "That's right."

Her lips quivered, her chin quivered. "But you're scaring me now."

"Why?" He rubbed the soft skin beneath her chin, hoping to soothe her. A riot of feelings bombarded him. She was all but naked and tied open beneath him, so lust was there, demanding attention. He hadn't realized quite how much he'd like the bondage stuff, but he had to admit it was an enormous turn-on.

Those deeper emotions were there, too, making him soft in the head, turning his muscles to soup. And the damn tenderness, choking him, making his own eyes damp—he wanted to cradle her close and tell her everything would be okay. But he didn't even know what the problem was yet.

"I won't hurt you, Becky."

She turned her head away until her nose was pressed deep into the lace-edged pillow. George smoothed her hair. He loved her hair.

Shit, he loved her.

No woman had ever plagued him the way she did. No woman had ever turned him on, turned him inside out, and made him generally nuts the way she did.

And right now, she was afraid of him.

To ease the way, he stalled for time. "I'm sorry to subject you to this, but now comes the ickier part."

Her brows drew together and she glanced his way. "Ickier part?"

"Disposing of the condom." He sat up beside her on the bed. He made such an indent in the mattress, her hips rolled toward him. George grinned, grabbed several tissues from the nightstand and peeled the condom off.

Becky watched in fascination. "I hadn't thought about that."

"Really?" At least she wasn't crying now. She was such an inquisitive little ex-virgin. "And you had this all planned so well."

She snorted. "Obviously not well enough." A hard tug on the restraints proved her point.

George dropped the condom into the bedside waste can. "You have more rubbers on hand?"

She sniffed, sounding very put out but also curious as to what he intended to do. She bobbed her head. "I bought a whole box. They're in the drawer."

"I like a woman who thinks positive." George retrieved a few more of the little silver packets—and noticed the wooden ruler in the drawer. "Ah, what's this?"

"What?"

George lifted it out, pleased that she had started to relax enough to converse. He waved it under her nose. "Planned to do your own calculations, did you?"

"Yes." She glared at him and her face was hot. "Before you ruined everything."

George dropped the ruler and rubbers on the top of the nightstand. He turned and rested his hand on her belly. "Ruined things how, babe?"

For long moments, she simply stared at him, utter defeat clouding her gaze.

"Come on, Becky," he encouraged, knowing he couldn't pull back now. "Explain it to me. Maybe things'll turn out way different than you expect."

"I'm don't want you—any man—to see me."

That totally took George off guard. He wasn't at all sure what he'd been expecting, but modesty over her body? It didn't make sense. He glanced at her sprawled form, which looked beyond delectable even in the dark shadows. Thank God for the night light or he wouldn't have been able to see her at all.

Her long skirt was twisted around her legs, her ankle socks were bunched, but the rest of her . . . well, she was naked.

She was his.

"Why the hell not?" Her pale breasts and belly showed up just fine. "You're beautiful."

"*No.*" She shook her head, mussing her hair once more. For a woman who starched her pillowcases, she sure had a problem keeping her hair in order. "I don't . . . don't look how you probably think I look."

"Is that right?" George cupped her breasts. Even now, when she was frantic to get away from him, her nipples stiffened under his touch and her heartbeat lurched.

"Let's see," he murmured, while playing with her pretty breasts. "These are real, not enhanced. A gift from Mother Nature, and they look even better than I'd imagined."

"George! I didn't mean that."

He slid his hand to her waist—and felt her stiffen. "No

girdle," he said, watching her closely. "You're not bone skinny, but your curves are all perfect."

She squeezed her eyes shut.

George moved his palm lower, over her hip and then under her to cup one round cheek through the corduroy of her skirt. "There sure as hell isn't anything fake about this great ass. So that leaves, what? Your belly button? Do you have two? An outie, maybe? Hell, Becky, I like outies. No? That's not it?"

"No."

He'd never heard so much misery in one word. George stroked her right thigh through the skirt—and heard her catch her breath against a cry. He knew he hadn't hurt her, so that had to mean her embarrassment was over her legs. But why? She did always wear long skirts, and even now, when they were in bed together, she had her legs covered. He frowned in suspicion.

Whatever bothered her, it wasn't going to be easy to convince her that he didn't give a damn.

He decided it was best to bypass that topic for now, and instead reached beneath her skirt and between her legs.

She went rigid, but for different reasons.

"You're awfully tight," George admitted, and pushed his middle finger into her.

She squirmed, gasped. Moaned softly.

"I like that, Becky. I really do. You squeezed me and I lost it." With gentle care, he pressed in and out, rasping against already sensitized, swollen tissues. She was so wet, still excited. He kissed her open mouth. "You were a virgin, weren't you?"

She groaned.

"I like that too, babe, though how the hell you kept your virginity for so long amazes me. A woman as sexy and sweet and beautiful as you is just made to be fucked."

She made a small sound of dazed excitement. George smiled. Becky liked it when he talked dirty to her. He'd noticed that early on, and right now, he wanted her insensate with lust. He wanted her to forget whatever inhibitions remained, whatever troubled her, scared her. He wanted her to trust him.

He wanted her love.

Looking at her with new insight, he asked, "Does this feel good, Becky?"

"Yes." That single word shivered almost as much as Becky did.

She was so precious, so hungry for physical contact and yet such a sweet innocent. The contradictions drove him wild, and made it impossible not to love her. "If I'm going to squeeze back into you again—and you can be damn sure that I am—we need to prepare you a little more. Let's try two fingers, okay?"

Her head tipped back, exposing her pale throat where her pulse raced. "Yes. Okay."

He smiled at her immediate, husky reply. She held her breath as he began working the second finger into her, not roughly, but with insistence. "Take deep breaths, that's it. A little more." Her feminine muscles squeezed his fingers as he pushed forward until he had them completely inside her. "I told you I'd fit."

Her eyes closed. "But you didn't."

"Only because you didn't let me get you ready. Remember me telling you that women need to be touched?"

She swallowed hard. "Yes."

"Especially here." He found her clitoris with his thumb and pressed.

"Ohmigod."

"Yeah, that feels good, doesn't it?" He watched her, loving the way her face, her chest and breasts pinkened. Satisfaction flowed through him as she began to tense. "Next time I slide deep into you, you'll be so wet and ready, you'll be begging me to hurry."

She opened one eye to stare at him in doubt. George

grinned and kissed her again. "Now, I'm going to scoot down just a little bit—no, don't get all antsy on me. I only want to get to your breasts. You have very soft, heavy breasts. They turn me on, and I especially love how your nipples taste."

"Oh." She arched, offering herself to him.

George tested her self-control by kissing just below a nipple, around it, touching with his tongue.

"George?"

"Hmmm?"

"Will you . . . um . . ."

"What?"

"Suck on me again?"

He'd already come not more than five minutes ago, and with just a small request, she had him painfully hard once more. "Yeah. You can bet I will." He went back to teasing her.

"George?"

Hiding his grin, he said, "Hmmm?"

"When?"

He curled his tongue around her and drew her into the wet heat of his mouth. Her moan was nice and deep and real. He liked it. He liked helping her forget her silly qualms about her body. What, did she have freckles on her legs? A birthmark? He'd show her that it didn't matter—after he had her mindless with lust and limp from a screaming orgasm.

Within minutes, Becky was squirming and gasping and George knew she was close. He wanted to be inside her when she came, but decided he could be generous. She deserved a lot of pleasure, and he'd enjoy giving it to her.

He kissed her ribs, down her belly.

Becky groaned. She jerked and pulled against the handcuffs, then flopped back in defeat.

"Sorry, babe, but you're not nearly strong enough to free yourself." He dipped his tongue into her navel.

"What . . . what are you going to do?" She sounded both anxious and worried.

He wanted her to enjoy her first orgasm with him, so he didn't push the issue of her skirt. Instead, he spread the skirt out across her wide-opened legs. Becky tried to bring her knees together but the footcuffs stopped her.

"None of that. You're open to me, and I can touch you, taste you, and look at you, as much as I want. Just relax and enjoy."

He ignored her continued struggles, her rasping breaths, and raised just the middle of the skirt, keeping her thighs hidden but revealing her mound. She went perfectly still.

Being the master of understatement, George said quietly, "Now isn't this pretty."

Becky groaned, but otherwise didn't reply.

He fingered the dark blond curls decorating her sex; they were damp with her excitement. "Very, very pretty."

Her heels pressed into the mattress, but she still didn't say anything. Unable to wait a second more, George carefully parted her. "All sweet and pink. You're beautiful, Becky."

"You're looking at me!" She sounded scandalized—and aroused.

"Hell yes." He stroked his fingers over her, opening her more, teasing her. "I love looking at you." He leaned down and kissed her deeply.

Her hips shot off the bed. *"George."*

He held her steady, keeping her poised high, and continued to taste and tongue and nip at her.

"Ohmigod, ohmigod, ohmigod."

The taste of her, her spicy female scent, filled him. He held her tight so she couldn't lurch away from him, found her clitoris—and suckled.

In that moment, George knew she forgot all about her worries. She thrashed and cried and pressed herself against his mouth, as much as she could, considering she was tightly bound to the bed.

She begged him with words and actions to continue. He stayed with her, carefully attentive to her reactions so he'd know exactly what she liked the most.

"Back inside you again," he whispered against her hot flesh when he felt her begin to tighten, felt her legs tensing. He pushed two fingers deep, out, in again—and she came.

It was pretty damn special, George thought, watching Becky come, tasting her release, hearing her low cries.

When she finally quieted, her body going boneless against the mattress, he reared up, grabbed another condom, and in record time, he was over her. She didn't have time to accustom herself or gather her objections.

George shoved her skirt aside, but kept his gaze locked on her face. Her eyes opened in startled alarm, met his, and went soft and vague as he thrust into her.

"You can take me, Becky," he ground out from between his clenched teeth. *"All of me."*

Her hands curled into fists, her head tipped back. George kissed her throat, bit her shoulder, and rocked into her. "More," he said as he felt her hips lift, shift in an effort to accommodate him. "More, more, more . . . ah, yeah."

Becky panted, her whole body dewy, drawn taut. He knew he filled her, that she felt strained. She was young and virginal and stretched tight around him, squeezing him, gripping him.

George slowly pulled out, moaned with her, and just as slowly drove back in. "Perfect," he said. "Fucking perfect."

Becky whispered, "Yes," and amazingly enough began to shiver in another release.

He wanted her to come again, with him this time. He slipped his hands under her satiny bottom and helped her to meet the rhythm that would drive them both over the edge.

"Faster," she begged, then, brokenly, on a whimper, *"Harder."*

George shuddered. The bed rocked with his thrusts. He felt Becky tense, felt her body go rigid, and it was enough. He held her closer, drove deep into her one last time, and they both shook with an explosive release.

George collapsed on top of her. Her body was small and soft and damp beneath his. Her hair tickled his nose. Her gentle breath brushed his sweaty shoulder. Her plump breasts cushioned his chest. He wanted to stay this way forever, the two of them still connected, their hearts beating together.

For the moment, Becky wasn't shy or apprehensive. She was sated. She was his.

He dreaded moving because he didn't want her to start shying away from him again, but he knew he was too heavy for her, and he knew her arms had to be tired.

Forcing his muscles to work, George braced above her. "Mmm," he teased, and kissed her slack mouth. "You're something else, lady."

As if by a great effort, her eyelids lifted. "George?"

Her love-soft voice made him smile. "Did you enjoy yourself, sweetheart?"

Her gaze roamed over his face, finally settling on his eyes. "You're incredible." Her sigh brushed his throat. "And very big."

"But not too big to fit."

"No."

George regretted what was to come. He drew a breath to prepare himself, then cupped her cheek. "Now, let's see what has you so shy, okay?"

All the sleepy satisfaction left her face. Instinctively, her arms jerked, trying to be free. She glanced up at the hand-cuffs still around her wrists, then back at him. She cried out. Her legs twisted and tugged, shaking the bed.

Disregarding her futile efforts, though they tore at his heart, George sat up. Knowing she watched him, he disposed of the second condom much as he had the first. The sound of her strenuous breathing filled the air between them.

When he finished, he turned on the bedside lamp and faced her. She squinted against the light, tried to twist away from it, from him. Her voluminous skirt was now bunched and tangled around her thighs.

"George, please . . ." she said, without much evident hope.

Her pleading tone ate at him—and strengthened his resolve. He shoved her skirt aside—and froze.

Becky gave a soft sob.

Her entire right thigh was marred with zigzagging scars, some deep, some shallow. The skin was puckered, pinkish in places, roughened in others. They feathered out around the front of her hip, then got worse, uglier, down her leg, her knee, and partially onto her calf.

Acting solely on emotion, George cupped his hand around her knee and bent closer. "Jesus, what happened?"

"Don't touch me."

Her flat voice brought out his frown. "Don't touch you? You're naked in bed, Becky. I've just finished making love to you, twice. You're the sexiest woman I've ever known, and regardless of what you think of me, I care about you. Of course I'll touch you."

"Go away."

"Not on your life." He was angry at her for not trusting him, for evidently considering him a shallow ass. He was angry that she'd hidden herself for so long, that she'd let it matter too much. Angry that she didn't know what a beautiful, amazing, unbelievable woman she was.

She didn't even realize he loved her.

"Tell me what happened."

Devoid of feeling, she said, "A car wreck."

He caressed her, from the inside of her knee to her groin then back again. Bound as she was, she couldn't do a damn thing to stop him. "How old were you?"

"Twelve."

"Surgery?" His heart threatened to break, thinking of his Becky at the tender age of twelve, so hurt, so emotionally wounded, too.

She managed a shrug despite the handcuffs. "Some. It helped me to walk again, but there was nothing they could do to make it look better."

Very gently, George said, "They're just scars, Becky."

"They're hideous. Kids . . . they used to make fun of me at school. The ones who weren't mean, who didn't tease, just stared instead. They'd look at me with pity." She spoke with no emotion at all. "My mom started buying me long skirts to hide my leg, but by then, everyone already knew."

"So you never dated? Never gave a guy a chance?"

She looked at him, her face almost blank. "I dated a guy once. When he saw my leg, he got sick." Her laugh scared him because it didn't sound like his Becky, didn't sound sweet and shy and innocent. "Needless to say, he never asked me out again."

George floundered for a proper reply, but all he could think to say was the truth. "I'm not him, you know."

"No?"

"Nope. It doesn't matter to me, Becky."

She laughed again.

George decided he'd just have to show her. He gave her a friendly slap on the hip. "You know what I want to do?"

Her gaze turned wary. "What?"

"I want to turn you loose, first. Much as I enjoy seeing you like this"—he leered at her, to make his point—"I know your arms must be getting tired."

"They are." She still looked doubtful.

"Okay then. We'll shower, probably fool around a little more, then I'd like to spend the night." He put his hand back on her belly, this time under her skirt. "Will you let me stay with you?"

"Why?" She appeared genuinely perplexed by his request.

"You mean other than the fact that I haven't gotten nearly enough of you?" He grinned at her expression. "All right, I'll bare my soul again. I'm a man in need of reassurance. I've got that damned reputation to live up to, but you only came twice and then only after I'd already acted like a pig and lost control. I need to know that you still respect me."

"George," she said, almost laughing but not quite.

He tickled his fingertips down her leg to her ankle, back up again to her hipbone. "I need to know that you haven't lost hope, that you'll give me a few more chances to show you that I can be a considerate lover. A great lover. A lover worthy of an awesome reputation." He bobbed his eyebrows. "I can't have you running back to work with tales of my shortcomings."

"Shortcomings?" She smiled past her tears. "You're a nut. You already know you're awesome."

"Awesome enough that you'll let me spend the night?"

The laughter was replaced with hope. "You really want to?"

"Damn straight." He unhooked her legs and massaged them in case they were stiff. He ignored her rigidity when he rubbed over the scars, pretending he hadn't noticed. "Feel better?"

A hot blush colored her face. "Yes."

George unhooked both her arms and went through the same process, rubbing and stroking. Then he looked down at her breasts. "I feel like Pavlov's dog."

She folded her arms around herself. "What do you mean?"

"I see your breasts, and already I'm conditioned to drool." He shook his head, a little stunned, a lot chagrined. "Damn, I want you again. Already. I'm insatiable."

Two heartbeats passed, and then Becky tackled him to

his back. She trembled, and she had a death grip on his neck. George, feeling his own throat close with emotion, held her tight. "Don't cry, Becky. I can't bear it."

She sniffed and snuggled closer. "George?"

"Yeah?"

"If I let you stay, you have to let me measure you."

He laughed and rolled her beneath him. "Deal."

George woke to an empty bed. He sat bolt upright in alarm, but Becky was nowhere to be seen. Frowning, he realized sunshine filtered through the drapes. When he looked at the clock, he was stunned to realize he'd slept so late. It was nearly ten, when he almost never stayed in bed after eight. Especially when there wasn't a woman in bed with him.

He frowned—then heard the feminine whispering in the other room. Becky had company, and he could just guess who it was. Asia and that damned Erica. Were they gossiping about him even now?

George grabbed up a sheet, halfheartedly wrapped it around his waist, and slunk to the door to listen. Yep, that strident voice belonged to Erica. Was she trying to talk Becky out of getting involved? She was so damned cynical about men, even when she was being amusing.

Because he couldn't hear anything clearly, George opened the door and slipped halfway down the hall. He heard Asia say, "You let him spend the whole night? Why, Becky, you little tart."

The women laughed, so he knew Asia was only teasing.

"Is it love at first lay, then?" Erica wanted to know, and George thought about storming out and muzzling her.

But Becky's next words stopped him cold.

"Of course not, Erica. I'm actually amazed that he even wanted to stay the night."

Both Erica and Asia asked, "Why?"

There was a long expectant moment, and Becky sighed. "There's something neither of you know."

George peeked around the corner in time to see Erica bound to her feet. "What did he do to you?"

"No, it's not like that."

Asia touched Erica's arm. "There's something she wants to tell us. Is that right, Becky?"

"Yes." But rather than explain, Becky stood. She straightened stiff and proud, and lifted her nightgown, showing her friends her leg.

George wanted to groan. He knew she expected them to be horrified, to be disgusted. If either of them hurt her feelings, he'd . . .

Asia whispered, "Dear God, Becky, what happened?"

And Erica asked with concern, "Does it still hurt?"

Becky dropped her nightgown back into place. "I was in a wreck when I was young. No, it doesn't hurt, but you see how ugly it is."

Erica turned militant. "Did George think it was ugly?"

"He said not. He said it didn't matter."

"Of course he's right." Asia stood to hug her. "You should trust what he tells you, honey."

Erica laughed. "True enough. George doesn't care about a few scars on your leg, Becky. He probably only cares about what's between your legs."

The comment sent George right over the edge. Dressed only in a sheet, he stormed into the room. "You don't know what you're talking about, Erica."

Erica stood, too, so that the three women grouped together to stare at him in shock.

Three sets of feminine eyes roved over him, from his naked chest and legs to his tenuous hold on the sheet at his hip.

Asia gulped.

Becky blushed. "George, you're naked!"

Erica recovered first. She gave a wolf whistle, then said

to Becky, "Honey, there are some things a woman never complains about. I think this might be just such an occasion."

George was too disgruntled to be embarrassed. "I don't like having you speak for me, Erica."

Asia raised her brows. "You're saying she's wrong? That you do care about Becky's leg?"

Becky looked horrified. "Asia!"

"Of course I care about her leg."

In a united front, Asia and Erica flanked Becky. They looked ready to castrate him. Becky looked devastated.

At the ragged end of his emotions, George stomped forward. When he touched Becky's cheek, his hand shook. "I love your leg, and what's between your legs, and your heart and your hair and your—"

Becky gulped out a laugh. Her face turned bright pink.

Beside her, Asia beamed. "Well now, this is wonderful."

Erica snorted. Before she could say anything, George reeled on her. "Isn't it your turn to go hang out in the porn shop?"

A heavy silence fell. All three women scrutinized him, Asia with a touch of guilt.

Becky breathed in accusation, *"You knew."*

George wanted things settled. "Damn right I knew." He cocked a brow. "Or at least I thought I did. You put a definite spin on things that I hadn't anticipated."

Asia and Erica leaned around Becky to look at each other. "A spin? Now that sounds interesting. Do tell."

George rolled his eyes and ignored them. "I didn't really give a damn what your so-called fantasy was, because all my fantasies are about you. No matter what, I couldn't lose."

Erica rubbed her hands together. "Better and better."

George growled, "Will you two go? I'd like to propose in private."

Becky blinked. "Propose? You mean . . . you mean . . ."

Knowing he'd just blown any chance for privacy, George groaned. Then, filled with determination, he cupped Becky's chin and demanded, "Marry me, Becky."

Asia squealed. Erica laughed. Next thing George knew, he was caught in their circle and they were all dancing and jumping and singing their way around the room like a gaggle of loons.

He damn near lost his sheet, and when he made a grab for it, he stumbled. "Damn it, she hasn't said yes, yet!"

They stopped bouncing around. Becky covered her mouth with a shaking hand. She looked at Erica, looked at Asia. Glowed at George. "Yes."

Satisfaction rolled through George, followed closely by a tidal wave of lust. "Good." He grabbed her wrist with his free hand. "Let's go back to bed."

Erica burst out laughing. "Men. They are so predictable."

George stumbled to an outraged halt.

Asia said, "Uh-oh. Bad timing, my girl."

He turned and stalked back to Erica. "You are next, right, Erica?"

She lifted her brows with mock confusion. "Next?"

"To visit the blasted shop." He had her cornered and they both knew it. He took swift advantage. "So tell us, Erica, what's your fantasy?"

"Wouldn't you like to know," she quipped, but Asia and Becky just crossed their arms, not offering her an iota of help. Asia even tapped her foot.

"You wouldn't understand."

"Why?" George put his arm around Becky, hauling her close. "Because I'm a lowly male?"

Becky said, "He's very understanding, Erica," and George couldn't help but kiss her.

"George will be family, soon," Asia pointed out. "So tell."

Rolling her eyes, Erica blurted, "All right, all right." She put her hands on her hips, thrust her chin in the air, and said, "Prepare yourself, kiddies." Then she named her fantasy with a taunting smile.

Asia and Becky went wide-eyed. George straightened in surprise. Thinking of what she intended, and what she'd likely get, George started to laugh—until Erica gave him a sloe-eyed, seductive look. He could tell that she expected him to poke fun, to ridicule her. Her opinions on men weren't overly complimentary.

Well, he wouldn't give her the satisfaction of reacting as she expected.

But he couldn't resist saying, "I pity the poor bastard who runs into you. He doesn't stand a chance."

"No, he doesn't," Erica assured him.

Giving up, George turned and dragged Becky back toward the bedroom.

Asia was still laughing when Becky yelled over her shoulder, "I think it sounds wonderful, Erica! You can start on Monday."

George pulled her into the room and slammed the door. He dropped the sheet, picked her up, and crawled into bed with her held close to his heart. "Wonderful, huh?"

Becky touched his chest. "Not as wonderful as you."

George stared into her eyes, watching her reactions as he slid his hands up her thighs, then spread them wide so he could nestle in between. Becky flinched when he touched her scarred leg, but George knew now that she'd get over that in time. In a thousand ways, he'd show her that she was the perfect woman for him. "I love you, Becky." He stroked her thigh. "All of you."

Big tears welled in her eyes. "I love you too."

"Is that right?" He was already hard, but hearing her say that made him burn.

"I've been hung up on you for a long time. What you said about me being your fantasy? You're mine. You've always been mine."

George smiled. "That's all I ever want to be." He kissed her. "Yours."

"George?"

She sounded so serious, George gave up his contemplation of her breasts to give her all his attention. "What, babe?"

"Do you think Erica is going to end up hurt?"

He rolled over and pulled Becky on top of him. "I think Erica is going to learn a very well-deserved lesson. But if you're worried about her, I can lend a helping hand."

"How?" Becky groaned as he began fondling her breasts.

"I'll make sure the right guy knows what she's up to." Cameron had helped him along, so George figured it was the least he could do.

Becky smiled. "Ah. And I know just the right guy."

He scowled, then caught her nipples in a tantalizing taunt. "You wanna rephrase that, Becky?"

She laughed, squirmed, and when he didn't release her, she groaned. "The right guy for Erica."

"That's better. Now enough about Erica. Come here and love me."

"All right." She peeked at him. "Can I handcuff you again?"

George's heart pounded and his cock flexed. Damn, seeing Becky in a frisky, kinky mood was enough to make any man lose the battle. "You know, I believe you can."

Naughty By Night

Janelle Denison

Chapter One

Chloe Anderson hummed to herself as she blended a batch of strawberry margaritas, her hips swaying rhythmically as she worked. Heated desire ignited in the deepest part of Gabe Mackenzie and spread outward, feeding the hunger she inspired. He watched her in silence, his presence in the kitchen of her apartment still unnoticed. Hell, according to her brother, Chloe didn't even know he was back in town. But she would. As soon as he'd looked his fill.

She was hotter and sexier than the sexual fantasies that had sustained him since the last time he'd seen her seven months ago. Her soft honey blond curls were clipped on top of her head and spiral strands wisped around her nape. He ached to press his lips to that vulnerable, exposed curve of her neck. Craved to taste and tease and coax her surrender in any way she'd allow.

Soon, he'd do just that.

His hungry gaze flickered lower. She wore a pair of well-worn jean shorts that rode low on her hips and a pink cotton camisole that was held up by thin straps he could easily rip apart with his bare hands. At the moment, he was feeling primal and possessive enough to do just that. The hem of her top ended at the inward dip of her waist, revealing a strip of tanned skin around her midriff. His fingers flexed, itching to caress her smooth flesh.

Her bare legs were endlessly long, the kind that inspired provocative images of stroking his hands up her sleek thighs as he pressed them apart . . . and more erotic visions of having those gorgeous, slender legs wrapped tight around his hips in the throes of passion.

The tantalizing thought made the temperature of his blood rise another notch. He lifted his gaze back to the classic lines of her profile just as she rolled a fat, juicy strawberry into a sugar bowl and took a big bite of the fruit. Juice dribbled down her chin and she caught the sticky sweetness with her fingers, then sucked each one of them clean . . . slowly, leisurely, thoroughly.

It wasn't difficult to imagine her tongue swirling and licking him in the same delicious way. Arousal settled low and deep in his belly, and he drew in a steady breath to keep his unruly hormones under control. A futile attempt, he knew. She'd always had an effortless way of revving his libido, and the damnable thing was, she had no clue the power she held over him. Had no idea just how much he wanted her. Had *always* wanted her.

Tonight she was going to learn the truth, and more. There would be no avoiding him, and no denying what he ultimately desired. Chloe. In his bed. In his life. In his future. Unfortunately, a huge obstacle stood in the way—gaining her forgiveness for walking out of her life six years ago.

He had less than a week to breach the barriers she'd erected since that cool spring night when he'd hurt her so badly. This time, he wouldn't allow her to reduce their conversations to polite chitchat as she now tended to do, or pretend as if what they'd shared for a very brief time hadn't meant anything at all to her. He knew better. The emotions he'd glimpsed in her eyes over the ensuing years told a different tale.

She still wanted him, too.

The attraction still burned hot between them and he intended to confront and pursue it—and her—by any means necessary. Including executing a shameless, all-out seduction she wouldn't be able to resist. Starting tonight, at the weekly Monday night poker game between Chloe and her brothers. And the one invited guest she wasn't aware of. Yet.

She turned the blender off, reached into the cupboard, and brought down a crystal glass. Wetting the wide rim, she dipped it into the sugar to coat the lip of the glass, still oblivious to his presence. But Gabe was very aware of the fact that his time alone with her was limited. All three of Chloe's older brothers were only a room away, setting up the table for the card game.

If he didn't act fast, the opportunity to shake up her defenses and stake his claim would be lost. "Chloe," he murmured in a low, silky drawl.

She spun around at the sound of her name, her bright green eyes widening with startled surprise when they landed on him. "Gabe!" His name escaped on a gasp.

Taking advantage of her shock, he closed the distance between them in three long strides, slid his fingers into the loose hair at the back of her head to keep her from pulling away, and claimed her mouth with his own. Her body stiffened, and she grasped the edge of the counter behind her for support. Amazingly enough her lips softened and grew pliable beneath the heat and persuasion of his, and he wasted no time slipping his tongue inside with a hot, searing stroke that stated his intentions in a way she couldn't misinterpret.

A faint, strangled sound rose in the back of her throat, which quickly coalesced into a soft moan of pleasure when he angled her head and deepened their kiss. A shameless, erotic embrace designed to make her weak with wanting, and mindless with need. She tasted like the sweetness of berries and womanly desire, and the ripe flavor was like an aphrodisiac to his already overloaded senses.

Beyond rational thinking, and with his sole focus on the woman he'd waited years to make his, he placed his free hand on her bare waist and feathered his thumb across the soft skin of her belly. She shivered at his alluring touch, and he boldly stepped closer, bringing her hips into intimate contact with the fierce erection straining the front of his jeans. He moved against her, a subtle roll of his hips, letting her feel exactly what she did to him. He wanted to brand this moment into her memory for her to think about later, when he took their simmering attraction to the next level of seduction.

Too soon for his liking, he lifted his head, untangled his fingers from her hair, and glided his open palm along her jaw in a tender caress. He took great satisfaction in the knowledge that not once did she attempt to stop his advance.

Her breathing was ragged and aroused. With every rise and fall of her full breasts the taut nipples pressing against her cotton camisole top grazed his chest. He enjoyed the feeling, enjoyed even more that she wasn't wearing a bra so that he could appreciate the way the soft material molded to those shapely mounds.

"That was a long time coming," he murmured, his voice low and husky as his thumb stroked across her bottom lip, still hot and wet from their kiss. "But definitely worth the wait."

Even now, when she could have found a way to evade his touch, she didn't back down or try to move away. Adopting an indignant attitude had never been her style. Stubbornness was more suited to her personality, and that mutinous characteristic made an appearance now.

She held her ground, bare toes to his sneakered feet, never once letting on that he'd managed to ruffle her composure with his spontaneous kiss, or that his nearness bothered her. He admired her spirit and fortitude, and knew those traits would work to his favor more than her own.

Her chin lifted, and her eyes flashed with a mixture of defiance and wry humor. "A simple hello would have sufficed just fine."

A bad-boy grin curved the corner of his mouth as his wandering finger found the pulse beating rapidly at the base of her throat. "Every simple, polite hello we've exchanged in the past six years has left me lukewarm when I know the two of us can burn red-hot."

"So, you decided to just walk into my place and kiss me like you own me?"

He tugged playfully on a stray spiral curl and dipped his head closer to hers, tempted to take her mouth again. "Got your attention, didn't it?"

She rolled her eyes in disbelief and moved her head back. The strand of hair slipped from his fingers, severing the connection between them. "You know, I don't remember you being so arrogant."

He shrugged, unwilling to admit that his actions had nothing to do with arrogance and were more centered on the need to claim what he'd forfeited that night so long ago. "It has its time and place."

With an audacious wink, he turned and exited the kitchen, knowing she wasn't ready to hear the truth about his feelings just yet. He'd fallen hard and fast for her six years ago, at a time when his life was in the midst of turmoil. He'd been drafted into the NFL, so very close to grasping his dream, and in a split second lost it all when he'd torn a ligament in his knee, which had ended his career as a professional football player before it ever began.

With nothing promising to offer her, and fearing he'd never claw his way out of the poverty that had always been his way of life, he'd walked away from her, believing he was doing the honorable thing by giving her the chance to find someone who could give her everything he couldn't.

The ensuing years had been good to him, in ways he'd never imagined or expected. Yet no matter how hard he'd tried to forget about Chloe and move on, she'd remained deeply rooted within his mind and heart. And since there was no purging her from his soul, this time he was playing for keeps.

For him, it could be no other way.

Chloe felt as though she'd been swept into the eye of a hurricane and spit back out, leaving her neat and orderly world tipped on its axis and her body still reeling from the aftershock. Gabe had returned. And with his unexpected and thorough possession of her mouth he'd staked some kind of primitive, male claim with his hot, unapologetic kiss. But why her and why now?

She touched her trembling fingers to her puffy, still tingling lips. She had no answers to that particular question, and he hadn't been forthcoming about those details, either. Obviously he believed he could barge right back into her life and pick up where they'd left off all those years ago. And she'd done nothing to stop his direct and explicit invasion.

Turning back to the counter, she poured the strawberry margarita mix into her glass with a shaky hand and her heart still beating wildly in her chest. If there ever was a man who could make her pulse race at the mere mention of his name, let alone a kiss, it was Gabe MacKenzie, a sexy, blue-eyed rebel who'd played a reoccurring role in every guilty, erotic fantasy she'd indulged in since high school. Unbidden, he slipped into her most private dreams and aroused her with wicked, forbidden pleasures, yet she always woke up with her breasts tight and aching, and her body throbbing with need. The same way he'd left her nearly six years ago, the night they'd finally given in to their mutual attraction.

A night that had ended in her first taste of heartbreak.

A lifetime ago, yet her recollections were as fresh as yesterday. Gabe had come home from Chicago during spring break from his senior year in college. After her brother Derek had stood him up for a hotter date, Chloe had offered to join Gabe for a casual pizza dinner. Afterward, they'd driven to a secluded hilltop spot that overlooked the city of San Diego. There, he'd told her about the knee injury he'd sustained during a football game that had ended his career as a professional quarterback and any chance at the NFL.

He'd been clearly upset and at a loss as to where his future was headed. When she'd spontaneously leaned across the console to brush her lips across his cheek in a comforting gesture, he'd turned his head and her mouth had landed on his. That's all it took for their suppressed desire for each other to flare out of control. After slow, deep kisses and caresses that had quickly turned intimate, he'd abruptly stopped his skillful strokes just as she reached the brink of a breathtaking orgasm. Without an explanation—just an oppressive silence hanging between them—he'd driven her home, leaving her unfulfilled and aching, as well as hurt and confused. But most of all, once he was gone, she'd missed the friendship they'd shared.

She closed her eyes and shivered at the provocative memory of that long-ago night, hating that he still had the ability to affect her so strongly after all this time. She'd become adept at keeping him at arm's length and protecting her emotions and in a moment of spontaneous passion he'd shaken her control and resolve.

Now Gabe was back, bold as he pleased, kissing her like he had every right to. She had no idea what his intentions entailed, but judging by that sexy gleam in his eyes she considered herself fairly warned.

She'd learned from the past. He'd broken her heart once and she wouldn't allow him to do so again. No matter how the man's kisses turned her inside out with carnal longings.

She took a big gulp of her frothy drink and waited for the double shot of tequila to settle her nerves while her mind debated a strategy of her own. She'd initially been thrown by Gabe's aggressive overture, but having been raised with three older, competitive brothers, she'd learned young to never back down from a dare, which her male siblings considered a sign of weakness they could pounce on and exploit to their benefit.

If anyone was going to be exploited tonight, it would be Gabe, because she was going to fight his brand of sensual fire with her own unabashed approach. She'd be just as brazen as he, only this time she'd walk away with her emotions firmly intact.

A private smile curled the corner of her mouth as she took another sip of her drink. Oh, yes, she liked the idea of giving Gabe as good as he dished out.

Feeling calmer now, she refilled her margarita, grabbed the snack mix she'd poured into a bowl earlier, and headed into the other room. Gabe's back faced her as he conversed with Scott and Chad, two of her other siblings. He'd picked up a cold long-neck beer somewhere along the way, and she took a brief moment to admire a body that had, amazingly enough, improved with age. He'd been the star quarterback in high school, always in shape, and still no excess fat clung to his waist. His shoulders were still as wide as ever, tapering to narrow, lean hips, and giving way to a nice, tight ass that deserved a lingering, appreciative glance.

Tearing her gaze from that enticing sight, she placed the bowl of snacks on the dinette table. The surface had been set up with a deck of cards and colored playing chips for their Monday night poker game, which had become a weekly ritual a few years ago and a way for her and her brothers to make time for one another outside of obligatory family gatherings. While it was just the four of them for the most part, every so often someone brought a guest to make the game more interesting.

And Gabe definitely livened up the evening.

She willed her legs to move forward and join her brothers in the living room. Deliberately, she came to a stop next to Gabe, just to prove she could stand this close to him and resist the temptation he posed to her body and senses. She glanced up and met his gaze, the dark irises still hot and smoldering from the kiss they'd shared minutes ago. Thick jet black hair was tousled around his head in a way that begged her to reach out and sift her fingers through the inky strands. The ebony color provided a velvet backdrop to his striking blue eyes, which had no doubt cajoled and enthralled many women over the years. Just as the heat and awareness glimmering in the depths seduced her now.

One deep inhale, and she realized he smelled good enough to take a big bite out of. Or nibble and lick leisurely. Every glorious, masculine inch of him. She could literally *feel* the sexual magnetism pouring off him, a natural confidence that kindled too much need and desire and the kind of craving no other man but Gabe had managed to stir within her.

She gave herself a hard mental shake. God, she was crazy to still lust after him, but the knowledge that he was still under her skin only served to reinforce her plan to take advantage of the opportunity Gabe had presented and indulge in a little sexual revenge of her own.

With effort, she transferred her gaze to her brother Derek, who'd brought Gabe as a guest. "Nice of you to bring fresh blood to our weekly poker game," she told him, an upbeat, sassy note to her voice.

Derek chuckled. "Shhh. I told him it would be a *friendly* game of poker."

"You didn't warn him just how ruthless Chloe can be with a new player?" Scott asked, amusement creasing his handsome features. "Why not just have Gabe empty the contents of his wallet into her purse and be done with it."

Chloe beamed at the compliment. She had to agree that

she *was* an impressive poker player, and she'd learned from the best. Her ruthless, card-shark brothers had granted her no leniency for being the youngest in the family, or for being the fairer sex. She'd learned quickly that it was either learn the game and play it well, or end up fifty bucks poorer every week.

She slanted Gabe a sly look. "I'll go easy on him, boys," she said, the promise not quite as pure as it should have been. Besides, she found the thought of beating the pants off Gabe MacKenzie too irresistible, in more ways than one.

He held her gaze, one dark brow raising, matching the subtle challenge she'd just issued. "No need to go easy on me, Chloe," he drawled lazily. "I can definitely hold my own in a poker game."

And with you, she read in his gaze. "Okay, consider yourself forewarned then." She smiled sweetly.

Her brothers moved away to make room for another player and put out the rest of the pretzels and peanuts. Alone with Gabe once again, yet all too aware that her siblings were within hearing distance so she needed to behave, she decided to stick with polite pleasantries for now.

"So, what have you been up to lately?" After the accident that had ruined his knee, Gabe had redirected his ambitions to representing some of the biggest names in the sports industry. "Still living the good life as a sports agent in Chicago?"

His broad shoulders lifted in a shrug. "I don't know about living the good life," he said modestly, "but yeah, I'm still doing the sports agent thing."

She caught the slightly wistful note in his voice and words, as if his life lacked something despite all that he'd achieved on his own. An amazing notion, considering the fact that he was highly successful and made enough money to be considered wealthy, though he certainly didn't wear or flaunt his monetary assets. She guessed a part of him still remained a cautious spender since he'd come from such an impoverished upbringing.

She took another swallow of her drink and slowly licked a bit of sugar off her bottom lip, just to torment him since that's where his eyes had chosen to linger. "What brings you back to San Diego?"

"My mom," he replied, and took a long, slow drink of his beer.

She tipped her head, recalling a bit of information she'd heard from her own mother. "Isn't she off in the Caribbean on a cruise with her new husband?"

He nodded, causing a lock of that silky hair to tumble across his forehead, adding to his virile appearance. "Yeah. She's selling her house here in San Diego and moving to Nevada where Clyde lives and works and she wanted me to go through what's left in my old room. So, I'm here for a week to pack up what I want and tie up other loose ends."

After that kiss he'd planted on her in the kitchen, she wondered if she was one of those other loose ends he intended to tie up. And what, exactly, did that resolution consist of besides a lusty, dizzying kiss?

"And what about you?" he asked, his gaze touching on her damp lips once again, the gesture as evocative as a caress. "It's been a while since we last saw each other. What are you up to?"

She was surprised he remembered their last encounter at a nearby restaurant, which had been very brief as he'd passed her table where she'd been eating lunch with a girl-friend. He'd stopped and asked about her family, his sinful eyes and demeanor as breathtakingly sexy as ever. After a few minutes of polite conversation on her end he'd continued on his way. But as always he'd left a lasting impression, which had carried her through the rest of the day and into the night.

She saw no harm in telling him what she did for a living.

"I just recently went to work for an Internet sales company designing web sites and databases for large corporations."

"Wow," he said, suitably impressed, then followed that up with a teasing comment. "You don't look like any computer geek I've ever known."

She laughed lightly. "Thank you . . . I think."

"That was definitely a compliment," he assured her with an easygoing grin. "Intelligence, a good sense of humor, and natural beauty all in one package is rare to find in a woman these days."

A warm blush swept over her cheeks, startling her, mainly because she wasn't normally prone to such coy mannerisms. But then again, the men she'd dated had never been overly interested in her choice of profession, nor had they seemed to appreciate her attributes the way that Gabe just did. His remark could have been nothing more than a flirtatious ruse, but judging by the serious set of his features, she didn't think so.

"Come on, you two," her brother Chad called from the dining room. "Put your money on the table and let's get the game started."

"We're coming." She turned to go when she felt the brush of Gabe's long fingers at the base of her spine—a fleeting touch that could have been as erotic as a deep, intimate caress for how wildly her pulse escalated. Her breath caught in her throat as she glanced back at him, and a slow, sensual grin appeared on his lips. He looked too damned composed, guileless even, while her entire body thrummed with heated awareness.

Gabe took a seat at the table, and she selected a chair across from him. Her glance encompassed all four men, but lingered the longest on Gabe. "I'm feeling very lucky tonight, boys, so no whining when I win."

"We'll see about that," Derek said, picking up the deck of cards to shuffle.

Gabe's piercing blue eyes remained steady on her as he

withdrew fifty dollars from his leather wallet and tossed it toward Chad, who doled out colored chips for everyone's cash. "I have to say that I feel like I'm going to get lucky tonight, too."

She lifted a brow incredulously, surprised that he'd go so far as to issue her a double entendre in front of her brothers, as well as an obvious dare. And judging by the curious looks her siblings sent her and Gabe's way, they were very aware of the sexual undercurrents between them.

Gabe was being very, very bad, and she decided it was up to her to teach him a thing or two about poker, and maybe a bit about seduction, too. Because if anyone walked away from tonight's game *satisfied,* it would be her.

Shoring up her confidence, she blinked lazily and said in a husky drawl, "Then by all means, let the game begin."

"Ante up," Derek announced, and tossed a handful of roasted peanuts into his mouth. Once everyone added their opening bet to the middle of the table, he dealt the first hand for seven-card stud and the fun began.

After two and a half hours of bawdy jokes, laughter, raucous teasing, and a subtle, seductive push and pull between her and Gabe, the game dwindled down to the last hand and a pot of chips that encompassed the last of everyone's money, except Gabe's, who'd been on a winning streak all night long and who held everyone's surplus in reserve.

Each of her brothers folded their current hand at the delivery of their fourth card because they didn't have enough money left to match Gabe's latest increase in the betting. Chloe was just barely able to remain in the game, and from the looks of her cards, she finally had a decent hand to play.

"I'm out." Chad huffed in disgust, and drowned his loss in a huge swallow of beer.

"Yeah, me, too," Derek echoed, tossing his cards, facedown, onto the table.

Scott did the same, his mouth pursed with exasperation

and his gaze narrowed on Gabe. "How in the hell did you manage to wipe us out?"

Gabe merely smiled and transferred his gaze to Chloe. "How about you, Lady Luck?" he drawled, laughter dancing in his eyes. "Are you willing to risk the rest of your money on this last hand?"

Her supposed luck throughout the game had been dismal, not that she appreciated him rubbing her nose in the fact. Nor was she about to bow out now and admit defeat to him in front of her brothers. She'd play to the bitter end.

To give herself an extra boost of confidence she finished off her third margarita and matched Gabe's current bet. "I'm in."

"You've got guts, I'll give you that," Gabe said, his velvet smooth voice wrapping around her like a long-denied addiction. Tempting, taunting, teasing her.

"Don't gloat too much," she shot back, striving for a bravado she didn't completely feel. "You haven't won yet."

"'Yet' being the operative word," he added, his eyes glimmering with deviltry and too much self-assurance.

The next card was dealt. Her brothers watched the game, adding amusing commentary while Chloe continued to match and raise Gabe's bets, increasing the stakes and tension between them until the final card was doled out. She glanced from her hand, to Gabe's, chewing absently on her bottom lip. As it stood, with four cards faceup, one down, and the last card just being delivered, it appeared that Gabe had a good chance at a flush of diamonds if one of his other cards came through for him, while she was sitting on a three of a kind of fours. Great, another losing hand, she thought grumpily.

Just as she was about to peek at her last facedown card, Gabe reached across the table and pressed his fingers to the rectangular card so that she couldn't lift it up and see what she held. Uncertain of his actions, she met his smoky gaze.

"How about double or nothing," he asked, his tone way

too low and intimate for her peace of mind. Especially with her brothers listening in on the conversation.

Her heart thumped beneath her breast. "That's a nice gesture, but nothing doubled is nothing," she rationalized, as if he couldn't have figured that out for himself. "If you haven't noticed, all of my money is out on the table."

"Yeah, I noticed." He smiled, a bit predatory, and traced a long tapered finger along the edge of her card. "I was thinking of something more along the lines of a personal, private bet to raise the stakes a little more."

She opened her mouth, then snapped it shut. He couldn't be serious.

Oh, but he was.

"Whoa," Scott said and abruptly scooted back his chair and stood, amusement evident in his tone. "I'm not sure I want to hear where this is going."

"I'm with Scott," Chad agreed. "As interesting as this game is getting, I think this is our cue to leave."

Chloe couldn't believe her brothers were ready to bolt out on her. "You don't have to go," she protested, not at all certain she wanted to be left alone with Gabe and whatever he had on his devious mind.

"Yeah, I think we do." Derek shoved his fingers though his sandy blond hair. "Whatever's going on between you and Gabe, and something obviously *is*, it would be better resolved without an audience."

A touch of panic curled in her belly. "*Nothing's* going on!"

"Uh-huh, sure," Derek said knowingly, and turned to Scott. "I came to Chloe's with Gabe, so would you mind dropping me off at my place on your way home?"

Scott grabbed his lightweight jacket and shrugged into it, anxious to be on his way, too. "Not at all."

Derek planted a hand on Gabe's shoulder as he passed his chair and murmured something beneath his breath that Chloe couldn't hear, though judging by the fierce look on her brother's face, he'd just issued Gabe a friendly warning about not hurting his baby sister. While she'd grown used to such protective gestures, Derek had nothing to worry about. She was old enough to take care of herself as far as this man was concerned.

Minutes later, the trio shuffled out of Chloe's condo.

"Thanks a lot, guys," she called after them. The door closed, and the air suddenly turned thick and warm with expectations and unbridled awareness. "Traitors," she muttered.

Gabe leaned back in his chair, the muscles across his chest rippling beneath his cotton T-shirt. "They're guys. They know when they're not wanted or needed."

She smirked. "You're a guy, and I don't see you heading out the door."

A sexy, too-confident smile flirted around the corners of his mouth. "That's because you want and need me."

Even though her mind screamed yes!, she wore her best poker face. "Don't be so sure of yourself."

He rested his elbows on the armrest of the chair and clasped his hands in front of him. "I'm confident enough to put my wager where my mouth is," he said, his voice a soft rumble of sound in the quiet, still room.

Knowing there was no avoiding the inevitable, and drawn to the innate sensuality in his gaze, she asked, "What kind of personal, private bet did you have in mind?"

"Have you ever wanted something so badly that you think about it all the time?"

It was a rhetorical question, couched in a low, husky tone that mesmerized and enthralled Chloe.

"At night it consumes your dreams, and it's the first thing you think of when you wake up. The desire and obsession grows, becomes nearly unbearable, like a fever in your blood you can't get rid of."

She swallowed hard, feeling exactly like that now, all hot and bothered and *needy*.

Her breathing deepened, her entire body flushing with desire. He was seducing her with his words, tapping into her most erotic thoughts of him and bringing them out in the open. It was as though he had a direct link to her thoughts and *knew* all the forbidden secrets she'd harbored for so many years.

"Have you ever wanted something that badly, Chloe?" he murmured silkily.

From across the table, his intense gaze remained locked on hers, delving deep into her woman's soul. This time he expected an answer, and her reply came boldly, truthfully. "Oh, yeah."

He looked pleased with her answer. "Then here's your chance to dare *anything.*"

She clung to one last bit of reality, even as her wildest fantasies begged to be a part of this last bet. "Even requesting that you leave and don't come back?"

"If that's what you truly want," he said, seemingly willing to accept whatever she requested. "But you'd have to win this last hand first, and do you really want to waste your bet on something that you don't really want?"

There was that bit of arrogance again, as if he knew exactly what she wanted, needed even. She glanced at his faceup cards again, then her own, and knew that the odds of her winning the last hand were strongly against her. She could end the game now, without a personal, private bet on the table. The opportunity to walk away from him just as he'd done to her six years ago presented itself, but turning down a challenge wasn't in her nature. Which meant she had to be willing to succumb to whatever he wagered.

His mouth tipped up in a beguiling smile. "What is it going to be, Chloe? A personal dare to spice up the pot, or are you going to call it quits?" His voice and words deliberately taunted her.

Backing out wasn't an option, and the man sitting across from her damn well knew it. She held his sensual gaze, realizing what an emotional risk she'd be taking if she agreed to his dare. Realizing, too, that he'd be gone and out of her life after this week. Chances were they'd never see each other again, so why not indulge in a fantasy or two of her own?

Scooting back her chair, she retrieved a pad of stationery from a drawer in the kitchen. Ripping out two pieces of the violet-hued stationery trimmed in feminine lace print, she tossed one of the sheets his way, along with a pen, then sat back down to jot down her dare.

Suspecting his final wager would be as explicit and sexual as his kiss had been, she decided that her bet would be just as wicked and scandalous. She'd put her deepest desires down on paper, just to shake Gabe up a bit and put them on equal footing when he won the last hand. To let him know she was game for *anything*.

She'd request a brief affair, a sexual fling . . . all the pleasures he'd denied her six years ago and everything she'd craved ever since. Sex. Lust. Desire. Her written fantasy would suggest it all.

With a deep breath and her hand steadier than the rapid beat of her heart, she added her folded note on top of Gabe's in the middle of the pile of chips. Then they both flipped over their final card, revealing their hand.

"I'll be damned," Gabe murmured in amazement. "A full house to my flush. It looks like you won."

"Oh, wow." Chloe stared at her three fours and the second ace she'd just revealed, giddy with the victory of beating Gabe and winning the huge pot of money . . . until it dawned on her that he was now honor-bound to deliver on the sexual and brazen request she'd suggested as her wager.

Which made her wonder what kind of proposition *she'd* narrowly escaped. She reached for Gabe's note, but he snatched it up and out of her reach before she could grab the piece of paper.

Startled by his quick move, and annoyed that he was denying her the chance to read his bet, she frowned at him.

"That's not fair." Standing, she rounded the table to his side, her hand palm out. "Hand it over, MacKenzie."

"Nope." He stood, too, and stuffed the note deep into the front pocket of his jeans, far out of her reach since she had no intention of wrestling him for it, which would entail shoving her hand down his pants. "Neither one of us stated any rule about the other person's wager being read out loud if they lost."

Her jaw tightened. The man was not only arrogant, but exasperating, too.

His blue eyes twinkled mischievously. "But, seeing that I owe *you* something, let's see what my fate is."

Plucking her folded piece of stationery from the table, he opened it, a dark brow raising high. "For the next four nights you're mine, to do with as I please." Gabe's low, rich voice swirled around Chloe as he read her private note out loud. "I want you as my sexual slave, willing and eager to attend to my every whim and fulfill all my erotic desires."

Lifting his head, he met her gaze and whistled long and low. "You're a very naughty girl, Chloe," he murmured, a sinfully sexy smile easing across his too-gorgeous face. "I wasn't sure you had it in you to admit what you really wanted."

Heat washed over her, making her feel every bit as wicked as he'd implied. She'd never been so straightforward with a man before, not that she was about to enlighten him of that fact. "Just goes to show you how little you know about me."

He flicked the piece of paper in his hand with a finger. "According to this very adventurous bet, I'm sure by the end of the week I'll know a whole lot more about you."

Not if she could help it. Their affair would remain strictly about physical pleasure, she told herself, for the sole purpose of satiating her lust for a man who'd remained a part of her fantasies for too long. Here was her chance to prove she could indulge in a fling and remain immune to him, and finally get him out of her system once and for all. Maybe then she could move on and give one hundred percent to another man, without thoughts of Gabe keeping her chained to a past and emotions that had consumed the deepest part of her soul. She'd pull out all the stops to have him, in any way she desired . . . and this time she'd be the one to walk away in the end.

And it all started here, and now, with her making the first brazen move to put the reins of control firmly in her hands. She was going to seduce *him,* his body and mind, and establish right up front who was in charge of this affair and that she'd call the shots. She had, after all, won fair and square.

Flattening a hand in the middle of his chest, she pushed him a few steps back, until his spine pressed against the wall and her body brushed along the front of his. Beneath his T-shirt, against her fingertips, his muscles moved and shifted. Dampening her bottom lip with her tongue, she slid her splayed hand lower, feeling the taut ridges in his abdomen flex in reaction.

His breathing deepened, and she cast him a slow, sultry, upswept look, gratified to see that her wanton move had surprised him. His eyes were dark and hot, and his face was etched with a fierce hunger that made her tremble deep inside.

She wasn't done shocking him. Or arousing him. Shifting to the side, she leaned more fully into him so that her knee slipped snugly between his hard thighs, then she feathered her lips along the corded tendons in his neck, all the way up to his ear. She inhaled deeply, intoxicated by his masculine scent, as well as by the feminine power that was hers.

Her tongue lightly traced the shell of his ear, and his big body shuddered. A large hand settled on the curve of her waist to pull her closer, and she gently removed it, unwilling to let him distract her in any way.

"No touching, Gabe, not just yet."

A frustrated groan slipped from his throat, and she bit back a delighted smile and continued to torment him.

"By the end of the week, you'll know exactly what I want before I even ask for it, and you'll know where and how I like to be caressed and pleasured the most." The hand on his belly traveled upward, and her thumb flicked across his erect nipples. "You'll find out how sensitive the inside of my thighs are when you kiss them, and how the slow, soft stroke of your tongue can make me quiver and moan. My breasts are very responsive, and just thinking about you taking my nipples into your warm, wet mouth is making me excited and my panties damp."

He released a harsh breath, the entire length of him radiating waves of heat, inflaming her in turn. "Chloe . . ." Her name escaped on a gruff, desperate note.

Before he could say anything more, she pressed her fingers to his lips. "Shhh. I'm not done yet." She placed a damp kiss on his jaw, removed her hand, and let her lips drift to the corner of his mouth. "I want to do things with you that I've never dared before, and be as uninhibited as I am in every one of my intimate fantasies. And you'll do whatever I say, and agree to anything I request." She smiled and met his gaze, which blazed with intensity and restraint. "And I think it's only fair that I tell you that it's been a very long time since I've had sex, and you're just what I need to take the edge off of all my suppressed desires . . . unless you're not up to the challenge?"

He laughed, the sound low and rough with arousal. "I'm more than up for it, sweetheart."

"Really?" she goaded.

A shameless smile made an appearance, showing off straight white teeth. "See for yourself," he dared.

Refusing to back down from his blatant challenge after coming so far, she slid her hand down his body, over the waistband of his jeans, and curled her fingers around the long, hard ridge of his penis. He filled her palm to overflowing, and as she stroked, the pulsing pressure of his erection continued to swell even more.

She swallowed to ease the dryness in her mouth, to quell the ripple of blistering heat infusing her veins. "Very impressive," she said huskily, and squeezed him tighter in her hand, undeniably excited by the heady thought of having all that male aggression buried deep inside her. "And all mine for the next four nights."

Sweat beaded on his forehead, and he groaned, instinctively rocking his hips forward into her hand.

She let him go and stepped away before they went too far for the first night, and he growled in pure disappointment. "You're a tease, Chloe."

"I just want to build the anticipation." And leave him aching and aroused, as he'd done to her six years ago. Walking to the door on shaky legs, she opened it wide for him to exit. "Pick me up tomorrow night at seven."

One side of his mouth quirked at her dismissal, but he played the game and respected her request. "As you wish." At the threshold, he stopped just long enough to place a soft, warm kiss on her lips. "Sweet dreams, Chloe."

Then he was gone.

Leaning against the closed door, she inhaled deeply and pressed a hand to her full, aching breasts. With her mind filled with prurient thoughts of Gabe and her body strung tight with shameless, carnal needs, she knew her dreams would be anything but sweet.

Chapter Two

With an hour to go before he picked up Chloe, Gabe stepped into the shower stall and under the warm spray, absolutely certain Tuesday had been the longest day of his entire life. He'd tried to keep busy sorting through the boyhood paraphernalia his mother had never gotten rid of through the years, but his restless thoughts kept replaying last night's events with Chloe. The brazen way she'd come on to him after winning. The candid, seductive words she'd spoken that had turned him on like nothing else he could remember in recent memory. And the impudent way she'd cupped and caressed his thickened shaft through his jeans.

Hoarse laughter escaped him as he glanced down the length of his dripping wet body to the erection he'd been sporting since last night's encounter. Arousal still thrummed hot and heavy through his veins, and he supposed he hadn't helped matters much by spending a good portion of the day imagining all the different provocative scenarios Chloe had in store for him. He'd envisioned how she'd look completely, gloriously naked, her slender figure sprawled on a soft mattress, thighs parted in invitation and a come-hither smile on her delectable lips. He'd tormented himself with thoughts of how incredible that first deep thrust into her lush body would feel, and couldn't stop from visualizing her on her knees in front of him, her tongue gliding across the tip of his rigid sex, her lips parting to take him deep inside her mouth.

With a low, frustrated groan, Gabe propped his hands on the tiled wall in front of him and dipped his head beneath the shower spray. Bracing his legs apart, he let the lukewarm water drench his hair and sluice across his shoulders and down his back. The rivulets of water followed the crease of his buttocks and caressed his heavy sacs like silky fingers, making them draw closer, tighter, to his body.

And just like a dozen other times today, he thought about taking his aching cock in his hand to relieve the tension and building pressure Chloe had instigated the night before. Two or three precise strokes and he knew he'd come hard and furiously. But the one thing that stopped him from following through on the most practical solution to his problem was the knowledge that one fist-induced orgasm wouldn't stop him from wanting and craving Chloe. Ultimately, he wanted to ride on the buzz of growing excitement, let the eagerness gradually increase until he was wild for his climax, begging for it even . . . with Chloe an integral part of his release.

A surge of unrequited lust pooled in his lower region as a wry smile tugged at the corner of his mouth. He wondered how long she intended to make him wait for that pleasure. Would she allow him more liberties this evening than she had last night, or would she weave her bewitching brand of temptation and tease and torment him for the next four nights with her uninhibited sensuality?

He had no answer for that particular question. He only knew that he'd be a willing slave to her every whim and satisfy her every longing and wish. He'd do whatever it took to gain her trust again, her forgiveness. To make her realize that this time he wasn't going to hurt her. Even if it meant sacrificing his own pleasure in the process. It was a small price to pay to prove to Chloe that he wanted her in his life for more than a handful of days.

Turning off the water, he stepped out of the shower, ran a towel across his body, then wrapped and knotted the end around his hips while he shaved his face and dried his hair. Once he was done, he padded barefoot down the hallway to the small bedroom he'd grown up in to get dressed. He tugged on his briefs, pulled an olive green knit shirt over his head, and slipped on a pair of casual khaki pants. After pulling on his socks and shoes, he strolled to the old, beat-up dresser his mother had bought for him at a yard sale over twenty years ago and shoved his wallet and keys into his pocket.

Catching sight of the folded piece of stationery from last night's final poker game with Chloe, Gabe smiled to himself. He'd taken a huge risk with his final wager, going so far as to take a chance on the depth of his feelings for her, figuring he'd had nothing to lose and everything to gain. Considering the cards he'd seen on the table, he'd never expected her to win. Neither had he anticipated her turning the tables on him with such an outrageous and tantalizing dare.

But as he lay in bed last night, unable to sleep, he'd come to the conclusion that her winning the bet worked in his favor. As she'd proved last night, without any pressure from him she'd set the pace of their relationship and held back nothing because she believed the control was hers. And he'd willingly let her cling to that notion if it meant she'd feel more secure and sure of herself.

During the course of the next four nights, he'd openly let her take whatever she wanted from him, because he planned to give her all that she desired, and more—physically and emotionally. From the very depths of his heart, he was ready to take a chance on the emotions he'd hidden for years beneath layers of doubt and the need to be more than a washed-up football player so that he had something substantial to offer her.

Chloe wasn't the only one who had a few fantasies she'd like to sate. He'd harbored a wealth of erotic dreams about her for more years than he cared to recall, hungered for her sweetness and acceptance for forever. And in satisfying her most forbidden longings, he hoped to fulfill his greatest needs.

"Drive faster!"

Gabe cast a quick grin at Chloe, who sat in the passenger seat of the convertible Camaro he'd rented for the week as they drove along the 15 Freeway toward Del Mar, per her orders. The woman apparently had a reckless streak and a need for speed, and he obliged her. Pressing his foot to the gas pedal, he accelerated the sleek car from a respectable fifty miles per hour to the maximum limit of sixty five.

"This is so cool!" she said, shouting to be heard above the lash of the wind.

She'd been so excited to find he'd rented a convertible sports car—a spontaneous, frivolous impulse on his part—and had insisted they drive with the top down. He'd accommodated her order, surprised and pleased with her request since he'd chosen the car and its vibrant red color because it screamed unbridled, sexy fun. But he'd never expected Chloe to share in that philosophy. While most of the women he'd dated in Chicago would have balked at having their hair mussed and the wind in their faces, Chloe reveled in the warm summer night air caressing her bared skin and was loving the wild ride.

And he was enjoying her uninhibited delight of such a simple pleasure. Her cheeks were flushed with exhilaration and her eyes sparkled brightly with the vicarious thrill of being exposed to the outside elements as they drove. The breeze caught and tugged at the honey blond hair she'd left down, tousling the wavy strands around her head, and she didn't bother trying to restrain the unruly mass.

The wind whipped through the front seat area of the open vehicle, playing havoc with the slip of a dress she wore, and his libido. Floral in print, the low-cut bodice was fitted and held together by a crisscross lacing of thin silk ribbon, which prominently pushed up her voluptuous breasts so the night air could kiss and tease the soft swells. One tug of the enticing little bow and she'd spill right into his hands, a sensual feast he'd never be able to resist.

He swallowed hard and shifted in his seat. If that tantalizing display wasn't enough to make him salivate for a taste of that creamy flesh, then the hem of her dress certainly did the trick. Standing, the soft, flirty skirt ended just above the knee and flounced against her slender legs and small bottom when she walked. Sitting in a butter-soft leather seat with the draft teasing and fluttering the material, she'd at first laughingly tried to hold down the hem as it billowed in the breeze, then had finally given up and let the skirt gather loosely at the very tops of her smooth, bare legs. Another inch up and he'd be able to glimpse her panties, their color and texture. He wondered if she still favored silk trimmed in lace.

Oh, yeah, there were definite perks to driving a convertible with a sexy woman intent on seducing him. The only downside to the top being lowered was that it made it difficult to carry on a normal conversation without shouting at each other to be heard. But the silence between them was comfortable and relaxing. Besides, they'd indulged in plenty of light, amicable, flirtatious banter at the pizza parlor where she'd requested they go for dinner—which had been the same Italian restaurant they'd eaten at on their date six years ago.

And now as she instructed him to take the Del Mar Heights exit, he had a sneaking suspicion that Chloe had deliberately planned both destinations in order to reenact that night so long ago. He wondered what she had in mind, and while he was burning with curiosity, he didn't ask. He figured he'd discover her motives soon enough.

Unnecessarily, she guided him through residential streets he remembered with too much clarity and up a curving two-lane road to where hilltop estates overlooked the city. The Camaro made the climb smoothly, and he came to a stop at the cul-de-sac that ended with a service road now secured with a gated fence that hadn't been there six years ago. A KEEP OUT sign had been posted to ward off unwanted trespassers and effectively kept Gabe from driving to the secluded spot just around the curve in the paved road.

Letting the car idle, he turned toward Chloe. "Looks like the owners got tired of people parking on their property."

"If that's the case, they didn't try very hard to keep them out. Or they're depending on the honor system." She grinned impishly at him. "There isn't a lock on the gate."

His brows rose inquisitively. "And you know this how?"

She shrugged nonchalantly, the movement drawing his gaze to her breasts. "I've been up here more than a few times over the years."

Unexpected jealousy sliced through him and his fingers curled into tight fists around the steering wheel. She was a beautiful, sexy woman and no doubt had had her share of boyfriends and lovers, but he hated the thought of her sharing *their* spot with another man.

She patted his thigh, and a few inches higher she'd discover how turned on he'd been since leaving the restaurant. "Sit tight and I'll open the gate for you to drive through."

Before he could insist on doing it himself, she was out the door and strolling toward the gate, her strappy, high-heeled sandals clicking on the pavement and hips swaying provocatively. Then his mouth went completely dry and his groin pulled tight as she stepped into the white glow of the car's headlamps. The beam of light was as effective as an X ray through the thin fabric of her dress, silhouetting the sweet curve of her waist, the enticing swell of her hips, and the slenderness of her incredibly long, toned legs.

Christ. He exhaled a harsh, aroused breath. She might as well be naked for all the luscious attributes she'd just revealed to his hungry gaze. The bright light cast a golden, shimmery halo around her tousled, burnished hair as well, but despite that heavenly bit of aura, tonight Chloe Anderson was no angel.

She was a temptress with sin on her mind, and he was her willing and enthusiastic victim.

Effortlessly, she pushed the metal contraption wide open for him, then secured the gate after he'd passed through. She slid back into the car as if she hadn't just turned him inside out with scalding sexual need, and he drove about a quarter mile up the road to the spot he'd discovered many, many years ago.

He shut down the engine and car lights, plunging them into pitch black darkness and absolute silence. He glanced out at the multimillion dollar view in front of them, then up at the clear night sky bright with twinkling stars, feeling content in a way that had eluded him all his adult life.

A soft, wistful sigh escaped her, as if she felt the same sublime connection. "It is so incredible up here," she whispered. "Like being in a whole different world."

"Yeah," he agreed wholeheartedly, then addressed a question that he couldn't shake loose. "So, how many guys have you brought up here?" He'd meant to ask the question in a light, playful manner, but the jealousy in his voice betrayed him.

She glanced his way, a vixen smile tipping one corner of her mouth. "You're making unwarranted assumptions, Gabe," she chastised gently, amusement evident in her throaty voice. "I didn't say anything about coming up here with men."

No, she hadn't, but she'd implied as much, probably to provoke that green-eyed monster that lurked inside him.

Her ploy had worked. "You come up here by yourself, then?"

"Yeah." She rested her head against the back of her seat and stared up at the velvet night sky, her expression relaxed and beautiful. "It's a great thinking spot. It's quiet and secluded, and the view is gorgeous."

Reaching out, he threaded a silky strand of her hair between his fingers. "Would you believe that before bringing you up to this spot I used to come here all the time, too?"

"With girls?" she asked.

He laughed and feathered his fingers along her neck. "Now there *you* go making assumptions."

"You had a slew of young, eager teenage girls panting after you in high school and wanting to make it with the star quarterback of Santana High School," she said wryly. "I figured this dark secluded place would be the perfect make-out spot for you."

"Never happened." Not in high school anyway. She'd been the one and only woman he'd ever shared this private spot with, but the timing had been all wrong and he'd screwed up his chance to finally take a risk on something more with her.

He'd wanted Chloe since he'd first laid eyes on her when her brother Derek had brought him home after school one day to work on a science project together. She'd been fifteen, pretty, and sweeter than anything that had been a part of his life up to that point. And he wasn't near good enough for her, or so he'd believed.

She'd accepted him as a friend, and even though there had been a wealth of awareness between them from the very beginning, he hadn't wanted to mess with his best friend's sister. Besides, his sole focus at that age had been working a part-time job after school to help his mother pay bills and studying to gain the GPA to nab the football scholarship that would admit him into a reputable college, and from there be drafted into the NFL. He'd attained his goals and achieved his dreams, and lost every single one of them in a shattering life-altering moment.

She tipped her head and regarded him speculatively. "You mean to tell me all those rumors I overheard in the girls' locker room about what a stud you were in bed were all false?"

"That's why they're called rumors, sweetheart," he said, then revealed, "I only went all the way with one girl in high school."

Her jaw dropped in obvious shock. "Only one? Get outta here!"

He nodded. "I swear it's true. And it was with Melissa Bender, the captain of the cheerleading squad. I lost my virginity to her my senior year, prom night."

"Were you a late bloomer?"

He grinned at her skepticism. "No, just . . . selective. Still am," he said meaningfully. "That night after the dance, one thing led to another, and the next thing I knew we were in the backseat of my mother's Ford Escort screwing like rabbits." And the whole time he'd been pumping furiously into Melissa's body he'd been thinking of Chloe. With his eyes squeezed closed, he'd fantasized that *she* was beneath him, wanting him, and it was that erotic vision that had finally sent him over the edge. "I can't say it was the greatest introduction to sex."

"The first time isn't always romance and fireworks," she said softly, giving him the impression she was referring to her first sexual encounter, too.

"I think the first time with the *right* person can be all that and more," he countered, looking deeply into her eyes.

She transferred her gaze to the glittering cityscape below. "Maybe." The one word was tinged with disbelief.

He held back the urge to argue her way of thinking. When it came to him and Chloe there was no "maybe" about it. He had proof that the two of them were capable of generating enough electricity and heat to power the entire city of San Diego. And before the next four nights were over, she'd experience romance and fireworks, too.

He returned to the original thread of their conversation. "Anyway, that night with Melissa was a huge mistake. She wanted a commitment, which I'd never promised, and she literally stalked me from class to class. She scared the shit out of me. My biggest fear was that she'd end up pregnant even though we used a condom, and everything I'd worked so hard for would get sucked down the toilet. That thought alone kept me celibate for a long time after that."

She laughed, the sound low and husky. "Poor baby."

"Don't feel sorry for me, Chloe," he murmured, touching the shell of her ear and eliciting a shiver from her. "For me, it's quality that counts, not quantity."

She flashed him a wicked smile. "I like the sound of that, especially since you're mine for the next four nights. And the last thing you need to worry about is me getting pregnant. I'm on the pill." She twisted in her seat so that she faced him straight-on, her eyes seeking his in the shadowed darkness. "Do you remember the night we came up here together?"

That evening was indelibly etched in his mind, their first slow kiss, which had escalated into heavy foreplay, the need and longing that had welled up in him as the fire between them had burned out of control . . . then came echoes of the self-recriminations he'd tried to escape for tearing a ligament in his knee and ending his football career, which had instigated a brusque ending to not only their foreplay, but to the trust Chloe had given him.

"I remember everything about that night," he told her.

She blinked slowly, lazily. "What do you remember most?"

"How much I wanted you." Honesty infused his rich voice.

A small frown formed between her brows as she stared at him for a long moment. He could have sworn he saw a flash of hurt pass over her features, and then it was gone, replaced by a sassy tilt of her chin. "You certainly had a funny way of showing it."

How could he explain that everything had happened between them so quickly, the connection and the intimacy. She'd felt so damn right at a time in his life where everything had gone so horribly wrong. He'd ached to make love to her that night, but had convinced himself he was doing the honorable thing by walking away. Now he had to wonder if he'd been a coward, afraid to take a risk when he'd never, ever done so in his entire life.

He was taking a risk now, but was he too late?

The question haunted him, and he refused to dwell on it. Instead, he sought to reassure the woman in front of him just how desirable he found her. "Don't ever doubt that I wanted you, Chloe." *Then or now,* he thought. "Hell, I was so goddamn hard when I got home that night—"

"You took a cold shower?" she finished humorously for him.

"No." He shook his head. "A cold shower is highly overrated and doesn't do much when you want someone as much as I craved you that night." Sitting back in his seat, he relaxed against the headrest and closed his eyes, determined to draw her into his fantasy and seduce her senses. "What I did do was strip off all my clothes, turned off the lights, and laid down on my cool sheets completely naked. I knew I'd never be able to sleep, not until I gave my body the release it was screaming for. So, I took my straining erection in my fist and pictured your hand stroking me, your mouth making me slick and wet." His eyes opened halfway, just enough to gauge her reaction, and was pleased with what he found. Her breathing was ragged and aroused, the upper swells of her breasts taut and nearly bursting from the bodice of her dress.

He went on. "Then I fantasized about you straddling my waist, moving on me, and the tighter I squeezed, the more I imagined being deep inside your body, feeling your inner muscles clutching me. And just like that I came in a hot, scalding rush that made my toes curl from the pleasure of it."

She touched her tongue to her upper lip, then the bottom, making her lush mouth glisten with silvery moonlight. "At least one of us had an orgasm that night."

He lifted a brow. "You didn't?"

She shook her head, and a sultry smile appeared. "I went to bed frustrated, my entire body throbbing." Her fingers touched her throat and leisurely drifted downward to her heaving breasts, tracing the edge of her bodice. "Up to that point I had no idea how to take the edge off of my desire."

He watched her caress herself, throughly caught up in her brand of seduction. "And now you do?"

She nodded and tugged on the ribbon securing the front of her dress. The little bow unraveled and the laces loosened, just as he'd envisioned earlier, giving him a glimpse of more pale smooth flesh. "Yeah, in this day and age, I discovered a girl has to depend on herself for certain things. Including her own orgasms."

"Ahh, Chloe, I'm so sorry," he murmured, knowing his apology covered more than just the release she'd been denied. "I never meant to hurt you . . ."

She pressed her fingers over his lips, cutting him off, seemingly not wanting to hear any excuses. Crowding closer to his side of the car, she pressed a damp kiss to his jaw, then whispered hotly in his ear, "Here and now, I want what you withheld that night six years ago." *An orgasm.* "Move your seat back and make room for me."

Her tongue dipped into his ear, and his breath whooshed out of his lungs. Oh, man, he was in big trouble . . . the kind he welcomed with open arms. Pushing his leather seat as far as it would slide back, he helped Chloe crawl over the center console and gearshift, then settled his hands on her waist as she moved over him and sat in his lap, her thighs straddling his hips. The position was tight and cramped, and devastatingly intimate.

"Hmm, I don't think I'm close enough," she said huskily.

Gabe just couldn't think, period. At least not with his brain. His penis was reading her signals just fine.

With a wanton gleam in her eyes, and a boldness he was beginning to enjoy and admire, she inched closer, if that was even possible. The wispy material of her dress bunched high on her thighs, until the unmistakable heat and softness of her femininity pressed against the hard, unyielding bulge in his trousers.

"Ahh, much better." She sighed. Her fingers fluttered at the waistband of his pants, and she tugged his shirt loose. "Now, let's see what we can do about making you a bit more accessible."

"Why do I need to be more accessible?" he asked, not that he was complaining if she wanted to strip him bare. "I thought this was about your pleasure."

"It is," she said impudently, "but I find I get more turned on when I'm visually stimulated, as well as physically aroused. And you have a magnificent body, one that is meant to be admired and appreciated and touched."

He laughed, and lifted his arms as she pulled off his shirt and tossed the garment into the backseat of the car. "That sounds like it ought to be my line."

"Tonight, it's mine." Her cool hands glided across his broad shoulders and down his chest, leisurely exploring his muscular contours. Her thumbnails scraped across his taut nipples, and he sucked in a quick breath.

She smiled, pleased with his reaction. "I told you last night that my breasts are very responsive, and right now my nipples are tight and hard, aching for your warm mouth and wet tongue." Grasping the hands that still rested on her waist, she guided them to the loosened ties of her bodice. "Open up the front of my dress, Gabe. I want to feel your mouth on my breasts."

There was no way he could refuse such a request, not when he wanted that just as much. He pulled on the ties until they unraveled completely, then he spread the front of her dress wide open. She wasn't wearing a bra, and he groaned at the voluptuous beauty displayed before him. The glow of the moon shimmered on her pale skin, enhancing the fullness of her breasts and the rosy hue of her engorged nipples.

She threaded all ten fingers through his hair and guided his head forward, until her velvety nipples brushed across his mouth. He parted his lips, breathing damp heat across her flesh, then stroked his soft, wet tongue over one luscious crest. He laved her slowly, languorously, before suckling the rest of her deep inside his mouth.

Her body shuddered and a helpless moan rose in her throat. Her knees flexed against his hips, and her fingers tightened in his hair, holding him close . . . as if he planned on going anywhere, he thought, consumed by a red-hot haze of desire that simmered like a ball of fire in his belly. Needing more of her, he cupped both of her breasts in his large hands, pushed the plump mounds together, and tongued both of her beaded nipples at the same time.

She writhed restlessly on his lap. "Gabe," she whispered raggedly, her voice vibrating with the same hunger and need flowing through his veins.

Without preamble, he lifted his head and claimed her lips in a hot, lavish, openmouthed kiss rich in passion, and primitive and greedy enough to brand and possess. With a soft moan, she returned the greedy, tongue-tangling kiss with equal fervor. Her hands slid from his hair and caressed his jaw while her lower body began a rhythmic, rocking motion against his erection.

Knowing her lap dance and simulated act of sex would have him coming in his pants, he pulled his lips from hers, steadied her sensual movements with one strong hand on

her hip, and met her gaze, which blazed with feverish longing.

He splayed a hand on her bare thigh, making his intentions known. "Let me touch you and make you come," he
murmured, seeking her permission. She was, after all, in
charge of this seduction.

She didn't hesitate, but took what she wanted. "Yes,"
she breathed, the one word infused with undeniable excitement and excruciating need.

Holding her gaze, he stroked his long fingers up the insides of her spread thighs, then grazed the scrap of satin
covering her feminine mound, finding her panties drenched
with moist heat and silky desire, for him. He pressed his
thumb along her slit, once, twice, and even through the
damp fabric he could feel the soft, swollen folds of her flesh,
and the distended nub seeking more pressure, a deeper caress.

Her hips thrust forward, her body trembled, and a moan
rumbled up from her throat. "Stop teasing me," she groaned.
"I've been waiting six long years for this."

Her words stunned him. For a brief moment he wondered if she'd meant she'd been waiting for the orgasm he'd
denied her, or for him. Either way, it was a heady thought
and one that boosted his self-esteem and made him want
this release to be the best she'd ever had.

Slipping his thumb beneath the elastic band of her
panties, he glided his finger along her slick folds, touching
her languidly, caressing steadily, delving deeper. . . .

She arched her back and moved on his hand rhythmically. "Oh, yes," she breathed, her lips parted and her expression near rapturous.

Overcome with the urge to devour her in any way he
could, he flattened his free hand in the middle of her spine,
forcing her to bend back even further. The position brought
her breasts to his mouth, and he ravished her with wet, hot
kisses with his teeth alternately nipping and gently biting

her tender skin. He swirled and flicked his tongue across her hardened nipples the same way he ached to flick his tongue along the clit pulsing beneath the press of his thumb.

He felt the tension within her build as her knees dug into his hips, heard the catch of her breath change as her climax rolled over and through her. Clutching his shoulders, her head fell back and a raw cry echoed in the quiet night air as she tumbled over the edge, her body shaking from the force of her release.

He lifted his head and watched her, his blood roaring in his ears, his heart threatening to explode from his chest, and his mind chanting possessively, *she's mine, she's mine, she's mine. . . .*

One last delicate shudder and then she opened her eyes and looked at him, a satisfied smile on her lips and the reflection of the stars above shimmering in her gaze. "Now *that* was worth waiting for."

"*You're* worth waiting for," he said, the truthful words slipping from him without a second thought. Withdrawing his hand from between their bodies, he traced his wet, slick thumb across her bottom lip. Ignoring her startled expression, he brought her mouth to his and licked off the dewy essence, then kissed her slowly, deeply, thoroughly, sharing the honeyed taste of her with his tongue. She relaxed into him, the feel of her breasts crushing against his chest an exquisite torture.

Reluctantly, he ended the kiss before his self-control snapped and he took her in the front seat of the cramped Camaro. Then again, judging by the mischievous gleam in her eyes, he knew that this evening's performance was solely for her gratification and he was in for another sleepless, tossing and turning kind of night. Payback for the way he'd let things end between them six years ago . . . in this same exact spot. He sighed, wondering how long she planned to make him suffer.

She pulled the front of her dress together and tied another bow, covering up her gorgeous breasts. "Ahh, one fantasy down, three more to go," she said, her breathy voice rife with sensual pleasure. "What do you say we make our rendezvous for the same time tomorrow night at my place?"

He grinned wryly. Did she really think he'd refuse? "Consider it a date."

Chapter Three

Revenge had never been so sweet.

Still reveling in last night's pleasure and her ultimate conquest, Chloe smiled to herself as she stepped from the warm, relaxing bubble bath she'd indulged in after work. Drying off with a fluffy towel, she spritzed her skin with a light cinnamon body spray and slipped into the silky, thigh-length chemise she'd bought on her way home today. The soft emerald green material draped along her curves, skimmed her flesh in a provocative caress, and aroused her senses.

She hoped it would have the same effect on Gabe.

Catching sight of her reflection in the bathroom mirror, she realized she'd spent the whole day at work with a contented smile on her face, which had drawn a few comments from coworkers about her exuberant mood and the glow on her skin. She had Gabe to thank for both. The shimmering, relaxing aftereffects of the incredible orgasm he'd given her last night had lasted through the night and into the day. Hell, she was still riding high on the rush of satisfaction, and feeling even more sexual and wanton than she ever had in her entire life.

She decided she loved being able to openly express what she wanted and desired. Her newfound boldness felt liber-

ating and exciting, and she knew from Gabe's numerous reactions that he enjoyed her brazenness, too. She'd always
traveled the safe path of being a good girl, letting the few
guys she'd slept with over the years take the lead in the bedroom, which had resulted in her getting left behind in the
orgasm and pleasure department.

Not this week. Being naughty was on the agenda, and
she was going to reap the benefits of embracing her femininity, as well as treating herself to the effect Gabe's pure
masculinity had on every one of her five senses.

Leaving her hair secured in the topknot on her head and
damp tendrils curling around her neck, she padded barefoot
into her small living room to set up tonight's seduction.
Fantasies came in all shapes and forms, and tonight's request was solely for her gratification and enjoyment . . . and
Gabe's, if he had a foot fetish of any sort, she thought with
an amusing grin.

She turned her stereo system on low to a soft-rock station and set up the coffee table in front of the couch with
the accessories Gabe would need to pamper and pleasure
her. While she worked, her mind and thoughts drifted back
to last night and what a good sport Gabe had been about
everything, considering she'd been the only one whose desires had been fulfilled. Unfortunately, his touch had an ad-
dicting effect on her, because she craved more caresses. More
of *him*.

The realization startled her on a deeper, emotional level,
but she was convinced that it was all a matter of getting him
out of her system—sexually, physically extricated from the
deepest recesses of her heart. Once she had her way with Gabe
and had accomplished that goal and he returned to Chicago
to resume his own life, she'd be able to go on with hers. In
the meantime, she'd tempt and tease and seduce him, and
drive him crazy with wanting *her* this time.

She brought out the fragrant cinnamon oil from the bedroom and added it to the other sensual items on the table,

which included the smooth, sleek vibrator she'd purchased at a friend's naughty lingerie party a few years ago.

She wasn't done making Gabe suffer for leaving her hot and bothered six years ago. Tonight was all about building tension and stoking the flame of hunger that burned bright in his eyes. Tomorrow evening they'd graduate to a darker, more forbidden fantasy of hers, one that would require Gabe to be just as adventurous and daring. She shivered and liquid heat settled low in her belly at the thought of where that particular fantasy would lead.

Switching off the lights so that the only illumination in the living room came from a lamp beside the couch, which added to the cozy, romantic atmosphere, she headed into the kitchen and poured two glasses of wildberry wine. She'd already enjoyed one serving during her bubble bath, which accounted for her current relaxed state.

Just as she set the drinks on the coffee table, a brisk knock echoed through her condo. With a leap of anticipation catching in her chest, she went to the door, opened it, and found Gabe leaning a broad shoulder against the jamb with his thumbs tucked into the front pockets of his jeans. His stance was a bit cocky, all confident male, and he literally took her breath away.

His slow, lazy gaze traveled down the length of her, taking in her silky chemise and bare legs. "You certainly don't look dressed for a night on the town," he drawled.

She lifted an amusing brow even as a hot ache of awareness suffused her entire body. "I never said we were going *out* tonight."

He thought about that for a few brief moments. "No, I guess you didn't," he agreed, meeting her gaze with a sexy-as-sin grin curving his lips. "I suppose I need to stop making assumptions."

"Yes, you do, because one of these times you're going to end up *very* disappointed."

"I haven't been disappointed with you yet, but definitely

surprised a few times," he murmured huskily. "Which is a good thing. I like a woman who keeps me guessing."

And so far, nothing between them had been predictable. Which she liked, as well, because her life, thoughts, and choices had been too sensible and practical for much too long.

Acting on the same impulse that had driven her since his arrival back in town, she grasped his muscular arm and tugged him inside. Shutting the door behind him, she entwined her arms around his neck and pressed her body against the scorching heat and unyielding hardness of his.

"Did you think about me today?" she asked, her voice dropping to a low, sultry pitch.

His nostrils flared at their intimate position, and his eyes turned hot, like burning blue embers. He settled his big hands at the small of her back, keeping their lower bodies aligned. "Only every second of every minute of every hour since dropping you off last night."

"Good answer." She inhaled his delicious male scent, and resisted the urge to bury her face against his throat, to taste his skin with her lips and tongue. Instead, she threaded her fingers through the soft hair curling against the nape of his neck. "I was a bit more disciplined at work, but then I stopped at a lingerie boutique on the way home and everything about the shop made me think of you."

A frown pulled at his dark brows. "Whoa. I refuse to cross-dress, if that's what you have in mind for tonight."

She chuckled. "Don't worry, seeing a man wearing my bra and panties doesn't do a thing for me."

He visibly relaxed. "Thank God," he muttered.

A genuine smile replaced her laughter. "I meant that while I was trying on various teddies, camisoles, and chemises at the boutique I couldn't stop from imagining the way your hands would feel against the silky, satiny, lacy material, how the fabric would caress my skin with decadent heat and friction." She let her lashes flutter closed and whispered near the corner of his mouth, "Rub your hands across the material, Gabe, so I can see how luxurious and sexy the silk and lace feels against my bare skin."

His large, flattened palms obeyed, skimming the small of her spine and gliding upward in firm strokes to where the back of her low-cut chemise gave way to smooth flesh. Her nipples peaked against his chest, and a purr of pleasure escaped her throat.

"That feels so, so good." She sighed.

"Yeah, it does," he agreed.

Hearing the gruffness in his voice, she blinked her eyes back open, noting the tight restraint clenching his jaw and feeling the thick, hard ridge of his sex pulsing against her lower belly. The poor man . . . did he have any idea he was in for another long, torturous night of sexual advances and provocative suggestions?

She continued with her seductive monologue. "And the scents they offered in sprays, lotions, and oils . . . well, the selection was absolutely incredible." With her hand cupping the back of his neck, she brought his head down to her arched throat. "See how good this smells. I bought this scent specifically with you and me in mind."

He pressed his nose to her neck and inhaled slowly, lingeringly, seemingly savoring the alluring fragrance clinging to her skin. "It smells hot and spicy. Like cinnamon."

"Yeah, that's it." He drew another deep breath, and she shivered as gooseflesh rose on her arms, her belly, her breasts. "Would you like to taste the flavor of the oil I bought to go with the spray?"

He lifted his head, a lopsided grin on his lips. "Oh, man, tell me you dabbed some on your breasts, your thighs, your stomach."

He sounded so aroused, so desperate to taste her, she couldn't contain her grin. "I rubbed some of the oil on my lips, but in a little while you'll be rubbing it elsewhere . . .

with my permission to sample anywhere you'd like. But for now, a kiss will have to do."

The length of his body shuddered and he lowered his head, catching her mouth with his in a soft, slow, sexy kiss that increased the wanting curling within her. His tongue stroked and teased her full bottom lip, and his teeth nibbled and ate at the sweet, hot flavor clinging to her tender flesh. His hands started to wander, gliding down her back, smoothing across her bottom . . . then his fingers caressed the back of her thighs, where the lace-edged hem of her chemise ended.

With a rush of exquisite pleasure making her legs tremble, she grabbed his wrists and pulled them away before he could venture into more intimate territory.

He dragged his mouth from hers and feigned a guileless look. "Did I do something wrong?"

She shook her head to reassure him. "I've got something very unique and exciting planned for tonight, and I don't want it over before it even begins." Lacing her fingers through his, she led the way into her living room, then made him sit down in the spot she'd cleared on the coffee table between her props and accessories. "There's something I've fantasized about for a very long time, and you're just the man to give it to me."

"I like the way that sounds," he said with an indulgent grin underscored with sexual promise. "What would you like me to do?"

She settled onto the couch across from him and braced her feet on the edge of the table between his spread thighs . . . right against the crotch of his jeans. "I'd like you to give me a pedicure."

He stared at her wriggling toes, dumbfounded by her request. Then he shook his head, hard, and met her gaze. "A pedicure?" he repeated incredulously.

The disbelief on his face nearly made Chloe laugh, but she managed to maintain an air of complete seriousness.

"Actually, I went to a salon on my lunch break today and had the pedicure done, so my heels are smooth and my toenails have been trimmed and buffed. But I left them unpolished so you could paint them for me."

"Chloe . . ." He shifted uneasily, which caused the pads of her feet to brush against the enormous hard-on straining the fly of his jeans. He sucked in a swift breath and jammed his fingers through his thick hair, his expression uncertain. "I don't know anything about painting a woman's toenails."

"There's nothing to it, really," she told him. "And considering you're obligated to cater to my every wish and desire, I'm not really giving you a choice in the matter."

"Okay," he said slowly, cautiously. "If it turns you on, then who am I to argue?" He rolled his shoulders and glanced to either side of him, quickly taking inventory of the feminine products she'd set out for him to use. "Umm, where do I start?"

"First, you can hand me a glass of wine, and the other one is for you."

He passed her one of the drinks, but didn't touch the other glass. "I don't think you want me painting your toenails under the influence," he said wryly.

She laughed lightly. "I just thought it might help *you* to relax." Taking a sip of the fruity wine, she reclined more comfortably against the couch cushions. "The best place to start is by painting my toenails, and from there you can massage my feet and rub oil on my skin to make it soft and supple. And don't forget about using the vibrator over there," she said, motioning to the left side of him.

"A vibrator?" he croaked, obviously having missed that prop during his first glance. But he saw it now, a thick, eight-inch towering phallus designed to bring a woman all kinds of erotic pleasures.

His breathing deepened, and when his gaze met hers again, the depths were filled with smoldering desire and hunger . . . just as she'd hoped. She swallowed and found her own voice. "I find it's great for relieving excess stress and relaxing tense muscles."

He braced his hands on his taut thighs and quirked a brow her way. "What muscles are we talking about here, sweetheart?"

"The ones in my calves, my thighs . . ." She let her voice trail off so he could draw his own conclusions, then shrugged. "Wherever you think I'm too tense."

He stared at her intently, accepting the silent dare she'd just issued with one of his own. "And you're going to let me be the judge of that?"

"Absolutely." She took another drink of wine, knowing she'd just given him free rein to use that vibrator anywhere and anyway he wished—which was all part of tonight's seduction and her ultimate pleasure. "But you need to paint my toenails first before we get to the massage part."

He rubbed his hands together in preparation. "Then let's get started."

Over the next few minutes, she instructed him how to insert the prefabricated foam piece between her toes to keep them separated so the enamel wouldn't smudge, and pointed out the soft shade of pink for him to use. With her right foot wedged tightly between his thighs and tipped at an angle for him to paint, he carefully, slowly, stroked the pale color onto her little toe, and worked his way from there.

His hand was amazingly steady, and his gorgeous face was a mask of intense concentration as he applied the first coat. There was something incredibly sexy about a big, virile guy like Gabe treating her feet and toes with such reverent attention and care. Only a man secure in his masculinity would agree to such a feminine task, and she couldn't help the smile that appeared at that thought, or the sweet, sentimental warmth that invaded empty places in her heart and gave her an emotional jolt.

Startled by that deep, intimate reaction, she took another

long drink of wildberry wine and sought to redirect her thoughts to something more conversational and ordinary.

"Tell me about your life in Chicago," she said.

Finished painting the toes of her right foot, he placed her arch against the edge of the table next to his hip and tucked her other foot between his leg and began the same process again. "What do you want to know?"

His nonchalant tone told her he was open to discussing anything with her. "Do you enjoy living in Chicago?"

He dipped the small brush into the liquid paint and swiped it across her big toenail in three quick, precise strokes, leaving behind a perfectly glossy sheen of enamel. "I think I'm *accustomed* to living there, if that makes any sense."

"Because that's where you went to college?"

He nodded and finished coating her middle toenail, his attention riveted to the task. "Yeah, that had a lot to do with my decision to stay."

But there was more, and she felt compelled to scratch below his superficial answer. "You could have returned to San Diego once you'd graduated."

"With my football career over and my future so uncertain, I couldn't bring myself to come back." He glanced up, honest emotions glimmering in his eyes and his expression revealing nuances of a deeper pain she didn't fully understand.

Then, he explained. "I felt like I let so many people down. Myself, my mother . . ." His rough voice trailed off, and he redirected his gaze and attention back to her pedicure. "I just wasn't ready to come back to San Diego to face family and friends . . . and my own failure."

She caught the surprising layer of insecurity woven into his casual tone, which struck a reciprocating chord in her she didn't want to feel. "I'd hardly call you a failure, Gabe," she said softly. His incredible achievements as a sports agent proved just how successful he'd become.

Finished with her second foot, he braced it against the

opposite side of the coffee table, so that her feet bracketed his hips and the hem of her chemise fluttered between her thighs. "When you don't and can't attain the goals you've had for years, the only word that described what I was, was *failure.*"

She was surprised to hear the self-condemnation vibrating in his voice and realized that she was seeing a more complex side to Gabe she'd never known existed. A part of him he'd obviously kept hidden from everyone beneath a durable facade. And now, he'd just given her a glimpse of something personal, private, and very painful for him.

She'd always regarded Gabe as strong and determined and confident. Always sure of himself, and never allowing anything negative to shake his resolve and ambition. He'd survived his father's abandonment when he was just a young kid, had made the best of the poverty that had become his way of life in the aftermath of that desertion, and had spent his teenage years struggling to be something more than a high school dropout.

He'd achieved so much to be proud of, yet his accomplishments were underscored with a personal anguish he'd carried with him internally, in deep, dark places no one could see or touch. And now, for the first time ever, he was sharing that emotional depth with her, letting her past external barriers to glimpse the multifaceted man he was, instead of the shallow cad she'd pegged him to be since that night six years ago when he'd seduced her, and then walked away without looking back.

Which made her question once again all his reasons for returning to San Diego and apparently making it his mission to pursue her. As an unsettled conquest from his past, or something more? The thrilling, hopeful possibility caused her heart to skip a beat.

No, no, no, her mind screamed. She wouldn't go that route with Gabe, not when she knew how easy it would be to fall for him again—only to experience more hurt and heartbreak. Nope, it wasn't going to happen. She didn't trust her feelings, didn't completely trust him with her emotions when he could tug on them so easily, so effortlessly. She was far safer keeping her thoughts grounded on their bet, enjoying any and all illicit pleasures, and getting him out of her mind, body, and soul.

Clearing the tight knot that had gathered in her throat, she transferred her gaze to her freshly painted toenails. "Nice job," she complimented.

"I've always been good with my hands," he said playfully, lightening the mood. "Now I know I can handle more than pigskin."

Yes, she was learning that his skills went much further than those nimble fingers catching a football. Finishing off her wine, she held the glass out to him. "Since you're not going to drink your wine, could I have it, please?" She smiled. "Then you can put those talented hands to good use and start on the massage you owe me."

"Yes, ma'am," he replied, and switched her empty glass of wine for his full one. Finding the bottle of oil among all the other pedicure paraphernalia, he poured a large dollop into his palm, rubbed his hands together, then massaged the warmed lotion onto her right foot.

Chloe moaned blissfully as Gabe's thumbs pressed against her arch and worked his way to her heel, then ankle, deftly massaging the oil into her skin and easing taut tendons and muscles. The arousing fragrance of heated cinnamon reached her nose, curling around her senses and coaxing feminine nerve endings to life. After making sure her polish was dry, he carefully removed the foam separator from her toes and slid his fingers between each digit, evoking erotic impressions unlike anything she'd ever experienced.

"Now I get to taste," he said, his eyes gleaming devilishly as he brought her foot up this mouth and lapped his tongue along her sole, slick from the aromatic, flavored oil.

She gasped in surprise, and her knee jerked back in an automatic response to the rippling sensation that shook her entire body. "Hey, that tickles."

A gust of low laughter rumbled against her foot and heightened her awareness of him even more. "Nice to know I can torture you a bit, too."

His lips and tongue did just that, making her alternately laugh and groan. "Ahh . . . I can't take any more . . ."

His dark blue eyes, filled with wicked intent, peeked up at her. "Yeah, you can." Ignoring her protest, he held tight to her leg, with one hand cradling her foot and the other cupping the fullest part of her calf as his mouth skimmed its way toward her toes.

She squirmed restlessly on the sofa, certain he meant to draw her toes into the warm, wet cavern of his mouth and suck on them. The provocative thought had her breathing hard.

Instead, he stopped short of her toes and gently, sensuously, sank his teeth into the pad of her foot, which sent bolts of electrical currents all the way up to the tips of her breasts. Her nipples peaked against silk, aching for the feel of his mouth tugging there, too.

After a few more well-placed love bites that had her alternately laughing and cursing him, he finally gave in to her pleas and moved on to knead his way up her leg.

She took another swallow of wine and sighed as his long oil-coated fingers rubbed the muscles in her calf then stroked over her knee to her thigh. His hands were indeed magic, and she went utterly boneless under his skillful ministrations and the relaxing effects of the wine.

Finished with one leg, he started on the other. Setting aside her empty glass, she closed her eyes, sank into the couch cushions, and enjoyed every nuance of his sensuous pampering, the heat of the cinnamon oil on her supple skin, and the silent tingling awareness building in her body and between them.

Until she heard the soft buzzing sound of her vibrator. Her eyes blinked open, and she found Gabe holding the twitching phallus, examining it, intrigued by the shape and size. And judging by the enormous erection straining the fly of his jeans, he was a whole lot turned on by the possibilities inherent in the sex toy.

A combination of excitement and startling uncertainty mingled within her. She wondered how far he'd go with her vibrator . . . and knew she'd given him carte blanche to use it wherever and however he wished. She'd done it to taunt and tease him, of course, but now the very real possibility existed that he'd call her bluff and use it on more than easing the tense muscles in her calf and thighs.

But that's where he started, anyway, rolling the gadget against taut tendons, dabbling behind her knees, coasting over the muscles in her inner thighs . . . and she had to admit the pulsating pressure against her flesh felt incredible. And incredibly arousing. Liquefying her body from the inside out. Making her tremble. Generating a sizzling heat and dizzying need so great her blood roared in her ears and her nerve endings felt vibrantly alive and poised on the crest of a greater pleasure.

Biting her lower lip, she sought Gabe's eyes. His hooded gaze burned with equal intensity as he moved off the coffee table and settled closer, between her legs, using the width of his chest to keep her knees spread and her open to him. Slowly, he lifted the vibrator and caressed the outer swell of her breasts, then grazed the flickering tip across her rigid nipples, the fleeting touch as erotic as a wicked, illicit kiss.

Lower, he explored, his bold, masculine features etched with uncompromising purpose and a darker hunger that made her shiver. He drew the vibrator down to her quivering belly, making her silk chemise dance and shimmer against her skin. With his free hand he bunched the soft material in his fist, drawing the hem up until her panties were revealed. Her knees automatically clenched the sides of his chest, but he merely leaned in closer, dominating her movements. He closed his eyes and inhaled deeply of her scent, his nostrils flaring at the combined essence of cinnamon and the damp evidence of her desire.

Oh God. The vibrator touched down once again at the elastic edge of her panties, leaving no doubt in her mind where his final destination would be. She trembled, the first stages of a mindless, shuddering orgasm pulling at her, willing to let the exquisite pleasure happen in all its glory and decadence. She could feel herself coming undone inside, unraveling physically as well as emotionally. Wanting, needing, *craving* everything she knew he could give her.

Somewhere along the way she'd lost control of the situation and he'd gained the upper hand, and the realization shook her up. Just as the pulsing shaft grazed her mound, she grabbed his wrist, stopping his descent.

He glanced up at her, his jaw tight with restraint and his gaze hot and earthy and unapologetically sexual. "You don't like the way it feels?" he asked, his voice low and rough.

How to explain how exposed and vulnerable she felt at the moment? "It feels too good," she managed. It was as honest an answer as she'd allow.

"That's not supposed to be a bad thing," he teased, his mouth tipping up in a beguiling grin. Letting go of the fabric in his fist, he splayed his hand on her smooth, bare stomach, adding a tantalizing pressure that stirred deeper desires. "Go all the way with the fantasy you started," he dared.

Could she surrender to this naughty fantasy in front of him? Heat scored her cheeks and doubts got the best of her good-girl sensibilities. "Gabe . . ."

He interrupted her before she could fully object. "After

all you've put me through these past two nights, don't turn shy and modest on me now, sweetheart," he chided gently. "Let me watch you come like this. Just give me that tonight. *Please.*"

The soft, reverent way he said the word *please* melted away her reserve. And if she were completely honest with herself, she wanted the orgasm he promised, was wet with wanting, and already buzzing from the anticipation of experiencing the kind of all-consuming release he'd given her last night. But this time she'd tumble over the edge in a very wanton, shameless way.

Before she lost the nerve, she released her hold on his wrist and whispered, "Go ahead."

She expected him to pull off her panties and strip her bare, but he left her covered, which proved to be even more titillating and thrilling as the knob of the quivering phallus glided over damp silk, lightly stroking, slowly tracing the swollen, delicate folds of her sex. She gasped and shuddered from the feverish imprint on her sensitive flesh and the hot, possessive look in Gabe's eyes as they searched hers.

Fearful that he'd see all the way to her soul and discover the depth of her feelings for him, she closed her eyes and let her head loll against the back of the sofa. She focused on the hedonistic pleasure radiating through her body instead of the selfless man who was *giving,* without asking for any satisfaction of his own in return.

But the need she harbored for him was inescapable, and even with her eyes squeezed tight he was intricately woven into the fantasy unfolding in her mind. Then fantasy melded into reality when she felt his lips skim the inside of her thigh, his hot, moist breath wafting across her skin, and finally his tongue lapping her up like a piece of cinnamon candy.

She couldn't contain the untamed groans that slipped from her throat. Another feathery sensation shimmered across the tiny knot of nerves and flesh between her legs, followed by the deeper, rhythmic stroke of the vibrator, his mouth, his tongue. Her mind reeled, and the combined sensations catapulted her into the most intense climax she'd ever had.

Voluptuous tremors rippled through her limbs, and she cried out hoarsely as her fingers clenched the couch cushions on either side of her hips in an attempt to hold on to *something*. Her back arched as she came in an overwhelming rush of passion and desire, her entire body trembling, shuddering . . . flying apart in the most glorious way.

It seemed like hours passed before she could breathe normally again and bring herself to open her eyes and finally look at Gabe. He was still kneeling on the floor, watching her, a look of pure male satisfaction on his face when she knew he had to be in excruciating pain with his own arousal still raging.

"You're incredible," he said, his voice deep and husky and filled with an abundance of honesty and emotion. "Absolutely amazing."

A portion of her heart melted, a dangerous thing when she couldn't afford emotional involvement with this man. Not a second time around.

She managed a smile and opted for humor. "And you certainly know how to give a good . . . pedicure."

He laughed, the sound rough with shared amusement. "At least I'm good for something."

"Oh, you're plenty good, Gabe MacKenzie." And almost more than she could handle.

"I'm glad you think so," he said, winking at her.

He stood, straightening up slowly, his burgeoning erection now eye level for her. She wondered what he intended, but he merely held out his open palm to her, and she placed her hand in his trustingly so that he could pull her up. Her unsteady legs wobbled and their bodies brushed, but he didn't take advantage of their close proximity.

Gently, he pushed a stray strand of hair away from her cheek, the tender gesture at odds with the sexy grin that slashed across his features. "Same time tomorrow evening?"

"Yeah, and another fantasy to fulfill." She ran her index finger slowly, seductively, down the middle of his chest. "And this time, *you* might just get lucky."

"Hmm, imagine that," he murmured.

And he did . . . all night long.

Chapter Four

A soft, distant voice invited Gabe to enter, and as soon as he stepped into Chloe's condo the next night and took in his surroundings, he knew he'd walked into a very provocative kind of seduction. After two nights of nonconsummated foreplay that had left him permanently hard and aching, he couldn't help but wonder what Chloe had in store for him tonight—fulfillment, or more sexual frustration.

The entryway and living room were dim, lit only by a dozen strategically placed candles that filled his every breath with the distinctive scent of vanilla underscored with arousing cinnamon. The flickering flames cast shadows in the room and along the walls, adding to the stimulating and very alluring atmosphere.

Hand still on the doorknob and his pulse registering the slow thrum of awareness flowing through his veins, he glanced around for Chloe but couldn't find her anywhere in the living room, though he knew it had been her who'd invited him inside. As he gave the ambiance another quick glance, the significance of this particular fantasy hit him, making him realize that the cloak of darkness was most likely Chloe's way of protecting her feelings and keeping her distance. The veil of obscurity was like a shield, keeping him from seeing all the emotions her expressive eyes couldn't conceal.

After everything that had occurred between them last night he suspected she was feeling a bit threatened emotionally and needing the reins of their affair back in her hands. He'd give her complete control over his body, his heart, his soul even, if that's what she demanded. But he refused to let her hide from him in any way whatsoever. She might need the darkness to feel safe, to believe she was protected from his ultimate intentions, but he only needed to feel her passionate, candid response to him to know the truth . . . that she cared for him more than she was willing to admit.

And it was that admission he sought. He had tonight and tomorrow to convince her that he needed her in his life and to make her realize that there had *always* been something more between them than just friendship, and now sex. Two more nights to gain her forgiveness and the love he'd forsaken six years ago, and he hoped like hell that she'd give him both.

"Lock the door, Gabe."

Chloe's soft, sultry voice wrapped around him, but he couldn't pinpoint the origin. He did as she requested, squinting his eyes as he waited for his pupils to adjust to the shadowy darkness. His nerves were on alert, anticipating how this latest scenario of hers would unfold.

"Are we playing hide-and-seek tonight, sweetheart?" he asked, his tone low and sexual. "Because if we are, I have to warn you that I play for keeps."

"You don't have to find me," she said somewhere to his left. "I'm right here."

He caught a movement as she stepped out into the open and the candlelight illuminated her slender body and the tempting sway of her hips. He watched her approach, looking like an ethereal vision in a white, gauzy blouse so sheer he could see the outline of her bra underneath, and a pair of white hip-hugging shorts. The flames added golden high-lights to the hair she'd left down, making the strands shim-mer and dance with a life of their own.

His stomach clenched and his groin tightened with un-quenched lust. She stopped in front of him and pressed her hand against his chest, right over his rapidly beating heart, which he was certain she could feel through his T-shirt. This close, the cinnamon fragrance was hotter now, the incan-descent sheen on her skin leading him to believe that she'd rubbed that exotic, delicious oil all over her body.

A vixen smile curved her luscious mouth. "I want you, Gabe . . . if you're daring enough to follow me into a night of decadent, forbidden pleasure."

His eyes caught and held hers, and an equally wicked grin appeared on his lips. "You should know by now that I'll dare anything when it comes to you."

"Perfect," she murmured, seemingly pleased by his promise. Gathering his shirt in her fist, she stepped back and pulled him until her spine flattened against the entry-way wall and his body imprinted the length of hers from breasts to thighs. She lifted her mouth up to his, a breath away from a kiss, and whispered huskily, "Dare to be my lover. Dare to fulfill my wildest, most erotic fantasies. Dare to surrender *all* to the carnal side of pleasure."

As if he'd say no to such a proposition. "Lead the way," he said, letting her set the pace, the tone, the direction of this intriguing seduction.

She did . . . blowing his mind with a deep, silky, tongue-tangling kiss that skipped all coaxing preliminaries. Her mouth was soft and sweet, assertive and greedy, and he matched her unbridled aggression yet was acutely aware that this was her fantasy and she was the one in control of where and how far they would take this impetuous adven-ture of hers. So when she lifted his hand to the collar of her blouse, he didn't hesitate to follow through on her silent order to undress her. Except his big fingers fumbled with the small, slippery buttons of her blouse, and he growled in frustration against her lips.

She pulled back, breaking their kiss. She was breathing hard, panting with need, and her eyes glowed with fire and passion. "Rip it off," she told him.

He didn't think anything she could say or do would shock him, but this request definitely gave him a jolt of surprise. And excited him beyond reason. And in that moment, the meaning behind tonight's fantasy crystalized and made complete sense. In the darkness she could be naughty, more outrageous, more sexually explicit. Without the lights on and his features obscured in shadows, she could imagine he was a faceless stranger.

But they weren't strangers, and no amount of pretending could change just how intimate they'd been with each other thus far. She was attempting to keep things physical between them, but what she didn't realize was that she was trusting *him* to be that faceless stranger, trusting him to fulfill her desires, yet keep the fantasy within the realms of reality.

His entire body remained tense, and her chin tipped up a fraction, taunting him. And then he knew. She was testing his resolve, wanting to see how far he was willing to go, if he'd play the part she'd asked, if he'd go all the way and *take her*. Hard and fast and without reserve. He had no boundaries with her, just so long as she was a willing participant, too.

Making his decision, he took a half step back, grasped each side of the flimsy material in his hands, and tore the blouse completely open with one firm tug. Those itty-bitty buttons popped, hitting his chest, the wall, the floor. She gasped as the thin fabric shredded beneath his hands, and he stared at a white bra so sheer she might as well have worn nothing at all.

He covered her lush breasts with his hands and bent his

head, scattering warm, moist kisses along her cheek, her jaw, her throat, all the way down to the fullest part of her heaving breasts. Cinnamon flavor tingled on his tongue, and grew hotter with every taste of her skin, making him burn all the way down to his burgeoning erection. Dragging his open mouth across the generous swell of flesh, he tongued her stiff nipples and plucked at them with his teeth through the stretch-lace material.

She whimpered and thrust her hands in his hair, arching her back to accommodate him, his mouth. He continued paying homage to her breasts while his fingers skimmed down her belly to her shorts. He unbuttoned and unzipped them with ease, then slipped his flattened palms just inside and followed the waistband around to the small of her back. He shoved the shorts over her hips so that he could fill his hands with her silk-clad bottom and tilt her pelvis against his. He moved against her, grinding his rock-hard sex between her legs, his movements slow, lazy, and precise.

As soon as he heard that sexy catch to her breath that told him she was gearing up for an orgasm, he stopped, drawing out the anticipation, the hunger. For both of them.

He lifted his head, connecting with her entranced gaze. In the soft candlelight he could see the flush of excitement on her skin and the blatant wanting etching her expression. His own heart thundered in his chest as he pushed her shorts down her thighs and long legs, and she kicked them aside. More stretch lace hindered his ability to touch her intimately, and he only hesitated a second before he ripped off the insubstantial panties and let the scrap of material fall to the floor at her feet.

Widening her stance with his sneakered feet, he slipped his hand between her thighs and grit his teeth at the bounty he discovered. Christ, she was so hot, so slick and wet, her essence drenched his fingers the moment he touched her. But it wasn't enough, and he filled her first with one long finger, then two, while using his thumb to stroke her soft, swollen vulva. She was tight, her inner muscles clenching around his fingers, and he thrust them in a little deeper while imagining how her snug sheath would feel enveloping his aching cock.

She sucked in a sharp breath and shuddered. Closing her eyes, she let her head roll back against the wall and licked her dry lips. "Gabe . . ."

There was more to that husky plea, and he wasn't about to make this easy on her when she'd been the one to issue the dare. "Tell me what you want," he said, kissing the corner of her mouth, coaxing her to state her desires out loud.

The pulse at the base of her throat fluttered wildly as she swallowed. "I want . . . I want you on your knees in front of me."

"I'm there, baby," he rasped and knelt before her, scattering kisses across her belly, dipping his tongue into her navel, inhaling deeply of her arousing scent, and finally replacing his seeking, gliding fingers with the heat of his mouth. Spreading her soft, pouty lips apart, he laved her with a slow, searing stroke along her cleft that made her moan and her legs tremble. He flicked the tip of his tongue over her clitoris, then drew the distended nub into his mouth, suckling her hard and strong.

A shuddering breath escaped her, and he felt her hands moving restlessly in his hair, heard the mewling sounds of pleasure she made deep in her throat as he increased the pressure and friction of his tongue. She rolled her hips forward to give him better access and widened her legs even more, enabling him to delve deeper so he could indulge in the sweet honeyed taste of her as her climax pushed her over the edge.

She screamed hoarsely, clawing wildly at his back as her entire body shook with the strength of her orgasm. Then her fingers twisted in his hair to pull his mouth away from the now-sensitive flesh that pulsed beneath the press of his tongue.

With one last defiant lick that made her whimper, he abruptly stood back up and fastened his mouth over hers, kissing her aggressively, giving her no choice but to accept the long, deep sweeps of his tongue as his lower body took up an ancient, gyrating rhythm against her mound. He was so hard for her, mindless with wanting, his groin throbbing, aching, craving her—a culmination of three nights of erotic foreplay and six years of imagining her just like this.

A desperate hunger rushed through him, along with the primitive need to brand and possess her as *his*. With that urgent thought filling his head, with his taut body keeping hers pinned against the wall, he buried his face against her neck and groaned . . . and finally gave in to a dark, forbidden fantasy of his own.

"I *have* to get inside you," he panted against her ear, his voice as raw, carnal, and emotional as the moment between them. *"Let me fuck you."*

The explicit, unrefined plea escaped him before he could curb his choice of words, but much to his surprise, his frank request seemed to excite her. A delicate shiver rippled through her, her breathing deepened, and she gave him the permission he sought.

"*Yes,*" she whispered.

He moved away from her for a handful of seconds, just long enough to yank off his shirt so he could feel her lush, naked breasts crushed against his chest when he took her, then unbuckled his belt. He jerked down the zipper and pushed his jeans just low enough on his hips to release the throbbing length of his penis. He shuddered, feeling triply erect and twice as thick as he'd ever been before.

He glanced back up and found her leaning against the wall, taking in his size and length, her eyes heavy-lidded with passion and her expression a mixture of fascination and hunger. He closed the distance between them, sandwiching her between the wall and his hard, muscular body. His massive erection slipped between her thighs and nestled between her nether lips, and he was instantly surrounded by the sultry heat and dampness of her desire. She moaned softly, her tongue darted out to wet her lips, and he knew once he was inside her it was going to be a quick, fierce ride.

"Wrap your arms around my neck and hold on tight," he ordered, his voice low and rough.

She did as he asked, entwining their bodies more intimately than before. His hands smoothed over her bottom and gripped the back of her thighs. Then he was lifting her, spreading her legs apart and tilting her hips up to him. He pushed into her in one long, relentless thrust that had her sucking in a quick gasping breath, and him growling deep in his throat at how perfectly they fit together. Locking her legs around his hips, he forced his way deeper, until she was utterly impaled on his cock and it was impossible to tell where he ended and she began.

He moved inside her, a slow, slick in and out glide that sent spirals of heat shooting up his spine. Her fingers clenched his shoulders, holding on tight, and her head fell back against the wall, her expression so incredibly beautiful and rapturous his heart swelled with indescribable emotions. He wanted this moment to last forever, but he was too overwhelmed with pleasure, too consumed by needs he'd denied for too long.

His body instinctively picked up the pace of his thrusts, his movements rhythmic, wild, desperate. His mind spun as his climax built, hot and fast, consuming him, searing him from head to toe. He drove to the hilt one last time, and stiffened and groaned as his orgasm slammed into him in a white-hot rush of ecstacy that seemed never-ending.

Once the tremors subsided, Gabe carefully lowered her feet back to the ground, keeping her steady with an arm around her waist. He slipped from the warmth of her body, still semierect, and silently berated himself for letting their first time together, no matter how earthy and torrid, be so one-sided. His jaw tightened in self-reproach. He'd never meant to get so caught up in his own satisfaction that he left her behind.

Determined to make it just as good for her, too, he gently pushed her torn blouse and bra from her shoulders, then lifted her limp body into his arms and carried her to the couch. He lowered her so that she was lying on the cushions, and admired the way the candlelight illuminated her body and cast a rosy-golden hued flush to her skin.

Absently, she touched her fingers to the upper swell of her breast and looked up at him questioningly. He said nothing as he quickly peeled off the rest of his clothes so that there was nothing to hinder the sensation of flesh against flesh. Nothing to get in the way of him pleasuring her.

Pushing the coffee table out of the way, he knelt beside the couch, and grasping her hips, he gently pulled her down to the carpeted floor with him. He turned her, positioning her so that she was on her knees and her upper body rested against the soft cushions. His gaze took in her spread legs and pert, slender bottom, upturned and ready for him. That quickly, that easily, he grew hard once again at the seductive image of taking her in such an erotic, primal way.

Lowering his head, he pressed his open mouth to the small of her back and ran his tongue up her spine, covering the length of her body with his own until they were aligned from shoulders to thighs and his rigid sex glided across the silky, damp flesh between her thighs.

A violent shiver rippled through her and she curled her hands into fists against the sofa. She looked over her shoulder at him, the brightness in her eyes underscored by a glimmer of uncertainty. "Gabe . . ."

"Shhh," he soothed from behind. Burying his face in her fragrant hair, he reached around and caressed her breasts in his hands, plucked at her nipples with his fingers, and smoothed a flattened palm down her quivering belly. "I'm not done with you yet. Just relax and go with the fantasy . . ."

She moaned when his fingers parted her folds, and sighed breathlessly as he slowly eased his shaft deep, deep inside her. His hips pumped against hers, slow and easy, and he stroked her swollen sex until she was rocking back against him, uninhibited and greedy, setting the pace and letting him know precisely what she liked.

Spearing his fingers through the hair at the nape of her neck, he wrapped loose strands in his hand, tenderly tugged her head back, and dragged his mouth across her cheek and along her arched throat. His lips blazed a trail up to her ear, and in the cloak of darkness, and in a rough, husky tone of voice, he whispered all the naughty, erotic things he'd like to do to her, the varied ways he wanted to make her come, and shared all the different, shameless ways he'd dreamed of taking her.

Her eyes fluttered closed, shutting him and any emotional connection out at the last possible moment, and her lips parted on a soft, keening cry as her entire body began to quake.

The convulsions started deep, an incredible rippling sensation that clenched and squeezed his cock like a tight fist. She sobbed his name, and the sound on her lips and the feel of her intense orgasm pulling at him triggered his own. And then he was swept away, lost in the heat and sensuality of Chloe, riding one long continuous crest of a shattering climax that left him lethargic and completely sated physically, but wanting more emotionally . . . like forever with this woman.

After a few moments, he separated their bodies, lifted her back up to the couch, and stood. She lay there, spent and languid, a drowsy, satisfied smile on her lips. In the candlelight her gaze finally met his, and something she witnessed on his own face made her expression change, drawing forth confusion, uncertainty, and a wealth of vulnerability.

He knew what she'd seen . . . love. He loved her. He'd carried the knowledge in his heart for years, since the first moment he'd laid eyes on her in high school. He just hadn't been able to embrace the feelings because he'd never felt worthy. Old insecurities died hard, but now, having finally come to terms with his past and the man he'd become, he was willing to risk everything for her.

"Chloe . . ."

"The fantasy is over," she said, cutting him off, a touch of panic in her voice, as if she *knew* what was tumbling through his mind. As if she wasn't ready to hear what he had to say.

Curbing the impulse to blurt out his feelings, he reached for his briefs and pants instead and quietly put them on. His shirt followed, along with his socks and shoes, and when he glanced back at Chloe a minute later he noticed she'd covered herself with the throw blanket that had been folded over the back of the sofa.

Feeling distinctly uneasy, a whole lot frustrated, and not wanting to leave with this subtle tension between them, he clung to what had ultimately brought them together. The bet. And regardless of how complex this game between them had become, he owed her one last night. "About to-morrow night—"

"It's all yours," she said softly.

He blinked, not certain he'd heard her correctly, or what she really meant. "Excuse me?"

"Tomorrow night is yours," she repeated huskily. With her hair tumbling wildly around her face, she pressed the blanket to her breasts, the barest of smiles brushing across her well-kissed mouth. "Whatever you want, whatever you desire, whatever fantasy you want to fulfill . . . It's yours."

Once again she'd thrown him off balance, made him wonder if she even realized the trust she was extending, and the implications of relinquishing her control to him. But he didn't question *why*, and he wasn't about to refuse such a generous gift and offering.

One he'd used to his advantage in every possible way.

He grinned wickedly. "I hope you're into bondage."

Her eyes turned a dark, velvet shade of green. "I can't say that I've ever been tied up for a man's pleasure, but I'm game."

Oh, he hoped so. Except what he had in mind wasn't only bondage of the physical kind, but of the emotional variety as well, and by the end of the night he wanted her complete and total surrender.

"I promise the pleasure will go both ways." Not wanting to shatter any of the illusions she'd created for tonight's intimate fantasy, he turned and left, leaving her in the same darkness in which the fantasy had begun less than an hour ago.

"Look what just came for you," Chloe's friend and co-worker, Anita, announced as she sauntered into her office with a huge floral arrangement in her hands. "Do you have a secret admirer you haven't told me about?"

Chloe smiled and set aside the contract she'd been preparing for web site services. She knew without reading the enclosed card who'd sent the gorgeous bouquet of roses, tulips, and carnations. A tiny thrill fluttered in her belly. No man had ever catered to her every desire, need, and fantasy, and she had to admit that she liked feeling romanced and pampered by Gabe. All part of a bet, yes, but she'd enjoy the feeling . . . for one last night.

"My lips are sealed," she told her friend. "That's why they call it a *secret* admirer." And Gabe was her very own sexy, private secret, one she'd share with no one.

Anita perched her skirt-clad hip onto the corner of Chloe's desk and grinned at her. "Well, regardless of who the lucky guy is, I have to say it's about time you let a man sweep you off your feet."

Chloe inhaled the fragrant scent filling her office, realizing that she'd foolishly let Gabe do just that. "It's just a temporary thing," she said, the brutal words causing an ache in her chest. "A fun, brief fling."

"You sure about that?" Anita's light brown brows raised questioningly. "From the blissful look that's been on your face all week, I'd say you're further gone than you realize."

Chloe knew that for a fact, and it was her own damn fault for letting her emotions intertwine intimately with the great sex she'd had with Gabe. "He's leaving to go back home to Chicago this weekend," she said, determined to put things back into proper perspective. "It can't be anything more than a temporary affair."

Anita tipped her head, regarding Chloe speculatively. "Who are you trying to convince, me or yourself?" Her mouth creased with a teasing smile, but there was too much wisdom and knowledge in her hazel eyes.

Anita's comment struck deep and lingered long after her friend left her office to get back to work. Leaning back in her chair, Chloe swallowed the tight, aching knot in her throat, wondering when a simple bet to finally get Gabe out of her mind and heart had become so complicated. And when had she started craving *more*?

The answer came too fast, too easily. She'd never stopped wanting Gabe MacKenzie, despite the pain of his past rejection. Now he was more entrenched in her heart than ever, and in the quiet and solitude of her office she was forced to admit that she'd missed him for six long years . . . the easy comraderie they'd shared, their friendship, the underlying attraction and awareness that made her body buzz with excitement whenever she was near him.

She'd been empty inside and lonely for too long. Now, with him, she felt fulfilled and joyous . . . yet there was no denying she'd experience that same vast emptiness once he left again.

No matter her feelings for Gabe—then or now—he'd

given her no other promises this week other than pleasure, which he'd given her in spades. By mutual agreement they'd embarked on an affair, which in itself implied temporary, and she'd walked into the situation with her eyes wide open. He'd given her exactly what she'd asked for, memories so erotic they threatened to singe her mind just thinking about them, and he'd obviously gotten what he'd come for, too. As he'd stated that first night at the poker game, he had loose ends to tie up, and those loose ends obviously included *her*.

Funny how he'd selected bondage for tonight's fantasy.

With a heartfelt sigh, she banned her tumultuous thoughts for now and reached for the small envelope tucked into the middle of the gorgeous arrangement. She retrieved the card inside and read the note Gabe had written in a bold, masculine scrawl: *Be at my mother's house at 7 P.M., and bring a big appetite. Love, Gabe.*

Love. Her heart leapt at the sentiment, and her thoughts tumbled back to the previous night and the intense emotions in Gabe's eyes after the second time he'd made love to her, how nervous and afraid she'd been that *she'd* say something to reveal her own feelings for him when she was so determined to be strong and in control of their affair . . . and her own emotions. Unfortunately, Gabe was one of her greatest weaknesses, and that was something she refused to let him know.

Judging by Gabe's past actions, once this week was over he'd leave, return to his life in Chicago, and quite possibly never come back to San Diego since his mother would no longer live here. Nothing had changed in the past six years . . . except his apparent need to make up for the chance he'd lost on that long-ago night up on the hill in Del Mar. And as she'd told him, she wanted the same thing, and she had only herself to blame for craving more now.

She fingered the satiny petal of a rose, forcing herself to

accept that unpleasant truth, and knowing that tonight would be the end of their brief relationship.

She'd given Gabe tonight's fantasy to do with whatever he wished because she wanted to know and experience his deepest desires. Whatever happened between them tonight would be another sexual memory for her to tuck away and dream about when the emptiness in her felt too all-consuming.

Ultimately, she'd enjoy the evening for all it was worth. She'd keep her emotions locked away, and after she enjoyed her final, glorious night in Gabe's arms, this time *she'd* be the one to walk away from him.

Chapter Five

"I have to admit I'm very impressed that *you* made dinner tonight." Chloe waved her fork over the entrées on her plate and glanced at Gabe, the two candles he'd put on the table making the ends of her hair glitter like gold dust and her eyes glow a striking shade of green. "Filet mignon made just the way I like it, roasted potatoes with hollandaise sauce, and a spinach salad with hot bacon dressing. Absolutely amazing."

He shrugged off her compliment as he chewed a bite of tender filet, though he was secretly pleased that she was enjoying what he'd selected for tonight's menu and appreciated the work he'd put into making everything just perfect for her.

She'd arrived earlier, all smiles and a sassy, teasing attitude, but there was no mistaking the subtle reserve beneath her breezy disposition, a barrier that had been erected since last night. Physically she'd been accessible and responsive to the kisses and caresses he'd stolen before serving dinner, but she'd managed to keep those vulnerable emotions of hers confined. Protecting herself, he guessed. From him, and what he had planned for her tonight, their last night together.

He didn't mind the steady stream of conversation because he loved talking with her about anything and everything, but no way was he taking this high-strung, anxious woman into the bedroom. Which meant he needed to figure out a way to make her relax and let down her guard a bit so she'd be more receptive to what was going to happen between them when they made love this time.

For starters, he lifted the bottle of wine he'd left on the table and refilled her glass. "I really like to cook," he told her, and topped off his own wine as well. "So tonight's dinner was a pleasure to make."

Her brows rose in surprise. "Really?"

"Yep." He smiled at her. "I think too many years of macaroni and cheese, hot dogs, and Hamburger Helper made me appreciate a good meal, though I can't say I eat like this all the time. When you're cooking for one, it's much easier to toss a frozen dinner into the microwave."

She laughed and nodded in agreement. "Oh, I hear you. And how did you know that I liked spinach salad? That was a risk to make, don't you think?"

"Not at all." He speared a potato with his fork. "Do you remember what you were eating the day I saw you at that restaurant eating lunch with a friend?"

She thought for a moment, then her eyes grew big and round in shocked disbelief. "OhmiGod, it was a spinach salad! That was over seven months ago. How in the world did you remember that?"

"When it comes to you, there's not a whole lot I *don't* remember." He let her think about that meaningful comment as he lifted his hand and wiped away a smudge of sauce from the corner of her mouth. "Hollandaise sauce," he murmured, completely turned on by the way her eyes darkened at his touch.

"Thanks." She glanced away and swiped at her mouth with her napkin, then focused her attention back on her dinner. "So, how is the packing coming along?"

Gabe recognized a switch in topic when he heard one.

He also suspected her question was a calculated reminder of his brief stay in San Diego. "I'm almost done. Most of the boxes are sealed and ready to be shipped back to my place in Chicago."

She chewed and swallowed a bite of meat. "Was it hard to pick and choose things to keep from your childhood?"

"Yeah." An indulgent grin curved his lips. "My mom saved everything, and I'm a sentimental old fool. I found a whole lot of stuff I'd forgotten about and couldn't bring myself to part with."

She tipped her head curiously. "Like what?"

"Like a very old snapshot of my dad that I kept hidden away. It's the only picture I have of him. I'd forgotten about the photograph, and my first instinct was to toss it, but I decided to keep it instead."

"Why?" she asked softly.

"Because for the first time ever, I could look at his face and not experience all the hurt and resentment I'd harbored for him walking out on me and my mother." He shook his head, amazed at the revelations that had come to him over the years and had solidified this past week. "I finally realized that for a man who'd never been a part of my life, he was actually the catalyst for everything I did and tried to accomplish."

Chloe pressed her hand to his arm in understanding. "You have nothing to prove to a father who was never there for you, Gabe."

He set his fork on his plate, and lifted his wineglass for a drink. "It's taken me a whole lot of years to figure that out for myself," he admitted. He'd spent most of his childhood and part of his adult life trying to make something of himself, to prove to his deadbeat dad, Darren MacKenzie, that he'd managed to do well without him as an influence. That despite leaving him and his mother nearly destitute, they'd managed without his support.

The accident with his knee had thrown his goals off

course, and it had taken him too long to realize that all he had to do was accept himself and the choices he made in order to be happy. And he was happy . . . except for the one thing missing in his life. The love of a good woman. The right woman. *Chloe.*

"What else did you find and keep?" she asked, bringing him out of his musings and keeping their conversation on track.

"A lock box I'd made in wood shop my junior year, a few baseball cards I'd held on to, my first *Playboy* magazine, which your brother, Derek, gave to me on my seventeenth birthday."

She laughed at that, the light, amusing sound fitting so perfectly into his life.

"And of course I kept my high school football jersey, along with my very first football that my mother saved up to buy me for Christmas."

A smile quirked her mouth. "You can take the man out of football, but you can't take the urge to play football out of the man, huh?" she teased.

"Football was my first love," he admitted, but knew his life had turned out better than he'd ever imagined, despite that huge loss. "Actually, I kept that memorabilia because I'd like to think that maybe someday I'll have a son of my own who likes to play football."

"Would you want him to?"

"As much as *I* enjoyed playing the game, it would be his choice," he answered honestly. "I'd want him to do it for nobody but himself."

Finished with her meal, she pushed her plate aside and studied his face for long moments. "You miss playing football, don't you?"

Leaning back in his chair, Gabe clasped his hands over his stomach, prepared to share insecurities and weaknesses with Chloe that no other woman had ever glimpsed. It was time if he expected the same openness from her in return.

"I did miss football, at first. It was all I knew and so much a part of me and my life for so long. It was also my way of escaping poverty and showing my old man that his son had grown up to be someone successful and important."

She sat quietly, listening and not judging his reasons and youthful logic.

"It was a difficult adjustment for the first two years after my knee forced me to give up a shot at pro football," he continued, "mainly because I had no idea what I was going to do with the rest of my life, or how I was going to make a decent living."

She braced her elbows on the table, clasped her hands, and rested her chin on top. "You managed just fine, and landed right back on your feet as a sports agent."

"Which took even more hard work and a whole lot of perseverance. And having contacts in the sports industry helped," he added, then finished off his wine. "Looking back on the past six years, though, I have to say that everything turned out for the better. I have a steady, if not hectic job that I enjoy, and I'm still a part of the game, but in a more behind-the-scenes kind of way. Now I see so many of my clients worrying about what they're going to do when their professional sports careers are over, and I'm so relieved and grateful that I've already been through that angst and I'm content and happy with what I'm doing."

"I'm glad to hear that," she said, her tone soft and sincere. Absently, she ran the tip of her finger around the rim of her wineglass. "So, what's left to accomplish in the life of Gabe MacKenzie?"

He shrugged nonchalantly. "What every man wants."

"A carefree, bachelor life filled with wild women and lots of hot sex?" she asked flippantly before he could explain what he meant.

Inwardly, he flinched, but he suspected her playboy image of him helped her maintain an emotional distance.

For the moment, he'd cater to her notions, because there was no point in forcing her to face his feelings for her when she wasn't ready to accept the truth. He had the rest of the evening to convince her otherwise.

No doubt she expected tonight to be all about hot, wild *sex* and believed she knew exactly what he wanted from her. But she didn't have a clue. What he desired went far beyond sating immediate carnal longings. He craved the love of a good woman. A lifetime commitment to a soul mate. A family to come home to. And he ached to share that with her, a woman who'd once been one of his best friends and was now his lover in every sense of the word.

Unfortunately, she wasn't ready to face what was between them, not when her defenses were a mile high. It was obvious to him that while she might trust him with her body, she didn't trust him with her heart. Not that he could blame her for being wary, considering his past track record with her. Which meant he still had his work cut out for him before he moved things to the bedroom.

Abruptly she stood and reached for his plate and utensils and stacked them on top of hers. Before he could say anything more, she'd disappeared into the kitchen, leaving behind a silence he felt all the way to his bones. Thrusting his fingers through his hair, he blew out a harsh breath, shook off his frustration, and joined her with a handful of dirty dishes he'd cleared off the table, too.

He came up beside her and set the serving bowl and their empty wineglasses in the sink, and she cast a quick glance and smile at him before redirecting her gaze to scrubbing a platter. "How about you clear the table, and I'll rinse everything and load the dishwasher?" she suggested.

Sensing her need to regroup, he didn't argue. "All right."

It remained quiet between them as he made a few more trips back out to the table, and by the last round into the kitchen he had to curb the impulse to take her right where she stood, up against the counter, and show her how much he wanted her, adored her, loved her . . . and wanted that intimacy with *only* her. No one else. But considering her own state of mind, using barbaric, caveman tactics to sway her would only make her retreat further, and that was something he refused to allow tonight.

Once they were done and the kitchen was spotless, Gabe grabbed a big bag of M&M's, and tucked her hand in his. "Come on," he coaxed, leading her back out to the living room. "Let's move on to the second phase of my fantasy." He sat down on the couch next to her and used the remote to turn on the TV and VCR. The cassette tape he'd slipped into the unit earlier whirled to life.

Her brows puckered with a confused frown. "Your fantasy is to watch a movie with me?"

"It's just *part* of my fantasy," he clarified, making sure she realized there was more to come.

She glanced back at the TV, then at him, her expression tentative. "Umm, what *kind* of movie are we going to watch?"

"Not the kind *you're* thinking," he said, and chuckled. "I don't need porn to get hot and bothered and worked up for sex. You do that to me easily enough. I picked out a romantic comedy I thought we'd enjoy watching together." He showed her the VCR box so she could see the title of the movie.

"Wow. You're throwing me all kinds of curves tonight," she murmured, smiling. Relaxing. Just as he'd intended. "Not many guys I know would willingly sit through a chick flick."

"I didn't think you'd appreciate a blood and guts kind of movie. Kinda kills the mood, you know?" Leaning against the far end of the couch, he pulled her into the crook of his arm and settled the bag of candy-coated chocolates on his lap. "But don't think that you're getting off easy," he said, grinning wickedly into her upturned face, "because I want you to hand-feed me the M&M's."

She laughed, breaking up any last traces of tension between them from dinner. "I think I can handle that."

For the next hour and a half Gabe cuddled Chloe in his arms while she kept him supplied with chocolate, which he shared with her as well. They laughed at all the humorous antics and scenes keeping the protagonists apart, and she sighed wistfully when the guy finally got the girl in the end.

By the time the credits rolled, she was snuggled close to his side and completely relaxed, making it easy for him to shift their positions so that she was beneath him. His body was half on top of hers and he stared into her soft, slumberous eyes.

She rested a hand on his shoulder and trailed her fingers down to his chest. "Did you enjoy that part of your fantasy?"

"Yeah, I did." He lowered his head and tenderly kissed her lips, her jaw, her neck, loving the scent and taste of her. "There's something incredibly satisfying about spending a quiet evening with a beautiful, sexy woman and having her all to myself."

She moaned as his tongue touched the sensitive spot just below her ear. "And now that the movie's over?" she asked breathlessly.

He met her gaze again, seeing the want and need reflected in the depth of her eyes. The same kind of hunger that flowed hot and molten through his veins. "I want to make love to you."

Her palm slid lower, to the waistband of his jeans, and she fumbled with the top button, her intentions unmistakable. "Out here, on the couch?"

He shook his head and gently stopped her advance, though he was rock-hard from the thought of her taking him in her hand. "I don't want something fast, hard, and quick." Tonight was about more than satiating mutual lust. It was about intimacy, emotion, and devotion, and by the time he was done with her she'd know how it felt to experience all three. "I want you on a nice soft bed so you'll be comfortable and I can take my time and do as I please to every single inch of you."

Moving off her, he stood and held out his hand, helping her up, too. Then he led her down the short hallway to his boyhood room. He turned on the dresser lamp to illuminate the room, refusing to make love to her in the dark. Tonight, there would be no hiding for either of them.

He brushed back silky strands of hair from her cheek. "You've been in this bedroom before," he told her.

Her perplexed gaze took in his stark furnishings—the same double bed and secondhand dresser he'd grown up with. Then she shook her head. "I've never been in your bedroom before."

"Yeah, you have," he refuted, and allowed a slow, sinful grin to lift his lips. "You've even been in my bed. *Naked.*"

She opened her mouth to deny that claim as well, and he pressed his fingers to her lips to quiet her. "As a teenager, I spent so many restless nights in that bed, thinking of you, kissing your lips, taking your breasts into my mouth and imagining what it would feel like being buried deep inside you. You were the cause of every wet dream I ever had."

Her breath caught at his explicit words, her expression equally stunned that he'd coveted her for so long.

"I've wanted you for what seems like forever, Chloe," he murmured huskily. "Years and years that seemed so empty without you in them. So tonight, you're fulfilling a huge fantasy of mine and finally making it a reality."

She swallowed, and an uncertain smile appeared. "I hope reality lives up to the fantasy," she said, her tone more serious than teasing.

He framed her face in his big hands and stroked her cheeks with his thumbs. "Sweetheart, it already has," he reassured her, and pressed his mouth to her lips, which automatically parted for the hot sweep of his tongue.

Cupping the back of her head, he kissed her long and

slow and deep. Endless, rapacious kisses that chased any lingering doubts from her mind. Their mouths parted ways only to help each other strip off their clothes, but always returned to continue where they left off. Once they were both completely naked, Chloe's hand curled around his rampant erection, caressed him from base to tip, and he groaned low and rough into her mouth.

She broke their kiss and stared into his eyes. "I want to taste you," she whispered.

He wasn't about to refuse her request, not when it was something he wanted just as badly. "I'm all yours, honey."

She pressed her damp, open mouth to his collarbone, his chest, and licked and nipped at his nipples while her palm cradled his penis and her fingers squeezed and stroked the length of him. She worked her way lower, scattering hot, wet kisses on his belly and followed the line of his hip with her tongue, all the way down to his groin. She settled on her knees in front of him, and he glanced down at her, taking in the silky hair that tumbled around her shoulders, the thrust of her breasts, and the dark raspberry hue of her aureoles as they brushed his thighs.

She teased him with a soft, swirling lap of her tongue over the swollen head of his cock, and he visibly shuddered, completely at her mercy. "Chloe," he groaned, the word a plea.

She tipped her head back to look at his face. This time when she smiled, it was pure seduction. "Is this part of that fifteen-year-old fantasy, too?"

He pushed his fingers through her hair and tangled the soft strands around his fist. "Oh, yeah. You're welcome to make it come true."

She opened her mouth and took him inside, as much of him as she could, and the reality of having her pleasuring him this way was so much better than he'd ever imagined. Her lips enveloped his shaft, suckling him, and her tongue pressed against the pulse throbbing along his hard length as she took him deeper still.

Incoherent sounds of need rose into his throat, and he shook with the force of the desire she'd incited. His stomach muscles clenched and his sacs tightened, warning him that it was only a matter of a few more strokes and he'd come hard and fast. And that's not what he wanted just yet.

With his hand still fisted in her hair, he gently urged her back up, and she came willingly. Lashes at half mast and a sultry, gratified smile curving her mouth, she licked her lips, and he nearly lost it right then and there. Within seconds he had the covers pulled down and her pushed back onto the bed and centered in the middle of the mattress. He straddled her waist with his heavy erection sliding against her belly and reached for the bright red silk scarves he'd stashed beneath one of his pillows earlier.

"I take it this is where you tie me up," she said, glancing at the bonds he'd produced.

"Yeah." He ran one of the scarves along his palm and through his fingers, taking his time and increasing the anticipation.

She eyed the feminine article in his hand. "Tell me you didn't borrow them from your mother's room." She looked worried and embarrassed at the thought.

"Nope." He grasped one of her hands, lifted it above her head, and tied her wrist to the wooden post on the headboard, then did the same with the other. "I went out and bought them today. I figured they might come in handy in the future."

She stiffened beneath him, and her eyes flashed with a hint of begrudging envy. He could only guess that she was thinking of him with other women. Good, he thought with a private smile. A little jealousy never hurt in a man's attempt to influence a woman to want him even more.

He gave her bonds one last tug to make sure the scarves were secure, but not hurting her in any way. Satisfied with his work, he took a moment to drink in the sight of her—naked, long-limbed, and blessed with generous, feminine curves.

She shifted restlessly under his scrutiny. "You look like you're about to devour me."

"Oh, you can bet I will, sweetheart," he drawled, and set out to fulfill that promise.

It was a night that allowed for no inhibitions, and he spent the next half hour worshiping her body with his fingers, his mouth, his tongue, leaving no part of her untouched. He branded her with the glide of his erection along her taut breasts, her soft stomach and sleek thighs, and discovered erogenous zones with his mouth she didn't even know she possessed. With slow, teasing foreplay he brought her to the peak of orgasm repeatedly, until she was begging, trembling, and pleading for release.

She strained against her silken ties as his mouth drifted once again over her belly, and she panted from the exquisite sexual tension thrumming through her body. "Oh, God, Gabe, please . . . *make me come.*"

Knowing he'd made her wild enough, he moved lower and gave her body what it ultimately craved. She was swollen, pink, and wet, her female flesh glistening with desire for him, and he covered her with his mouth, grazed her cleft with his teeth, and swirled his tongue against the nub of her clitoris. Her stomach quivered, her thighs clenched against his arms, and then she was unraveling and screaming as an intense orgasm raged through her.

While she recovered, limp and boneless, he reared up and untied the scarves, freeing her, then pushed her thighs wider apart with his knees. Settling between that warmth and softness, he moved over her so that they were finally face-to-face. Holding her gaze, he sank into her welcoming heat in one long, smooth thrust. The thrill and perfection of being sheathed inside her made him shudder.

Her hands were all over him, sweeping down his back

and grasping his buttocks to urge him deeper. Her hips rolled, undulating eagerly against him, and he tightened his jaw to keep from giving in to the temptation to make love to her hard and fast, as she seemed to want.

Grabbing her wrists, he held them down at the side of her head and pinned her squirming, gyrating body with the length of his. "Ms. Chloe," he managed in a low, gruff tone of voice, "this is *my* fantasy, and I'm gonna dictate the speed, so you might as well settle in for a long, slow ride."

Her lashes fluttered closed on a protesting moan that vibrated against his chest.

"Look at me," he said, refusing to let her retreat now, after everything they'd just shared. "Don't shut me out. Not now. Not tonight." *Not ever.*

She opened her eyes slowly, gazing up at him through a heavy haze of passion. And that's when he saw the emotion he'd been waiting for . . . a longing that wrapped around his heart and touched his soul.

He did his best to touch hers in return. "I gave you romance with flowers, a candlelight dinner, and a romantic movie," he murmured, moving slowly, lazily within her. "Now it's time to make our own fireworks."

The implication and intimacy of his words registered in her eyes, but she didn't deny what he was asking for. Instead, her body embraced his, met him stroke for stroke and matched the pulsing rhythm he set. And then they were both falling, tumbling together in a burst of brilliant heat and scorching passion. He watched her come for him, with him, as his own orgasm crested. The intensity of the moment stole his breath, made his pounding heart skip a beat, and utterly drained him.

Long minutes later he moved off her so he didn't crush her with his weight, and she automatically scooted closer, cuddled up to his side, and smiled up at him. "That was *incredible.*"

He smiled back and kissed her temple. "Yeah, it was," he agreed, still recovering from the encounter.

Resting her head on his shoulder, she draped an arm over his stomach and slipped her slender leg between his as if they'd been sleeping together for years. She felt so good and right snuggled next to him, and he finally had her right where he wanted her . . . in his bed and in his arms. Tomorrow morning would be soon enough to hash out the past and plan their future.

Chloe awoke before the break of dawn, with Gabe cuddled up to her from behind. His face was buried in her tousled hair, his warm, even breath caressed her shoulder, and a heavy arm kept her back secured close to his chest. While her body was replete and sated from a night spent fulfilling provocative fantasies, her emotions were in tatters and Gabe was far from being purged from the deepest recesses of her soul, as she'd hoped.

If anything, the past four nights had entrenched him more deeply into her heart. She'd witnessed a kind and caring man who'd grown up with a wealth of insecurities, but had managed to make something of himself despite all the obstacles thrown in his way. She'd experienced tenderness and an intimacy with him she'd only dreamed of finding for herself, and he'd given her a wealth of sensual, erotic memories to take with her.

So why did she feel so empty and cold deep inside?

Because it was over. The painful thought caused a swell of aching tears to gather in her throat, and she resolutely swallowed them back. Gabe had paid his bet in full, as well as tied up his loose ends with her, and in a matter of days he'd be returning to Chicago. She'd gotten exactly what she'd bargained for, and the last thing she wanted was to face an awkward morning-after scene with him. She'd leave him a brief note, slip out of the house quietly, and end their affair with as much dignity as she could muster. And with no guilt or regrets for either one of them.

More tears threatened to fall, and she shifted next to Gabe, doing her best to slip from his embrace without waking him. He sighed deeply in his sleep and turned onto his back, freeing her to move off the mattress without disturbing him. Quietly, she grabbed her clothes from the floor to put them on in the living room, and stopped at his bedroom door to look at him one last time.

He looked so peaceful in sleep and overwhelmingly sexy with the covers slung low on his hips and one bare, muscular leg exposed. The urge to return to bed and make love to him one last time was strong, but she forced herself to turn around and be the one to walk away this time.

Unfortunately, she'd be leaving her heart behind when she left.

Gabe blinked his eyes open with a start, glanced over at the empty side of his bed, and instinctively knew that Chloe had snuck out on him. A note lying on the pillow beside his confirmed his suspicion: *Your bet is paid in full. Have a safe trip back to Chicago. Chloe.*

"*Shit,*" he muttered. Tossing the piece of paper aside, he flopped back on the bed in frustration. He glared up at the ceiling, wondering how in the hell she could doubt the depth of his feelings for her after everything they'd shared last night.

But he knew the answer to his own question—after his past track record, she feared him leaving again. Didn't trust him to stick around for the long haul. Didn't believe he wanted her for anything more than scratching a six-year-old itch.

She couldn't be more wrong. He'd given her up once, and he refused to do so again. This time he wasn't about to leave for Chicago without confronting her with the truth about what he truly desired. Their bargain wasn't even close to being paid in full when *his* demands included a life-time commitment.

A faint sniffling sound from the living room caught his attention and jumpstarted his pulse. Was Chloe still there? Driven by the hopeful thought, he scrambled out of bed and yanked on the pair of jeans he'd worn the night before, zipping them up but not bothering to fasten the top button. He padded quietly down the hallway, stopped at the entrance to the living room, and found Chloe bending over by the couch to pick up the sandals she'd left there the night before while they'd watched the rented movie together.

She slipped the pair on her feet and swiped her fingers beneath her eyes, wiping away the moisture dampening her cheeks. His heart twisted in his chest and he had to forcibly resist the urge to go to her and take her in his arms . . . He wouldn't take such liberties with her until she invited him there.

She reached for her purse, and he spoke before she could grab the leather bag. "Going somewhere?" he asked, his voice still raspy with the remnants of sleep.

She spun around, her eyes big and round and puffy from crying, and looking as though she couldn't decide whether to stay rooted to the spot or bolt. True to the Chloe he'd grown to love, she stayed put and her chin lifted mutinously. "I . . . uh, just thought it would be best if I was gone when you woke up. No sense us dealing with an uncomfortable good-bye."

He leaned against the wall and crossed his arms over his bare chest. "You're assuming I *want* to say good-bye."

"Saying good-bye is inevitable, and we both know it, so why make things any more difficult than they need to be by stringing it out?"

He shook his head, openly discounting her logic. "Haven't you listened to a word I've said all week?" he asked, his low, calm tone contradicting the uncertainties he couldn't shake. "I want you, Chloe."

"You've had me for four nights," she refuted, her defenses in place.

"I want *you*," he clarified, and pushed off the wall so he could close the distance between them. "And four nights doesn't even come close to what I have in mind for us."

She stared at him, her wariness apparent. "You want to have a long-distance affair?"

He stopped in front of her, but didn't touch her. Yet. "I can't say that appeals to me, but I'll take you whatever way I can have you."

Her gaze narrowed and her mouth pursed with annoyance. "Why are you doing this, Gabe? You got exactly what you came for. You tied up your loose ends in San Diego, so don't make this any harder than it already is for me." In a huff, she paced away from him, but turned back around to finish her tirade. "Dammit, you're the one who walked away six years ago and we both made up for lost time these last four nights, but it's *over*. You're free to go back to Chicago and resume your life, and I'll do the same here in San Diego."

He inhaled a steady breath, wondering if he'd ever be able to heal the devastating hurt he'd inadvertently dealt her that long-ago night. He was willing to spend a lifetime trying to make amends, if only she'd let him.

"What if I don't want things between us to be over?" he asked, refusing to give up on her, on *them*. "What if I want what we shared this week to be the beginning?"

She shook her head jerkily, causing her disheveled hair to swirl and shimmer about her shoulders. "It's not enough," she whispered, the words escaping on a note of anguish.

His entire body tensed, and knowing he had nothing left to lose, he laid his soul on the line. "What if I tell you that I love you?"

More tears flooded her eyes, and she valiantly blinked them back. "Don't mess with my emotions, Gabe."

His heart squeezed tight. "Sweetheart, after this week,

how can you even doubt the way I feel about you?" he asked gently, sincerely.

"Because I thought you cared once before and you walked out of my life without looking back or giving me a second thought."

He felt as though she'd punched him in the gut, deservedly so for the emotional upheaval he'd put her through. Once again he moved closer, and when she didn't step away he reached out and caressed his thumb along her taut, stubborn jaw.

"Ahh, Chloe, I'm so sorry about that," he murmured. "More than you'll ever know. I swear there isn't a day that goes by that I don't regret the way I handled that night up on the hill, but I was so damned confused and the last thing I wanted to do was cause you any pain, and I did that anyway."

"Why, Gabe? Why did you leave and not contact me again until now?" She searched his face for answers. "I have to know."

He nodded sagely. "Yes, you deserve to know everything." He rubbed at the back of his neck, hoping and praying that she'd understand and accept his reasons. "When I came home six years ago I was still recovering from my knee injury and I knew my career as a professional football player was over. The goals I'd worked so hard toward, all the years of training and single-minded determination to make it to the big leagues, gone. And all the insecurities I felt growing up came flooding back, and all I could think was that I was never going to claw my way out of the poverty that had been my way of life since I was a kid."

She continued to listen, and he went on. "I wanted you so much that night, but I knew I had no right to make love to you, not when my life was such a mess and I had no idea what was in store for me or how my future would turn out. I believed you deserved to find someone who could give you everything I couldn't."

"What gave you the right to take that decision and choice away from me?" she asked, a thread of anger vibrating in her voice.

A wry grin tipped his mouth. "I thought it was for the best. Sort of like you thinking it best to sneak out on me this morning without saying good-bye."

She bristled, ignoring his attempt at humor. "So, you came back, intent on seducing me and making up for that night up on the hill?"

"Yeah, something like that. I've always made goals for myself and set out to achieve them. You've always been an unattainable dream for me, and I need to finish and solidify what's always been between us."

"I think we accomplished that this week."

He shook his head. "That's not what I mean." Unable to find the appropriate words to explain, he decided to give her viable proof of his intentions from the very beginning of their affair. "I have something to show you. Stay put," he told her, and headed back into his bedroom.

He returned seconds later with a folded piece of paper in his hand, which he held out to her.

She eyed the note, but didn't take it. "What's that?"

"Don't you recognize your stationery?" he asked, tipping his head. "It's the personal, private bet I put out on the table during our last poker hand. I want you to read what it says, Chloe."

Tentatively, she plucked the note from his fingers and read the message he'd written as his bet. " 'Be mine forever,' " she read, then looked up at him, her gaze shining with hope and the need to believe.

He cupped her cheek tenderly in his hand and gave her all the proof she needed to trust in him. "For six long years I couldn't stop thinking about you. I couldn't stop loving you, and I was finally willing to take a risk to have you in my life. *I deserve you,* and I'm so damn lucky that some other guy hasn't snatched you up before now. And just for the record, I'm not letting you go again."

A smile wavered on her lips. "No man I dated ever stood a chance against you, Gabe."

"What are you saying?" He held his breath as he waited for her to answer.

"You've had my heart since the moment I met you." She swallowed hard and clutched his note to her chest. "I love you, Gabe MacKenzie."

An overwhelming wave of relief made him shudder. "Be mine forever, Chloe. In every way. As my best friend. My lover. My wife." He brought her mouth to his and kissed her softly, reverently. "*Marry me.* I need you in my life, in my future."

The misty longing in her eyes made his heart soar, as did her joyful reply. "*Yes.*"

He secured their promise with a long, deep kiss that left them both breathless and aroused. "Come back to bed with me," he urged. "Let me make love to you, and this time wake up in my arms, right where you belong."

She sighed. "I'd like that very much."

They made their way back down the hall to his bedroom in between kisses, caresses, and the removal of their clothes.

"We'll make a relationship work whatever way we need to," he said as he stripped her dress and bra off and ran his hands over her breasts. "And we might have to do the long-distance thing until I settle everything in Chicago and find a new agency to work for here in California."

She caught his head just as he lowered his mouth to taste her puckered nipples, and brought his gaze back to hers. "You would do that for me?"

"I would do *anything* for you," he said, and meant it. "I don't want to take you away from your family, and I want our kids to grow up with their grandparents and uncles nearby. I'm ready to come home, Chloe."

Smiling, and with her heartfelt emotions shining in her

eyes, she gave him a light shove, toppling him backward onto the bed. He grabbed her around the waist, taking her with him, and they rolled on the mattress until she was on top and he was sprawled beneath her. She peeled his jeans off, straddled his thighs, and reached for the red scarves on the nightstand.

She fluttered the strip of silk across his belly and swirled it around his erection, her expression mischievously wicked. "Hmmm, after everything you put me through the past six years, I think you need to grovel and beg just a little bit more."

He groaned, prepared to do just that. By the time she had his wrists secured to the bedpost and her soft hands and damp mouth had traversed the length of his body, he was harder than a spike and delirious with wanting her.

"Ride me, Chloe," he pleaded in a raspy tone of voice, needing a deeper, more intimate connection with her. "Make me yours."

With a shivery sigh and desire etching her beautiful features, she impaled herself on his heat and took him to heights he'd never known before. With her heart, body, and soul, she sealed their future, surrendered her love, and welcomed him home.

. . . And When They Were Bad

Were Bad

Donna Kauffman

Chapter One

His woman had smooth, tanned skin, flashing eyes that said "make me," a confidant attitude that assured him it would be worth his while . . . and a body simply begging to be licked. All over.

She was waiting. Just for him. For his tongue, his lips, his hands, fingers . . . and every other part of him. She was here, at Intimacies. And for the next two days she would be his.

All he had to do was find her.

"Mr. James, sir?"

Cameron turned to find a young man dressed in what apparently passed for a club uniform—low-slung tropical swim trunks and a white muscle tank with the club emblem stitched over the heart. White teeth gleamed against a deeply tanned face; he was relaxed, fit, and exuding vitality. The epitome of what Cameron had come here to discover in himself. The guy with no worries, the guy looking for a good time. The guy looking to discover his inner wild man. If he had one. Dear God, he hoped he did.

Cam cleared his throat. "Yes. Sorry for the delay. I had a meeting—"

"Not a problem," the young man assured him with a smile that invited him to leave the pressures of the real world behind. If he only knew the magnitude of that invitation.

"I'm Brian," he said, offering his hand. "The Jeep is right this way, sir."

Cam shook his hand, then they both ducked against the wind coming off the private seaplane propellers as it scooted away from the dock, heading back out over the crystalline waters in preparation for takeoff.

Good-bye James & Son Industries, Cam thought, taking Brian's silent invitation to heart. *Good-bye divorce lawyers, good-bye IRS agents, good-bye rehab therapists and defense trial lawyers.*

Good-bye Cameron James IV, perfect son, perfect husband, perfect company man.

"Mr. James?"

He turned back to the young man waiting to escort him to Intimacies, the new private club tucked away on its own island in the Caribbean. "Call me Cam," he instructed and hefted his soft leather bag over his shoulder.

Because he'd been delayed leaving Atlanta, the sun was already setting on his first night. He wondered now why he hadn't just canceled the meeting with his dad's latest team of defense lawyers; they wouldn't win an appeal anyway. His dad was guilty as hell and as far as Cam was concerned should sit right where he was, paying his debt to society. He should have flown out first thing. He should have ditched the stop by Rosewell to talk to the latest in his mother's endless line of rehab specialists. All of whom gave her the attention she craved, none of whom would ever help her, as she had no plans to ever help herself. He supposed he should be thankful he hadn't heard from Claire's legal team, although after their last settlement, he expected she'd be busy spending his money for at least the next several months. But none of that mattered here.

The closer they got to the club, the more he felt the various and numerous shackles of his life falling off, like so many rotted shingles. He'd spent his entire life doing what was best for others, being there for them whether they deserved his loyalty or not. For the next two days ... and nights, he was going to do only what pleased himself.

Intimacies promised every sort of hedonistic delight a man—or woman—could think of ... and several more they'd never dreamed of. He planned to explore every one of them.

As they bumped over the dusty road, Cam ducked as the occasional palmetto frond or other tropical undergrowth fanned into the truck. "What's on tap for tonight? Or have I missed all the fun?"

"Did you receive the club itinerary?" Brian asked, then waved a hand. "Never mind. I'll run down the list." He shot Cam a wide grin. "And no, you haven't missed anything. The fun is just getting started."

Cam returned the grin. "Fill me in."

"There was a welcome reception earlier. As you've probably read in the brochure, the island is divided into two sections: clothing banned and clothing optional." He said it matter-of-factly, with no emphasis on either.

Cam hadn't really given the options a lot of thought. He supposed he'd just go with what felt right.

"We have a main dining lodge," Brian continued, "though there are other smaller, more intimate places to eat around the club grounds as well, each with their own theme. The main lodge is the one place where guests from both sides of the club can meet and mingle. Minimal dress is required there"—he grinned again—"but not all that strictly enforced. Which works out okay, since it gives those considering switching sides a chance to test the waters, so to speak."

Cam honestly tried to imagine wandering around among strangers buck naked and couldn't summon the image. He had no problem imagining everyone else doing it, however, and smiled to himself. So maybe he'd test some waters himself. After all, that was why he'd chosen to come here. Who knew, he could be naked and loving it by morning.

"The main lodge is surrounded by a lagoon with bars set up on both sides in the water," Brian went on. "There are recreational huts on the beaches and themed bungalows in other various spots on the club grounds. During the day there are organized sports activities listed for each hut. At night . . ." He laughed. "Well, there are sports activities as well, but of an entirely different nature. The bungalows are available at any time, as long as they're not occupied . . . unless of course the inhabitants don't mind company." He glanced at Cam. "You're welcome to join in as many club activities as you wish, or none at all. It's up to you what kind of vacation you wish to have here."

Cam's imagination exploded and his body responded willingly to the carnal visions that filled his mind. Oh, he planned to participate all right.

"The hot-tub relay starts in about forty-five minutes," Brian offered. "The mango body race is on then, too. You can watch or wade in. Whatever feels good, that's the club motto."

Cam wondered how the board members at the newly resurrected James Industries would feel if he introduced that as the new company motto upon his return. New CEO, new company name, might as well have a new motto. Then Brian was whipping the Jeep around a circular drive lit with tiki torches and pulling up in front of a large, round building with a faux thatched roof. "Main lodge," he announced. "I can check your bags for you and you can pick up your key later if you'd like to dive right in. We have you staying in the Cherry Wild bungalow on the other side of the grounds. Anyone at the desk will be glad to direct you there personally whenever you're ready."

"Fine," Cam said, distractedly. Two women and one gentleman had just exited the building. The man was wearing a narrow strip of wildly colored cloth tied around his hips, just barely covering himself. The women were less modest, wearing only a scrap of lycra on the lower half of their bodies and nothing at all on top. Cam immediately noticed—and approved of—their lack of tan lines.

"Hey, Brian," one of the women called out. "You in charge of the body puzzle tonight?"

Brian flashed a grin. "You bet. See you there?"

Both women laughed. "We're voting you captain of the Tab Team," one said with a wicked grin. "See you later," the other said, and gave a little wink and wave.

All three quickly disappeared around the side of the building and Cam climbed from the Jeep.

Brian already had Cam's bag. "I'll send this to your bungalow, Mr. James. Cam," he corrected himself with a smile. "There's a list of tonight's events on the board next to a big map of the club right inside the main hall." He pointed to the path the others had taken. "Right down there, around the back. Have fun!"

"Thanks," Cam said and waved as Brian disappeared into the main building through doors that silently whooshed open, then shut behind him. The brief wash of cool, conditioned air felt good . . . but he didn't want anything as civilized as that tonight. He wanted to feel the heat, the humidity, cling to his skin. He wanted to feel vital, earthy, animalistic.

He was halfway around the building before he stopped and looked down at himself with a rueful smile. *Oh yeah, you're a wild man all right.* Here he was at the premiere private club, whose brochure beckoned their guests to leave all their civilized ideals behind . . . and he was wearing trousers—perfectly pleated and cuffed—a white linen shirt expertly tailored for his broad shoulders . . . and a silk tie. A goddamn silk tie.

He debated heading back inside after Brian and going to his bungalow to change clothes. But he didn't want to postpone the start of his hunt a moment longer. So he yanked off the tie and stuffed it in his pocket, then untucked his shirt and unbuttoned it, rolling the cuffs up his forearms. His designer leather shoes were kicked into the bushes, his socks and belt following shortly thereafter. He rolled his pants up to his calves and continued down the path, enjoying the feel of the smooth stone path, still warm from the day's sun, on the soles of his feet. Then he caught sight of himself in a small, glass-surfaced lagoon and sighed. He stuffed his glasses in his other pocket and raked his hand through his hair a few times.

There. Not exactly a wild man. But not exactly Cameron James IV, good guy, either.

"Now," he murmured as he returned to the path, "where are you, my wanton partner in sin?"

His first impression of the main lodge was that it wasn't the thriving Mecca of bacchanalia he'd expected it to be. But it was interesting all the same. And stimulating.

Narrow tables filled with all kinds of fruits, juices, and finger foods wound their way around the sinuous design of the place. Small tables were tucked into curved alcoves, while round tables were placed here and there, beckoning larger parties to make themselves at home. Lush tropical foliage filled the nooks and crannies and draped over the backs of the alcoves, heavy with brightly colored blossoms whose fragrance mingled with that of the abundance of food being offered. The effect was heady, sensual . . . almost insisting that one partake of the bounty being offered.

There were people everywhere, though due to the clever design of the place, it didn't look at all crowded. At the core was a gleaming mahogany bar that snaked around in a circle, with smooth, tanned leather stools lined up along the outside. Next to it was the map and huge board Brian had mentioned. It was hard to miss as the activities had been chalked in hot red, bright yellow, neon green. Cam shook his head, thinking of the dry erase board in his staid meeting room. He used black markers, and on rare occasions, blue. He made a mental note to invest in bright green and hot red. Maybe even tangerine orange.

A nervous laugh caught his attention and he swiveled his head from the list of activities to the bar, where a young woman sat between two fairly beefy guys.

It was apparent from the first glance that she was even more of a fish out of water than he was. Her artificial blond hair had been piled artlessly on top of her head, her eye makeup applied with a tad too heavy a hand, her lips too glossy. Pink flamingo earrings hung heavily from her tiny lobes, stretching them downward in a not-too-flattering way, but worse was the colored shell necklace she wore that dipped down into her pale white cleavage. Cleavage that had apparently only been achieved with the help of a super-human Wonder Bra along with the tropical blouse that was tied tightly just beneath them. Even with all the help, there was very little spilling out of the unbuttoned silky shirt. Not that this had deterred her companions.

"Come on," said one of the men, "just let me undo that knot." He fingered the thick knot of silky fabric just below her breasts.

She laughed nervously and took a too-big sip of the obscenely large tropical drink that sat on the bar in front of her. Leaning forward caused what little nature had given her to be pushed almost beyond the bounds of the cóntraption she'd strapped them into. Both of her companions made no attempt to hide their overt appreciation of the display.

The one man continued to finger the knot, his hand splayed across the smooth white skin of her stomach. "Come on, honey. Just undo this one little knot, then we'll take you over to other side. You'll love it. Promise."

The other man leaned in and whispered something in her ear that turned her pale-as-pearl skin bright pink.

She tried to laugh as she swatted at him, but Cam saw her swallow nervously . . . and take another lunging sip from her curly red straw.

"What can I get you?"

Pulled from his observations, Cam turned to find a young deeply tanned woman on the other side of the bar. She had a red flower tucked behind one ear, a cascade of thick, dark hair, a welcoming white smile, and just enough bright yellow and green material tied around her voluptuous body to cover what needed covering . . . and make him want to rip it off her. Now *this* was more what he'd had in mind.

He moved closer to the bar. "What do you recommend?" *And are there more women like you who happen to be guests?* Even the way she moved aside and gestured to yet another smaller chalkboard listing the club specials was sinuous and inviting. Her hips were wide, her waist impossibly tiny. Her breasts, barely covered, sat up perfectly without any wires or unnatural support. They'd fill his hands and then some. And those hips, the way she moved them . . .

"See anything you like?"

Cam had to bite back a grin, mentally shaking his head. He was thinking like a randy teenager. But then, as a teenager he hadn't had time to think randy thoughts. He'd been too busy taking care of his mother, whose "spells" had become rather frequent at that point. And when he wasn't doing that, he was studying so he could graduate the top of his class, just as Cameron James numbers one through three before him had done. And then had come Harvard Business School, then working for his father, and finally marrying the perfectly bred corporate merger wife. Of course, that had been followed by dealing with his father's federal embezzlement trial, his mother's latest relapse, discovering his wife in bed with both her tennis instructor *and* Missy, her doubles partner, all the while holding the century-old family company together as the IRS tried to tear it apart.

No, he'd never had time to be randy. But where in the hell had being the good guy gotten him?

"I don't suppose the club employees do much mingling with the guests," he ventured.

She smiled and leaned against the bar, her manner relaxed and very inviting. His body stirred with an instant R.S.V.P.

"There are rules," she said, then shifted a little closer as she softened her voice. "But at Intimacies, rules are made to be broken."

"Are they now?" Cam responded, shifting his weight and leaning on the bar. Could it really be as simple as this? "You might be able to help me out then, as that's exactly what I came here looking to do."

He was interrupted by a little shriek, followed by masculine laughter. Unwillingly, he shifted his gaze back to the pale blond woman. One of the men had successfully undone the knot and she was clasping both hands to her breasts, easily covering them with her small palms.

"Now, now," she scolded with a laugh, trying for all the world to sound as if she could handle the situation she found herself in when it was obvious to anyone paying attention she'd long since gotten in over her head.

Cam knew he should just turn away. After all, she was a grown woman who wouldn't be here unless she wanted this kind of attention. She was on her own. He'd left his white knight membership card at home. He turned back to the bartender, whose sexy green eyes were all but devouring him. She fingered his collar. "Nice."

He could have told just how nice, but he was more interested in getting out of his clothes than discussing where he'd had them tailored. "Thank you. Interesting outfit you have on there. Very . . . provocative."

White teeth flashed, her full lips curving in a knowing smile. She was quite probably a half a dozen years younger than his thirty-two, but probably just as capable of making him not care.

"I'm glad you're . . . provoked," she said. "Have you decided on your drink order yet?"

He shook his head slowly. "Too busy trying to decide if I

could actually undo that knot on your hip"—he held her gaze and went for broke—"with my teeth."

Dark pupils shot wide and she licked her lower lip. Heaven have mercy but he wanted to taste that lower lip.

Another squeal punctured the intimate cocoon he was weaving around them.

The bartender looked over at the woman at the same time he did. She sighed, but quickly smiled at him. "Let me take care of this."

Cam noticed that one man was nibbling the blonde's earlobe, while the other was busy trying to explore what lay beneath those hands, almost white-knuckled now in their attempt to keep their protective shield up over her breasts. Then someone else came up to the bar asking for a drink and Cam swore under his breath. "I'll handle it," he told her, thinking that he'd do whatever it took to break up the unfortunate threesome while his wanton fantasy island barmaid fixed a few drinks. Then he could return and set up a rendezvous with her when her shift was over. Maybe they'd have their own private mango body-rub race.

As with most things in his life of late, however, events didn't exactly go as planned.

Chapter Two

Allison Walker clutched her breasts as if they were life rafts. Of course, it came as no surprise, given their size, that she was sinking fast.

"Really, Todd, you're too cute," she said, wriggling away from him and the tongue he was presently sticking in her ear. Unfortunately, this only served to move her more deeply into Oscar's personal space. Octopus would have been a better name for the guy. She smiled up at him. "You have such big hands," she said, trying not to grit her teeth, "I can barely breathe." She scooted backward, but the stool refused to scoot with her. And to move the stool meant removing one or both of her hands, which wasn't going to happen. She'd had visions of exactly this sort of scenario happening since she'd gotten the Intimacies brochure. Two men, vying for her affections. Two men, willing to do whatever she commanded of them.

Of course, in her fantasies, she'd been turned on by all this. As it turned out, reality wasn't all that arousing.

She shrieked in surprise when Todd the Tongue suddenly nipped her earlobe. "I can do that to your nipples," he breathed into her damp and not throbbing ear.

Not in this lifetime, she wanted to say, but part of her commitment to herself this week included handling just this sort of situation . . . and not running away. Again, she'd sort of hoped she wouldn't have wanted to run away. Screaming. Any screaming she'd imagined had had to do with multiple orgasms. Multiple partners optional.

She wriggled free once again and tried to laugh in a way that told these two men that she was totally in charge of this situation. Somehow, looking at the gleam in both of their somewhat bloodshot eyes, she didn't think she was pulling it off.

She'd only been at the bar fifteen minutes and already she had men wanting her body. This should be cause for celebration. The only thing men had ever desired before was her knowledge of computer technology.

It was the blond hair, she thought, and the makeup. And the clothes. None of which cried "Allison Walker, nerd." Judging by the men she'd attracted however, she was forced to admit that instead of saying "wanton, powerful woman looking for strong, confidant man" her new look apparently screamed "bimbo in search of immature losers."

The night had barely begun, though. Best to cut her losses. Fast. She smiled at Tongue, then at Octopus as she carefully shimmied off her stool. "Well, guys, the hot-tub relay is about to begin, and I promised Bruno I'd be his partner. Maybe we can catch up later on." *Like in my next life.* "Thanks for the drink." Of which she'd had far too much. Her head swam a bit as she stood unsteadily on her too-high slingy heels. The sarong wrap mini skirt had wedged up almost to her fanny by the time she got off the stool, but she hardly cared at this point.

"Bruno?" Todd asked skeptically.

It was the best she could come up with on a screaming-orgasm-fogged brain. "You've probably seen him," she said, trying to back between the stools, still covering her breasts with her hands. "About six-five, three hundred and twenty pounds? Shaved head, tattoos?"

Todd said, "Never seen him," but Oscar laughed and

said, "That's okay, sweetheart, Todd and me can take him. Come on with us." He got up and took her by the elbow, almost dislodging her death grip on her left boob.

"No, really. I promised," she said, trying to exude confidence despite her growing concern.

Todd leered then. "And you always keep your promises, right? Like your promise to come back to us later tonight?" He took her other elbow. "Why don't we just escort you up to the hot tubs and tell Brutus you're otherwise engaged. We have Bungalow Three reserved a bit later."

"It's Bruno and— What's Bungalow Three?" She probably shouldn't have asked, but the question was out before she could think better of it.

"Leather Lounge," Oscar said, almost salivating.

Leather? In all this humidity? How uncomfortable, she thought, not to mention slippery. "Well, I'm sorry, but I really have to—"

Both Todd and Oscar tightened their grip on her arms. "Come on, babe, it will be fun. You'll like being tied up. Trust us."

Tied up? "No, really," she said, knowing she sounded nervous now.

"It's what you need, to build your self-confidence," Todd assured her.

"I have plenty of self-confidence," she stated, tugging back as they tried to tug her toward one of the shadowy paths exiting the bar area.

Oscar and Todd laughed, which both hurt her feelings and made her mad. She did have plenty of confidence. When it came to computer circuitry and running a soon-to-be Fortune 500 technology business, anyway. When it came to being a sexual creature, desired by the opposite sex . . . well, okay, so her self-confidence level was somewhat lower. Okay, okay, nonexistent.

But she was doing something about that by coming here. And if she had misfired a bit in her approach, so what? The bait had worked, even if the catch was going to be thrown back. Her look still needed a bit of modification; she could accept that. What she could not and would not accept was these two behemoths pawing at her one second longer.

"One hour in the Leather Lounge and you'll be spitting fire," Todd assured her.

"And whipping up a frenzy," Oscar agreed with an eager laugh.

She yanked her arm free, angry enough now that she barely realized she'd also freed her right breast. "The only thing that's going to be whipped is your—"

"I beg your pardon, gentlemen, but I believe the young lady has made it clear she has other obligations."

Allie spun around, intent on telling whoever was trying to help her out that she could deal with these morons herself, but somehow the words got all tangled up in her throat. He was an Adonis. All smooth skin, golden eyes, and hard, all-business jaw. His white shirt clung to his broad shoulders, his trousers hung carelessly around his narrow hips. His feet and calves were bare and somehow a tremendous turn-on. The way he stood there, solid and in control, yet relaxed and apparently unconcerned, spoke to her. Something about mixing business with pleasure, she thought as her gaze drifted back over his flat stomach to his tightly held jaw.

Hmm, not so relaxed after all. In fact, now that the sensual fog was clearing from her brain, she realized he was irritated. And if she wasn't mistaken, that irritation extended beyond the gruesome twosome behind her . . . to her. Well, what had she done except get hit on by two slobbering idiots? It wasn't like she wasn't trying to extricate herself from the situation.

"I can take care of this," she informed him a bit coldly, "but thank you for your concern."

"Yeah, butt out," Oscar added. "We were just having a bit of fun here."

"I'm not sure the young lady shares your definition of fun," he said smoothly.

Too smoothly. Something about his tone irked. "I'm not sure you know the meaning of fun," she muttered, deciding the world was filled with jerks, even ones that looked like gods, and she was a magnet for all of them.

He turned that molten look at her. It was the only thing hot about him, though. "Excuse me then, I'll leave you to dealing with this yourself."

It was clear he'd never wanted to interfere in the first place—so why had he?—but when Todd stepped up and breathed on her neck, making it clear he wasn't the least bit ready to relinquish her, she suddenly decided Molten Man was the lesser of two—make that three, she amended when Oscar closed in—evils and stepped after him.

"Perhaps you could show me where the hot tubs are," she said brightly, moving so that he now stood between her and the two men.

"Brutus failed to give you directions?"

So he'd been listening in on her conversation as well. She didn't know what to make of this guy. Was he into voyeurism or something? Of course, if that had been the case, he'd have only had to follow them to Bungalow Three to get a real eyeful. She shuddered and decided it was better to eat some crow with him than eat . . . God knows what in Bungalow Three. "Listen, if you get me out of here, I'll buy you a drink later, or whatever," she said under her breath. "I really appreciate it and I'm sorry I wasn't more receptive to your help earlier. It's just that, I came here with the idea that if I can run a boardroom, I should be able to—"

"I'll take you to the hot tubs, okay?" he cut in, obviously impatient and just as obviously not remotely interested in her personally.

"Fine," she said, stung. "And it's Bruno," she muttered as he hustled her toward the door. Allie glanced over her shoulder and sighed in relief as she spied Oscar and Todd already slithering over to another unsuspecting pair of women who'd just come into the bar. "I hope they like leather."

"Where are the hot tubs anyway," Molten Man asked, not paying any attention to her.

"I can take it from here," she said, stepping away from him, thinking it figured that just standing near the guy made her nipples hard. Why was it the ones she was attracted to never even saw her? "Thanks again. Sorry to inconvenience you."

He looked back and also saw that Todd and Oscar were now deeply involved, then gave her a quick nod. "No problem. But you might want to rethink what you're advertising if you aren't really ready to go to market."

She'd already figured that out, but hearing it from him brought back all the feelings of inadequacy that had driven her here in the first place. "I'll take that under advisement," she told him evenly.

Her sharp, businesslike tone earned her a momentary surprised look, then he nodded and turned back down the path to the bar.

"And if you ever figure out how to have fun, the hot tubs are right up there," she said, knowing she shouldn't have given in to the jab, but his indifference just pushed one too many of her buttons.

He looked back, then followed her gesture to the ceiling of the main lodge.

It gave her some level of satisfaction to see the momentary shock cross his face. So, he wasn't so indifferent as all that after all.

She walked away and left him staring at the glass-bottom hot tubs that formed the roof of the hut. She remembered her own shock when she'd realized that the ceiling wasn't some kind of moving mosaic. From her one glance, it appeared that the banned side had taken over the tubs tonight, she thought, stifling a giggle.

She wanted to turn and see if he was still staring at the

scene above . . . and if it was having any other effect on him other than shock, but it was at that moment she realized that the entire time she'd stood there with him, delivering her lines with such frosty aplomb, she'd completely forgotten she'd been bared from the waist up.

She flushed hotly and quickly hooked the front clasp of her super bra and tied up her blouse, then hurried on her way. The body puzzle game was starting soon, which gave her about twenty minutes to work up her nerve to join the Slot Team.

She wasted a minute wondering if Mr. Good Deed would ever consider joining the Tab Team, then quickly shut down that path of speculation. She was no more interested in his type than she was in Tongue or Octopus. Okay, so she was interested in his body type. But it was exactly his kind of attitude she'd suffered from all too often. The "she's smart and brainy in the boardroom, so she must be boring or frozen in the bedroom" attitude. And she knew it didn't help matters any that she had few curves . . . and even fewer notions about how to use what little she did have to her best advantage. She'd been too busy earning multiple degrees to get much practice in college, and now there simply weren't many willing partners available to experiment with.

She'd hoped that here, thousands of miles away from that boardroom, she could find out what it was she needed to do to spark things up a bit in her bedroom. She was as committed to being open to new ideas, to trying new things, stretching her personal boundaries, expanding her comfort zone, as she was to making her company one of the most successful firms in Silicon Valley.

So what had she gone and done? Turned down her first offer to try something really new.

"Leather Lounge, huh?" she murmured to herself, thinking maybe, just maybe, she should at least go and give it a look. But not with Octopus and Tongue.

Images of Molten Man tying her up with thin leather

straps stopped her dead on the path. She'd never even fantasized about being tied up. So why did the mere idea of him leaning over her, securing her wrists— Dear God she was wet just thinking about it.

She looked behind her, back toward the main lodge and the bar. Should she go back there? Do whatever it took to make herself more visible to him?

She looked down at her hastily knotted shirt and gave a rueful snort. "Oh, you've already been about as visible as you can get with him." Short of stripping off her sarong-style miniskirt anyway. And somehow she doubted that would have him swooning at her feet either.

Maybe she'd get lucky during the Body Puzzle, she told herself, sending one last lingering glance down the path. Besides, she wanted a guy who knew how to have a good time. And even more importantly, how to show her how to have a good time. Somehow, she thought Mr. Good Deed might have as many hangups as she did. Not a good match.

"Tell that to my wet panties," she muttered as she hurried to Lagoon West. Hurrying anywhere in the stupid mules she'd decided to wear tonight proved a fruitless endeavor. She'd picked them hoping they'd show a flare of calf, but she suspected all they showed was her lack of co-ordination in anything higher than a sensible one-inch heel. Finally she kicked them off altogether. Then she undid the knot, readjusted her pump-me-up bra, and buttoned her shirt properly before tucking it into the sarong skirt. There wasn't much she could do about the skirt. Or the hair, or the makeup. She did unfasten the dumb earrings and necklace she'd bought on impulse at the airport and hooked them around the strap of her heels.

Maybe she should just observe the Body Puzzle tonight. Observe the women who played it, how they dressed, what they did to attract the opposition.

"No," she decided instantly. She hadn't come here to be an observer. She'd had twenty-nine years, three hundred and six days of observing. Before she turned thirty she was going to discover her inner slut. Or at least her inner multi-orgasmic self. Okay, even a singular, mind-altering orgasm would be worth the three-day all-inclusive club fee.

She took a deep breath. *Okay. Slot Team, here I come. Come hopefully being the key word in that phrase,* she added, yanking down her skirt again and adjusting her wonder cups. Then she laughed. She might have a ways to go on the orgasmic thing, but if she was lucky, by the time this night was over, she'd have at least discovered her inner Slot.

Chapter Three

Cam's wanton island maiden had already become deeply involved breaking rules with two other guys by the time he'd returned to the bar, so he'd opted to set off down a path and enjoy whatever scene he stumbled across.

Which didn't explain why his thoughts continued to stray back to the silly blonde. Only, in their brief time together, he'd already figured out she wasn't remotely the airhead he'd assumed her to be. He wondered why she'd chosen that getup, what she'd been after. It certainly hadn't been being pawed by two men. So what was she doing here?

"And why do I care?" he murmured. She wasn't what he'd come here to find; in fact she was the antithesis of his dreamed-of wanton island woman. Slender, pale, with no discernible curves and clearly at a loss as to what to do with the ones she did have. Perky nipples, he'd give her that, but he was looking to have his senses overwhelmed here, and for that he needed a woman who called to his animal instincts. A woman who could only be described as lush, bountiful, sensual. The blonde—or whatever her natural shade was—wasn't any of those things.

He was still trying to imagine her up in hot-tub heaven. His lips quirked as he imagined her talking herself into being the only one in her own tub. All things considered, she'd probably be safer that way.

He rounded the bend in the path only to find himself at a crossroad. There was laughter mixed with gasps of pleasure coming from his right. He stepped in that direction, only to freeze when he heard the shriek of nervous laughter coming from the opposite direction.

He knew that nervous laugh.

He groaned and shook his head. *You're not going to do this.* More gasping and moaning just down the path in front of him. Another squeal behind him. *She got herself into whatever she's into now, she can get herself out. Go for the pleasure moans,* he told himself, but somehow his feet were already carrying him in the other direction.

He'd just take a peek, he told himself. So he wouldn't be distracted by wondering just what she'd gotten herself into this time. Probably it was nothing; probably it wasn't even her.

It was her.

Cam stood stock-still on the path, trying to assimilate the scene before him. It had taken him a moment or two with the glass-bottomed hot tubs to believe what he was seeing. But this— He supposed he should have read the chalkboard before leaving the bar, if for no other reason than to prepare himself for the kinds of games they played here.

He could only assume this was the Smear Fruit All Over Your Half-Naked Partner game. Except the blonde was the only one left half naked. There were some thongs and bikini briefs on some of the other participants, but for the most part it was a sea of naked flesh covered in what looked like mango pulp. And his blonde was smack in the middle of it.

After a moment or two of study, he began to get the gist of the "game." It was a relay of sorts, where you had to pass an overripened mango from one teammate to another, without using your hands, or teeth. He supposed the first team to complete the relay won something, but none of the six or so teams seemed too concerned with that at the moment. Whenever a mango was dropped to the plastic—and by now quite slippery—mat, another was given to the beginning team member and they started again. Several of the team members had come up with rather . . . ingenious ways of passing their fruit, he noticed.

She was in the middle of the third line, about four deep in her team. Literally smack dab in the middle of all the chaos. It went without saying that the lineup was man-woman, man-woman. Somehow, she'd ended up man-woman-man-man. Three men were trying very hard to, well, pass her fruit. Mango juice sieved all over her pale flesh. Her shirt was glued to her skin and her various contortions had shoved her skirt up to her hips, revealing a startling pair of hot pink panties with a big red pair of lips curving across her surprisingly shapely little fanny. He found himself fighting a smile. He also found his body stirring. Which was ridiculous. Not that the scene wasn't erotic. Some of the women out there would have been right at home in a centerfold layout.

So why wasn't he watching them?

She slipped then, and two of the men "accidentally" slipped with her. The mango was on her stomach and the men weren't giving up on the relay. One man tried to tuck the mango under his chin, which had the fortunate side effect of pushing his face right into her breasts. He took his sweet time trying to capture the soft piece of fruit. Her other teammate was urging him to push the fruit between her breasts, breasts he was helpfully holding and pushing together to form a trap of sorts. The third teammate jumped in—literally—at this point and straddled her legs, which were thrashing around as she squealed hysterically under the ministrations of the other two. Her hands were trapped beneath the men and she bucked and gasped as they continued to have their merry way with her.

Cam found himself getting more than a little aroused, which made no sense. She was apparently having a great deal of fun, which was fine for her, but forcibly holding a woman down and having his way with her had never been high on his list of fantasies. In fact, it wasn't on the list at all. But there was something almost . . . primal about watching her squirm beneath their joint attentions. Not that he wanted to join in. If he were ever of the mind to try something like that, he was fairly certain he'd want to be the only man in the scenario trying it.

And yet, he couldn't take his eyes off her. There were other couples in far more sexually explicit contortions, several of whom had long since forgotten about the mango and, for that matter, the race altogether. They were far too busy licking juices off one another . . . among other things.

But his gaze kept going back to her. Maybe it was the shrieks. The men were laughing with her and no one appeared to be doing anything they weren't all enjoying. He should go back down the other path now and investigate the source of those pleasure gasps and moans he'd heard. But just then her head reared up, and despite the squeals of what sounded like delight, what he saw in her eyes was full-blown panic.

His desire to be a bad boy and go back to his wanton-woman hunt warred mightily with the instincts telling him she needed help. "Well, it doesn't have to be my help," he muttered to himself. There were plenty of club employees—pleasure directors he'd discovered they were called, P.D.'s for short—observing the action. All she had to do was call out and one of them could rescue her.

Her head thrashed wildly from side to side, her wide eyes searching for something—someone? A P.D. maybe? She opened her mouth, perhaps to call out, but it was immediately claimed by the man now on top of her, who'd finally rolled the mango up beneath their joint chins. Her face was blocked from him then, but the way she bucked and kicked told him she was not as willing a participant in this as he'd thought. He doubted her partner—partners, actually—had any clue. If he hadn't seen her eyes, he wouldn't have known either. And he knew they weren't interested in what her eyes held as much as what the remnants of her super bra did.

He should call one of the directors. It was the sensible thing to do, then he could go on with his night. So why, a moment later, he was the one wading into the fray, was beyond him. Two P.D.'s were on him immediately, genially pulling him back, all smiles as they told him he'd have to go join in at the end of the line. He tried to tell them he didn't want to play, that he was trying to help someone.

"Sir, we're sorry, but if your girlfriend chose to play, that's her prerogative. You know the rules. You'll have to discuss it with her when it's over, but you can't disrupt the—"

He yanked his arms free. "She's not my girlfriend. I don't even know her! I just noticed she was in trouble—never mind." He was only a foot or so away at that point, so he lunged and was on top of the man on top of her a second later. He tried not to think about the mango juices now ruining his linen shirt. He managed to slide the man off her, using one bare foot to dislodge the man holding her legs and a good forearm to the chest to get the third one off of her.

"Hey, dude, what the hell—"

"You can't just—"

"What the—?"

But he didn't care about the spluttering men, or the P.D.'s. Suddenly he realized that now he was the one directly on top of her. She was still thrashing, still thinking she was the main course in the mango buffet line.

"Hey, it's okay. Stop. Stop!"

She paused just long enough to focus on his face. "You!"

Mango squished along his stomach. He grimaced. "Yeah, it's me."

She stopped thrashing and the P.D.'s finally gave up and redirected her other partners back to the game. Cam barely paid them any attention.

"We really have to stop meeting like this," he said.

"I don't believe I asked you to meet me anywhere, much less"—she squirmed a bit—"like this."

His body responded sharply to the feel of her beneath him. Must be all that slippery skin. Anyone would react. "I just saved you from being made into a human smoothie and you act like—"

"Like a woman who didn't ask to be saved?"

"Anyone could see you needed saving."

"But only you thought it appropriate to barge into the middle of the game and ruin it."

"Ruin it?" A quick glance proved that her teammates had indeed found another mango and a far more willing participant and weren't wasting any time passing their fruit. "Hardly," he said, looking back down at her. "In fact, I don't think anyone's even noticed."

For just a brief second, something flickered in her eyes. Such a pale, pale blue, he noticed. And what he'd seen in them had been . . . hopelessness. Resignation.

She squirmed again. "You're heavy," she said pointedly. "Would you mind letting me up?"

His body jerked again as she rubbed against him, but he wanted nothing more than to dislodge himself from this melee and go back to being the captain of his own destiny. Which he was determined would have nothing more to do with hers. But instead he found himself staying right where he was, in the midst of fruit-flinging insanity, saying, "You had three men on you moments ago and you weren't complaining."

"It's—not the same."

"Why? Because I'm actually focused on you and all they

were focused on was copping a feel? And maybe a lick or two?"

Her eyes widened for a moment, then narrowed. "I could have handled them." Her jaw set. "With both hands tied behind my back."

Visions of her tied up, with rivulets of thick mango juice running all over her creamy white skin, of him licking up each trickle, making her thrash and buck and shriek, only this time with no doubt as to whether she was enjoying it or not, exploded into his mind, completely uninvited.

Something of those thoughts must have registered on his face, because her pupils shot wide and she went completely still. And then he was leaning down, to do what, he had absolutely no idea. At the last possible second, she turned her head to the side and very quietly said, "Please. I want to get up. Now."

It was that very quietness that had him moving off her. He was on his feet, helping her up, before he could assimilate the knowledge that in that split second before she'd turned her head, what he'd seen in her eyes hadn't been panic. Or hopelessness. Definitely not resignation.

What he'd seen was desire. A bright, microsecond burst of want, before she'd shut it off, turned it aside. Turned him aside. Why? And, again, why did he care?

They both slipped and almost lost their balance as they gripped each other's forearms for support—slimy as it was—and made their way through the melange of sticky bodies.

As soon as she got off the mat and regained her footing, she let go of him. She pushed back her hair, which now hung in loose, mango-covered ropes around her head and squared her partially bared shoulders in an attempt, he supposed, to retrieve some semblance of her dignity.

"I suppose I should thank you, even if I didn't really need the help."

He fought a grin, another nonsensical reaction. He'd

come here looking for passion, lust, wild monkey sex. And instead, he'd spent his first couple of hours playing Good Samaritan. And it wasn't even appreciated. His grin surfaced then and he shook his head.

"What's so funny?" Then her lips quirked and she gave in and laughed.

It was the first real laugh he'd heard from her and the difference was remarkable. For all her pale-skinned, non-curvy, basically unnoticeable-type self, her laugh was full-bodied, rich, and infectious.

She motioned to how they both looked and said, "I take the question back." She looked at him again, a bit of sparkle in the depths of those eyes now. "And I'm sorry for being such a snot back there. It's just . . . I came here hoping to learn more about myself and I'm discovering that's hard enough without . . ." She glanced away, then after taking a breath, looked back at him and finished. "Without someone reminding me every other minute just how incapable I am in the first place. I mean, I'm incredibly capable of a lot of things. But this"—she waved blindly behind her—"doesn't appear to be one of them."

He started to respond, though he had no idea what he'd have said, but she waved him silent.

"Listen, you're a nice guy and obviously were just trying to help me out of the jams I seem to have a special skill for landing myself in here. It's refreshing, especially after tonight, to know there are still nice guys left out there. But I know doing good deeds can't be why you came here. I'm sure you're here to have a good time and I'm just as sure you didn't plan to have that good time with someone like me. So—and don't take this the wrong way—please stop saving me, even if it's only from myself. I need to do this my own way, even if it lands me in over my head. Deal?"

Cam simply stared at her. A nice guy. Apparently he wasn't having any more success achieving his goals here than she was. "Why do you say that?" When she looked confused, he clarified, "That I didn't come here looking for someone like you."

She smiled again, this time more ruefully. "Let's just call it a well-educated guess. You didn't look exactly thrilled at having to rescue me the first time. Now I've managed to ruin your good clothes, to boot. Somehow I'm thinking it's not because you hoped I'd try to get them off you later."

He grinned, shaking his head. She really was something. "I don't know what I thought," he replied, realizing now just how truthful a statement that was. "But you're right about one thing. I didn't come here to be Mr. Nice Guy. In fact, I've spent a lifetime being Mr. Nice Guy and you know what? It's not all it's cracked up to be."

She tilted her head, studying him, then smiled. "Well, then, I'm sorry I brought out the worst in you."

He laughed at that and she joined him. She really did have a hell of a laugh. Then their laughter faded and they were left standing, in the midst of chaos, staring at one another.

She cleared her throat first. "Well, I suppose I should go clean up. I'm sorry about your clothes, if you want me to have them cleaned I—"

"It's okay. It was my choice to jump in."

She lifted a hand, then let it drop. "I hope you enjoy the rest of your night." She turned to go.

He should have let her walk away, should have turned and gone back down the path toward the pleasure moans he'd heard earlier. But he didn't. His life was full of "should haves." Why should this be any different?

Chapter Four

"Wait."

Allie turned back, her heart picking up speed despite her repeated silent warnings not to. Whatever had happened between them back there, or almost happened, it didn't change the fact that she was right. He was here looking for a level of action she wasn't up to providing. He'd even admitted he was here to find his inner bad boy. Probably he'd want someone who had some clue about what to do with it when he found it.

And yet, she was stopping, turning.

"The bungalows," he said, suddenly looking a bit uncertain himself.

She wondered if he was giving in to his Good Samaritan side again and really, truly wished that, just for once, she wasn't the type who inspired that instinct in a man. She wanted to inspire other kinds of instincts, the kinds that had to do with predator and prey. Dear God, just once she wanted to be the prey. Thinking about the men she'd met so far, she amended that to a predator who would know what to do with his prey once he'd captured it.

"Bungalows?" she managed, her throat suddenly tight.

"I meant the guest bungalows. They're that way." He

pointed in the opposite direction from where she was heading.

"Oh. That." She tried to stifle her disappointment, failing miserably. "This way leads to the beach. They have these waterfall shower things down there and . . . anyway, I know where I'm going. But thanks."

"Waterfall shower things?"

She nodded, uncertain where he was heading with this. The longer he stood there, the more she wanted him. And she wanted him badly. Making it all the harder to reconcile herself to the fact that she couldn't have him. If he would just go away, she could go stand under a waterfall, rinse off . . . and fantasize for a few really nice minutes, before returning to the fray.

"What exactly are they?"

She went still, watching him come closer. Why wasn't he leaving? What game was he playing? *Maybe he's just curious, Allie, ever think of that?* Considering the night she'd had, it wasn't surprising she'd become wary.

He was looking at her expectantly, so she went ahead and answered him. "You know how most beaches have showerheads to rinse off the sand when you leave the beach?" He nodded. "Well, they have the same thing here, only instead of showerheads, they have these little alcoves made of natural rock with a waterfall cascading over them. You just sort of tuck yourself inside, step under the water and rinse off . . . or whatever." She faltered a bit at that last part. Because after discovering one this afternoon after her windsurfing lesson, she'd done a lot of thinking about that "or whatever" part.

"Sounds . . . creative."

Oh, if you only knew.

"As it happens, I got in late and haven't checked into my bungalow yet," he was saying. "I really don't want to hike back to the main lodge and go through all that right now. Would you mind if I joined you and rinsed off here?"

Would you mind if I climaxed, oh, one or a dozen times while we do it? "No," she said finally, the word coming out somewhat hoarsely. It was the best she could manage given the circumstances.

He just smiled, apparently oblivious to her inner turmoil, and lifted a hand, gesturing her to lead the way.

Great, just great. Now she would have to stand under the rush of water with Mr. Adonis here, and still be forced to fantasize to get a little action. How pathetic was that? She should have worked up the nerve to play Body Puzzle. How much worse could it have been hoping she got the right tab for her slot? Of course, she'd thought the mango race would be a bit tamer, which proved right there she shouldn't trust her instincts.

Lesson number one, she ruminated silently as he followed close behind her. *Nothing is tame at Intimacies.*

"Except this shower," she muttered.

"I'm sorry, what did you say?"

She jumped slightly, not realizing until he spoke just how close he was. "Um, exceptional shower." She glanced at him and forced her lips to curve upward, aiming for that happy-go-lucky smile that said, "Oh no, you're not turning me into a mass of quivering need just by breathing on my skin. Nonsense! Guys like you breathe on me all the time. I'm totally unaffected."

Totally unaffected my ass, she thought, turning her back to him and trying like hell not to give in to the urge to disappear into the darkness before he realized just how totally affected she was.

She heard the soothing sounds of rushing water and knew it was too late. They were here. She brightened with relief as it occurred to her that her problem was actually easily solved. There were, after all, more than one of these alcoves. She could slip into one and he could find his own. And maybe, if she was really lucky, she could stifle her

224 / Donna Kauffman

moans as she made herself climax at least once. Just to take the edge off, of course. She certainly deserved at least that.

But her relief was short-lived as it became clear that they weren't the only ones seeking out the waterfalls tonight. And from the sounds she could hear over the rushing water, she realized most of the people here were enjoying that "or whatever" part she'd fantasized about.

"Maybe they'll all be taken," she murmured under her breath. "Maybe I'll be lucky just this once. Maybe—"

"Here's one," he said, oh-so-helpfully.

She made a face into the dark, then pasted on a smile before facing him. "Great."

She hadn't actually used the alcove this morning, so it came as a surprise that, once they moved inside the intimate circle of stone, the sound of the water cascading over the rocks above their heads created the illusion of total seclusion. Where they could do anything. Privately.

After several long moments, she realized she was still standing there, staring at the water. She imagined him moving under the water, watching it pound down on those shoulders, then that angular jaw as he tipped his head back and . . . She tightened her thighs against the little quiver that scenario produced, then darted a glance at him, wondering why he wasn't getting wet. After all, watching him was the one guaranteed thrill she would get this evening. Only he wasn't interested in the water. He was staring at her.

"Everything okay?"

She snapped out of her little reverie and took a small breath. "Sure, of course. Why wouldn't it be?" Not giving him a chance to reply, wanting only to just get this over with, she stepped beneath the full force of the water . . . and gasped as it cascaded over her. Not because it was cold, it was actually about the same temperature as the air. Balmy, in fact. She gasped because it felt good. Wonderfully, amazingly, good.

And then he was in the water beside her. And she simply had to look. One peek. Well, one peek turned into a lingering glance, which evolved into a full-fledged ogle.

Damn, he was as wonderful as she'd imagined. Better even. He tilted his head back, worked his fingers through all that thick, gorgeous hair and let the water pound down on his chest. His shirt clung to every ripple in his back as he turned beneath the spray, the muscles in his arms bunching quite perfectly as he raked his hair back and enjoyed the flow of water over his skin.

Her nipples pebbled and it had nothing to do with the feel of the water spraying her own skin. In fact, she'd all but forgotten about her own shower.

And then he opened his eyes and looked directly into hers. "Feels incredible," he said, his voice somehow deeper, more intimate sounding. It made her shiver. "Cold?"

She'd never been so hot in her whole entire life.

"Here, turn around," he said, "I'll help you get the stuff out of your hair."

She had no idea what he was saying, only that his lips were moving, because his hands—big, wide, and warm— were on her shoulders now and nothing else mattered except that he was touching her.

He shifted her so her back was to him, then his hands moved up into her hair. He tilted her head back under the heavy stream of water and slowly began to work the pulp from the strands. The pressure of his fingertips felt incredibly good on her scalp. Her skin came alive under his confident ministrations. A moan slipped out before she was aware of it. His fingers stilled for just a second and she held her breath, hoping like hell she hadn't just ended what was, so far, the highlight of her vacation.

Then his fingers started massaging again and she sighed deeply in relief and let herself lean back, just a tiny bit, into his hands. Hands that were moving, down her neck, back to her shoulders. He was turning her again and she worked hard to come out of her sensual fog and stifle her extreme disappointment that shower time was over. "Thank you," she managed.

He left his hands on her shoulders, looking into her eyes the whole time. It was all she could do to merely hold his gaze in return, and not grab his hands and drag them to her breasts and the nipples that were all but screaming for attention. His attention. His very explicit attention.

Just as she went to step back, to end this before she did something humiliating, his hold tightened. Just a flexing of fingers, and just for a moment, but a telling one. As if he, too, were warring with some inner decision.

"I—I should probably—" she began to stammer.

"Rinse your shirt out," he finished, fingering the sodden silk plastered over her collarbone.

Her heart hammered as they continued to stand there, gazes locked on one another, his fingertips playing over the wet fabric of her shirt. Was he offering what she thought he was offering? And if so . . . "Yes," she blurted before common sense could reassert itself. "Yes, I should."

Then he grinned. And she quivered.

The grin faltered just a bit, a brow raised in question as his fingers stilled. She covered his hands before he could take them away. He'd offered, dammit, and he was going to follow through. "I'm okay. It's just—" What the hell, she thought. "There was nothing 'nice guy' about that grin."

And then it was back, full-blown and far more dangerous than she could have imagined. "That's the best thing anyone has said to me all day." He stepped closer. "All year, in fact," he added, his fingers sliding down along the edge of her shirt to the bare skin between her breasts. "And God knows, it's been a hell of a year," he murmured, leaning his head closer to where his hands were lingering.

She had no idea what he was saying. She was using all her concentration to keep her knees locked and herself upright. When he began to peel the silk off her damp skin, her grip slid from his hands up to his wrists, then to his fore-arms, which flexed ever so perfectly beneath her touch.

He nudged her backward, just slightly, so the water hit only the bare skin of her breasts, beating lightly against her nipples, which were obvious now even through the soaked padding of her bra. She wanted to feel him touch her there, wanted to feel the water pummel her overly sensitized skin as he rolled her nipples between his fingers.

But when he started to undo the front clasp of her bra, she had a moment—a very brief one—of hesitation. It was an instinctive reaction, borne from too many less-than-enthusiastic reactions when she'd revealed her less-than-bountiful self to a prospective lover.

Lover. Dear Lord have mercy.

But she couldn't think about that now. Focus on his hands, she schooled herself. It was all she could handle any-way. But his hands didn't move, so she opened her eyes, only then realizing she'd closed them.

"Are you okay with this?"

She could only nod. Water clung to his thick lashes, framing eyes that looked like sparkling bits of gold in the moonlight. He smiled and shifted his forearms just a bit and she flushed, realizing she had a death grip on him.

"It's not like we haven't already revealed this part of you tonight," he said, only a hint of amusement in his tone.

She flashed a rueful smile and gave what she hoped was a carefree laugh. Which was difficult as this had somehow become far from carefree. For her anyway. "It was the sur-prise that you'd want to see them again that gave me pause."

He didn't even blink. His grin grew wider as the look in his eyes turned almost . . . predatory. She shivered in response. Feminism be damned, she thought, there were times when being the prey was good. Very, very good.

"Can I tell you something?" he murmured.

Anything! "What?"

"It's your nipples."

"My wha—?" But the word ended on a gasp as he brushed the tips of his thumbs over them.

He dipped his head a bit, then he looked up at her through those impossibly sexy lashes and said, "Ever since I first saw them, I haven't stopped thinking about how they'd fit into my mouth."

She had no idea what her reaction should have been, but probably not the laugh that burst out of her. It was part in amazement and part in nervous shock. This man—this Adonis—wanted her nipples? "Well," she managed finally, "I think you should definitely find out."

He dipped down and blew across the very tips of them, then said, "I was hoping you'd say that," just before extending his tongue and lightly flicking the water droplets that clung to their engorged tips.

Chapter Five

How in the hell had this happened? At the moment, however, he couldn't seem to string his thoughts together enough to care, much less find the answer. Damn, but her nipples were perfect. Dusky rose and fully budded, they just beckoned to be rubbed, licked, and sucked.

He'd gone rock-hard at the thought of getting to put his mouth on them. Once he'd heard that throaty little moan of hers and remembered how she'd looked, standing half naked back on that path, nipples puckered beyond belief, he'd discovered a burning, almost desperate need within himself to learn how those plump buds would feel between his lips.

He pushed at the clinging fabric of her shirt and the sodden cups of her bra, until her breasts were bared completely to him. Small, softly rounded, they wouldn't even fill his palms. But tipped so sweetly with those perfect nipples, it didn't matter. He stroked his thumb over one, making her gasp and shudder, then placed his tongue directly beneath the other and lapped at the water cascading over the reddened tip. Again and again, he let the tip of his tongue gently stroke the bottom edge, causing that perfect nub to tighten further as he continued to play with her other one.

He was dying to pull it into his mouth, but something

kept him teasing her. He switched allegiances and stroked her other nipple with his tongue, a long, swirling swipe all around it, as he rolled the other one between thumb and forefinger. She moaned and her knees dipped. He nudged her backward, so her back pressed against the stones behind the waterfall for support. The water cascaded down his back now, her nipples wet with sparkling droplets of water, but no longer under the steady stream. Now they were all his.

Her hands drifted shakily over his shoulders, then she slid her fingers into his hair. "Please," she rasped.

"Please what?" he demanded, knowing when she shuddered hard that it was the right direction to push her. And he discovered he wanted to push her. This seemingly competent woman when it came to everything else, had no idea what to do with this. So this is exactly where he wanted to take her. Push her. Into an area she had no confidence with. So she'd be forced to follow his lead, to trust in wherever he took her.

It was a wild train of thought, one that aroused him unbearably, and yet made no sense to him. He'd come here looking for someone to drive him, push him, take him into those new arenas. But when he finally succumbed and moved his mouth over that perfect nipple, pulling it deeply into his mouth and suckling it so that she bucked against the wall and clutched at his hair, he realized that he wanted to be the one driving, the one pushing, the one taking. This was where he would find that inner wild man he'd so hoped to discover.

No tidy, man-on-top, one-orgasm-apiece interlude; this wasn't going to be like a corporate merger, all laid out ahead of time where everyone knew what to expect. No, this was going to be whatever he wanted it to be, whatever he could make it be . . . whatever he could make her do.

He used his tongue on her, growing harder, if that were possible, as she moaned and began to thrash her head from side to side. Then he moved over her slick skin, dragging his tongue from one nipple to the other. He toyed with it, flicked at it, until she grabbed his head and tried to shove his mouth on her. "Do it," she commanded. "For God's sake, do it."

He grinned against her wet skin and felt his hips buck a little as his body began to demand its own release. "Do what?" he asked, flicking at the tip once again with his tongue. He gripped her hips suddenly and pulled her forward so that the water once again rushed over her breasts. She gasped and her hips bucked and he thought he could swallow her whole right there. Her back arched to him and her head tipped back as she thrust her breasts at him, reduced now to following her body's demands, willing to beg him.

And that very idea almost set him off. The idea that he could make her beg. He, Cameron James IV, who'd never in his entire life done something so . . . impolite as to make a woman beg him for anything.

"Do what?" he growled again, grappling now with his own self-control, his mind reeling almost drunkenly with this new arsenal of possibilities.

"Touch me." She was shivering, shuddering, grabbing at his head, trying to make him do what she wanted.

He resisted, just enough to make her struggle. "How," he said roughly. "How do you want me to touch you?"

"You know," she almost whined, her fingers twisting in his hair now. "Like . . . like you were." She panted, then gasped again when he flicked his tongue across first one tip then the other. "Yes, please, yes."

"Tell me—" It was then he realized he didn't even know her name. "Your name, what is it?"

She tipped her head forward then, her gaze a bit disconnected, as if she were trying to focus outwardly but couldn't quite manage it. It only provoked him further.

He brushed his thumbs lightly over the tips, making her jerk and gasp. "Your name. Tell me."

"Alison," she managed, breathless. "Allie."

He looked up into her eyes, his mouth poised right next to where she was so desperate to have it. "Then tell me, Allie, tell me what you want me to do to you."

She tried to move and press her nipple between his lips, but he gripped her hips and kept her right where he wanted her. "Tell me."

"Your mouth . . . on me," she said, then gasped, as once again he shifted her so that the water brushed over her.

"How," he kept on, the torture almost as unbearable for him as it was on her. Exquisitely so.

"Your . . . tongue." She panted. "Please."

"More, tell me more."

She whimpered a little, then bucked hard when he lightly flicked the ends yet again.

"Say it," he commanded.

"I—please." Her thighs were trembling visibly, her body fairly quivering with need. A need he had driven her to, and with only his tongue and fingers. She wasn't even fully naked. It made him wonder what else he could do to her, with her.

He had a momentary, almost violent need to rip off that silly sarong, and simply ram himself right into her. She'd be dripping wet by now and he knew he could take her screaming over the edge, and himself with her. It was such a shocking vision he stilled for a second. And that was all it took for the tide to turn. She yanked his head back and looked blindly down at him. "Suck them," she demanded hoarsely. "Dammit, do it!"

He grinned then, feeling wildly primal and seeing the same mirrored in her flashing, ever-so-pale eyes. This was even better, and he hadn't thought it could be better. Dueling for control.

"Now," she said.

"Yes, ma'am," he murmured, then pulled her nipple deeply into his mouth, making her moan long and hard the entire time he suckled it. He moved to the other, keeping his hands on her the entire time, until she could barely force her legs to hold her up. He had just started to slide his tongue down the center of her belly, when she suddenly pulled away.

"I can't—you have to—I've never—Jesus," she finally panted.

He straightened, but didn't move away from her. His body had gone well past demanding release to actual pain. He willed it to subside, just a little. He wasn't done pushing her . . . or himself. Because he knew right then he wasn't going to end this hastily. Oh no . . . the night wasn't even half over. So what if she wasn't the wanton maiden of his fantasies? He had another full day and night to find her, discover other games, other needs . . . other satisfactions. This night belonged to them.

And he already had a long list of things he wanted to do with her . . . make her do for him.

He crowded her back against the wall with his body. "I told you your nipples fascinated me."

"They're beginning to fascinate me too," she managed, followed by a slight, almost giddy laugh. "I never . . ." But she couldn't seem to finish and let her head loll back against the rocks. Another little laugh escaped her and his body twitched—hard—at the rich, inviting sound. "I almost—" She broke off, shaking her head as a taint of red stained her cheeks. "I didn't think I could," she said, almost more to herself. "Just from . . . you know."

His grin returned even as his body continued to prod him. What was it about her that was just so damn stimulating? In a crowd, or even sitting alone, he'd have never noticed her, never looked twice. Yet, here he was, all but dying to get a real taste of her. "Why did you stop me?"

Her lips quirked then. "Because I'm hopeless?"

Is that how she saw herself? And yet, wasn't that the impression he'd gotten the first time he'd seen her? That she was somewhat clueless about her own sexuality? Or at least with what to do about it? Well, tell that to his still rock-hard cock.

"Not hopeless," he said, because he knew now it was true. She simply needed . . . guidance. A steady hand. And tongue.

When she opened her mouth, presumably to argue, he shifted his weight against her, so she could clearly feel the hard length of him against her. "Actually," he said, his own voice suddenly tight, "I was thinking more along the lines of hope*ful*."

She blinked, then looked at him again. "Hopeful?"

He pushed against her. "Very hopeful. Almost demand-ingly so."

Her hands came up against his chest, in what felt like an instinctive move more than a conscious one. Her body was primed, beyond primed, and he felt this renewed spurt of power that he could probably push her exactly where he wanted her to go. But would he do that? Could he simply take what he wanted?

He twitched with the need to follow through on his thoughts, right here and now, but her eyes widened just slightly at the movement and he silently cursed as the nice guy put the wild man in a half nelson . . . and held him there. He wanted to push her, but he wanted her to be ready to be pushed. He shifted back, just slightly, just so he wasn't pressed right up against her.

Her fingers pressed into his chest, surprising him, stilling his retreat. "So . . ." she began, trailing off as he looked into her eyes.

"So?"

"Do I get a turn?"

His cock all but leaped in response. "I, uh . . . yeah."

She smiled, and it was the hint of uncertainty in it that undid him the rest of the way.

"Do with me as you will," he said, smiling at her.

She moved away from the rock and pushed him so that

he took her place, his back to the wall of stones. She pushed at his shirt until she'd shoved the soaking wet fabric off his shoulders, leaving it bound around his biceps, trapping his arms to his sides. He had no idea what she was about, but he was primed and ready to find out.

So he was going to be taken, driven, after all. He almost smiled as he looked at whom he'd chosen to be in the driver's seat. And yet, he couldn't remember ever being poised on such a high-perched brink as he was right at that moment. It must be the location, he thought, some kind of island fever, the shackles of societal conventions gone so that anything felt good. With anyone.

Then she dipped her head, almost tentatively, and flicked her tongue across his nipple. A short, fierce exhalation followed and it wasn't until she forced that sound from him again by flicking the other one that he realized he'd even been the one to make it.

She rubbed her fingertip over whichever nipple she wasn't sucking on and suddenly it was his knees that weren't so steady. "Sweet . . . Jesus," he said, ending somewhat forcefully as she sucked him a bit harder, flicked the tip of the other one a bit harder. How had he missed out on this bit of knowledge before?

Then she lifted her head, but kept her gaze averted from his, as if intent on what she was doing and afraid he might stop her. She stepped closer, cupped her own breasts, and—dear, merciful God, that felt so goddamn good—she rubbed those plump nipples of hers across his chest, lifting up on tiptoe so that she could brush his . . . with hers. He groaned loudly then and when she went to move away, he gripped her and forced her to renew contact.

His hips bucked outward of their own free will, seeking, searching, damn near demanding. He slid his hands down her back and cupped her sweet backside, almost blindly seeking some kind of release. He buried his face in her neck and had to forcibly keep from begging her to let him take her right then. In fact, he had no idea why he didn't. He was pretty damn sure she wanted the same thing.

But there was something about this . . . whatever the hell it was they were doing to each other . . . that begged to be prolonged, spun out to its furthest length, stopping only before one of them snapped.

He decided then he wanted to push this as far as he could. The rest of this night if possible, see how far he could drive them before they gave in to it.

He tipped her head back and looked into her eyes and knew right then that, at the end of this, she was going to give in to it.

But not yet. Not yet.

"I think we're clean." He slid out from the wall, willing his cock to subside . . . just enough so that he could walk. He didn't think he'd fully subside until he was buried inside her. He took her hand when she simply stood there, suddenly looking uncertain. "Come on. We're going exploring."

"We are?" She held her ground.

And that's when he realized just what it was about her that so intrigued him. She was this odd amalgam of strength and vulnerability. And he was never sure which part was going to surface at any given time.

"Oh yes," he told her, wondering just what depths this exploration would take them to . . . and dying to find out. "We are."

Chapter Six

Allie thought they'd been doing some pretty damn fine exploring right here. "Wait," she said, pulling her hand free. When he turned back, she almost knelt to the ground right there. Did he have any idea what he looked like? He didn't seem to have any arrogance about the fact that he was built like a god, that those eyes of his made her feel completely wanton with nothing more than a glance. "I—" What was she going to say? *I want to know why in the hell you want to have anything to do with me?*

She wasn't that pathetic, was she? And did it really matter why? She'd come here to learn how to go for it, hadn't she? *So go for it already.*

"I don't know your name," she said finally. "If we're going to . . . explore together, then I want to know—"

"Whose name to scream when you come?"

She gasped. So he had a little arrogance about him after all. But in this case, she was fairly positive he could back it up. Okay, she was dead certain. She tossed his grin right back. "It's only fair. After all, you already know whose name you're going to be screaming."

Big words, Allison Walker. But, dear God, was she looking forward to backing them up. Or trying to, anyway.

When he didn't laugh in her face, she figured she was going to find out if she could.

"Cameron," he said, then flashed that wicked grin she was coming to know and lust after. "But you can scream Cam if you want."

"Big words," she said, heart pounding.

He reached out and tugged her flush up against him. "I don't have a problem with big. Do you?"

She swallowed against a suddenly tight throat. Tight lots of things, in fact. "No. Not at all." She could feel the hard length of him pressing so perfectly against her. If she just went up on her tippy-toes and moved the tiniest bit— His eyes flared and she flushed even hotter. "Is it time to scream yet?" she asked with a little laugh.

He moved back and she had to fight the whimper that rose in her throat. He took her hand instead and she decided that any contact with him was apparently incredibly carnal. His hand was so big, his palm so wide it swallowed hers. Could a person come just from palm-to-palm contact? His thumb stroked the length of hers and the muscles between her legs actually clenched. That's a big yes, she decided shakily.

"Shall we?" That light was back in his eyes. Eyes full of promises. Promises of pure pleasure.

Oh, we most certainly shall, she responded silently. "Lead on."

He squeezed her hand and led her back to the main path, then paused at the first crossway. Three choices. One, she knew, led back to the mango race, or probably more aptly by now, the mango orgy. She sighed in relief when he turned to study their other options. She'd had enough mango pulp to last her a lifetime.

The one on the right, she knew, led down along the beach. Hmmm. Sex on the beach. She smiled privately. Not just a drink at the bar anymore.

"What's so amusing?"

She glanced up at him, unaware he'd been watching her so closely. It was a heady thrill, his attentiveness. It sort of intimidated her . . . but in a good way. He seemed so determined to see this through, all she had to do was not screw it up by freezing up.

Right now being cold in any way seemed beyond the realm of possibility. She was aching hot. And wet. In ways that had nothing to do with waterfalls and mango juice.

"I was thinking that the mango race has likely progressed beyond the, uh, finish line at this point."

He smiled, nodding. "My thoughts as well." He stroked her palm with one thick fingertip. "And I'm not ready to cross the finish line anytime soon."

She clenched again. "Me either," she said, a bit hoarsely.

"So . . . which way?" He pulled her close, slid her in front of him, then pulled her back against him, so that they faced their choices together. He wrapped their joined hands across her waist, pressing her to him so that he prodded her right between her buttocks. She had to fight to keep from grinding back on him and wondered briefly what he'd do if she did. She was maybe a second away from finding out when he lifted his free hand and toyed, almost idly, with one of her nipples.

She gasped, then moaned a bit as he continued playing with her, finally letting her head loll back on his shoulder. She realized, distantly anyway, that she should have been shocked to realize they'd left the seclusion of the waterfall alcove with her totally bared from the waist up. Not that anyone else would notice, as she was still overdressed by the standards of most of the guests. But not by her own standards. And yet the idea of covering herself up right at the moment was completely abhorrent to her.

Especially since she knew he had a thing for her nipples. Who knew having sexy nipples could be so empowering? Her lips quirked, just before she moaned again as he shifted his attentions to her other breast. What would it be like when she finally convinced him to play with some other part of her?

"Which way?" he murmured, his lips brushing her temple.

All the way? "The way you're doing it is just fine," she breathed.

He laughed and she felt the rumble of it against her back, the tickle of his breath along her temple . . . the promise of it right down between her legs.

"You're so damn responsive," he said, then dragged their joined hands upward. "Do you ever pleasure yourself this way?" He brushed her own palm over her breast.

She couldn't even answer; her throat had closed over. Sure, she knew how to give herself pleasure. It was that or go insane, given her love life. Or lack thereof. But it had never occurred to her to—She sucked in a breath as he pulled her palm up and licked it, then rubbed it over the peaking tip of her breast.

"Cam—" It was part plea, part protest. She wouldn't last much longer like this before she was reduced to begging him to finish her off right there on the path.

He pulled their hands away and turned her around to face him, keeping just an inch or two of completely excruciating distance between them. Her backside actually mourned the loss of the sweet pressure of him nudging her. She wanted to swing right back around and plant herself on him, wriggling until he damn well did something about it.

So, she thought, only mildly shocked at the idea, it appeared she was well on the way to finding that inner slut after all. She smiled.

"This way," he said decisively, pulling her toward the path she hadn't contemplated at all. She had no idea where this one led, having taken the main one when she left the beach that afternoon.

He had her so aroused now that even the balmy night air caressing her bare, damp breasts made her twitchy. Just twenty-four hours ago she'd been in a high-stakes merger meeting, reciting flow-chart statistics to a bunch of very serious businessmen wearing stiff three-piece suits, wearing a stiff gray suit of her own, with matching sensible pumps, topped off by her favorite horn-rimmed glasses. She swallowed a smile, wondering what those men would think if she were to recite some stats dressed as she was now?

Would they think she had sexy nipples, too?

She imagined slapping her pointer on the long, sleek board table to draw their attention back to her charts. Maybe she'd keep the horn rims on. But the sensible pumps would definitely be traded in for something sharp and spiky. Her boardroom dominatrix fantasy was abruptly interrupted by the sounds of moaning. And for once, it wasn't her.

Cam paused as well, just before a bend in the path.

Cameron. Figured he had a sexy name. Nothing so Plain Jane as her own. She glanced down at his left hand, wondering at his marital status. Not that it mattered here. Intimacies had a thorough screening process they put their prospective guests through, including a detailed medical history that required a complete physical with all the appropriate testing done, before they'd approve the registration. However, marital status wasn't something they were concerned with. The club was about fulfilling fantasies, or at least providing their guests with every opportunity to fulfill their own. What and who you were before you came . . . and after you left . . . didn't matter.

So long as you played by the rules while you were here.

She'd observed more than one couple checking in together and had wondered at the pressures of being a couple in a place like this. Then she'd laughed at her naïve-minded self as she realized that some of those couples might have come here specifically looking for . . . increased opportunities. Either solo . . . or together.

The moaning erupted in a shriek. A shriek of ecstasy, pulling Allie's thoughts once again back to the present. She immediately tugged on Cam's hand. "Maybe we should—"

He grinned down at her. "Take a peek?"

Her eyes widened, which made him laugh. "What?"

"Why so shocked?" He leaned in. "Doesn't suit my Mr. Nice Guy image? All the more reason to do it."

She gulped, but couldn't deny that the gleam in his eye further aroused her. "I just thought we should give them some privacy."

"Sweetheart, if they're out here, they're not concerned with privacy."

Allie wasn't so sure she agreed with this logic. What had happened at the waterfall hadn't been planned, not on her part anyway. But as soon as he'd started toying with her nipples, she hadn't thought once about the fact that someone—anyone—could have been watching them. Some little part of her sparked hard on that scenario, which she immediately ignored. She was on sensory overload enough at the moment, thank you.

Cam tugged her hand. "We'll just walk by, then. You don't have to look if you don't want to. The path is here for all guests to use, right?"

Allie didn't respond. Eyes on the path, she told herself. Though it wasn't like she hadn't seen some pretty lascivious scenes this evening already, but this was somehow different. This wasn't a club event they were about to stumble over. This was—she drew in her breath as they rounded the bend and she came to a dead halt. "Dear Lord have mercy," she whispered.

"I don't think she's looking for mercy," Cam murmured back.

On a spongy-soft grassy area right off the path, a woman lay on her back, completely naked. There were four small stakes in the ground, each with a padded velcro strap attached. Both her wrists and ankles had been secured in the straps and she was being . . . attended to and quite thoroughly so, not by one man, but by three.

So that's what you'd do with three of them, Allie found

herself thinking, unable to tear her gaze away from the erotic tableau. Not that it mattered as the foursome was completely caught up in what they were doing.

One man was kneeling behind her head, rubbing the tip of his hard cock along her lips, but not allowing her to take him fully in her mouth, despite her attempts to do so. Another man was alternately sucking and toying with her nipples, making Allie want to rub at her own suddenly aching breasts. But it was the third man who had her clenching her inner thighs together. His head was between her legs and from the way she bucked and writhed, he was driving her madly insane with his tongue.

The woman was alternately begging and commanding him to finish her off, but he'd only lift his head when she did, until she whimpered and quieted, whereupon he'd make her shriek with pleasure by spearing her with his tongue once more.

Allie twitched and rubbed her thighs together, knowing she should be aghast at herself for standing there, staring, but she was helpless to look away.

"Would you enjoy something like that?" Cam murmured in her ear.

"In my dreams maybe," she answered honestly. "But I'm not sure about reality."

Cam chuckled. "Maybe if we started with just one man . . . and worked our way up?"

Allie shook her head slowly, gaze locked on the foursome. "I'm not interested in anyone else," she said, then realizing how that sounded, she did look up at him. "I mean, I'm not ready. Not tonight. I hope you don't mind."

Cam held her gaze steadily. "I'd prefer to have you all to myself as well." He shifted his gaze back to the scene in front of them, his finger drawing lazy circles on her palm. "There are probably more velcro straps around . . . Would you like to find a set?"

Allie imagined herself splayed like that, fully open and

vulnerable to whatever Cam wanted to do with her, and clenched almost convulsively. "I—couldn't."

"Oh, yes you could," he said, that deep voice of his vibrating against her skin.

She shook her head. "Too . . . public for me."

"I could make you forget all about the public. Or maybe even make you very aware of them . . . and like it."

She shuddered . . . in pleasure. But shook her head again. "Not tonight."

Cam said nothing and Allie wondered if she'd just jeopardized her night with him. But he didn't leave, didn't pull away. Instead he leaned down and said, "I wonder if she'll have all three of them before this is over."

Allie couldn't say anything. The very idea of having more than one man enter her during the same lovemaking session . . . was just too far-out to contemplate.

But apparently it wasn't too far-out for the woman strapped to the ground. Her hips were pistoning now and finally, finally, the man between her legs dragged his tongue from her, up along her belly as he climbed over her and positioned himself between her legs.

"All of you." The woman panted. "I want all of you."

"You'll have all of me," he growled.

Her head thrashed to either side. "All . . . three . . . of . . . you." She was moaning, panting. "Same time."

"Same time?" Allie whispered. "Ouch."

Cam chuckled, but she noticed he was having a hard time standing still.

Allie gasped as she realized just what the woman meant. As the first man kneeled between her legs and pushed into her, the man behind her head pushed himself into her mouth, while the third man had straddled her chests and held her breasts together so that he could stroke himself between them. All four of them were grunting and moaning now and Allie knew she had to look away, knew she shouldn't be watching this. It wasn't right.

Instead she found herself shifting in front of Cam, then pushing herself back on him. He jumped as though he'd been scalded, finally doing the impossible and tearing her attention away from the foursome to him. "I'm sorry," she said immediately, "I was only, I just—"

Cam's eyes looked a bit unfocused and he was breathing a bit unevenly. "No, it's okay. I just didn't expect you to—I was—" He broke off with a half laugh. "I was right on the edge. And the feel of your sweet backside on me was going to push me right over it." He moved closer to her until he filled her immediate space, making her forget all about the people behind him, which, given the screaming crescendo they were all racing toward, was a pretty impressive feat.

"When I come tonight, I'm not going to be standing half clothed on some path," he said hoarsely.

She held his golden gaze. "You're not?"

He shook his head, looking straight into her. "Oh no. I'm going to be buried deep inside you." He lifted his hand and stroked his fingers over her lower lip, making her tremble. "I do agree with you on one thing."

"Which is?"

He pressed the tip of one finger between her lips, then pressed a bit further, until she took it into her mouth. "I want to be the only one entering you tonight."

She shuddered, her gaze locked on his as she nodded. The feel of his long, hard finger pushing into her mouth, moving in and out, only served to drench her further. The muscles between her legs were so tightly clenched now they hurt.

"And I plan to enter you every way you'll let me."

He slid his wet finger from her mouth as she gasped, "Yes."

Chapter Seven

Cam throbbed and twitched at the feel of her soft tongue on his finger. Damn, but he'd never been this hard, this needy. This determined.

It was all he could do not to take her up against the nearest tree. She had him tied in so many knots, he didn't think he'd survive even that long. He could tell himself it was the setting, the . . . entertainment they'd witnessed, but right now all he saw was her. Those soft blue eyes searching his, burning with a desire only he was going to fill. It was heady, exciting . . . and not a little empowering.

His gaze dropped to her lips and he was stunned by the sudden realization that he hadn't yet tasted them. How was that possible? Given the intimacies she'd allowed, the things she'd made him feel, how was it he'd never kissed her?

He began to lower his head, then stopped. Something about taking her mouth with his own almost seemed more intimate than taking her body with his own. It made no sense, but he wanted to savor that moment, taunt himself and her with the exquisite sensations they were both going to experience when their lips, and tongues, finally met. And somehow, he knew it would be beyond anything so simple, so unremarkable as any kiss he'd ever shared with anyone else.

He pulled on her hand, suddenly unwilling to lose another precious second, much less share the time they did have with anyone else. They had all weekend, he reminded himself, or did if he played his cards right. And even though they'd done hardly anything yet, he already had a feeling that two days . . . and two nights, were not going to be enough. He made a mental note to find out more about her.

He glanced down at her and found himself smiling. Her face looked as determined as his. Find out everything about her, he amended. Every last thing. His wanton island woman.

They came across a small marker that read BUNGALOW 9. "Privacy," he said, looking at her. "What do you think?"

"Um, I'm not sure all the club bungalows are set up to be private."

"Shall we find out?"

She opened her mouth as if to say something, then stopped and nodded.

He wanted to drag her inside right then and there, but something in her expression . . . "You sure?"

She nodded again, then said, "If it's not . . . if it's set up in a way that—" She shook her head and laughed a little. "I'll stay but not if it's some kind of torture chamber or anything. I know they have some pretty wild bungalows set up."

He knew he shouldn't, but he immediately envisioned her all strapped in black latex, with impossibly spiky heels on . . . and maybe a whip. It shouldn't have turned him on; he was not one for those games. Or he'd never thought he was. "Why don't we take a look, then decide? Who knows, it might already be taken anyway."

But there were no sounds coming from the small, round building. The club bungalows were different from the guest bungalows in that they were of varying sizes, all of them smaller than the ones the guests stayed in, pretty much appearing to be one main room, with maybe enough room for a bathroom or dressing room of some kind. Each one decorated and set up with some sort of theme in mind.

Cam pushed at the door. "Hello?" he called out, but the inner room or rooms were dark and silent. He stepped inside and pulled Allie in with him. "Unoccupied," he whispered.

She moved in close behind him and he twitched at the feel of her warm breasts brushing his arm and back. "Is there some kind of light switch?"

Cam turned to face her, intending to reach behind her to feel along the wall, but paused as he looked down at her. There was just enough of a glow from the small path lights to cast her face in pale relief, leaving the rest of her shrouded in velvety darkness. He ran his hands down her arms, enjoying the resulting shiver. "Maybe we should keep the lights off. Feel our way around." He drew his fingertips back up along her arms, careful to brush the sides of her breasts and nipples as he did.

She gasped, then shook her head. "I want to—to see you."

His eyes widened, surprised by the request . . . but it was a request he approved of. He wanted to watch her come apart for him as well. But he wasn't quite ready to relinquish the darkness that enveloped them. He moved forward, his big body nudging her smaller one back toward the wall behind her. She brought her hands up to his chest, but to brace herself, not to push him away. Her fingers brushed over his nipples and he, too, shivered in awareness. Hyperawareness. He wondered if he'd ever be able to recapture this exact level of awareness once he left this place. He planned to find out. He wondered if she'd be there to find out with him.

When she came up against the wall, he kept moving in until his body was right up against hers. He pressed himself against her belly, struggling not to continue to thrust his hips. He didn't think he'd ever been hard for such a long period of time. He should be in physical pain by now, but instead the forced control only jacked up the arousal until he thought he might simply explode. He had a few other things he wanted to do before that happened.

He leaned his head down and pressed his lips to her temple. "Do you realize we haven't kissed yet?"

She stilled for a moment, then said, "I—no, I guess we haven't." She lifted her head, putting her mouth ever so close to his. "We could change that."

He brushed his mouth along her chin, then her cheek, even lightly dragging them across her lips, but moving away as she opened them for him. "We could. But we won't. Not yet."

He could hear her breath coming in shorter pants now. "Okay," she said, her voice a tight whisper.

He surged again, realizing the gift she'd just given him. She was going to let him guide, lead. Dictate. At least for now, he thought with a smile, remembering how swiftly she could turn the tables on him. Best to begin then, he thought. He drew his hands down along her arms until they circled her wrists. Slowly he pulled them up until they were all the way over her head.

He saw her eyes widen, but she allowed him the liberty. He pulsed with the power of her acquiescence. He switched his grip so he held both wrists together with one hand. The other he drew lightly down over her face. He moved his body so it brushed over her bared breasts as he once again pressed his fingertip to her lips.

She moaned and twitched a little.

"Hold yourself still," he commanded softly.

She gasped and looked sharply at him, then nodded tightly and held herself perfectly still.

"Take my finger into your mouth." He pressed it slowly between her lips.

She allowed him to enter her lips, her gaze steady on his. There was a duality of power here, he realized instantly. She didn't have to let him do this, they both knew he'd stop if she said the word. The fact that she allowed him these liberties also put her in a position of power with him. She had to know what this was doing to him . . . and he suspected she was enjoying wielding her power every bit as much as he was. Damn, but he wished this night would go on forever. That he could last forever.

You can have her again tomorrow, he reminded himself. And tomorrow night. And all the following day. Right up until it was time for them both to leave.

Leave. His body clenched at the very thought of her disappearing from his life, and not in pleasure. He hadn't even kissed her and he couldn't imagine having her beyond his immediate reach, beyond his control.

Control.

He leapt in response once again to the very idea. This, right here, right now, he controlled. And would continue to until they chose to end it.

"Taste me," he said roughly, stroking his finger along her tongue, pushing it deeper into her mouth until she had to tighten her mouth around it to keep from choking. "That's right," he schooled, brushing her body with his again, almost moaning himself when she gasped and pulled him more deeply into her mouth in doing so. "Suck on me, Allie," he commanded gently. "I want to feel how soft and strong your mouth is."

She continued to hold his gaze with great deliberation, and began suckling his finger. He pulled it halfway out, then let her pull it back in with the force of her tongue. He repeated this again, and again, until he thought the torture of one more stroke would kill him. Then she flicked her tongue over the tip and along the edge and he abruptly pulled it all the way out, panting now himself.

She grinned, but said nothing. She knew exactly what she'd done to him. Or almost done.

He found himself smiling, too. "There are other things I

plan to push into you," he said, enjoying her almost convulsive shudder. "Hot things, hard things, wet things."

Her body trembled, but she continued to hold his gaze and struggled to keep herself still in his grasp.

"Shall we find out what lays in the darkness behind me?" Before she could respond, he leaned in next to her ear and whispered, "Whatever it is, will you trust me to find some way to make you scream with pleasure before we leave?"

She nodded.

"I didn't hear you." He leaned away just enough so that he could look into her eyes. "Tell me, Allie."

"Yes," she whispered.

He could feel the pulse in her wrists tripping wildly as she held his gaze steadily. "Yes, what?"

"Yes," she said, "I will let you make me scream."

His cock twitched hard at her softly spoken words and the slightest curve of her lips told him she'd felt it, that she knew the power she wielded in this scenario was, at the very least, equal to his.

And he wouldn't have it any other way.

He reached behind her with his free hand and felt along the wall. When he found the switch, his hand hesitated. "Ready?"

"Ready."

Chapter Eight

Allie wanted to close her eyes as Cam flipped the light switch, remaining in the darkness where anything seemed possible. But she was also dying to see what lay in store . . . for them both.

Instead of harsh lights, a dim, rich glow filled the small bungalow as gas lamps leapt to life. There was a sconce just beside them next to the door, and one somewhere behind Cam as well. There was just enough light so that when she turned her head toward the door, she could make out the small, delicately hand-painted sign on the door.

"Victorian Villa," she read.

Cam saw it the same time she did, then looked back at her with a fake pout. "No whips and chains."

"Don't be so sure, the Victorians could be an . . . interesting lot."

Cam pulled her wrists down, still holding them in the span of his one large hand. He massaged her palms and fingers as the blood flowed back into them, then tugged her away from the wall. "Let's find out what we have here."

He turned them both around at the same time, and she wasn't sure who gasped first. The small round room was a study in Victorian lace. The bed dominated it, sitting right in the middle. It was a small, but commanding four-poster that sat so high off the floor there were stools on either side for help in climbing up on it. It was covered in a downy coverlet with mounds of lacy pillows, all pristine white, as was the draping that hung from the posts, like misty clouds.

"Definitely not leather and whips," Allie murmured, wondering what Cam thought of this ultra-feminine décor. The sole nightstand had a lace cover and held only the gas lamp and nothing else. The sconces on the wall barely emitted enough light to show what else might lie about for them to employ in their enjoyment, but it looked as if the elaborate bed was to be its own toy. The visual of Cam, all big and tawny gold, reclining in the midst of that sea of white linen and lace, was a bigger turn-on than she'd expected.

"Think you can still fulfill your promise to me here?"

When he shifted his gaze to her, she realized he wasn't the least put off by the décor. His eyes all but blazed into hers, his grin downright carnal. "Oh, I think I can elicit a scream . . . or three."

She shivered, then almost laughed herself. In glee. She wanted to pinch herself to make sure this was real. Considering how the evening had started, this was turning out to be way too good to be true. She spent another second or two wondering if she would be enough for him, enough to convince him not to end this when the night itself ended. He tugged her toward the bed and she decided right then and there to be whatever she had to be in order to keep him around. At least until the sea taxi arrived to take them all back to wherever they came from.

Her body and mind both instinctively rejected the idea of letting him simply walk away from her. But that was part of the allure of this place, right?

She refused to answer that on the grounds that it would make her crazy if she let herself go there. *Enjoy what you've got, Allie, while you've got it.* It sure as hell was more than she'd ever hoped for.

Cam paused beside the footstool. "Climb up onto the bed," he instructed.

Allie felt the buzz of his intently spoken words hum through her entire body. She liked hearing his deep voice issue those oh-so-velvety commands. Maybe it was because she already knew he was a Mr. Nice Guy at heart that she was able to trust him to guide her. And maybe it was because she hoped to be the one to make him be Mr. Bad Boy.

Whatever the case, she stepped onto the stool.

"Wait," he said, tugging her back. When she looked questioningly at him, he said, "You still have far too much covering your delectably pale skin."

She'd been self-conscious about her pasty white skin since she got here. She'd hoped to hit a tanning salon before coming, or at least use one of those tanning creams but with the merger going through had never found the time. She was probably the only woman in California with no visible tan.

Then he stroked a fingertip along her collarbone and said, "It's so creamy, so pure, I want to lap up every inch of it."

One look into his eyes proved he meant it. And suddenly she felt . . . well, if not beautiful, at least desirable. And that was more than enough.

"I want to see every inch of it," he said, then let go of her and moved back a foot or so away from her, leaving her all but swaying with one foot still perched on the small, padded stool. "Take off your clothes, Allie. Take off that skirt and peel those ridiculous panties down your sweet hips."

Allie had never undressed for a man before in her life. Sure, she'd had sex with the lights on, but undressing had either been a clumsy, groping affair . . . or done in the bathroom while her partner undressed in the bedroom.

He's already seen most of you, she reminded herself. And yet as she felt along her waist for the knot that held her sarong skirt up, she couldn't stop the fine trembling of her fingers . . . or of the muscles in her inner thighs.

"Undo the knot, Allie." He looked from her fingers, to her face, and continued the dual attention as she fought with the damp fabric. The water had made the knot so bound up there was no way it was coming loose. Her brief visual of undoing the knot and sexily flinging the sarong away fled. *Well, doesn't this figure?*

He took a step toward her, but she held up her hand. No, dammit, she wasn't going to let him help her get around this. This was why she was here, to learn how to handle exactly this type of situation with feminine finesse. There had to be a way to get this thing off without—

She smiled then, perhaps a bit wickedly as the solution came to her . . . and had double the pleasure of seeing his eyes widen a bit as she regained her confidence in herself. She turned just slightly, so he could see her hips . . . and that sweet backside he'd mentioned . . . and slowly began to nudge the sarong down over her hips.

She tried the best she could to dip her hips and roll them, hoping it looked suggestive. Her panties got caught up in the fabric and were being pulled off with the sarong, but she didn't pause. They were going to have to come off anyway, she told herself, turning so her back was more fully toward him. She continued to push and slide, moving her hips as she did. Praying he wasn't trying not to laugh.

Then the fabric was past the swell of her hips and dropped to the floor. She stepped gingerly out of them, hoping she didn't trip, but kept her back to him, wondering what he was thinking. Then she felt him walk up behind her and it took everything she had to keep still.

"You're perfect," he said, his voice tight and almost raw with tension.

She let out the breath she hadn't been aware she'd been holding, but resisted the urge to melt back against him. It was a heady thing, turning a man on like this. She liked it. A lot.

"Hardly perfect," she managed.

She felt the warm tip of one blunt-edged finger brush the nape of her neck. He trailed it all the way down her spine, undoing her self-control as easily as he might have undone a zipper. She shuddered and was forced to clamp her thighs together against the aching need that pooled there.

His finger continued past the base of her spine, down along the curve between her buttocks. The feel of his finger, so close . . . drenched her further.

"Step up onto the stool," he commanded hoarsely.

She no longer questioned this, or him. She wanted whatever he wanted to do to her, with her. She stepped onto the stool.

"Brace your palms on the bed."

She did, and in doing so had to push her cheeks ever so slightly toward him. He ran his fingertip again along the dip between her cheeks, causing her to convulsively flex the muscles between her legs.

"Move your feet apart. Just a little."

She could feel his breath on the skin of her lower back. She closed her eyes, intent on all the things he was making her feel. Somehow she'd thought facing him, stark naked, would make her feel the most vulnerable, especially when he was still dressed. However, exposing herself to him this way was far more intimate, far more vulnerable than she could have ever imagined. And it thrilled her no end.

She moved her feet apart.

Again, she felt his fingertips trace down along her buttocks, but with her feet slightly apart, she couldn't clench as tightly against the need. It left her open there, and aching, and so wet she didn't think she could stand it a moment longer.

She wanted to scream at him to move his fingers lower,

to touch her there, to give her some relief. But his touch was removed once again. She moaned and heard a similar noise come from him.

Maybe she should beg him, she thought, maybe that's what he wanted. She was certainly willing to; at this point all she cared about was getting him to put an end to this ache he'd built up inside her.

"I said I'd enter you tonight," he said roughly, before she could do anything.

She quivered. "Yes," she managed. *Dear God, yes.*

He traced several fingertips along her buttocks now and she had to fight every urge she had to keep still. Again his fingers left her just before touching her where she most wanted to be touched. She moaned again.

"Would you like that?"

"Yes," she said tightly, wanting to scream.

He shifted so he was beside her. "Look at me."

She turned her head and watched him put one of his own fingers into his mouth and wet it.

She moaned again, softly. "Please."

His eyes glittered. "Please what, Allie?" he said when he freed his finger, now all wet and shiny. "What would you like me to do with this finger?" He wet it again, then slid two fingers in his mouth.

She groaned now and twitched hard. "Dear God."

He turned so that he could continue to hold her gaze, and drew his wet fingers along her buttocks. "Tell me," he said, as his fingers went lower . . . and lower.

"I want—" She gasped and shuddered against the lightest brush of his fingertips against her wetness. "Please, do it. Now," she begged, beyond caring.

"Do what, Allie?" He leaned forward and ran his tongue along the shell of her ear. "And say my name when you tell me what you want."

His fingers were right there, poised to do exactly what she so desperately wanted them to do. She swallowed against the tight knot in her throat, wanting badly to just wiggle back onto his fingers and be done with it. But she couldn't deny the dark thrill this game gave her, and she knew then she would play along until she'd seen it all the way through. "I want . . ." His pupils shot wide when she stopped to lick her suddenly dry lips. And it was seeing his need, clearly matching her own, that gave her the will power to do what she so badly wanted to do. "I want you to push your fingers inside me." She turned her head just slightly so she could look directly into his eyes. "All the way inside me. Cam."

He groaned and in the next instant, she was filled with him. No gentle slide, no torturously slow entrance. His fingers filled her full and yes, she did scream. In complete, saturated pleasure. She collapsed onto her elbows as he slid them back out. *"No,"* she gasped, pushing her hips up, seeking, wanting.

"Again?"

"Please God, yes." She'd been so close, so close. She'd barely acclimated to the shock of his entrance to get beyond that to the climax that was just right there.

"You're so wet for me," he said, and she could hear him fighting his own needs to keep his voice steady.

The power that gave her had her lifting her hips again. "Fill me again, Cam," she ordered.

"Oh, you'll be filled."

She shuddered again, wanting to lower her breasts to the soft linen and rub them against the downy fabric.

But then he was moving behind her and she could no longer see what he was doing.

"Cam?"

Then his hands were on her hips and she sighed. Oh thank God, he was finally going to enter her. For real. She wanted him to fill her up, and from what she'd felt earlier when he'd pressed every hard inch of himself against her, she knew he'd fill her and then some. Sweet Jesus, it was going to be glorious.

"Lean farther over," he told her.

Yes, yes, anything you say, just fill me up. Now.

She felt something soft, downy, like hair, brush over her buttocks. She held her breath, tried not to squirm as she waited to feel the velvety warmth of him press between her legs. Instead she gasped when his wet tongue brushed over her instead. She swallowed hard and gritted her teeth against a long, keening moan when he flicked his tongue over her again. And again.

She moved against him when he continued to lap at her, trying in vain to push down enough so that he'd finally, blessedly take her clitoris between his lips and drive her screaming over the edge.

He was moaning now, too, and she could no longer keep her hips from bucking back against him. "Jesus God, yes," she panted as his tongue dipped ever closer. Then he was gripping her hips and lifting her forward onto the bed, rolling her onto her back before she knew what he was about.

Her legs dangled over the side of the bed as he knelt on the small footstool, his head positioned right between her spread thighs.

"Hold on," he told her, looking up at her over the flat, creamy expanse of her belly and breasts. "Grab the sheets and hold on."

She did, her head lolling back, then thrashing side to side and he blew a warm breath over her quivering, wet skin. She was all but whimpering at him to put his mouth back on her, trying to lift her hips, but he kept her firmly braced on the bed. "Please," she whispered hoarsely.

"I'll take you there," he promised.

"Now," she commanded.

"Patience," he said, sounding a bit rough himself.

"Cam," she warned.

He chuckled then, and she should have hated him for it, or herself for not caring that he was making her beg. But the fact was she'd never been so primed in her entire life and she was loving every single second of this torture.

Then he lapped at her, just one quick lick that made her shriek.

"Again," she ordered. "Slower, longer." She could have sworn she heard him smile.

"Not so shy now," he said.

"Don't . . . be . . . smug," she ground out, then gasped again when he brushed his tongue over her. "Dear God, you're killing me."

"Then we're both going to die very happy," he said, and buried his tongue inside her with one, bold thrust.

Her hips pitched violently off the bed as she climaxed instantly, violently. And he was right, he'd made her come screaming. But he didn't stop there. He continued to flick his tongue back and forth over her as she twitched and thrashed beneath him.

Then, just when she thought she might pass out from the torturous pleasure, he slowly began suckling her, and simultaneously slid one finger inside her.

Again she was ripped over the edge, again she screamed. Again she begged him for more.

Her entire body was so sensitized by now she couldn't lie still. Her legs trembled, her hands grasped convulsively at the coverlet as he continued with his tongue . . . and stroking her with his finger.

"Move on me," he said, lifting his weight from her.

She pushed on his finger, moving her hips, clenching as tightly as she could on him, but she was so wet. So amazingly, gloriously wet, it was hard to grasp him tightly. He solved that by sliding another finger inside her. She groaned and bucked even harder. Then he trailed his other hand up over her abdomen . . . and lightly pinched her nipple.

And she screamed again as another climax was torn from her, and she came once more against his mouth.

"Enough," she gasped. "I can't—can't—"

"Oh, yes you can," he growled. He gripped her hips and shoved her back across the bed, then crawled on top of her.

She'd never wanted so badly to be proven wrong. She was all but clutching at him with her hands and heels, pulling him down on top of her, wanting—wanting more badly than she'd ever wanted anything—to feel him push, no thrust— hard—inside her. Over. And over.

She had no idea when he'd undressed and felt a fleeting disappointment that she hadn't gotten to watch. Later, she thought, almost mindless with need now. *I'll make him strip for me next time. Make him.* Yes, she thought wildly, next time it would be her turn. And there would be a next time.

"Now, for God's sake, do it now!"

But he braced himself just over her, keeping just out of reach of her pistoning hips.

"Look at me, Allie."

She swerved her gaze blindly to his. "What?"

"I wanted to watch your eyes when I do—this." And he thrust fully into her with one long groaning slide.

Chapter Nine

Cam had intended to stop once he was buried inside her, to pace himself. To savor the tight, wet feel of her gripping every inch of him. But the self-control he'd exerted thus far had taken a toll and the sweet way she tightened around him ripped the last shred of it away in one velvety squeeze.

"Yes!" she screamed as he pumped into her again, then again.

She'd locked her legs around him with surprising strength and kept him tight up against her as she rocked with him, thrust for thrust.

He was groaning now, done with grappling for control, blindly seeking the release her perfectly lithe little body promised him.

"Oh God," he groaned as he felt the rush coming over him.

"Look at me," she commanded, reaching him through the thick haze of lust and carnal need that had gripped him the moment he'd entered her.

His eyes flashed open at the command.

"I want to watch you scream," she panted, then tightened her heels on his back and pushed hard up against him as he buried himself in her once more.

His climax roared through him like a rocket on takeoff.

He shouted, groaned, and, yes, screamed as she continued to take his thrusts as he poured himself into her.

When the shuddering convulsions finally stopped, he was barely able to shift and collapse on the bed beside her. "Dear . . . God," he managed, shaken by the power of what he'd just experienced.

"Amen," she said, reverently.

He smiled then. She did that to him, too, made him smile when he least expected to.

He turned his head to look at her. Her eyes were closed and her expression could only be described as . . . blissful. He wondered if his looked the same. He certainly felt it.

She rolled her head toward him then and opened her eyes. Those pale, yet so intensely passionate eyes. "Hey, sailor," she murmured.

"Hey," he said quietly.

They said nothing else for long seconds, simply lying there, looking into one another's eyes as their breathing gradually slowed and returned to normal.

The connection he felt to her went beyond the physical, he realized, as they continued their silent communication. He liked that she didn't know him beyond what he had revealed to her here, and yet he couldn't help but feel she knew him better than anyone ever had. Ridiculous really, yet he couldn't shake the notion. Or chalk it up entirely to mind-blowing sex.

He wondered if she felt the same thing . . . or if she was merely thinking about wanting to go another round. He had to know, and he knew exactly what he had to do to find out. Make the one intimate connection with her they'd yet to share.

And suddenly he was nervous, which was even more ridiculous. After what they'd just done together . . . But somehow this was more important than anything that had happened thus far. Her eyes flared as he shifted toward her, leaned in closer . . .

"Cam—"

A little moan escaped him at the sound of his name, murmured so lazily, so contently. "I need to kiss you," he said. "Like I need my next breath." And the instant he said it, he realized he wasn't exaggerating.

She trembled . . . and reached for him.

His heart rate tripled at her touch, then he cupped her face and leaned over her, lowering his mouth to hers . . . and touching her lips. They were warm, soft, and the most inviting thing he'd ever tasted. It was like coming home.

Then she parted her lips and tentatively tasted him with the tip of her tongue. His own lips parted as a groan sounded deep in his throat and he took her inside him. It was a perfect joining, one of tongues . . . and souls. He couldn't explain it and didn't dare try. But this wasn't going to end here, tonight. Not if he had anything to say about it.

He rolled onto his back and pulled her across his chest, continuing their deep kiss without a break. He felt his body stir again and wondered at this power she had over him. She straddled him and moved over him, stirring him further. The brush of her breasts, her peaking nipples, over his chest caused a leap of response and as she continued to plunge her tongue into his mouth, her hips moving atop him, he gradually grew fully hard once again. Amazingly again. Mercifully again, as he badly wanted back inside her.

"Slide down over me," he managed when she finally ended the kiss.

"Patience," she said, flashing a dry smile down at him.

"Allie," he warned, but smiling, too.

"You'll get what you need," she reassured him.

He grabbed her hips and tried to position her where he could do what he so badly wanted to do, but she wriggled free. "Please," he said, surprised to hear himself beg, but not caring so much when she grinned.

"Please, what?"

He pushed his hips off the bed, discovering it was as

much fun being the follower as it had been being the leader. Still that didn't mean he had to play fair. Catching her gaze and holding it with his own, he said, huskily, "Please take me inside you and hold me more tightly than I've ever been held before."

She gasped even as she continued to evade his maneuverings. But instead of doing as he'd pleaded, she bent back on her knees and dipped her head down to lap at his nipples, surprising a moan from him. She looked up at him and said, "Grab the sheets and hold on." Then she licked him again before pulling one of his flat nipples between her lips and tugging ever so lightly. He groaned . . . and grabbed for the covers.

She continued her torture, her position on her knees causing her belly to brush lightly over his now throbbing erection. "Keep your hips still," she commanded.

"I—can't," he ground out.

She lifted her body off his then, kneeling upright as she straddled his thighs. "Oh, yes you can." She grasped him, wrapping her hand fully around the steely length of him, eliciting another groan as she stroked him.

"Lie still . . . and let me have you."

It took every last scrap of control to keep his hips on the bed, but he couldn't help the way he twitched and pulsed in her hands. Not that she seemed to mind.

Then she lifted herself over him. "Watch me, Cam," she instructed. And he did, as she slowly pushed him inside her wet, hot body.

The instant she was fitted fully on him, he groaned and his hips pumped, his self-control shattered. It didn't matter; she leaned back, bracing herself on her hands, and let him push and pump, the angle letting him deeper inside her than ever before. He didn't know who moaned louder and didn't care.

He tilted his head up and watched himself enter her, watched her writhe on him, until he couldn't take it an instant longer. He reared up and pulled her legs around his hips, so she was in his lap, impaled on him, her breasts crushed to his. "I want to be tasting you, kissing you, when I come in you," he all but growled.

She was already there, kissing him before he finished speaking, taking him, forcing him to take her. They dueled and fought, with both tongues and bodies, battling the sensations they each wrought in the other, until both their screams filled the night air.

This time when it was over, there were no words. Cam simply pulled them both up to the pillows, and sank gratefully into their cool softness, tugging her into his arms and stroking her hair as her breath steadied, then deepened as she fell asleep on him.

Mine, he thought, holding her tight as sleep claimed him, too. *Hers.*

He awoke to the sound of someone tapping softly on the bungalow door. It took him a second to recall where he was . . . and only another moment to realize he was alone. He sat up abruptly, forcing his sleep-drugged brain to clear. Another tapping sounded at the door had him crawling off the bed, almost tripping over one of the stools in his haste to get to the door. She'd gone out early, he thought, striving to keep from panicking, and the door was locked. She was back now.

But he knew, even as he opened the door a crack, that it wasn't going to be Allie.

"I'm so sorry to interrupt, sir," said one of the young P.D.'s. "We just need to know when you think you'll be done so we can send in the maids to ready the room for later use by other guests."

"Give me a few minutes," he managed.

"No hurry."

"A few minutes."

The young man nodded, with a cheery smile that Cam

barely resisted slamming the door on. He clicked the door shut, thinking it was unfair for anyone to look so happy when he felt so . . . lost.

Yes, that was how he felt. Where had she gone? And why?

He looked around and realized that only his clothes littered the floor. Actually, only his pants and briefs. His shirt was gone. A spark of hope filled him and he hurriedly dressed, deciding the shower could wait until he'd checked into his own bungalow. After he'd found Allie. They could shower together. Perfect way to begin the day, he thought, forcing himself to think positively. In fact, today he intended to find out everything about her, tell her anything she wanted to know about him. And if he was really lucky, maybe convince her to take showers with him every morning.

But when he checked in at the main lodge, there was his shirt, neatly folded, with a note in the front chest pocket. She'd checked out earlier that morning and taken a water taxi to a nearby island. He waited until he was alone in his room to read the note.

Dear Cam,

Words cannot express the way you made me feel last night. It was beyond my wildest fantasies. I thought I'd spare us both the risk of spoiling such perfection with an awkward morning after. But I wanted you to know that I'll never forget what we shared, and what you taught me about myself. For that I'll owe you forever. I hope you enjoy the rest of your vacation. I'm leaving this morning. After all, I found what I was looking for. More, in fact, than I ever dreamed. And I know you don't want to hear this, but, Cameron, you are a nice guy. The best kind of nice. I hope that doesn't ever change.

She'd signed it, simply "Allie."

Cam sat on the side of his bed and read the note again. And again. "It wouldn't have been awkward, dammit," he said, torn between feeling angry . . . and desolate. "It would have been perfect."

And she hadn't even given him a chance. But then, maybe she wasn't looking for more. *I found what I was looking for.* One hot night in a tropical paradise.

Well, dammit, he might have come here looking for a hot fling, too, but he'd found more. So much more. She said she'd never forget him. He didn't want her to have to try. Nor did he want her to be merely a memory, even if it was the best damn memory of his life. She said she'd found what she'd come for. Well, ultimately he'd come here looking to find himself. And in making love to her, being made love to by her, maybe he'd discovered just who he was.

Not a man who selfishly put his own needs first. Allie had been right about that much. He wasn't now and never would be a bad boy. But he had realized something else. He might not be a bad boy, but he was no longer the man who simply did what was expected of him and hoped that would be enough. Because it wasn't enough. And it never would be. If he was going to be happy, fulfilled, then he was going to have to be a man who knew what he wanted . . . and went after it. And he knew exactly what he wanted.

Allie.

Chapter Ten

Allie looked down at the doodles she was making in the margin of her merger notes. She couldn't seem to pay attention to what the CEO was saying. Which was not a good thing as this was the final meeting before she and said CEO signed an agreement to join their respective companies.

She'd already played her mental dominatrix game, something she'd taken to doing over the past several weeks since her return from Intimacies. Her own little form of entertainment during otherwise mind-numbing board meetings. Meetings she was usually chairing. But role-playing scenarios weren't holding her attention either. All it had earned her this morning was a suggestive look from one of Maxwell's board members. A rather dashing and handsome member, too. One who had already made it clear during lunch that he'd be interested in comparing . . . notes, later.

But she couldn't work up any interest there, she thought as she doodled the shape of a man's hand, a hand with thick long fingers. She shifted in her seat a little, trying hard not to picture Cam's hands, and what they could be doing to her right now.

Cam. Now there was definite interest there. In fact, too much of it. She thought about him far too often, dreamed about him even more.

It was a weekend fling, she reminded herself for the millionth time. *You got way more than you bargained for.* And her little adventure had brought about the desired results if Mr. Handsome and Dashing's reaction was any indication. She'd gone shopping immediately upon returning and chosen business wear that was more flattering to her figure. She'd even taken the time to learn how to apply more than just mascara and lip gloss. But more important than the surface changes was the way she felt in her own skin. Comfortable. Sexy, even. Definitely female.

And she had Cameron to thank for all of it.

Cam. She wondered for the gazillionth time what he was doing, wondered again if she'd done the wrong thing by ending it so abruptly. But it had seemed the right thing to do that morning when she'd awoken to find him sleeping so beautifully next to her. He'd looked even better, slumbering amidst all that white lace and linen, than she'd imagined.

Her heart had tripped, dangerously. And she'd known even another day with him, much less another night, and her heart would go beyond tripping into a giant, headlong, free fall. And neither of them had gone there looking for that.

Love. She swallowed a sigh. She could have loved him. *You don't even know him. You ran away before you could.* Guilty as charged. But she'd asked herself if it was better to wonder "what if" than to risk living through his Mr. Nice Guy rejection when he realized she wanted more than a weekend fling. Better to leave when it was still the perfect memory.

"Ms. Walker? Does that meet with your approval?"

Allie jerked her attention back to the long conference table and the ten men and two women seated around it. She was at the opposite end from Ted Maxwell, CEO of Soft-More, Incorporated. His business created software programs for high school and college courses. Her company was going to provide the technology to integrate his software into a nationally available online curriculum that would benefit schools and universities all over the world.

She was very excited about the merger and all the possibilities it entailed, the first of which was going to be a relocation of the bulk of her company to the East Coast, to be closer to SoftMore's parent company's headquarters.

Given all that, the very last thing she should be thinking about at the moment was how much she missed Cam.

"I—" She was saved from having to bluff her way through an answer when there was a tap on the door.

"Enter," Maxwell stated, and a slim brunette slipped in the door and quietly passed him a folded piece of paper. Maxwell read it, then nodded to her. He turned back to the table and said, "I'm very sorry, but I have to step out for a brief moment."

Allie nodded, then sighed in quiet relief at the reprieve she'd been given. *Get a grip,* she scolded herself, all the while smiling confidently at Maxwell's board of directors. *This is your whole life here. Pay attention.*

The seconds ticked away and she returned her attention to her notes. But they were a blur. She was wondering if Cam had been upset to wake up alone. Or relieved. She remembered how it had felt, having him pull her protectively into her arms as they both fell asleep. Not the actions of a man wanting to make a quick getaway. But he'd been exhausted, satiated. Come morning, in the light of day, he might wonder what in the hell had gotten into him.

Nonsense, she told herself. She knew there had been something between them. *Knew* it. She should have stayed. Should have found out more about him. His last name would have come in handy. But it was too late now.

Her whole life was about to change in a major way. And yet, despite her excitement at the challenges that lay before her, she knew the real change had happened on a bed of Victorian lace in the Caribbean.

Maxwell's secretary poked her head into the room again

and cleared her throat. "Ms. Walker? Could you step out here for a moment?"

Surprised at the request, Allie smiled and nodded, calmly excusing herself and following the secretary into the hallway while wondering wildly what this was all about. Had she been so out of it that Maxwell had noticed? She didn't think so. Besides, today's meeting was really more formality than anything, a chance to introduce her to his board of directors. He'd met hers the week before. But it was important that she make as good an impression as possible to ensure that the transition went as smoothly as possible.

"Right through here," the secretary said, motioning her to Maxwell's personal office.

"Thank you," Allie responded, wondering what Ted wanted that couldn't be said in front of the whole room. Bracing herself, she pasted on a smile and entered the room— and froze. She blinked, certain she was hallucinating. But he was still there, standing across the room, smiling at her.

She opened her mouth, but the words refused to form.

Maxwell cleared his throat, dragging her attention unwillingly to him. "I, uh, this is highly unusual," he stammered.

Allie was peripherally aware that Maxwell was uncomfortable, not angry.

"As you know," he went on after clearing his throat, "Soft-More is a subsidiary of James and Son, Indust—"

"Just James, now," the man by the window said. "James Industries."

"Right, right, sorry, sir." Maxwell darted a gaze between the two of them, apparently as aware as Allie of the tension arcing around the room. He cleared his throat again but Allie couldn't stop staring . . . and not at him. "James Industries is headquartered here in Atlanta as well, and Mr. James here—"

"Ted," he said quietly, "if you could just give us a few minutes?"

"Certainly," Maxwell said, looking enormously relieved as he hurried to let himself out of his own office.

And then they were alone. Allie . . . and the man she'd never thought to see again.

"Say something," he said softly, looking so directly at her she felt her entire body flame in response.

But they weren't at some private sex club now. They were here, smack in the middle of the real world. Her entire world. Allie's thoughts careened wildly. Well, now she knew his last name. James. As in Cameron James IV. Owner of a good percentage of all the technology industry on the East Coast. Had he somehow discovered she was the Allison Walker behind Walker Technologies and was going to call off the deal because of what had happened between them? "What—what are you doing here?" she finally stammered.

"I hardly recognize you," he said in response.

She fingered the hem of her fitted suit jacket, then smoothed her dark hair back from her face. "I . . . wasn't really a blonde."

He held her gaze. "I know."

She flushed, unable to stop the heat from climbing . . . everywhere. "Yes, yes. Of course you do." She cleared her throat, remembering exactly how he'd know that. "I . . . dyed it back, when I got home." She tried to laugh lightly and failed miserably. "Blondes do have more fun, but being a brunette is more my speed."

"It suits you. Your skin glows."

She shifted her weight, wanting badly to squeeze her thighs together to assuage the fierce ache that had already sprung to life there. "Thank you."

"I'm making you nervous."

"I'd be a lot less nervous if I knew why you were here."

"Did you not want me to find you, Allie?"

"I—I didn't know you would come looking."

"Didn't you?" he asked, and for the first time she noticed the tension beneath the calm. He leaned, seemingly relaxed, against the windowsill, but his knuckles were white. "After what we shared, did you honestly think I'd let you go?"

She stilled. "What do you mean?" She should be angry at his presumption, as if he owned her or something. But explain that to her libido, which was raging . . . or her panties, which were soaked through.

He finally pushed away from the window and walked toward her. It took everything she had to remain where she stood. Mostly she managed it because she wasn't sure that if she did move, whether it would be to run from the room . . . or into his arms. "What do you want?" she asked again, only this time there was a tone of command in her voice. And maybe a touch of panic.

If he touched her, she was fairly certain she'd let him do anything he damned well pleased . . . right here in Maxwell's office. Hell, right on the boardroom table. With the entire board of directors watching.

That was the effect he had on her. And in that moment, she knew he always would. No matter where they were.

He stopped just in front of her and lifted his hand.

"Don't," she whispered, and he stopped. If she wasn't such a knot of need and confusion, she'd have smiled. Still Mr. Nice Guy, no matter what. "Tell me what you want. What you came here for."

"I came here for you."

She looked into his eyes then. "This isn't about the business?"

"That's the other thing I wanted to know. When I pursue you, personally, is it going to bother you that, technically, I'll own a piece of your business?"

"Pursue?"

"I hated waking up alone, Allie."

She looked into his eyes and saw that he spoke the truth. "I've missed you," she said, finally, softly.

"Then why did you go?"

"I—" She stopped, shrugged, looked away. "It was the

most perfect night of my life. And I guess I knew that it was about more than the sex." She looked back at him. "I was already starting to . . . feel things. For you. I didn't want to put you in an awkward position. I know that's not what you came there looking for."

"Maybe I didn't know what I was looking for. Until I found her."

"But—" Now that she knew who he was, it was impossible not to put the pieces together. Within the industry it was no secret what he'd been through in the past couple of years, from the salacious details of his mother's bouts in rehab to the media highlights of his father's trial. With some juicy tidbits of his divorce tossed in just for fun.

He must have read it in her eyes. "Don't let what's happened to me, what you think you know about me, change what you already know to be true."

"But I don't know you."

"Oh yes, you do. You know the real me, Allie. The me I want to be. With you."

She wanted to deny that, but she'd had the same exact thought about him, that he was the one person in the world who really knew her. "How did you find me?"

"It wasn't easy. Part of it was serendipity, with our companies joining. I suppose if you believe in such things, that would be some sort of karmic sign or something, that we belonged together all along."

She smiled a little. "What are the odds, right?"

His lips quirked a little, but the tension lines still bracketed his mouth. "Exactly. What are the odds, Allie?"

She knew what he was asking. "I don't know." Trembling now, she lifted her hands and tentatively laid them on his chest. "But I'm willing to play them and find out."

His self-control snapped the instant she touched him. He pulled her almost roughly into his arms and his mouth was on her a second later.

Allie all but blossomed beneath the heat of his kiss, like a flower that had lain dormant in the dark, until the sun rose again.

She grabbed at him, unable to get him close enough to her. There were suddenly far too many layers of clothing between them and she'd have given anything to be alone with him. Truly alone.

"Tell me again, Allie," he murmured against the now damp skin of her neck.

How she was ever going to go back into that boardroom she didn't know . . . and didn't much care. "I missed you, Cam, missed seeing you, hearing your voice." She looked up at him and stroked her fingers over his face. "Missed tasting you."

His pupils all but exploded with desire. He pulled one of her fingers into his mouth, making her gasp, then swallow hard against the need to moan.

"I like knowing I can make you wet, just by looking at you." He tugged her hips snug up against his own and almost growled when the rigid length of him pressed between the juncture of her thighs. "Do you like what you do to me, just by looking at me with those incredibly beautiful blue eyes of yours?"

She did moan then, and moved against him. "Yes," she managed, "yes, I do."

"I could take you, right here. On Maxwell's desk."

"Yes," she said, a pleading note in her voice that secretly thrilled her. "Yes, you could."

"Should I lock the door? Or does the chance of discovery thrill you?"

She laughed then, but it ended on a gasp as he pushed her back against the back of the tall, padded leather chair that fronted Ted's desk. "I think you know how I feel about that," she said. "I only like an audience of one." She grabbed his tie and slid the knot open, then tugged it off altogether. "You."

He grinned then and she finally relaxed and let herself believe this was all really happening. She was going to have this man. And, blessed merciful God, he was going to have her. As long, and as often as possible if she had any say in it. And, she decided, a bit wickedly, she most certainly would.

She let his tie dangle from her fingertips and ran her other hand along the side of the chair behind her. "You know, I never did get back to Bungalow Three."

"Bungalow Three?"

"The leather lounge."

His eyes darkened and she felt electric with the need that pulsed in her. He went to Ted's desk and pressed a button on his phone. "Sandy, please tell Ted we'll need his office awhile longer. The merger plans are fine. We're just working out the . . . details. He can dismiss the board." He looked over at Allie and she nodded. "Ms. Walker will sign the final papers tomorrow morning."

He let go of the button, then crossed the room and flipped the lock. "Just so you'll feel more secure."

"Once a Mr. Nice Guy, always a Mr. Nice Guy," she said with a smile.

He crossed the room directly to her and whipped his tie from her fingers. "You know, speaking of things we never got to do," he said, fingering the long length of silk and looking at her wrists.

She shuddered . . . but didn't resist when he took them in his hands and turned her around, pulling her wrists behind her back.

"You know that saying, don't you, Allie?"

"Saying?" she managed, a bit breathless already, need pulsing in her, the ache between her legs already beyond her ability to assuage by clenching her thighs together.

He tugged the silk into a knot around her wrists, then turned her back around . . . and pushed her legs just a few inches apart, making her whimper at the loss of the one thing she could do to give herself even a measure of relief.

He held her gaze as he slowly began unbuttoning her suit jacket. "I missed the taste of your nipples."

She shivered. "That's a saying?" She gasped as he opened her blouse, then undid the front clasp of her bra, baring herself to him . . . and leaving her vulnerable to whatever he wanted to do to her. Thank God.

He leaned down and flicked first one nipple with his tongue, then rolled it between his fingers while he pulled the other one into his mouth. She moaned and her knees threatened to buckle.

He turned her around then, and bent her over the chair, pushing her skirt up her hips. She was immensely gratified when she heard him gasp. "Garters," he said on a strangled moan. "Dear God."

"My taste in lingerie has improved," she said.

"Yes," he said, "yes, it has."

He traced his fingertips along the edge of tender skin at the tops of her silk hose. Making her thighs twitch. He moved in behind her as his fingers slid from the silk hose, to the silk panties just above them. He fingered the slender band of elastic, until she was barely able to remain upright, thankful to be trapped between the heavy chair . . . and his hard body. Oh, so deliciously hard.

"Tell me what you want," he whispered against the side of her neck.

"The saying," she gasped. "Tell me."

"Oh, right." He teased her by sliding one long finger over the silk panel between her legs, pressing the cool fabric against her wet, sensitized skin until she moaned.

"Cam, please."

"That's Mr. Nice Guy to you."

"Yes, it is. You are. Now please, I don't give a damn about the stupid saying."

She felt him grin against the nape of her neck as he moved in closer, pressing himself between the cheeks of her buttocks, while his hand slid around the front of her body . . . and right back down between her legs.

"The saying goes like this," he murmured, groaning a little as she ground her hips back against him. He slid one finger under the edge of elastic. "When they were good . . . they were very, very good." He slid another finger under the edge, and moaned as he encountered her wetness. Slowly, he slid both fingers inside her. "And when they were bad," he growled, sliding them out, then back in again, until she had to swallow the sounds of her first climax.

"They were perfect." She gasped, shuddering as she came hard.

"Exactly," Cam said, right before he slid his belt from his trousers. "Now, about this leather fantasy of yours . . ."

Please turn the page for an exciting preview of
NEVER TOO MUCH
by Lori Foster.

An October 2002 release from Brava.

The damp, sultry night air felt thick with the threat of a violent storm. Not a single star glimmered through the ominous gray clouds gently crowding the dark sky. It was the type of night that stirred a man's blood, made him think of warm mussed sheets and a warmer, mussed woman.

Ben Badwin needed a woman, and he needed her now. Tonight.

Breathing slow and deep, Ben let his mind wander to the carnal image of uncontrolled sex, of raging lust. His muscles tensed as he dredged up several female possibilities, but then he dismissed them all as not quite right. A muggy breeze ruffled his hair, drifted against his heated skin through the open collar of his shirt. Ben turned his face up to the night and smiled. He knew what he wanted.

A challenge.

Lately, the thrill of the chase, the chance to seduce, had been missing in his life. But he was a man, and damn it, he *liked* the chase. He liked testing himself and coming out the conqueror. He liked being a dominant male.

Tonight, the bar and grill attached to his motel was packed. For the most part the crowd remained friendly and free-spending, allowing Ben to take a moment to himself. He stood just outside the entry door and surveyed the parking lot. Flood lamps lit the area, showing a collection of shadowed cars and trucks. Business was good, booming even. On that level, at least, Ben was very satisfied.

On another, he burned with edginess.

A little ways down, in one of the ground floor rooms, a door opened. Two attractive, chatty women, probably in their early thirties, emerged. They laughed together as they moseyed toward the bar along the walkway. From all indications, they'd already been drinking. They neared Ben, and one with short, stylish blond hair winked and gave a three-finger wave.

Ben smiled back, polite as always, yet uninterested. "Ladies."

A leggy brunette cocked out her shapely hip. "Helluva night to be hanging outside." She eyed him up and down and up again with lascivious significance. A long scarlet fingernail touched his naked chest just inside his open shirt. "You should come on in and let me buy you a drink."

Wishing he felt even a spark of interest, Ben raised his arms in mock regret. "An offer that sweet is hard to refuse, but refuse I must."

She leaned forward, showing an impressive bosom to advantage. "I promise not to bite."

Ben couldn't help grinning. He adored women and their antics, the games they played and how they flirted. "Sweetheart, I don't believe that for a second."

The women laughed in delight. "You sure you don't want to join us?"

The blonde added, "I promise it'll be fun."

"Can't." Ben shook his head, and lied. "My time is already taken."

"Your loss."

"I'm sure it is."

They went inside and promptly found new game. Amused, Ben crossed his arms over his chest and leaned back against the clapboard wall. He enjoyed the business, he definitely enjoyed the female attention.

But these days he simply needed more, and he refused to settle for less.

A low rumble, probably thunder from the approaching storm, stirred the air. Ben looked to the sky for lightning, but saw none. The rumbling increased and seconds later the headlights of a truck came around the curve, briefly flashing into Ben's face before swerving into the landscaping business directly across the street.

A few weeks ago Ben had noticed that the shop, after being abandoned for several months, was turning operational again. He'd seen workers putting the rundown business to rights with new paint, repaired shutters, a clean sweep of the cluttered gravel lot. Truckloads of mulch and plants and such had been delivered and arranged into neat rows.

Ben watched the old battered truck come to a jarring halt with grinding gears and a spattering of the loose rock and dirt. The headlights died, followed by a slamming door. He stared through the darkness, strangely alert.

Inside Ben's bar, someone started the jukebox, and the rousing tune of "Bad to the Bone" emerged. The base was low and thrumming, reverberating in his chest, in his head.

That's when Ben saw her.

She came out of the shadows and started across the street toward him. Spellbound, Ben watched as fog seemed to part around her, giving her an ethereal appearance. Somehow her steps, slow and rhythmic, matched the beat of the music, and the beat of his heart.

The reflection of a street lamp glinted off her reddish-brown hair. It was tied into a high ponytail that might have been neat at one point during the day but now straggled loose and sloppy around her face. A fringe of bangs, stringy with sweat, hung half in her eyes. She wore a dusty white sleeveless shirt under a pair of coverall shorts with unraveled hems and a pair of brown work boots over rolled gray socks.

Ben wouldn't call it feminine attire, but maybe fetish attire? Whatever. It sure got his attention.

Despite being midnight and hotter than Hades, her stride was long and sure and fluid, matching that provocative music. *Bad to the Bone.*

She had the walk of a satisfied woman, and it turned Ben on.

Because he stood in the shadows, she didn't notice him until the last moment, when she was a mere three feet away. Their eyes met and she faltered. Her lips parted in surprise. Slowly, intently, she surveyed him.

Ben didn't move, didn't alter his relaxed pose against the building. But inside, interest roiled, kicked up his heartbeat, and sent his senses on full alert.

Knowing he looked too enthralled, Ben managed a nod—just barely.

The woman inched closer, but now her every step seemed weighted with caution and curiosity. When she was directly in front of Ben, her wide, lush mouth tilted and her eyes smiled. She shook her head, as if bemused.

Or disbelieving.

"You ought to be illegal." Her laughing comment, low and throaty, broke the spell. "It's a good thing I have a stout heart."

With that strange remark, she strode on past and into the diner.

A little amazed at his aberrant reaction, Ben realized he hadn't said a single word. He turned to view the back of her and his interest expanded. Her ass looked great in the coveralls, soft and cuddly and rounded just right. Her legs were strong, shapely, lightly tanned.

The rousing music faded away, but the scent of heated woman touched by the damp outdoors remained. Ben grinned.

Oh yeah, the chase was on.

And here is a seond preview that
will whet your appetite for
BEHIND CLOSED DOORS
by Shannon McKenna.

A September 2002 release from Brava.

Nine forty-six P.M. Almost time.

The monitor glowed with eerie blue light in the darkened room, but the mosaic of windows on the screen remained stubbornly dark. Seth Mackey glanced at his watch and drummed his fingers against the desktop. Her schedule never varied. She should be home any minute.

There were more important things for him to be doing. He had hundreds of hours of tape to process, and even with Kearn's new kick-ass rapid-filter software, it still took time to run the analyses. He should be studying the specs for the new generation of Colbit mikes, or at least conducting a random sweep of the other surveillance sites.

Still he stared at the monitor, trying to rationalize away the buzz of hot excitement in his body. The dozens of hours of vid that he had on file for her wouldn't do the trick. He needed her live, in real time.

Like a junkie needed his fix.

He spat out a curse at the passing thought, negating it. He didn't *need* anything, not anymore. Since Jesse's death, he'd reinvented himself. He was as cool and detached as a cyborg. His heart rate did not vary, his palms did not sweat. His goal was sharp and clear. It shone in the still, cold darkness of his interior landscape, as brilliant as a guiding star.

The plan to destroy Victor Lazar and Kurt Novak was the first thing that had aroused Seth's interest in the ten months since they had murdered his little brother. It had rendered him a miracle of single-minded concentration—until three weeks ago.

The woman who was about to walk into the rooms monitored by the screen in front of him was the second thing.

The light-activated camera monitoring her garage flicked suddenly to life. He tried to ignore the way his heart rate spiked, and glanced at his watch. Nine fifty-one. She'd been at the office since 7:30 A.M.

Her car pulled in, the headlights switched off. She sat, slumped in the car for so long that the camera switched itself off and the window went dark. He cursed softly through his teeth and made a note to himself to reprogram the default from three minutes to ten.

The second two cameras activated themselves as she unlocked the front door and headed for the kitchen. She took a bottle of spring water from the refrigerator, tilted her head back, and drank. She took off her ugly horn-rimmed glasses and rubbed her eyes, clutching the edge of the kitchen sink for balance. The miniscule camera embedded in the macramé knots of the plant hanger framed her oval face, her stubborn jaw, the shadows under her large, heavily lashed eyes. She looked at the mascara smeared on her fingers and closed her eyes. The sweep of her lashes was dramatic, shadowy, and soft against the delicate curve of her high cheekbones. She looked exhausted.

Being Lazar's new sex toy must be more strenuous than she had bargained for. He wondered how she'd gotten herself embroiled with him. Whether she was in too deep to ever get out. Most people who got involved with Lazar soon found they were in over their heads. By then, of course, it was too late.

There was no objective reason for him to continue to

monitor her. According to the personnel file he'd hacked into, Lazar Shipping International had hired her a month ago as an executive assistant. Had it not been for the fact that she was living in Lazar's ex-mistress's house, she might never have come to his attention at all. Lazar's visits to that house had warranted surveillance, and Seth had been watching it for months.

But Lazar didn't visit the blonde, or at least he hadn't yet. She came straight home from the office every night, stopping only to get groceries or to pick up her dry cleaning. The transmitter he had planted in her car confirmed that she never varied her route. A weekly phone call to her mother revealed only that the woman had no clue about her daughter's latest career move, which was understandable; a young woman kept for pleasure by a ruthless criminal slimebag might well choose to hide the knowledge from her family. She knew no one in Seattle, went nowhere, had no social life that he could discern.

Kind of like himself.

The blonde stared almost directly into the camera with big, haunted eyes. She disquieted him. She looked . . . God, *sweet* was the word that came to mind, even though it made him wince.

He had never before had moral qualms about spying on people. When he was a kid reading comic books, he'd picked out his superhero mutation of choice right away. X-ray eyes won, hands down. It was the perfect mutation for a suspicious, paranoid control freak like himself. Knowledge was power, and power was good. He'd built an extremely lucrative career on that philosophy. Jesse used to tease him about it.

He shoved that thought away fast, before it could bite him.

He'd watched Montserrat, Lazar's former mistress, with business-like detachment. Even seeing her writhing in bed with Lazar had left him cool and unmoved, even a little repulsed. Never once had he felt guilty. But Montserrat was a professional, a player who knew the rules. He read it in her sinuous, calculated body language. She wore a mask all the time: when she was fucking Lazar, even when she was alone.

The blonde had no mask at all. She was wide open and defenseless and soft, like whipped cream, like butter, like silk. It made him feel sleazy for watching her, an emotion so unfamiliar that it had taken him days to put a name to it. The hell of it was, the sleazier he felt, the more impossible it was to stop. He wished he could shake the nagging sense that she needed to be rescued. He wasn't the white knight type to begin with, and besides, he had Jesse to avenge. That was enough responsibility.

He wished she weren't so fucking beautiful. It was disturbing.

A shrink could probably explain his fixation; he was under stress, projecting his deprived childhood fantasies onto her because she looked like a fairy-tale princess. He'd read too many comic books as a kid. He was alienated, depressed, obsessed, had an altered perception of reality, blah, blah, blah. You name it, he was afflicted with it.

And the sight of that woman's stunning body had altered reality beyond recognition. It had shocked his numbed libido violently into life.

She drifted wearily into the range of the micro-camera nestled inside the carved latticework of a hanging lamp in the bedroom. The lamp had been left behind by Montserrat, who had departed so abruptly that she hadn't even taken the time to pack the personal items that she had contributed to the apartment's décor.

The blonde had brought nothing of her own to the apartment, and had shown no interest in changing or moving the pieces that were already in place, which was good. The lamp commanded an excellent view of the mirror on the armoire, a detail for which he had reason to be grateful. She opened her armoire, and he enlarged the image until it filled the whole screen, pushing away the now-familiar pang of guilt. This was his favorite part.

She removed her tailored jacket and clipped the skirt to the hanger, which left her clad in a pale silk blouse. Not for the first time, he wished he'd installed one of the color cams, at least in the bedroom. He'd seen no point in it at the time, but with the black-and-whites he couldn't tell if the blouse was white, ivory, yellow, pink, baby blue, or ice green. He wanted to differentiate between every tiny gradation of her perfect skin, from pale cream to pink to blush rose to deep crimson. He wanted it almost badly enough to break into the house again and upgrade. Almost.

She stretched up on tiptoe to hang up the suit, and the tail of her blouse hiked up to reveal prim cotton briefs that stretched tightly across the swell of her rounded ass. He knew her evening routine as well as if it were the opening credits of an old television show, but still he hung on every detail. Her artless, unself-conscious movements fascinated him. Most of the good-looking women he knew played constantly to an imaginary camera; checking every reflective surface they passed to make sure they were still beautiful. This dreamy-eyed girl didn't seem to particularly notice, or care.

She peeled off her hose, flung them into the corner, and slowly commenced her clumsy, innocent nightly striptease. She fumbled with her cuffs until he wanted to scream at her to get the fuck on with it. Then she fussed and picked at the buttons at the throat of the high-necked blouse, gazing into the mirror as if she saw another world entirely.

His breath hissed sharply in between his teeth when she finally shrugged off the blouse. Her full, plump breasts were sternly restrained by a plain white underwire bra. It was not a sexy, rich man's plaything scrap of lingerie. It was fullcoverage, wide straps, practical and unadorned—and the faint hint of cleavage it revealed was the sexiest thing he'd ever seen.

He rearranged his throbbing private parts inside his jeans and dragged his hand over his hot face with a groan. He had no business getting anything more than a purely casual, incidental hard-on for one of Lazar's toys. It was deadly stupid, and it had to stop.

Except that now it was time for the hair. God, he loved that part.

She tossed pin after pin into the china tray on the dresser, and uncoiled the thick blond braid from the bun at the nape of her neck. She unraveled the strands, shaking them loose until they rippled past the small of her back, tapering down to gleaming wisps that brushed tenderly against the swell of her ass.

His breath sighed out in a low, audible groan as she reached behind herself and unhooked the bra. His hands tingled as he stared at her plump, luscious breasts, crowned with pale pink nipples. He imagined them taut, flushed, and hard against his fingers, the palms of his hands, his feverish face, his hungry, suckling mouth. His heart began to pound.

She peeled off the panties, and stretched her beautiful body. Rolling her shoulders, her neck, arching her back until her breasts thrust out, enjoying the sensual freedom of being naked and alone. Unmasked and defenseless. Whipped cream and butter and silk.

The nest of springy, dark blond curls at her crotch didn't quite hide the shadowy cleft between her shapely thighs. He wanted to press his face against those soft ringlets, inhale her warm woman scent, and then taste her, parting the moist, tender pink folds of her cunt, licking and suckling her until she collapsed in pleasure. Video was not enough. He needed more data. Colors, smells, tastes. He was starving for it.

And then, the gesture that always undid him. She bent from the waist and flung her hair over her head, arching her back and running her fingers through the wavy mass. The placement of the camera and the mirror guaranteed him a spectacular view of her soft, rounded thighs, the creamy globes of her ass, the enticing divide between them.

Sweet Jesus, it was enough to wake the dead.

Eichmann's Executioner

EICHMANN'S EXECUTIONER

A NOVEL

ASTRID DEHE and ACHIM ENGSTLER

Translated by

Helen MacCormac and Alyson Coombes

THE NEW PRESS

25 YEARS

NEW YORK
LONDON

The idea for this novel and some of Nagar's words came from
Netalie Braun's film *The Hangman (Hatalyan)* (Pardes, 2010).

Requests for permission to reproduce selections from this book should be mailed to:
Permissions Department, The New Press, 120 Wall Street, 31st floor, New York, NY
10005.
Published in the United States by The New Press, New York, 2017
Distributed by Perseus Distribution

ISBN 978-1-62097-301-1 (hc)
ISBN 978-1-62097-302-8 (e-book)
CIP data is available

The New Press publishes books that promote and enrich public discussion and
understanding of the issues vital to our democracy and to a more equitable world.
These books are made possible by the enthusiasm of our readers; the support of a
committed group of donors, large and small; the collaboration of our many partners
in the independent media and the not-for-profit sector; booksellers, who often hand-
sell New Press books; librarians; and above all by our authors.

www.thenewpress.com

Book design and composition by Bookbright Media
This book was set in Goudy Oldstyle and Erased Typewriter

Printed in the United States of America

10 9 8 7 6 5 4 3 2 1

One

A narrow street in Holon in the industrial suburbs of Tel Aviv. A short, stout man, in his early seventies or maybe older, steps out from one of the small houses huddled beneath blocks of high-rise buildings. He is wearing a black coat, white shirt, and black trousers. A carefully trimmed white beard frames his weathered face, there's a black cap perched on the back of his head, and white curls hang down from his temples. He is holding a small suitcase in his right hand.

His dark eyes are alert; the old man looks around cautiously before he closes the door, he walks down the path cautiously, and cautiously opens the gate. Once he's on the pavement, he is filled with unease. He scurries down the street with hurried steps, looking over his shoulder all the time, stepping into the road, then back onto the pavement. In the end, he starts running sideways like a crab trying to keep an eye on what is ahead and behind at the same time, as if he dare not turn his back on anyone or anything.

He is on his way to the outskirts of the neighborhood. When he gets there, he is distressed and exhausted and doesn't calm down until he sees the sheep pen in front of him. He sets down the suitcase and wipes the sweat from his brow. As he turns around one more time, his eyes scour the cypresses and palm trees, the rundown huts at the foot of the hill, the fences made of corrugated iron.

Everything is as it should be. The old man goes to a shed beside the pen, made from rough planks of wood. He swaps his black coat for a blue smock hanging on a nail. Then he puts on a blue apron, opens the suitcase, and takes out a pair of thick rubber soles, a towel, and a wooden box. He ties the soles to the bottom of his shoes.

He opens the latch on the gate. The animals know his voice and he talks to them while he holds one back and pushes the others away. He forces the chosen sheep to the ground, binds its legs together with two ties. Then he heaves it into the wheelbarrow. Its body hangs over the side, the bound legs stick out. The animal is calm. It stares at the old man, as if it has been stunned. He opens his wooden box, takes out a knife and a whetstone, slides his thumb along the blade, holds it up to the light, and then starts sharpening it with rhythmic movements. The sheep watches. His skilled hand makes the steel ring; again and again the old man tests the blade, there's not a single nick left to be felt or seen, but he carries on sharpening the knife. There are nicks a human eye can't see, a human thumb can't feel. Nicks from tongues of flame and dark wings. Away with them! The law insists on purity—of spirit, not steel, sharpened beyond the blade.

The old man takes hold of the sheep's head, gently lays its ears across its eyes.

He says a prayer.

He cuts the animal's throat; separates arteries, veins, windpipe, and gullet in a single stroke.

On the other side of the compound, a man is pushing someone in a wheelchair. They are on their way to the meeting place, an improvised space in between the chicken coops and backyards with a fire for cooking meat and making tea, a wooden counter, a plain wooden table, folding chairs. It has a makeshift roof, planks supported by seven poles, which would hardly withstand a heavy shower.

The man in the wheelchair is pushed to the table. He doesn't move his head and his pinched features stand out. He is clean-shaven, his gray hair is cut short, and he's wearing a checked scarf around his neck to keep him warm. The other man, sturdy, with a beard, puts a hand on his shoulder, then goes to the fire, where he sets a saucepan of water to boil.

When he returns, he is carrying three mugs of steaming-hot tea. He pulls three pears and a knife out of his coat pocket, slices the fruit, and sets the pear halves beside each mug before he slips the knife back in his pocket. Then he sits down on one of the folding chairs. The sounds of the chickens, ducks, and geese surround them—a rising and falling antiphony to confirm the birds are there.

The sturdy man's chair is too small; he keeps changing his position, as if he would rather be standing. The man in the wheelchair hardly moves at all. His legs are paralyzed and his other movements are restricted. He can't lift his hands up high or turn his head very far.

The old man arrives still wearing his smock and the blue apron, which is now stained with blood. He sings as he walks and then starts to hum when he reaches the meeting place; he hums when he touches the sturdy man's shoulder and the shoulder of the man in the wheelchair. Then he sits down between the two of them and starts drinking his tea.

All three men are wearing the kippah, the flat cap that covers the back of the head and signifies fear of God. The old man is the only one with forelocks. He takes another sip of tea, leans back, folds his hands on his chest, and starts to tell his story: How was I supposed to know who Eichmann was? Adolf Eichmann. I'd never heard that name before.

The old man is Shalom Nagar. The sturdy one is my friend Ben. The man in the wheelchair is me, Moshe.

Nagar brought Eichmann back. I had nearly forgotten about him. The folders where I kept the newspaper clippings about him and the trial lay in a corner of my shelves, buried beneath my music scores. Books about his crimes are sealed with cobwebs, books that I used to keep at my fingertips and studied for such a long time. At some stage I just left them lying there. Why? I don't know the answer. Maybe because I didn't understand; maybe because I'd lost sight of what I was trying to understand. Eichmann went away.

He returned when Ben took me to see a film, a documentary called *The Hangman*. It was about Shalom Nagar—prison guard, kosher butcher, healer—Eichmann's executioner. Later we heard that Nagar had been invited to attend the film, but he hadn't shown up.

I know him, Ben said. He lives here in Holon, not far from you. We can visit him, if you like.

I didn't know if I wanted to. Eichmann, I thought, if he were Eichmann, I would want to meet him. Alone. But did I want to meet Eichmann's executioner?

Ben picked me up the next day. He pushed me past Nagar's little house, pushed me to the outskirts of our neighborhood, he pushed me past the sheep pen and over to the meeting place.

There was the old man, looking just like he did in the film, sitting there as he'd done in the film.

Shalom, this is Moshe, Ben said. An old friend of mine. He would like to meet you.

Nagar looked at me with dark restless eyes, nodded, and started to speak, said what he'd said in the film, introduced himself with his story, the text that has become a part of him: How was I supposed to know who Eichmann was? Adolf Eichmann, I'd never heard that name before. I came from Yemen when I was just a boy, you see, thirteen maybe fourteen years old. They'd told us about the war, not about all those other things. Eichmann? Who was he? I didn't find out about him until I had to guard him.

Eichmann's executioner? There are doubts. Was it really Shalom Nagar who pressed the button on May 31, 1962, opening the trap door through which Adolf Eichmann fell with a rope around his neck? And during that night, was it Nagar's hands that pushed Eichmann's body into the oven, to burn him to ashes?

Nagar insists this is the case; he is possessed by this person. Eichmann is still there, he believes. Eichmann is out to get him. He, Shalom Nagar, Eichmann's executioner, will be the final victim. Because there is one missing. Nagar believes Eichmann wasn't done. There is still one Jew left on his list.

How was I supposed to know who Eichmann was? Adolf Eichmann, I'd never heard that name before. I came from Yemen when I was just a boy, you see, thirteen maybe fourteen years old. They'd told us about the war, not about all those other things. Eichmann? Who was he? I didn't find out about him until I had to guard him. Now I know him, he is here every day, I know everything—

Who is here every day?

Eichmann!

Eichmann is dead, Shalom.

I was his bodyguard, Ben. I was with him in his cell. There were three guards, one in the cell, one in the hall, one in the next room. I was with him in his cell. I went with him everywhere, even to the toilet. I had to.

You had to smell his stench?

No, no. The Germans are clean, Ben. So clean! They are evil. Eichmann was evil, too. When he went to the toilet the first thing he did was pull the chain. There was water running the whole time while he did his business. He didn't want me to smell anything. Then he stood up and closed the lid and washed his hands, twice, three times. If I hadn't known who he was, I'd have thought: What a saint. They've caught a saint. He never did anything wrong. He thanked me for everything, *gracias, gracias,* he said. That's Spanish for thank you.

Do you speak Spanish?

No. How could I? We communicated with our hands. It was the only way—he couldn't speak Hebrew, I couldn't speak German. But we understood each other. I had to fetch Eichmann's food. I always put it on a special tray with a lid that had a lock. I had to make sure that it stayed closed all the way from the kitchen to his cell. So that no one could put anything in it. They could have paid someone to put poison in his food.

Who's they?

People who wanted revenge. And the ones who didn't want him to talk. Everything had to be secure. Eichmann poisoned in prison! Imagine the scandal. It was an international trial after all, the whole world was watching. I went into his cell with the tray. But before I was allowed to give him the food, I had to test it first. He said: You must test it first, Shalom!

Who said?

Merhavi, my commander. Once I asked him: Why do I have to test his food? Why can't someone else do it? He said: Listen, Shalom, if we lose a Yemenite, that's not a problem. Many Yemenites have died. But Eichmann mustn't die. It's an international trial.

If you spend a long time looking out for someone, you get close, familiar. You start to feel sorry for him. I could never have hit him. I never struck a prisoner, ever. Merhavi came to me after the sentence was announced, Eichmann was supposed to be hanged, but he had done something—he didn't want to accept the judgment.

He appealed?

Yes, and no one knew how long it was going to take. Merhavi came to me and asked: Shalom, when it is time, would you be prepared to press the button? I told him that I didn't want to. Everyone else wanted to, I was the only one who didn't. In the end we drew lots. And Merhavi said: This is an order, Shalom. You won, you have to do it.

When the day came—I had the day off that day—they came to fetch me. I was out for a walk with Ora and our little boy, and then a car stopped next to us; the door was opened, the commander pulled me inside, and we drove off to the prison. Eichmann was going to be hanged that evening.

Everything went very quickly. We lowered the rope, put the noose over his head, and I—I went over to the table. I pressed the button. And the trapdoor opened and he dropped.

I was twenty-six years old at the time, not really an adult yet. What did I know? I had never seen a man hang before. I saw his face as soon as I entered the chamber, white as a sheet. If you are strangled, the blood stops flowing to your head. And the eyes get forced out of their sockets. They came out.

His eyes had fallen out?

Bulged out. As if they were trying to touch you. And his tongue hung out of his mouth down to here.

To his chest? His tongue?

To his chin. His tongue hung down past his chin, I don't know why. It was all bloody. That was from the pressure of the noose on his throat. The mere sight of it made me ill. I hid behind my colleagues, so the commander wouldn't call me. But then Merhavi shouted: Nagar, come here! I said: Leave me alone, Chief, I can't bear it, I can't look at him. He said: Get over here now, Shalom, no discussion. This isn't a game.

So I climbed onto the gallows to pull Eichmann up so that Merhavi could remove the rope. Eichmann hung there with his head to one side, watching, he almost touched me with his eyes. I started to shake. And then he said something.

Who?

Eichmann!

How could he? He was already dead.

He had said something before he died. It's like the radio. When you pull out the plug, it carries on playing for a moment before it stops. When people die talking, the same thing happens. Their last words stay with them when they die, and if they can, if there is any air left, they still have their say.

That's what happened with Eichmann. I didn't know his stomach was full of air, so I grabbed him round his belly and out it all came. I couldn't understand the actual words, but it was a curse. He cursed me. And all the blood shot out of his mouth with the words. He spat in my face. The commander was safe behind me. All the blood hit me. The little Yemenite.

And then—

That's enough for today, Shalom. Moshe needs to get home.

No. Wait, Ben, I want to finish the story. You know I tell true stories, not nonsense. One guard on either side and Eichmann in the middle. That was the order. When his lawyer came, when he was allowed onto the roof, whenever he went to the toilet: I tied him up—

His arms or his legs?

Arms and legs.

How on earth could he go to the toilet then?

When we got there, I removed the ties. That's how it was, one guard on either side, and Eichmann in the middle. And then when I went back to work, it was me who had to be guarded!

What do you mean, Shalom? Why were they guarding you?

They protected me! After—after that night I was given three days off—to recover—and then I was supposed to go back to my duties. But I couldn't. I could hardly manage to climb the stairs. I didn't dare go up to the second floor where his cell was, Eichmann's apartment we called that wing. I was sure he was waiting for me there. That's why they gave me the guards: two colleagues who walked on either side of me when I did my rounds. The commander didn't like it, of course. My colleagues were needed elsewhere. It was very embarrassing. But what could I do? I couldn't get Eichmann out of my head.

Week after week, month after month, I still needed the guards. A year went by. A whole year of fear and nightmares every day. Because of Eichmann, because he spat that blood all over me. When I was awake, I was afraid he might appear; when I was asleep, he haunted my dreams.

When the year was over, I went to Merhavi and said: This has got to stop, Chief, let me do my rounds on my own again. I want to get over this. He agreed.

It seemed all right at first. No problems on the ground floor, or on the first floor. I felt fine. But then, when I was on my way up to Eichmann's apartment—I was nearly at the top of the stairs—I heard his voice.

Eichmann's?

Yes! Quite clearly.

How?

I don't know how—it was just there, Ben. I was on the stairs when I heard him. I walked on, slowly because my knees had turned to jelly. I'm walking along the corridor and can't hear anything. I reach the first door and take the keys out of my pocket. My hands were shaking. I could hardly fit the key into the lock. I unlock the door. Everything is quiet. I unlock the second door and walk into the hall. Just a couple more steps to his cell door. The hatch is open. One step. My legs don't want to move. Another step. I can't go any further. I stand on tiptoe. The light from the hallway shone into the cell through the hole in the door—a bright square at an angle to his bed.

And there he stood, staring at me, like this, with his head on one side.

I felt giddy, couldn't find my keys, managed to get out of there somehow, ran through the corridor. When I reached the stairs, I heard him shouting, *gracias, gracias,* and then—I woke up in hospital. I had fallen down the stairs, broken my leg and cut my head. Merhavi wanted to know what had happened. I told him everything. You saw your shadow, Shalom, he said.

He only feels safe when he's at the shed beside his sheep, his hens and geese, the animals he takes care of, feeds, and kills. Eichmann doesn't come here, he says.

Why not? Ben asks. He's happy to give Nagar the prompts he needs to weave his story. Why not?

He can't stand the sight of blood, Ben. If the prison doctor wanted to do a blood test, Eichmann had to lie down, or else he would have fainted. One time when he visited a bullfight he really did faint. His bosses didn't care. They sent him to the East. It was his job to report on . . . how the Jews were being murdered. They were shot. Hounded into pits, naked, and then the Germans shot them. Eichmann couldn't bear to watch. He looked away and waited until the pits were full and covered with mud. At one of these shootings, his black leather coat got splattered with blood. He took it off straight away even though it was freezing. It was no use, though. They drove back past the pits. They were sealed with a layer of mud so Eichmann thought he could risk taking a look, and then a fountain of blood shot up right next to his Mercedes.

Shot up, how?

I don't know, I wasn't there, and Eichmann didn't explain. Maybe there were just too many bodies piled on top of each other, the pressure kept building up until the blood came spurting out—

Onto Eichmann's Mercedes?

Or just next to it. Eichmann felt sick, the driver wanted to stop, but couldn't because of all the blood. They had to keep going. It was too much, I was exhausted, Eichmann said. I felt as if I had been beaten. I do not have the required robusticity of feeling.

The what?

Robusticity—he used words like that.

Did he say that during the trial?

No, to me.

How do you know what he said? You can't speak any German.

He said it in Spanish.

But you can't speak Spanish, either.

But he thought I could because I'm from Yemen, I'm a Sephardic Jew and the Sephardim come from Spain. That's what he thought.

Nagar makes it up as he goes along. I was tired when Ben took me home. Tired but filled with a strange kind of energy. Eichmann, Eichmann, Eichmann was back.

A few days later, Ben took me back to the meeting place. Nagar wasn't there. Ben made three mugs of tea, fetched three pears from his coat pocket. There was no sign of Nagar.

A storm was coming. Lightning struck somewhere; then it started to pour. There were puddles and streams everywhere, including where we were sitting. Ben stood up to keep a lookout for Nagar. He didn't catch sight of him at first, but then he saw him standing under the porch of his sheep shed where it wasn't too wet. Ben signaled to me, grabbed the wheelchair, and started pushing me along as fast as he could.

In some places there were huge puddles blocking our way, while in others the ground was so saturated the wheels got stuck. Ben pushed, pulled, steered this way and that. Somehow he managed to keep the speed up. The wheelchair slid and lurched all over the place, but I enjoyed the wild ride. It was the price we had to pay to get to Nagar's safe shelter—or so it seemed to me. I held on to the armrests and egged Ben on, shouting instructions as if we were trying to win a race. Two old men behaving like children.

We reached the shed soaked through and laughing. Nagar was just drying his hands. A bedsheet had been fastened to the wall, and a plucked chicken hung on a string in front of it.

Ben was still charged with energy and stared at the chicken for a moment before giving it a little push that set it gently swinging to and fro, while pale red liquid dripped from its slit-open gut.

Nagar was not amused by his antics. He didn't approve. He grabbed the chicken and held it tight. He sounded ceremonious all of a sudden. The sound of his voice was forever changing to suit his mood. Now, he rallied it in a darker tone: A woman from the neighborhood is ill, Ben. She won't eat or speak, no one knows what is wrong with her. The doctors can't help. They are relying on me. I have healed people before. They say: You have the gift, Shalom. I don't know about that. I take a chicken, wrap it in a sheet, and wave it above the head of the person who is ill. I pray, and they get well. What did I do? Not much. I prepared the chicken, no more, no less. It has to be drained of blood. That's the main thing. The soul's dwelling is in the blood, it needs to get away, must not be touched. The chicken has to be completely drained of blood.

That's what Shalom does. That's how he heals. The words and the way they were said had the desired effect. Ben didn't say anything; he felt ashamed. And even Nagar seemed moved by the scale and significance of what people believe he can do. They are all in awe of Nagar the healer.

It wasn't pouring as much as it had been, but large drops of rain still smacked the ground and pelted the iron roof of the shed. Thick, dark clouds were everywhere and there was no sign of it getting any lighter. Ben looked at the sky anyway; Nagar stood beside him, his arms folded across his chest.

It is always raining in Germany.

That's not true, Shalom. What makes you say that?

When the Romans tried to conquer Germany, they got stuck in the mud. And the Germans, what were they called in those days—

Teutons?

The Teutons took their chance. They charged out of the woods and defeated the Romans. Every Teuton carried a weapon, men, women, children, even the elders, everyone. The Teutons always kept their weapons within easy reach. It was a question of honor. It was all that mattered. Honor! The Germans are evil. Eichmann—

What does this have to do with him?

Wait. Eichmann followed orders. Always carry a weapon. The Teutonic code. Of course Eichmann obeyed. He was always armed with a gun.

Even in bed?

He kept one in his bedside table. And he had secret drawers in his desk where he hid loaded weapons. The thought of actually having to shoot someone disturbed him, though. So he was constantly giving his guns away. His adjutant got one, so did his driver, even visitors were urged to take a gun from him. Here, take my gun. I insist. Yes, Herr Obersturmbannführer! *Jawohl!* But every time he gave one away, he was given two more. And there was a gun cabinet in his Mercedes packed with anything you can imagine, pistols, hand grenades, machine guns—

But he didn't shoot?

Never! He was too scared. He never shot anyone in his whole life. He couldn't. He can't stand the sight of blood, he can't shoot a living thing.

I don't believe you. He was in the war, he must have shot people.

He was in his office! He was responsible for transports, he ordered Jews onto trains. Trains, railway lines, timetables—that was Eichmann's world, Ben. He didn't have to shoot. Later on, he would moan: I was not allowed to be a soldier, I was never a commanding officer, I never got to see the front. Actually, it was what he wanted because he was scared. I still can't understand it.

What can't you understand?

How can someone who's evil be afraid?

You'll have to ask Moshe, Shalom. He thinks about that kind of thing, not me.

Nagar turned around and looked at me. He seemed to hesitate. So far he had only talked to Ben or into the space between us, as if there were another, greater audience out there somewhere. He had never spoken to me directly. Perhaps he was shy, or it could be a precaution. Ben was someone he knew. Ben fed him cues, Ben allowed him to make things up and go his own way. But who was Moshe? The man in a wheelchair who listened in silence, never showing any kind of reaction to Nagar's stories? Nagar knew nothing about me and couldn't tell that, in a different way, I was as close to Eichmann as he was. Or did he suspect something and that was why he ignored me? Could he sense that my thoughts were like music accompanying his stories, critical comments, corrections, detours, enhancements? Some of Nagar's words would unlock troves of memories in my head. In his office! Did Nagar know that Eichmann's office was nothing more than a briefcase in the beginning? Eichmann was a newsman when he started out; he collected news about Jews straight from the Jews. A newsman needs to be agile, pop up all over the place. He couldn't line them up in front of his desk because he didn't have one. So they met on the stairs, going up, going down, Eichmann listened, Eichmann asked the right questions, Eichmann learned, Eichmann took notes, created a position for himself as the expert on Jewish matters. He was given an office and it was as familiar to me as if I'd been in and out of it every day. As if I had walked the long diagonal from his desk to the door. It was a gargantuan desk and he liked to sit behind it, leaning back into the shadows while his desk lamp lit up the person opposite him. He wrote his transport orders at this desk, forced Jews into trains—a hundred, a thousand, hundreds of thousands—with one stroke of his pen. But one time—was it just the once?—he sent someone into a new life, set him free, didn't shout him down; instead, he shook his hand. Called him comrade, not half-caste or a pig. That was just as evil. An angel can fall, but a devil can't rise. There was no way back for Eichmann.

Nagar came over to me without saying a word. He leaned forward and studied my face, as if he were searching for traces of the words he could sense in my gestures but couldn't hear. How can an evil man be afraid? The answer?

I didn't have an answer.

Nagar turned away, winked at Ben, and shook his head in mock disappointment: Moshe's not saying anything.

Moshe is tired, Shalom. We're going to go now, even though it's raining. You should go, too. Ben pointed at the chicken still hanging in front of the white sheet. Your neighbor will be waiting.

She has been waiting all her life, Ben. She is a lonely woman. Everyone is dead. Her husband, her sons, and still she waits. I'll go to her.

Nagar took the chicken down and undid the string. Hold the sheet, Ben, but be careful. Don't let it touch the ground. It has to be clean, without any stains.

Ben held the sheet while Nagar wrapped it around the chicken and then tied the bundle up with string.

Let me tell you a story.

We're going now, Shalom. Moshe needs to get home.

It's raining far too hard. I'll tell you a different story.

Not too long?

No, no, a short story. What do you say, Moshe? One last short story?

I raised my hand to stop him, but either he misunderstood the gesture, or else he simply ignored it.

In the prison in Ramla, the prisoners were supposed to clean their own cells. They were each given a cloth and bucket. Most of them never bothered. They didn't mind the dirt. But when Eichmann arrived in Ramla, he said he would need two cloths: One to mop the floor and one to wipe it dry. And I would ask you to change the cloths once a week, he said. That's how neat and tidy he was! He swept the cell floor from corner to corner, wall to wall, every day. You could see your reflection in the tiles. Every morning he made his bed, shook out the blankets, folded them up, and put them one on top of the other. Once a week, he beat the mattress and turned it over. Twice a week, always on the same day, he washed his clothes, his shirts first, then his socks and undershirts, and finally his underpants. He hung them up to dry on the bars of the window in the bathroom, always the same way. Before he sat down at the table to write or read, he dusted the table top and the chair with his handkerchief.

He was pedantic.

He is German, Ben. Germans are like that. They won't tolerate filth. They want it gone. It has nothing to do with them, it should not be there. Away, away! Be gone! Eichmann had a project, what was it called—

Deportation?

No. No. Before that. Nisko! The Nisko Project. Nisko was a place somewhere, I don't know where, an awful place in the middle of nowhere. The Jews were filth for the Germans, so they were sent to a filthy place. Eichmann collected thousands of Jews, builders, carpenters, mechanics, and transported them there. When they arrived, they had to march for miles and miles. Then he made a speech. They were to build a camp with wooden barracks. But be careful, he said. Do not use the local water. There is typhoid and cholera in this area, the water in the wells is contaminated. You will have to dig new wells. Get fresh water at all costs. Or else— and then he paused and smiled: Or else you will die. That is how evil he was. That is why he liked things to be clean. Everyone had to be clean. The Germans think they are saints. White people!

He wasn't really white, Shalom. He was darker than most of them.

Yes, but he liked to have everything as white as possible. During the war he had an affair with a noble lady who only wore white dresses and white hats. After the war, he kept white chickens. Then he bred angora rabbits, each generation whiter than the last. And still it wasn't enough. The commander showed me a photo of Eichmann in Argentina. A barren landscape, covered in stones and dust, but Mr. Eichmann is wearing a white shirt and trousers. And sitting on a white horse! And then—

Shalom, stop!

That was a few months ago. We still visit Nagar at the meeting place or in his shed. Ben picks me up once or twice a week. Every time he takes me home, I think: That's it. I've had enough! Nagar can't stop, we know now. As long as we go to see him he will tell us his stories. And if we don't visit him he will tell someone else.

Shalom Nagar is laden with tales of Adolf Eichmann—they come pouring, splashing, spouting out, never ending, never stopping. Eichmann, Eichmann, Eichmann. Nagar has lived with him for fifty years. His life revolves around him. He's always repeating or contradicting himself, his stories are full of gaping holes. But it doesn't matter. He doesn't care. He's trying to protect himself. Nagar needs to spill blood to wash away Eichmann's blood, he needs to talk about Eichmann to drown out Eichmann's curse. Blood for his blood, words for his words, it's how he lives with what happened on May 31, 1962, the night that will never end.

He upsets me, he fascinates me, he poses a challenge. Nagar talking about Eichmann—the way he talks about him—feels like a reproach. What did I do instead? I hid Eichmann behind a white sheet. I made myself pure, I thought I was holy! All lies. I didn't forget Eichmann—that's another lie. I kept him secret!

I can't play the violin like my father or Eichmann anymore, so I compose music. I write themes that don't remind me of Eichmann, choose time signatures that distance me from him, and tones that sound nothing like what I heard in the courtroom during all those hours. How many hours? Hundreds, perhaps, while I watched Eichmann, saw his mouth twitch, studied his bearing when he rose to answer a question from the prosecutor or the judge.

And then this little old man comes along, folds his hands across his chest, and starts telling his stories.

This morning I took my file of newspaper cuttings from the shelf, wiped the dust and cobwebs off my Eichmann books. I am going to write. I am going to write about Eichmann. About Eichmann and Nagar, about the trial and everything else. The gallows, the rope, the prison director, the preacher, the president. The oven. I have no idea where this will take me. Perhaps I will begin to understand something that can't be understood. Perhaps not. But there is something out there that I must face. It is getting closer, it's closing in. The noise is destroying my music. I've run out of notes.

Two

A train rattles in the distance. The prisoner raises his head.

For a moment, his heartbeat merges with the rising and falling sounds in which he gradually recognizes the familiar driving rhythm, this iron pulse he once beat himself.

What is the cargo? he wonders. Victims? Then he needs numbers; he closes his eyes, counts the carriages, there are not enough, there were never enough. His life was too short for the fanatical art of transport.

Reluctantly he shakes his head, opens his eyes again, and now the silence falls around him, the suffocating isolation of his cell, which has no windows, is surrounded by other rooms—occupied by guards—and empty corridors, along which they march him once each day when he is allowed to go outside. Here, too, there are only guards, no one else at all sees him, he sees no one, and whatever it is he can hear has no name. It is not a train. Do trains even run in this country?

The prisoner, that's Eichmann?

Yes.

You're writing about Eichmann?

About Eichmann and you, Shalom.

Why?

When Ben picked me up, he saw the typewriter on my table.

Are you typing music?

I've run out of notes, Ben. I'm writing.

You're going to be a writer?

I'm writing.

What are you writing?

I told him.

You're writing down what Shalom says?

I'm writing what I think about while Nagar tells us his stories.

Can I have a look? Ben asked. I didn't want him to. You read to us, then, he said. We'll go to the meeting place, like we always do, and you read what you've written.

No, Ben. That's Nagar's meeting place. It's where he tells his stories. I write here.

Writers need an audience, Ben said.

But I'm not a writer, I just write.

For yourself?

I didn't know the answer.

You're writing about Shalom, Ben said. He needs to know.

Nagar needs to tell stories, Ben. He doesn't listen. He needs to talk. About Eichmann, his Eichmann. The Eichmann at the meeting place belongs to him.

He tells stories, you write them and read them out loud, Moshe, Ben said. Two voices, why not?

In the end, I put the papers in my bag, the few pages I'd written, and Ben wheeled me to the compound. He made tea, as always, and cut up the pears. We drank, we ate, Nagar didn't come. At some point the chickens grew louder; it sounded as if they were complaining. Ben stood up, kept watch. He's coming, he said. Soon I could see him, too. He wasn't carrying his black case today, he had a white bundle instead, but he was singing as usual as he came over. I couldn't understand what he was singing, words in a language I'd never heard before, a happy melody, softly rising and falling. Maybe a song of praise to the day and the work done. As always, the singing turned to a hum when he reached us. He shifted the bundle onto the table, between the cups and pears, collapsed into his chair, studied his hands, rubbed them together.

My chickens—they've got wet feathers.

It rained a lot the last couple of days, Shalom.

It's not the rain, Ben. It's from within; they're restless. We've got to be careful. Let me tell you a story. Eichmann was given the same food every morning, two slices of bread—

Moshe has been writing, Shalom. He wants to read to us.

I want to tell you the story. You know I tell true stories, things that really happened.

Let's listen to Moshe's writing.

All of a sudden Nagar stood up. But he just took off his jacket and hung it on a nail. Then he sat down again, sat there in his white shirt in front of his white bundle, stared at my white pages. Said nothing. I picked up the first page, started to read.

```
A train rattles in the distance. The pris-
oner raises his head.
```

Nagar edged forward in his chair while I read, straightened up, lifted his chin—that's how he sat in Eichmann's cell, I thought, on his chair by the door. When I reached for the second page, he interrupted me.

The prisoner, that's Eichmann?

Yes.

You're writing about Eichmann?

About Eichmann and you, Shalom.

Why?

I want to know how it was.

I tell you how it was, Moshe! Again and again, I tell you!

Other people tell stories too.

Other people? My words echo across the compound like a threat. Nagar narrows his eyes, he's disappointed, disappointed and angry. Two voices? There's only room for one voice here. I've broken the law of the compound, Nagar's law, I curse myself, curse Ben, who talked me into it. He'll leave now, I think.

But Nagar didn't leave. The guard doesn't leave. He remains seated, he does not yield.

If you're writing about Eichmann, why call him the prisoner? There were lots of prisoners in Ramla, but Eichmann was Eichmann. You have to say Eichmann! A train rattles in the distance. Eichmann raises his head.

I call him the prisoner, Shalom. Then I say the accused, the condemned man.

Why? Are you afraid of saying his name?

As soon as I say Eichmann, I might as well stop writing. Everyone has heard of him, everyone knows what he looked like, everyone has their own Eichmann in mind and deals with him accordingly, an inner process that's triggered whenever his name is mentioned. That's not what I want.

What do you want?

I want Eichmann to be—

Like the first man? Adam?

If Adam stands for any man, for all men, then yes. We inherit the apple, not the sin.

But victims, why do you say victims? He's thinking about Jews, this German man. He transported Jews! It's us, the Jews, he wants to exterminate. You have to say Jews, Moshe.

I can't, Shalom. It wouldn't be right.

Why not? We are Jews!

That's why it wouldn't be right. I can't say Jews when I write about Eichmann. I'll stand before God as a Jew, not before the Nazis. And ye shall be unto me a kingdom of priests, so it is written. Day by day, hour by hour, we are Jews standing before God, who made a covenant with us, we are loyal, we are obedient, we keep his law. If I say extermination of the Jews, I place everything that makes us who we are before the Nazis. If I say victims, I keep us apart, standing before the Lord. That's how it was in the trial, too; the attorney general accused Eichmann in the name of the victims. The witnesses testified as victims. Jews like us, they testified as victims. He was judged in the name of the victims.

No, Moshe. They were crimes against the Jewish people.

There are no crimes against a people who have a covenant with God, Ben. The kingdom of priests cannot be defeated by man. Their faces are turned toward God! No man can defeat them. When they get beaten, they are victims. It should have been crimes against the people of the victims. And that's what I write.

They persecuted us because we are Jews.

Yes, but we cannot give them our Jewishness.

They took it!

Then we must take it back! They never had the Jews. They never had a single Jew. Never! Not a single one! Only victims. They had victims!

They don't understand. Ben looks confused, Nagar distraught, he jabs his finger in the air, points at me as if he wants to gore right through me.

Jews!

Victims!

I have to say victims, why don't they understand? Nagar runs his hand over the bundle on the table. Why is that? Superstition? Is he healing me? Himself? Us Jews? I see my hands shaking; I can't hold the pages anymore. They rustle as they fall to the ground.

Ben looks away. He picks up his tea, holds the cup in two hands.

That's your business, Moshe. You write, we listen.

His advice could mean one thing or another.

Ben touches his kippah, Nagar lays a hand on his arm. Ben passes him a piece of pear. Nagar waves him off. Reaches behind him, searches for something in his coat pockets, something he chews and then spits out again.

Let me tell you a story.

The sounds of the chickens surround them once more. Moshe's text nothing but an interruption, powerless in this place, alongside the shochet and healer. Finished before it's really begun. The overture a finale. Why did I let myself be persuaded?

Let me tell you a story.

Tell us. We'll keep them apart. Your Eichmann, my Eichmann. But, Nagar, the day will come when they will meet despite us. One will hang. And the other? Let's wait and see. You tell the story, I'll continue to write.

Let me tell you a story.

Eichmann was given the same food every morning. Two slices of bread, two kinds of sausage, a cup of coffee. I fetched the tray; still in the hall, I tasted everything, had a sip of coffee, ate a small piece of bread, a bit of each sausage. Then I took the tray into Eichmann's cell. Eichmann stood to attention, I set the tray on the table, he sat down and started to eat. When he was finished he cleared his throat very politely, ahem, ahem, and I took the tray away. It went like clockwork. One morning—

Shalom—

No, wait, Ben. I want to tell you the story. One morning I made a mistake. I was restless and lost in thought because our little boy was ill. He'd been running a fever for days. So I forgot to taste Eichmann's breakfast. I set down the tray, sat down on my chair, and thought about our son.

Eichmann starts eating. I look up at one point, he's still eating. Deliberately, as is his wont. He's taking his time today, I think. He's eating like this, slightly strange somehow, grinding his teeth and swallowing all the time. I'd never seen him eat like this. I had no idea, is he savoring the bread or doesn't he like it? I study him, take a closer look—and all at once I realize that I didn't taste his food!

I break out in a sweat, I leap to my feet, he is just putting the last piece of bread into his mouth, his eyes question me. I point to the plate, make signs, like this, can he tell me does he feel ill? He doesn't understand at first. When he does understand, he shakes his head, hints at a smile, points at his plate, holds up two fingers and puts them down again, holds up six fingers. That was it: They'd given him six pieces of bread instead of two! I hadn't noticed. And Eichmann had eaten the lot.

I had no choice, I had to report it. Merhavi cautioned me severely, it was a serious offense. Then he started pondering: If Eichmann had eaten all six slices of bread, maybe the portions had always been too small? Merhavi asks the director, he asks the prison doctor, who says they should ask Eichmann.

And? What did Eichmann say?

No, no, Herr Director, Eichmann said. Two pieces of bread are perfectly sufficient. But if I am given six, then I must eat them all.

Orders are orders.

Exactly, Ben.

If you'd given him twelve, he'd have eaten twelve.

Twelve slices, *jawohl*!

Nagar laughs. He's pleased, he's in a placating mood.

Are you hungry? I've got some mutton—

No, Shalom. Enough for today. Moshe needs to get home.

Nagar nods, heaves himself off his chair, starts picking up the papers that are strewn all over the floor, dusts them off, folds them, and puts them in my coat pocket.

You'll read more tomorrow, Moshe.

There are finger marks on the pages when I pull them out of my pocket in my apartment, my outer shell. I wipe them off as best I can. You'll read more tomorrow, Moshe? No. No! I won't let them hear what I've written again.

The Inner Guard

The prison structure has no core, it is
makeshift and crude, blocks of varying
lengths and heights stuck together, a space
created from crimes that deny all contact
with the outside world.

There is only one route to the prisoner's
block. They must climb several floors,
cross yards, pass through nine locked
doors. The final door opens into the inner
area, made up of five rooms.

The first hall leads to the guards'
lounge area. The second leads to the cell
and the meeting room in which the prisoner,
surrounded by guards, sits behind a heavy
glass panel opposite first his lawyer, then
a preacher, and, on just one occasion, his
wife.

The prisoner's cell measures three by
four meters. Whitewashed walls, dark tiled
floor, a single bulb hanging from the white
ceiling. A bed, table, and chair are lined
up against the wall opposite the door. The
prison bed has a thin mattress and four
woolen blankets, which serve as the prisoner's bedsheet, blanket, and pillows.
While he sleeps, his checked felt slippers
sit neatly beside his bed, always on the
same tile, which is just the right size.

The books stacked on the plain wooden table
have pieces of paper sticking out of them
at all angles. A folding chair sits by
the table, back against the wall. There is
another chair next to the door. The first
guard sits on this chair; he watches the
prisoner. The second guard sits on a raised
chair outside the cell door; he watches the
first guard and the prisoner through the
open hatch in the door. The third guard
sits a few meters away, watching the second
guard. The guards work in shifts; twenty-
four hours on, forty-eight hours off. During their shifts, they sit for three hours
and then have three hours' rest, before
spending another three hours sitting on the
chair assigned to them. During his shift,
Shalom Nagar is the first guard. For four
lots of three hours he sits in the cell,
opposite the prisoner.

Nagar is twenty-five years old, short and
stout. His wide, smooth face is adorned
with a mustache, which is reminiscent of
Errol Flynn's and so does not suit him.
Before he was transferred to the prison service Nagar worked for the border troops as
a military engineer, defusing mines. Sometimes he says he used to be a paratrooper,
too, which always makes his colleagues
smirk a little. He was chosen to be a guard

```
in this block because he is not a victim,
he knows nothing of the extermination, and
does not speak either of the prisoner's lan-
guages, German and Spanish. But the pris-
oner thanks Nagar in Spanish, whenever the
guard carries out one of his rare requests,
and Nagar has learned to understand these
few words. Otherwise they communicate with
gestures. None of the guards carries a
weapon, none has the key to the room in
which he sits. When a guard enters one of
the rooms he locks the door behind him and
passes the key through the barred hatch in
the door to his colleague on the other side.
Every guard locks himself in. The last
guard, the inner guard—Nagar—locks him-
self in with the prisoner.
```

Are you still writing, Moshe?

Yes.

Are you saying Jews now?

No.

And Eichmann, are you saying Eichmann?

No.

It's his business, Shalom. Moshe writes what he writes.

I'm not saying anything. He can write what he likes.

And then Nagar stops talking. With his arms folded over his stomach, he stares at the ground and stays silent. This time he's the one to break his own law, undermining the purpose of this place. The law says stories are told here; the law says Nagar tells his stories here. Right from the start, I always assumed that Nagar had built this place for this very purpose, rough-and-ready like the sheep pens. Had made himself a little stage to do what he had to do. Tell stories about Eichmann. And now he is silent.

Ben is silent, too. Somehow, Nagar's law applies to him as well. Nagar tells stories so that Ben can ask questions. Directly or coupled with objections. Why? How? Didn't you just—? If Nagar is the storyteller, then Ben is the questioner. Someone who doesn't have stories of his own to tell. We met in a kibbutz when we were young, then we lost touch, and didn't find each other again until I got sick. Ben's wife was my nurse. She was the one who told me that he had been a bricklayer and then a policeman, that he hated being in the house, that he always left early in the morning and didn't come home until late at night. He had never told me anything about himself. Instead, he asked me questions. Even his greetings were questions. And so were his goodbyes. The same compulsion, I thought. Ben needs to ask questions the way Nagar needs to tell stories. Not because of the answers. I think Ben asks questions to keep things moving, to give everything its own proper order. He doesn't set the pace, but he keeps it steady. Endless questions, on and on. If he can't ask questions, can't keep the story moving, then he needs to move, like now; he stands up, takes our cups, although they are still half full, goes over to the fire.

Nagar shuffles his feet, twiddles his thumbs. Stays silent. The place is shocked by this breach of law. No sound at all. The spell isn't lifted until I take my eyes off the silent, shuffling Nagar and look across the compound, my gaze passing over chicken coops with wire mesh that has been mended time and again. Now I hear the squawking ducks, the honking geese one by one, and then all together as the noise swells, a clamoring backdrop cloaked in clouds of dust. Then the animals quiet down, as if on command. A dog barks somewhere. Ben returns with steaming cups of tea. Nagar stops shuffling. He takes a sip, it's too hot.

Let me tell you a story. Eichmann—

What about Eichmann?

Eichmann wrote, too!

He was a writer? Is that what you mean?

He wrote, every day. I don't know what.

He wrote in German, you don't understand German.

He writes differently now.

Differently? How?

So that I can understand. When he comes—you know what it's like when you've had a high fever and you start to feel better? Everything seems different. You hear things differently, you touch things differently, your feet touch the ground differently. It's different ground. Perhaps the world is different? That's how it is for me and Eichmann. He reads, and suddenly I can understand. He comes, takes his papers out of his pocket, holds them very near to his eyes, he hasn't got his glasses, you know, they were left in the cell—his eyes bulge out, they came out you see—his eyes read, and I understand.

Eichmann doesn't read to you, Shalom. Not with his mouth and not with his eyes. Eichmann is dead.

The Walk to the Roof

They monitor the prisoner's health and
safety; he must remain alive. He is to see,
hear, and breathe until the trial is over
and the verdict has been given. He is to be
alive when the sentence is carried out.

The guards are under strict instructions
not to give or allow the prisoner anything
that he could use to harm or even kill himself. These fears are rendered pointless
by his fervent obedience. He knows what is
required of him and he obeys. The guards
are more generous toward him as a result.
Of course, the lenses in his glasses have
been replaced with plastic; of course, any
staples and paper clips are removed from
documents before they are given to him; and
the ten cigarettes he is allowed each day
are lit by one of the guards. But they let
him keep his watch and give him writing
materials, all kinds of different pencils,
carefully sharpened.

He is examined regularly by a doctor, he
is well fed, and all food placed in front
of him is tasted first by Nagar. They want
to be careful; even here inside the prison,
some would have reason to kill the prisoner. The poison meant for him would result
in Nagar's death instead.

Once each day the prisoner is allowed to
get some exercise, on the building's flat
roof. When the time comes, Nagar knocks on
the door of the cell and his colleague on
the other side passes the key through the
hatch. Nagar opens the door, the prisoner
gets up and follows. He is flanked by two
guards, with Nagar in front. They walk
across the hall and pass through the nine
doors, cross the inner courtyard, the main
building, enter the stairwell, climb up
floor after floor.

It is usually quiet on the way up to the
top; shouts can sometimes be heard from
another wing, and then the guards hurry the
prisoner on until they reach the roof.

Barriers have been erected on the roof-
railings covered with sacks, designed to
stop anyone from being able to see the prisoner. He walks along the path created by
the railings, changing direction several
times before emerging into a square that the
guards call the sports ground. This area
is also screened off on all sides. A folding chair, just like those in the cell,
sits in front of one of the walls. Perhaps
they had expected the prisoner to use the
time to do gymnastic exercises, perhaps
they put the chair there as a piece of appa-
ratus that would allow him to stretch, to

bend, to revive the muscles wasting away
from sitting and lying down in the cell,
to ensure he is ready. The guards give the
prisoner some space here, too, having stayed
by his side all the way up. He could do
anything he wanted.

But the prisoner just walks with even
steps, his arms crossed over his chest, his
head bowed. That is how he interprets the
command to do yard exercise, which for him
means a walk on the roof. Or is he daunted
by the sudden freedom, scared by the expanse
of sky that gapes above him? Does he not
trust the ground?

He takes a deep breath, then starts walking. He paces up and down the square as
always, step by step, as though that could
increase the space around him. He walks
down the side, turns around, walks halfway back, crosses the square, turns around,
walks back to the start. A pattern that
makes no sense, but that seems to be the
only one possible for him. He has never once
changed this pattern.

Today, however, the prisoner stops at the
end of the side wall; he seems to be listening, then he looks at Nagar's colleague,
who pauses too, he raises his left arm,
moves his hand up and down, points upward.
Nagar and his colleague follow his arm,

his hand, his outstretched finger. There
is nothing to see, although the prisoner
is not only pointing, he is explaining
something too, he talks continuously, as
though with friends, but says only one sentence, over and over. Always the same sentence, a German sentence.

Nagar searches the sky. No cloud, no bird,
no plane, just unequivocal blue, unmistakable as a piece of evidence. Is that it?
Or perhaps the prisoner does not even mean
something in the sky, perhaps he is simply
indicating a direction, beyond the wall.
That is where he came from, that is where
his house is, there, somewhere, was his
world?

The prisoner repeats the sentence once more
and then falls silent, crosses his arms
back over his chest, lowers his head again,
starts to walk. Tomorrow the verdict will
be given.

The Court

The next day they take the prisoner to the
capital; the procedure has long since become
a routine, and as with every routine it
feels like it will never come to an end.
None of the guards could say how many times
they have traveled this way over the last
few months—fifty, sixty? The prisoner will
know. Their destination is the Beit Ha'am, a
new cultural center that has been temporar-
ily converted for the trial. Rooms have been
set up for the judges, the court archives,
the prosecution, the defense, for those
watching the proceedings, and for media
representatives from all over the world. The
courtroom is the hall intended for concerts
and performances.

There are screened-off walkways here,
too. Nagar's colleagues flank the prisoner,
Nagar himself walks ahead. At the door to
the courtroom they stop, wait for the session to begin. In the room—

The day before yesterday, Nagar suddenly denied that he'd ever
been in the Beit Ha'am with Eichmann. I've stopped being surprised by the fact that he's always contradicting himself, but this
was too much for me, too much for Ben. As if he wanted to retell
the whole story without him in it.

I don't know what Eichmann said at the trial.

What is that supposed to mean, Shalom? Of course you know. Every single word he said in court was translated.

I wasn't in the courtroom, Ben.

Don't say such nonsense, Shalom. It was you who told us how Eichmann arranged his pencils, how he stared at the defense, before he put on his headphones—

I heard all that, Ben. I didn't see it. My colleagues told me all about it. I was Eichmann's guard after they'd convicted him. Afterward! They announced the verdict and then I was made his guard. I wasn't with him in court. That was someone else who looked like me. Even Merhavi mixed us up sometimes. Yoram, he said, but he meant me, Shalom.

You said there were twenty-two guards in Ramla, from the beginning until the end!

There were, Ben. But they swapped out Yoram. He was—he was dismissed. I don't know why.

And then they took you because you looked like him?

It was an order, Ben. What could I do?

The television cameras of the Capital Cities Broadcasting Corporation are already running in the courtroom, hungry for pictures as they have been every day of the trial, they show the room in its entirety, pan across the ground floor, up to the gallery, where the chairs are still empty. The public waits outside; crowds of people started gathering at the gate hours ago, bringing with them a build-up of grief and hatred, and a call for retribution. The people

talk, discuss, demand, laugh to lighten
their souls.

Inside the hall it is quiet, so quiet that
the half-darkness seems even darker and the
shapes in the room become hazy. Everything
closes ranks, the place for the perpetra-
tor, the victims, the judges. The attorney
general and the defense lawyer are already
there, deep in conversation next to the
huge cupboard that separates the stage and
the auditorium. A picture without sound;
the microphones on the tables are still
switched off. The camera moves, dissatis-
fied, until it finds what it has been looking for: a trapezoid-shaped box, built
against the left-hand wall of the room, in
front of a door that forms the back of the
box. The remaining sides consist of wooden
panels reaching up to waist height, on top
of which stands a frame construction, made
of white metal. Thick glass panels have
been fitted into the frame on both sides,
unbreakable and bulletproof. The front,
which faces toward the three high chairs
of the judges, is left open. There are three
chairs in the box too, two plain chairs at
the back against the door and one in front
with armrests, pushed under a narrow shelf,
which is fixed between the two side walls.

The television camera captures the box

like a still-life painting. An arrangement of objects whose minimalist imagery
was perhaps intentional, perhaps coinci-
dental, the result of practical necessity
and improvisation. Someone is supposed to
be made visible here, exposed to all glances
and yet protected at the same time.

A box but also a stake for the prisoner,
not the center of the room but still the
vanishing point. The ambiguity is reflected
in the uncertainty of the name: glass box,
booth, cage? The prisoner says: my glass
cell, the dock.

The doors are opened now. The gallery and
ground floor fill up and a low, polyphonic
murmuring penetrates the room. The men and
women, victims, relatives of victims, journalists, politicians, writers are restless,
exhausted by the tension, preoccupied with
themselves, their stories, their dead, with
everything in this room that they want to
hear, see, understand.

And, as always, they miss the moment when
the door to the glass box opens and the
accused is brought in. They do not see him
until he is already sitting down, motionless as ever, his forearms resting on the
narrow shelf that acts as his table, a
writing case beside him, pencils in front
of him, arranged as neatly as his tie. A

man of medium height, mid-fifties, thick
glasses, receding hairline. A clerk type,
whose ability to appear unnoticed never
fails to amaze. It is as if he circumvents
time, as if one could stare at the box with
the utmost concentration and still miss
the transition from empty glass box to the
box in which the accused sits. But perhaps
the guards also use the protection of the
murmuring, the unrest, the distraction,
to bring him into the room. His arrival
should not be an entrance. This is not
a show.

Three syllables are heard in a rising melody, as if a horn is being blown. The usher
has announced the start of the session.
The words are not comprehensible, although
according to the journalists he cried Beit
Mishpat—house of justice. The three judges
enter the room, everyone rises, and with all
eyes on him the accused, too, rises, lively
and lithe.

Nagar wasn't with Eichmann in the courtroom, he insists on that.
The man the cameras show beside the glass box is someone else,
someone who looked like him, with the same build, the same
astonished gaze, wearing the same odd mustache. Yoram, the man
they dismissed. The Nagar in the courtroom wasn't Nagar. Yesterday he went a step further: Eichmann wasn't Eichmann, either.

Let me tell you a story. Us guards worked double shifts. Twenty-four hours on duty and then we had forty-eight hours off. My shift always started in the evening. Merhavi had set it up that way. First the night with Eichmann and then the day with Eichmann. Handing over to the colleagues on the next shift, reporting to the director. When that was done, I packed my things and went to the bus station. I always waited there by myself, no one else ever took the bus at that time of day. But on this evening—

Which evening?

The one I'm telling you about.

Which one are you telling us about?

You'll hear soon enough, Ben. On the evening in question, someone's waiting, and turns around as I approach. He was wearing a large coat, a hat with a broad rim and a pair of dark glasses, sunglasses, even though it was getting dark already.

This sounds like a film, Shalom.

Hush! It happened just the way I'm telling you. I was tired, you see, I wanted to get home. And then there's this guy standing there with sunglasses on, although it was getting dark. His hands were hidden in his coat pockets. It was spooky. I wanted to turn around and go back to the prison at first. But I was wearing my uniform. You never run away when you are in uniform. You know that, Ben. So I stay where I am—then he says something to me. Don't you recognize me, Salaam? he asks. He spoke Yemeni! And he knew my name. I take a closer look, then I recognize him: an old friend from Sanaa. When I came here, to Israel, we lived together for a while. We hug each other, start talking about all sorts of things, he tells me that he's working as a journalist, I tell him I'm a policeman now. I know that, Salaam, he says. I know you're guarding Eichmann. I was waiting for you, I need to talk to you. It's important, Salaam, he says.

But Merhavi had forbidden us guards to talk to anyone about our work. We couldn't even tell our wives anything. Ora had no idea that I was guarding Eichmann, until—until the day. But my old friend knew. I said: Look, I can't talk to anyone about it. All right, Salaam, he said. I can understand that. I'll do the talking.

I didn't want to listen. I stared down the road to see if there were any car lights coming our way. Nothing. The bus didn't come either. What could I do? My friend spoke and I listened.

It's all a huge fraud, Salaam, he said. What are you talking about, I asked, and he said: The trial. The trial is one big fraud. The man in the glass box isn't Eichmann. He's just pretending to be Eichmann. It's all a farce, a play for the TV cameras, he said.

A madman. What are you telling us, Shalom?

Wait and hear, Ben. The man in the glass box isn't Adolf Eichmann, he said. The real Eichmann works for the Israeli secret service. They need him here. He's the best there is. Did you know that he was a news specialist for the Nazis before he organized the transports, Salaam? Gestapo, do you know what that means? Secret state police, he says. Mossad, do you see? And as no one is allowed to know—

Know what?

That Eichmann is working for our secret service!

Rubbish!

That's what you say, Ben. He said the whole thing is complicated. He can't tell me details, but he has got proof. Eichmann works for Mossad, at the highest level. And because no one must ever know, they've decided—

Who?

I don't know. All he said was: They've decided to let Eichmann die. For appearances' sake, of course. So they make up a fantastic story: Adolf Eichmann kidnapped in Argentina. Brought to Israel. Questioned, put on trial, sentenced. The Nazi pays for his crimes! But in fact it's the other way around, Salaam, they are paying him. They give him money, a lot of money, to teach them everything he knows. He's their master. No one must ever know. That's what the trial is for. A farce. The script was written by a famous American author. And you are guarding the leading man, Salaam, he said. You and your colleagues, you are guarding an actor. While the real Eichmann watches behind the lines. He's probably laughing because the man playing the prosecutor is such a ham, but maybe he's annoyed, too, because they've chosen such a slow, untalented guy to defend him.

Day after day you've been sitting in a cell with an actor, Salaam, he said. You taste the food for an actor to eat. You go to the toilet with an actor, you take an actor up onto the prison roof. Do you think the real Eichmann would grovel like that? Do you think he'd let himself be kidnapped just like that?

Mad. Mad, Shalom!

He can prove that Eichmann disappeared after the war, he said, with cases full of gold. They hunted him in the Alps, but he was in Argentina all along. He built himself a white villa in a park that was patrolled by guards with German Shepherd dogs day and night. He was friends with President Perón, walked in and out of the Government Palace whenever he liked. He received visitors from all over the world. Everyone came to seek his advice, Salaam, he said.

Mossad was watching Eichmann even then, of course. They were informed of his movements. And at some stage they decided that he shouldn't be working for Perón anymore, he should be working for them. They broke into his home, lay in wait for him, and made him an offer he couldn't refuse. Since then, he has been living in Israel with his wife and his sons. But no one knows that he is Eichmann. They have given him a new name and a new identity. You actually know him, Salaam, he said. But it is too dangerous to let you know who he is.

I didn't know what I was supposed to think. My friend talked at me, quickly and excitedly, and smoked one cigarette after another. My head felt clouded in fog. I couldn't think straight anymore.

I can see you don't believe a word I've said, Salaam, he said. I can understand that very well. I can prove everything I've said, but there is no time, I've got to be careful. Listen: The real Eichmann fractured his right hand in a motorcycle accident. He had to have several operations, it took months before he could use it again. During that time, he taught himself to write with his left hand. Later on, he went back to writing with his right hand, but then he fell down the stairs at his office and broke his right hand again. Since then he has always written with his left hand. And now, think, Salaam, which hand does the man you guard write with? I didn't have to think: He uses his right hand, I said. There you go, Salaam, my friend said. They didn't think of that. And they've made more mistakes. For the final proof, I just need to talk to the man you are guarding. A thousand dollars if you can find a way to smuggle me into his cell. Think about it, Salaam. I'll be waiting here for you at the end of your next shift.

And then?

He didn't turn up, Ben. I never heard from him again.

But you didn't believe him?

What was I supposed to believe? Everyone said: That is Eichmann.

The Verdict

The accused is charged with crimes against
humanity, crimes against the people of
the victims, and war crimes. The charges
include fifteen counts and the verdict is
given over a period of fifteen hours, during which the three judges take turns to
read. From the tangle of facts and puzzles,
explanations and ambiguities, confirma-
tions and doubts that are laid out on the
table after more than one hundred days of
trial, they have created a noose. A noose
that bears the burden of the victims and of
the law, a noose that will be used to hang
the accused.

Barely a soul in the room doubts what
the outcome will be, barely a soul follows
every part of the argument. The accused may
be the only one who never loses the thread.
He listens intently, hardly moving. Only
the left corner of his mouth, a tic that is
already well known. Occasionally he sits up
straight, reaches suddenly for one of the
pencils lying in front of him, scribbles
a word or two on his notepad, leans back
again, bends forward, puts down the pencil,
straightens it in line with the others.

Nagar, who is sitting by the half-open
side of the glass box, watches the accused

in the same way as he watches him in his
cell. He is the only one in the room close
enough to reach out and touch him. No need.
He can feel this man already, against his
will.

The onlookers, prosecutors, and judges
put the shifts between stillness and sudden movement in the glass box down to a
nervousness that the accused is struggling
to control, a desire to flee, triggered
by growing fear—Nagar senses a kind of
rhythm, a beating pulse that grows stronger with every twitch, every sudden movement forward, every pencil-grabbing motion.
Stronger and louder. A sound pattern is
created in Nagar's head, interfering with
the voices of the judges—the rattling of
trains on the track. The accused, Nagar
thinks, is following the judgment like
a timetable; he notes the sections of the
argument like passing stations, recognizes the movement of the points, the sid-
ings where the account occasionally pauses
before returning to the main track and
pressing on, unstoppable.

The man cannot escape who he is. He
remains the specialist whom he has declared
himself to be, the master of transport, even
though it was not he who ordered this particular journey, who named the destination,

and this time it is his own fate hanging
in the balance.

For better or worse he has chained himself to the trains. Since the days of the
cross-examinations, those carriages filled
with victims that shipped thousands, hundreds of thousands, millions of people to
their deaths according to schedule have
become his symbol.

In the Reich, which fell sixteen years
earlier, the accused was head of the sub-
department known as IV B 4. Responsible for
matters relating to victims and eviction.
Eviction, but also resettling, evacuation,
and transportation, which saw communi-
ties ripped apart, divided into victims
and perpetrators. The victims, it was
decided, must be eliminated from the German people, a sanitary procedure, which the
accused describes as a political solution.
Division of space in order to ensure that
the borders of the state were the same as
those of the people. First the victims were
ordered to leave the country, then they were
transported away. Transport means bringing people or goods from A to B using an
appropriate vehicle. The appropriate vehicle
for carrying the victims to the specified
destinations was the train. The transports
were organized and overseen by the accused.

```
Under the growing shadow of war, the polit-
ical veil finally slipped.
   What had begun as a division of space
eclipsed into a division of being, the
final, irreversible division. The Reich
transported its victims to their deaths,
orders were given for their physical exter-
mination. Gas chambers were erected at the
destination stations, beside them crema-
toria. The transports were organized and
overseen by the accused.
   The accused—
```

They keep interrupting me. I write as if they are watching me all the time; I write as if I have to justify myself. To Nagar, because I'm still saying victims, still won't say Eichmann, keep on saying Nagar, saying Nagar was in the courtroom, although, in fact, it was someone else, someone who looks like him. And to Ben, because I've lost my real purpose and have started writing a report, instead of telling Nagar and Eichmann's story.

Why are you giving us a history lesson, Moshe? Eichmann, the Nazis, what they were, what they did? I don't want to know about that. It's got nothing to do with Shalom.

Moshe's got us mixed up, Ben. It's a different Nagar sitting there in court beside the glass box, being made to listen.

You don't understand, Shalom. I mean—

I know Shalom doesn't understand. But me, I do understand, Ben. I know what you mean, I know why you're asking. I am writing about Nagar and Eichmann. I'm taking Nagar's lead, I follow him, I see Eichmann with him, see Eichmann over his shoulder, see Eichmann in a way I could never see him in court. Eichmann has come into his own; he acts how he acts because he did what he did. This isn't a history lesson, Ben. It's a step back in order to see the bigger picture. To see the order of things and the disorder that is part of it all, just as Nagar is a part.

The Nagar in my head protests: Another Nagar, Moshe, someone else; the Ben in my head still isn't happy. Neither of them wants to listen to me. Nagar rocks in his chair, he's started to hum, Ben stands up and looks away. I write against their humming and contention.

Gas chambers were erected at the destination stations, beside them crematoria. The
transports were organized and overseen by
the accused.

The accused does not deny this: After the
intended purpose of IV B 4, the political solution, had failed, naturally we were
recruited for the next stage of the final
solution. My orders were to oversee the
transports, and I knew that some of these
people would be killed in the camps, I must
admit that. But I had nothing to do with
the killing. My responsibility ended when
the transports were delivered to the destination stations according to the timetable.

A clear distinction must be made between
transportation and killing, he says. I
delivered the transports, but I did not
kill any of the victims. I have never

killed a single person. IV B 4 was responsible for transportation and in some cases
registration, but we were not involved in
the rest of the matter; our part was over
once we had created the timetables. We had
nothing to do with any atrocities, we simply carried out our duties in a decent
manner.

The spectators, among them victims who
had survived and countless relatives of
victims, had to bear these words for hours
on end. Everyone here in the room would
later be able to quote them, distraught,
disgusted, nauseated by the fanaticism of
this separation, which is embodied by the
accused. In his lost Reich he separated
people, in line with his orders, obediently;
now he severs these crimes, cuts a part out
from them, his part.

IV B 4 was responsible for obtaining the
train materials and creating the train
timetables. Period. As if this were all
just about objects, about iron and steel,
timings and routes, not about people. The
accused in fact consistently avoids this
word, talking instead about contingents,
numbers transported, numbers killed. Terms
so far removed from living languages
that for their own sakes the interpret-
ers attempting to translate the accused's

German into English and Hebrew have to
paraphrase, reducing the stark coldness
of his words. And yet still they remain
unbearable.

As if the victims were being exterminated
for a second time. In the accused's world
they exist only in trains, as goods to be
transported, as numbers to add up. Only
the matters that fall under your responsibility are real. IV B 4 was responsible
for transports; the rest did not concern
us. That the victims were ripped from their
homes, robbed of their possessions, driven
through streets, did not concern him. That
they were taken from the carriages at the
destination stations, forced into the gas,
burned to ashes that were blown back by the
wind, did not concern him. He saw trains,
not death, heard carriages rattling on
the rails, not the cries of the dying. The
boundaries of his responsibility were the
boundaries of his world. And the boundaries
of his world are, he says, the boundaries
of his guilt.

The judges reject these statements, unde-
terred and decisive. To them this is all
bureaucratic hair-splitting, lies told for
self-protection. Something that is whole,
they say, cannot be divided.

What do you mean, whole? The Ben in my head won't quiet down.

The judges mean the extermination of the victims.

The Nagar in my head rallies against me, stubborn, unequivocal. It's not right to say extermination of the victims. You must say the extermination of the Jews.

No, I won't say Jews.

The extermination—whose idea was it?

Hitler's.

Did he say: Exterminate the Jews?

I think so, yes. The order was never written down. But it existed in their minds.

In Eichmann's mind.

Yes. Eichmann didn't organize the transports because he loved watching trains roll.

Did you know that Eichmann never traveled by train? Never! He always went by car, a black Mercedes—

How could Eichmann ever travel by train? Trains went to the front or to the camps, full of soldiers, full of victims. There were no carriages for Eichmann. You can tell us what you like, Nagar, but not here at my desk. Tell your stories in your own space; tell them when I'm sat beside you. I am writing now. By myself.

A black Mercedes! A fast car with bright headlights, black leather seats, everything in black. Eichmann had his own driver. He sat in the back, with a gun cabinet to his right and a bar on the left he'd had built in, stocked with bottles of schnapps and red wine. The driver drove while Eichmann drank. They never stopped to rest, always looked sharp. They had so little time, the Germans! One day Eichmann had been somewhere, I don't know where, maybe where that project was being run—

In Nisko?

Nisko, yes.

No, Shalom. Nisko was before the war. You know that.

A camp! He'd been to a camp, Ben. Inspecting the ovens, making sure they were in working order and that everything was running smoothly. Things like that. So they drove back, late at night, they'd been on their feet all day, and then the driver fell asleep at the wheel. The car swerved and came off the road. Nothing else happened. But Eichmann still ordered his driver to get out and walk the rest of the way. Many, many kilometers—

How many, a hundred?

Not a hundred. But it was dark, it was winter, everything was covered in snow. The man nearly froze marching home. Eichmann didn't care. In the end the driver got sacked, not because he'd fallen asleep but because he stole a toilet seat from Eichmann's building. Dismantled it and took it away.

Why would he do that?

I don't know, Ben. Eichmann just said he dismantled it and took it away.

```
The physical extermination of the victims
was a single, all-encompassing action,
based on a single, all-encompassing order.
It cannot be divided up into individual
acts based on responsibilities. Regardless
of where a person entered the black river,
they were carried along to the mouth. The
main task of the accused, say the judges,
was not to procure railway carriages but
to procure victims to fill the carriages.
Each railway train filled with a thousand
```

people whom the accused sent to a place
of extermination, means he took part in a
thousand murders. Because this murderous
act forms a whole, the responsibility of
the co-perpetrators is equal to that of the
main perpetrators, that of those who carried out the crimes equal to that of those
who gave the orders. The accused is guilty
on all counts.

After the verdict is read, the accused is
permitted to give his closing statement. He
rises. Now, perhaps for the first time, people notice his broad shoulders.

His tone is sharp, his sentences, unusu-
ally for him, are short. In my hope for
justice I am disappointed, he says. I cannot accept this guilty verdict. He understands that the people of the victims
demand atonement for everything that was
done to them. But the crimes were not committed on his will. My wrongdoing is my
obedience, he says. I am not the monster
I am made out to be. I am the victim of a
fallacy.

On the following day, the court pro-
nounces the sentence. The accused stands
to attention. The accused is sentenced to
death.

Demons

Death remains strangely far away. The
condemned man spends as little time considering his own end as the millions of
deaths that cling to him, that should
mar his body, his face, beyond recognition. Nothing. Just a man, medium height,
mid-fifties. Dark blue suit, white shirt,
blue striped tie.

The sentence does not touch him either; it
is as though somehow it were lost between
the judges' chairs and the glass box.

If the sentence had not been spoken, but
had been presented in writing, Nagar would
have had to hand it over to the accused;
he is an extension of his arm within the
courtroom. Stand up, climb the steps up to
the judges' table, take the note from the
chair, climb down the steps, walk to the
glass box, hand the note to the accused, sit
down. Nagar would not have been able to do
this, he can feel it. Each step toward the
glass box would have taken him further away
from the accused. There is a gap that has
not closed. No one has penetrated the inner-
most depths of this person. People stand
before the wall of his castle, take aim
from there, even fire, but the space behind

those walls—the yards, the chambers, the
last room—remains unconquered.

Something is waiting there still.

The accused is guilty on all counts.

I am the victim of a fallacy.

The accused is sentenced to death.

This is a juristic death, a mere
possibility—no one knows if the sentence
can be carried out. Will the condemned man
be hanged, like the other German perpetrators in Nuremberg? A rumor passes around
the guards that he will be sold abroad.
Exorbitant sums are named; he is worth
these sums because he is the only one who
knows where the alleged treasure of the
fallen Reich is located. As soon as the war
ended, he singlehandedly moved it across
the Alps in an armored snow plow. The name
Blaa-Alm is heard, there was a cabin there,
the sentenced man was going to shoot the
landlord but he did not take his pistol out
of its holster; instead, he placed a bottle
of schnapps on the table and drank with the
landlord until he passed out. Nagar's colleagues crack their jokes, but he does not
join in their laughter.

The commander told him that every company
for which the accused has worked since the
war has declared bankruptcy. Nagar cannot

shake this thought from his mind, it
makes him feel uneasy. He sees the accused
working—apparently, he had started off as
a lumberjack—he sees the trees falling, sees
the axe, the sweat on his forehead, feels
the drive, the commitment this man takes to
work. That is not disconcerting. What is
disconcerting is the chain of bankruptcies.
Like an infection that spreads through contact. No one is immune.

The day after the sentence is given is
Nagar's day off. The breakfast table is
covered with newspapers, Nagar pushes them
aside, he does not want to read anything.
His wife, Ora, on the other hand, is eager
to read them; from the very first day she
has followed the trial in the media. All
the newspapers she has bought are piling up
in the shed.

Nagar is going to burn them, he does not
want an archive, does not need any commentary or printed pictures. He already has
too many in his head. He pushes his scrambled egg around his plate morosely. Picks
an olive out of the salad in front of Ora.
And then another.

Listen, says Ora, who has opened the evening newspaper. Immediately after the sentence there was a telephone survey. What
should they do with the condemned man? Exe-

cute him, not execute him? A third of the
participants are in favor of carrying out
the sentence, either here in this country or
there where the camps are that the condemned
man supplied with his transports. The vast
majority, however, want to keep the condemned man alive; if it were up to them, he
would be damned to a life of forced labor.
The same was said by an Italian poet and
chemist, himself a victim, in verse:

> Oh son of death, we do not wish you
> death.
> May you live longer than anyone
> ever lived.
> May you live sleepless five million
> nights.

Nagar is happy that no one asked him. He
would not have known how to respond. Neither does he know how to respond to the
gloomy prophecy that Ora finds in the edi-
torial of the second newspaper: Now, only
now our demon dance begins. He simply
shrugs his shoulders.

Ora continues reading aloud, Nagar listens with only half an ear. They had
expected the death sentence . . . there
was no other choice . . . the defense will
start an appeal . . . Supreme Court . . .

```
three to four months . . . legal options
exhausted . . . state president. People
expect an appeal for mercy, but also that
the condemned man could be prepared to die.
Then he must be killed. But by whom? There
are no executioners in the country of the
victims.
   Nagar stands up, they are expecting
friends for lunch; he goes into the yard
where he keeps chickens in a small coop,
reaches for one of the hens, takes it into
the shed, lays it on the stained workbench,
takes a knife with a nicked blade, and cuts
off its head.
```

I wait for protest at this point, but the Nagar in my head simply raises his hands, to explain, to apologize. I wasn't a shochet back then, you see. What did I know about knives? I grew up with chickens; we even kept chickens in Sanaa, when my parents were alive. You feed chickens, slaughter them, pluck them, I knew all that. We'd use any old knife, cut off their heads. I was such a fool. You are permitted to kill, so it is written, but only in accordance with the law.

```
The animal twitches, its legs kick out, dig
into Nagar's lower arm. Now, only now the
demon dance begins? Nagar shakes his head,
waits for the twitching to stop. Then he
begins to pluck the chicken.
```

Whoever Rides the Tiger

The prisoner writes. He wrote while waiting
for his sentence, and now that it has been
delivered he carries on writing. So much to
say. So much still to explain.

He is happy that the guard, this strange,
small man, leaves him in peace. There are
already enough interruptions. The medical
exams are particularly arduous. The doctor now comes twice a day, as though they
are all afraid that his heart could fail
at any minute. Absurdity. Death does not
frighten him. It is only time he is lack-
ing, he needs time to tell it how it really
is, he barely got to talk in court, they
always had to wait for the translations and
they always cut him off, for sixty days of
proceedings he just had to sit there and
listen to the prosecution's witnesses. The
victims, the victims. Yes, yes. Was that
it now?

The victims had been given enough time
to talk, to give vague recollections, to
lie brazenly, protected by their suffering.
They suffered, sure. Suffered terribly. But
he, too, is a victim! A victim of his obedience, of his loyalty to his oath, a victim of the speed at which his superiors and
employees changed their stories, those who

pinned everything on him after the war to
save their own soft skins. As though he had
run the Reich, as though he alone had dealt
with five or six or however many million
enemies of the Reich. Absurdity, insanity,
against which he had to defend himself—I
had to follow orders, I would never have
had the authority to act on my own initia-
tive, even when carrying out the evictions.
I had to present all matters to the head
of department IV for a decision and ask
for instructions. I could only do what my
department head ordered me to do.

The documents provided by the prosecution
prove this. I had to learn during the trial
that there are countless documents that
bear the seal of my department and my signature, but always and everywhere before my
name come the words "representative" or "on
behalf of." And when it says I, I instruct
and so on, that is just official German
language, the use of the first person does
not mean anything. "I" means only the competent authority, the one giving the order.

Of course, when someone takes out a single
document and plays it as the trump card,
as the attorney general did, then the whole
matter is turned on its head. You must consider the whole page in your hand. Then
things look very different. If you read

all the documents in chronological order,
everything looks different. Then it is
clear that IV B 4 was not involved at all
in these matters, I want to call them the
leading command processes. It was ordered
and so it was carried out. I had to obey.

And I did obey; I always carried out every
order I received, and I am still proud of
that today, because I fulfilled my oath.
The oath of allegiance is the highest duty
that can be given to a person, higher than
any so-called morals. Whoever fulfils
this duty ties themselves to their ances-
tral people and blood and must defend this
to enable the entire community to live.
These thoughts led me to subordinate myself
and to obey. Not as a stubborn receiver of
orders—that would have made me an idiot—I
shared these thoughts, I was an ideal-
ist. I came up with ideas, felt the joy in
creating something, and privately dedi-
cated myself further to this outside of my
working hours. But when I presented these
ideas to my department head he just smiled
thinly, as if to say: Yes, very good, but I
can't do anything with that. And then I was
dismissed. I might as well have explained
it to his wastepaper basket. It was the same
throughout the years I spent trying to pro-
cure territory and land for the victims.

I wanted a humane separation, but all my
ideas were burned and smashed to pieces,
whether it was the project in Nisko on the
river San or the planned relocation to Mad-
agascar. It was as though everything was
jinxed. Whatever I planned and wanted and
did and wanted to do, fate somehow got in
the way and put a wrench in the works.

It was no different with the transports.
In general, the whole matter proceeded with
a great deal of hope; in the beginning the
trains ran and people could say it was a
matter of glory, but then there were stop-
pages that often lasted for several weeks.
We faced problem after problem, everyone
possible got in the way, so many people
stuck their oars in from outside or from
within that I had no idea what was happening anymore. Every authority felt they
needed to get involved, and in the end it
all went wrong.

IV B 4 battles with the Reich Transport
Ministry for transport materials, wins the
battle, the transport is approved despite
all the resistance, and then the bureaucratic machine stalls, there are no victims because there is too much red tape. A
thousand victims are needed for the transport to run, there are only one hundred
and fifty in total, the local commander

does not feel able to come up with replace-
ments at such short notice, the train is
canceled. Again and again, it happened
that way.

I was always in favor of the political
solution, that was my field from the very
start, which I plowed together with leading representatives of the victims. When the
chief of the security police summoned me
to him one day, said a few words, and then
announced: The Führer has ordered the physical extermination of the victims, everything started to sway. I was done. I had
never thought it would come to such a violent solution. But whoever rides the tiger
is no longer able to climb down; he grabs
hold of the fur, like a small child, and
presses his head into the beast's neck.

I had nothing to do with the gas. If a
camp commander says he spoke to me about
the gas trials and we chose the method
together, that is a blatant lie. I played
absolutely no part in this matter, I had
no role at all, and I also had no power. I
knew the cardboard circles were being used
to kill, I cannot deny that, the camp commander showed them to me during a visit,
but IV B 4 was not part of this in any way.
When I discovered that my permanent representative had become involved with the gas

affairs, that he had somehow found a different way to get hold of the gas, we had
a big disagreement. Why are you getting
mixed up with the gas, I asked him, it's
got nothing to do with me. IV B 4 was not
involved with the gas, we could not give
any orders, we could not stop anything. We
had to deliver the transports in accordance
with our timetable, and that is where our
responsibilities ended.

But that is how it goes. Those who would
have been able to explain what happened are
either dead or have passed the matter on in
an attempt to exonerate themselves. And now
they are stamping my name on everything
that refers to what was done to the people
of the victims. So it was, and so it will
probably remain. I maintain today that the
entire human coexistence, at least in the
last two thousand years—but surely before
that, too—is one big and violent symphony
of lies and betrayal. People want someone
to blame, not an explanation; they found
their culprit, they kidnapped me, sneaked me
into this country, the country of the victims, where they prosecuted me and sentenced
me. Complicity, responsibility as one of
the main perpetrators, the public heard the
sentence, the cameras sent this fallacy out
into the world. It is the greatest consola-

tion for me: The dogs always bite those who come last.

I am not stupid enough to believe that I could fight it. The die is long since cast. But one day it will be history that will judge, not the people of the victims. Historians from all faiths and peoples will study the trial down to the very smallest detail, for the next fifty years and more. And depending on the spirit of the times it will be seen in different ways. Perhaps students will discuss it for more than fifty years. After all, it is complicated and confusing. There is so much material, I would be interested to read all the dissertations and theses written about my trial over the next hundred years. The truth about me will only be revealed some decades from now. A library of books will first spin legends about me. Until the web becomes weak and the spider shrivels up from a lack of fresh sustenance. But life is eternal; a new spider will start spinning the web of truth.

They cannot kill me in this country. There is no end for me, just as there is no nothingness.

I wrote all through the night, hounded and beaten by this voice, which grew louder and louder as I wrote, which separated each sentence as if it were an entity meant to quiver, sound, and shatter, a cacophony—and yet, with the last word complete, it was a composition after all.

```
There is no end for me,
just as there is
no nothingness.
```

I had fallen asleep at my desk, completely exhausted, and only woke up when Ben knocked on the door. My limbs ached. He frowned when he saw me, headed into the kitchen, made coffee, got me something to eat. I ate although I didn't feel like it and drank the coffee which was too strong.

Ben went to my desk, placed his large hands on the surface, stared at the pages I had filled with writing. Then he took one of them, went to the window, and started to read. At first, he mumbled to himself, then he started to read aloud, like an eager schoolboy, in his typical flat-sounding Ben-voice; wrong, it sounded all wrong, I couldn't stand it. Give that back! I demanded. Give it to me. I'll read! Astonished and baffled, he gave me the page. And I read.

Barked the sentences the way they have to be barked, hardened the beginning of each word, rolled my r's like Hitler, added the pauses after each conjunction so typical of Eichmann's speech, made periods sound like exclamation marks, kept time with the palm of my hand on the table.

```
It was ordered and—and so it was
 carried out!
I had to obey!
And—I did obey!
I always carried out every order I
 received,
and—I am still proud of that today!
Because—I fulfilled my oath!
```

Ben paced around the room while I read. Suddenly he stopped and leaned over me, looking angry. What are you writing, Moshe? What are you writing?

I didn't understand the question.

You are writing like Eichmann!

That is Eichmann, Ben! His words! I didn't invent them, I wrote them down.

Groaning, Ben straightened up, lashed out, sent the coffee mug flying. What?

Yes, Ben. That's Eichmann's voice. Listen:

```
A thousand victims are needed for the
transport to run! There are only one hun-
dred and fifty in total! The local com-
mander does not feel able to come up with
replacements at such short notice! The
train—is canceled!
 Again and again, it happened that way.
 Again and again!
 Again and again and again, it happened
that way!
```

```
I was always in favor of the political
solution—
```

Stop it! I don't recognize you, Moshe. I don't recognize you anymore.

```
I had nothing to do with the gas!
  If—a camp commander says—
```

Stop it, Moshe, stop it! You're a Jew, how can you give that monster a voice! I'm a Jew, how can you read to me like him!

Because he is a voice! Eichmann is a voice, Ben. I want all voices to have their say.

Ben doesn't understand. How could he, anyway? Like a stranger, he pushed me to the meeting place, pushed a stranger in front of him. The tension between us was palpable. Nagar, who was already there waiting, noticed it at once. Instead of greeting us, he started to hum, looked from one of us to the other and hummed more loudly when Ben avoided his gaze, leapt up and walked over to the fire.

Have you been arguing? he asked, when Ben came back.

Moshe is making Eichmann speak!

So am I, Ben. I'm telling you what Eichmann said, too.

I know, but Moshe makes him—he makes him appear. Lets him tell his lies! Eichmann is dead. We are Jews. We don't need to hear him anymore!

Did you know that Eichmann recited the Shema Yisrael?

What? What did he do?

He said our prayer, Ben. When they caught him, outside his house in Argentina—they'd been waiting for him, you know, he took the bus home from work every evening, they waited until the bus was gone, drew up beside him, one of them threw open the door while the other one dragged him into the car. They tied him up and gagged him and put on a sleeping mask—

What?

If you want to sleep and it's too light outside—

I know what a sleeping mask is, Shalom. Why, is what I'm asking.

So he couldn't see where they were going!

But it was dark!

They drove through town, it was light enough!

Okay, okay. A sleeping mask. Eichmann was wearing a mask.

The men from Mossad drove him through town to their hideout. In the hideout, it was a house they'd rented, he was put on a bed and they tied his feet to the bed frame. Then they undressed him and put him in a pair of pajamas—

How could they do that? Weren't his feet tied to the frame?

They untied him, and then they tied him up again.

And the sleeping mask?

Will you let me tell you, Ben! You know I'm telling the truth. Something that really happened. One of them, he was called Kenet, stood in front of Eichmann with a list. He read out loud: How tall are you? What size clothes? What size shoes?

Shalom—

They wanted to know if it was him, Ben! Imagine if they'd got the wrong man! Eichmann gave all the right answers. What's your party membership number? Eichmann told them the number. What's your name? Ricardo Klement, Eichmann said. Are the scars on your chest from an accident during the war? He said yes. What's your name? Kenet asks for the second time. Otto Henninger, Eichmann says. Kenet looks at the list and reads out two numbers. Are these your SS numbers? *Jawohl.* So, what is your name? My name is Adolf Eichmann, he says. Then everything was clear.

So? What's with the Shema Yisrael?

Hang on, Ben. So they knew they'd caught the right man. Everyone could relax a bit. Eichmann, too. He asked for a glass of red wine and they gave him one. He drank it and looked at them all one after the other. There were four agents. I knew who you were right away, he told them. I can speak Hebrew, you see: *Shema Yisrael, Adonai Elohenu, Adonai Echad. Baruch shem—*

I'd have grabbed him by the neck, I'd have shoved the words down his filthy German throat so that he choked on them! Miserable bastard!

You can't stop Eichmann, Ben! Nobody can. When they took him to the hideout he didn't say anything at first—

You just told us that he answered their questions and recited the Shema Yisrael!

They dragged him to the hideout, tied him to the bed, stripped him, then they took off the mask—he was in shock, you see? When you are shocked—

You start to pray? Your victims' prayer?

You can't control yourself! But then—he'd had some wine, he was Eichmann once more. And he didn't say anything else. Not a word. He turned over and stared at the wall and refused to respond to anything. There was just one of them, someone called Aharoni, he liked him somehow. When Aharoni came, Eichmann turned around and looked at him. Perhaps he reminded him of someone.

Aharoni would start to ask him questions. Wanted to know this and that. Aharoni asked him a question and Eichmann looked at him and said nothing. And it went on like that, quietly. Because Aharoni stayed calm, Eichmann trusted him. And suddenly he started to speak and didn't stop. Aharoni wrote down every word, whole notebooks filled with notes.

When Eichmann got to Israel, in the prison in Yagur, he was questioned some more, by a captain, a very polite man: Please, Herr Eichmann, he'd say, do have a cigarette, Herr Eichmann, may I repeat my question, Herr Eichmann. So Eichmann trusted him, too. And was willing to talk, for months on end. Everything was recorded on tape and copied out, thousands of pages. He had no one to talk to in his cell in Ramla. None of us guards could speak German, but he'd been given pencils and paper so that he could write. And he wrote. Wouldn't stop writing. The lights were never turned off, they were left on night and day, that's what the rules said. If they hadn't ordered him to go to bed, he would never have stopped writing. Then the trial started and he talked even more. And when he had to listen, to the witnesses talking, or when the prosecutor spoke, he filled his notebooks with writing. When they took him back to his cell in the evenings, what do you think? He sat down and wrote some more! Before the verdict: He wrote! After the verdict: He wrote! He'd often grimace when they came to take him to the visiting room, if his lawyer or someone else was waiting to see him. Because he had to put down the pencil then, you see, he didn't like that. He didn't want any visitors, he wanted to write.

Why?

I don't know. Maybe he thought that was how he could stay alive. That they can't kill him if he writes.

Why not?

Because whatever he wrote would be read, Ben. He knew things that no one else knew. And everything he wrote was kept, too! Every page landed on the prison director's desk, and he locked them all in his safe.

Oh, yes. Eichmann wrote. Six, seven, eight thousand pages. And Moshe allowed him to write, copied his words, spoke in his voice. I hope I didn't write off a friendship. A friendship based on the premise of shared beliefs and ideas about what it means to be Jewish, or to live in this country and deal with our past. Ben trusted me without knowing my circumstances. My background, my burden—he has no more idea than Nagar does. This has to stop. I've got to tell them.

But where? Where is there room for Moshe's story? The compound is Nagar's territory: I know his Eichmann will not tolerate anyone else. No, they have to sit here, facing me; this is where I can and should tell my story. But will Nagar come? He keeps to four or five familiar paths, and can hardly manage those, he tackles them, scared, driven, hounded by Eichmann, who's on his tail.

I need to tell you a story, Ben, I said, when he came to pick me up. You and Nagar. An Eichmann story you've not heard before. One no one has ever heard. Bring Nagar here. Take him by the hand, blindfold him if need be, let him sing and hum all the way, but bring him to me.

Now here they are, sitting on my small sofa while I sit opposite in my wheelchair. They are like brothers jostling one another, wearing the same clothes—black jacket, black trousers, white shirt, black kippah—both equally ill at ease. Everything is different here; no grubby wooden table in front of us, no folding chairs that will fit one of them like a glove and always be too small for the other, no earthen floor to keep us grounded. No pens, no chickens, geese, or sheep, no nail to hang up an apron or smock. No one has made tea, no one has cut up any pears. Only the first sentence is familiar. Just this once I say it myself.

Let me tell you a story. It begins in Germany.

Did I say it begins in Germany? It begins German, is what I should have said. My story is decisively German in the beginning, and ends helplessly so. No, it doesn't even end—there isn't an ending, yet.

It begins in Germany, in 1935, when the Nazis passed their so-called race laws. The Reich citizenship law. The law to protect German blood and honor. The law to protect the pure bloodline of the German people. Decrees written to supplement these laws determined what it meant to be German.

A history lesson! If Ben were not wedged in next to Nagar, who is unsure what to do with his hands, who tugs at his beard as I speak and plays with his fingers, this outburst would surely come. You're giving us a history lesson, Moshe! Why do we have to listen to this? Why do we have to know how German the Nazis wanted to be?

What do you say, Ben? Should I start like this: Oberscharführer Schneider was bent on killing himself? Would that make sense? You see! You have to know Schneider's reasons, have to understand how things suddenly came crashing down around this man.

But Ben isn't protesting! He's sitting quietly, staring at the floor. He even copes with my pauses.

So back to the race laws: Decrees defined what it meant to be German. For the Nazis, being German was a consequence of not being Jewish. People who are German, the decrees said, have neither Jewish parents nor Jewish grandparents. This had to be proved. To be a citizen of the Reich you had to produce seven birth certificates; your own, and those of your parents and your four grandparents. And all their marriage certificates. If one of the grandparents was Jewish, the person was classed as a quarter Jew or a Mischling of the second degree, with two Jewish grandparents they were a half Jew or a Mischling of the first degree, with three Jewish grandparents they were a full Jew. That's how it was.

Members of the SS, like Eichmann, were required to be even more German than ordinary citizens of the Reich. They had to trace their family tree back to the early eighteenth century. Not a single ancestor was allowed to be a Jew. When this requirement came into force, two or three years after the race laws, the SS had already been around for a while. And until then, no one had asked for a pedigree. The men took the oath, swore allegiance to the Führer and to the people, and joined the black league. Now, suddenly, there were divides here, too. Many SS men discovered that they weren't as German as required. As they compiled their ancestries, they stumbled across Jewish ancestors they'd known nothing about, or who hadn't concerned them because it had never mattered before. But it did now. Suddenly, a faded birth or marriage certificate decided everything.

One of Eichmann's men, Oberscharführer Giselher Schneider, was found to have Jewish ancestors. In fact, Schneider was a full Jew, non-German from tip to toe. In these cases, the men who failed to prove their own ancestry could expect no more than a final handshake from their old comrades. They were left in a void. They were no longer what they wanted to be and had always believed themselves to be, and they neither wanted, nor were they allowed to be what they were. Many of them fled, disappeared without a trace, for others the only way out was to shoot themselves. Schneider was one of these. But that's not what happened.

Eichmann liked Schneider, he valued him as an employee and as a person. They had also played music together, in the Rothschild Quartet, named after the Palais where Eichmann's department was based. Eichmann had even allowed Schneider to play first violin, as the Oberscharführer was a far better musician than he was. And now this man was a Jew. A full Jew. Could they ignore this, cross it out? Eichmann couldn't do that, it went against his honor. He summoned Schneider, to talk about his future. Schneider stood to attention. It's hard luck, Sturmbannführer! he said. We had a good time, but now it's over, no one can change that. What will you do now? Eichmann asked. My heart is German, Schneider replied, but my blood belies that. I'm going to kill myself.

Eichmann looked at him, calmly, searchingly. He liked the man, even now. Our honor means loyalty, comrade Schneider. To the people and the Führer. You can keep this honor. How, Sturmbannführer? Schneider asked. You must leave the Reich, that is clear, Eichmann said. Go to a country where this—these matters, are of no importance. Marry a German woman, father sons, who will in turn marry German women. In just a few generations the Schneiders' blood will be pure. And your descendants can return to the Reich, as Germans.

Schneider listened without moving, growing increasingly pale with every word. To be thrown from heaven to hell and then shown a way back, that was too much for him. Eichmann urged him to sit down, gave him a Cognac, offered him a cigarette. Schneider drank, Schneider smoked, and gradually he calmed down. Will you do it, comrade? Eichmann asked. *Jawohl*, Sturmbannführer, Schneider said. They drank another Cognac, to loyalty, and discussed what Schneider was going to do. I could go to Switzerland, Schneider said. He had friends there. How will you support yourself? Eichmann asked. I could be a musician, form a dance band. Eichmann liked the idea. He gave Schneider money, he gave him a passport, he promised that Schneider would be able to cross the Swiss border without any trouble. As they were saying goodbye, Eichmann shook his former Oberscharführer's hand for a long time, refusing to let go. Father a son, comrade Schneider, he said. Father a son!

Schneider did what Eichmann had told him to do. He went to Switzerland, formed a dance band there, married a German, a Catholic girl from Constance, and together they had a son, whom he named Adolf, in honor of Eichmann.

Adolf Schneider had a Swiss passport, but he felt German. He was brought up that way. All his relatives lived in Germany, and it was always assumed that the Schneider family would return there one day. Almost every week, his father dreamt up a new plan about where he could work or where they would live. Then Adolf's mother became ill, so ill that a move was out of the question. Adolf's father was changed by his wife's illness. He became curt and distant, he hid in his office. He never played the violin at home now; when he got back from concerts, he left his instrument in its case.

One night, when Adolf was almost asleep, his father suddenly appeared in his bedroom. He turned on the light, sat down on the edge of the bed. I have to show you something, my boy, he said, and took a worn photo from his jacket pocket. It was a portrait of a man in uniform. His head seemed rather small under his large cap with the death's head on its black peak. The man had boyish features, a crooked nose and a soft, almost feminine mouth. But his expression was sharp, although his eyelids drooped oddly. Adolf felt as though he were being scrutinized as he looked at him.

Do you know who this is? The boy shook his head. This is Obersturmbannführer Adolf Eichmann, his father said. It is thanks to him that I have a son. It is thanks to him that I have you. And he told Adolf his story. The boy listened sleepily, and when his father had finished, simply asked: So we're Jews? Not Germans? Did you not understand, Adolf? I'm a Jew, you're not! You're a half Jew, a Mischling. Your children will be quarter Jews. And their children, your grandchildren, my great-grandchildren, will be Germans. True Germans, Adolf. Like Obersturmbannführer Eichmann.

I can still feel his hand in mine, son, he said in a gruff voice. Then he leaned down and hugged his son, holding him for a long time. You must go back, Adolf, promise me. Back to Germany.

His father's emotions moved the boy more than his revelation. Adolf wasn't exactly pleased about being half German all of a sudden and the half Jewish part sounded a bit unpleasant somehow, but he wasn't too deeply affected. *Jew, Jewish*, these words meant nothing to him. He knew nothing about anti-Semitism or the hatred of the Jews. And he didn't know who this Eichmann was, either. He found that out a few years later, in a history lesson. His teacher, a strict man with a stoop, stood in front of the class, took off his jacket, rolled up a shirt sleeve, and showed them the number that was tattooed on his arm. Then he told them about Auschwitz, explained about the persecution of the Jews, the transportation of the Jews. Spat out names like poisonous morsels: Himmler, Heydrich, Höss. And Eichmann. Eichmann, again and again. Adolf listened as though the teacher meant him. He started to sweat; he wanted to run, out of the classroom, away from this unrelenting man with the number on his arm, away from Eichmann, Eichmann, Eichmann. The teacher knows, he thought. He knows Father's story, my story. And at the end of the class, he will reveal it all, point at me: Him. Adolf! Named after Eichmann.

Of course, the teacher didn't do that, but from that day on, Adolf felt like a stranger in his class. As if he didn't belong there anymore. Just his luck. Where did he belong? To the Jews, the victims? Or to the Germans, the perpetrators? He carried both inside him, he persecuted and was persecuted; driven by Eichmann, he persecuted the Jewish Adolf, and driven by his father's ancestors and six million victims, he persecuted the German Adolf. He turned on himself, going around in ever-decreasing circles until there was no ground beneath his feet, nowhere for him to stand. He drifted, floundering as though caught in a storm, helpless against the forces that tore at him: Eichmann, hurrying toward him in his black uniform, his father, naked with his death's head cap beside him on the floor. Here, Jews were forced into carriages, there, Eichmann shook a Jew's hand; here, his teacher rolled up his sleeve, there, his father hugged him. How could he live like that? Should he exterminate the German within him because that part of him was doomed, a fatal legacy? Should he hate the Jew within him because he owed it to his father, who had brought him into the world? His father, who belonged to the perpetrators, who worked with Eichmann, for Eichmann, to exterminate his own people. This man was inconceivable, he countermanded himself and should never have existed. This man had Eichmann

to thank for his son. And he had continued Eichmann's work in
him, Adolf Schneider! Because what was this act of mercy ordered
by Eichmann other than a further step toward exterminating the
Jews? Didn't he spill his Jewish seed in a German womb so that
the Jewishness, the impurity, would be halved, then quartered in
the next generation and would eventually disappear, fading like
smoke blown away in the wind? The Shoah was within him. And
he, Adolf, was the tool!

His confusion turned to anger, anger at Eichmann and his dev-
ilish duplicity, anger at his father, who had allowed himself to be
used, who used his son, and wanted to use his son's sons and their
sons after them.

It was a curse. And in that instant, Adolf knew how it could be
lifted. He would preserve what Eichmann and his father wanted to
destroy, would begin what they wanted to end: He would become
a Jew. The thought came with a tremendous feeling of liberation.
Become a Jew.

He knew almost nothing about Judaism. So he sat in the library
after school and read. In his rigorous way, he started with the
Old Testament. Then he read a three-volume history of Judaism, a book about the Jewish festivals, and finally Theodor Herzl's
The Jewish State. And that was just the beginning. He needed to
learn Hebrew, and taught himself as best he could. He did hardly
anything for school, just scraped a pass in his final exams, but he
didn't care. He'd made up his mind.

One evening, Adolf took his courage in both hands and
knocked on the door of his father's study. He found him sitting in
front of a bottle of Cognac, tired, lonely, gray. I'm going to Israel,
Father, Adolf said. I'm going to be a Jew like you. His father raised
his head and looked at him. His eyes hardened, but Adolf held his

stare. His father stood up, went to his desk, took something out from among his papers, held it out to Adolf. The photo he had shown him once before. Eichmann, wearing an SS uniform. You will not betray him, his father said. And you will not betray me. You will go to Germany! Horrified, Adolf snatched the photo, tore it to pieces, and let the scraps fall to the floor. His father leapt up and struck him in the face. Adolf staggered backward, tears springing to his eyes. You're the traitor! he shouted. It's you! And then he confronted him with everything that had been stewing inside him since the day his teacher had revealed who Eichmann was.

His father turned pale. He stared fixedly past his son at the wall, and as Adolf finally fell silent he replied with a single word: Lies.

The next day, his father kicked him out of the house. Adolf moved in with a friend, found work as an unskilled laborer, saved money, and when he had enough, he packed his suitcase, took his violin, and left for Israel. He changed his first name, called himself Moshe, worked in a kibbutz, became a musician and formed a string quartet, for which he also wrote music. He lived as a Jew, saw himself as a Jew. A part of the kingdom of priests as all Jews should be. Yet he felt different from the others. Different, because he was a Jew out of protest.

It's you?

The two men on the sofa had remained so silent throughout my story that I almost thought I'd asked the question myself. But it was Ben. His question was painfully matter of fact, with no hint of horror, shock, or empathy—the question sounded as though he were simply confirming a casual assumption.

I am no Nagar. I lack the warmth, the indulgence of his

storytelling that can take a joke, enjoys diversions, and calmly puts up with disbelief. My story is too real for that. Too German.

It's you?

Yes. It's me, Ben. I am Adolf Schneider. Or I was. I cut off my roots all those years ago. My mother was already dead when I came to Israel, my father no longer existed in my eyes, I broke off all contact with my family. My background was erased, including Eichmann.

Then came May 23, 1960, the day David Ben-Gurion declared to the Knesset: We've captured Eichmann. The news hit me like a shock. I had always assumed he was dead, had taken poison like Himmler or Göring, shot himself like Günther, his ever-faithful deputy, or had died in the last days of the war like Heinrich Müller, his superior in department IV. And now he was here, in the country I had chosen! As if he had come to get me. Me, the man who was only alive because of him, whose existence he had commanded so that a tainted tree could bear good fruit once more, and who had turned traitor to his cause, the German cause.

Eichmann was alive, he was in Israel. Nothing could change that. This time he wasn't just a photo I could tear to pieces. This time he was here in the flesh. I had to face him. I had to see, grasp, understand this man. You must swallow him, I thought, and you must digest him. Then you can flush him out, and he will leave your body for good.

I read every newspaper article that was written about him, compiled folders, bought books about the extermination—*The Final Solution* by Gerald Reitlinger, *The Third Reich and the Jews* by Poliakov and Wulf—and eagerly awaited the start of the trial, the moment I'd look this man in the eye.

On the first day of the trial I sat in the gallery, too far away to get a good view of Eichmann. So then I went a bit earlier every day until I was one of the first to arrive at the Beit Ha'am and got a place in the front row, as near to the glass box as possible. I studied Eichmann day after day, his tic, his posture, the way he spoke, his expression when he was listening. Above all, I watched his hands, which never stopped moving; large, yet strangely delicate hands, hands that seemed happiest leafing through a folder, hands that glided across the paper when Eichmann made a note of something, as though his pencil were a natural extension.

And I could never look at these hands without thinking of what my father said as he hugged me for the first, and I think only time in my life:

I can still feel his hand in mine, son.

His hand. Eichmann's hand.

I can't go on. I never get any further than Eichmann's hand.

Neither of the men spoke, Ben, my old friend from kibbutz days, and Nagar, who is a friend now, too. No comfort, no condemnation. My gaze gropes through the silence that rings in my ears, past their faces, to the window, where everything is just as it was. The world didn't implode, but what was I expecting? The eversame roofs opposite are as ugly as ever, spotted with a mix of gray and black satellite dishes. Sponges that absorb everything, funnels into which anything that travels through the ether is poured, no matter how trivial or significant it might be. All of them—I never noticed before—are pointed toward my apartment.

Let me tell you a story.

Nagar has found his voice again. Maybe he just waited a

moment. Allowed a few minutes to pass after my last words, for courtesy's sake.

Eichmann had lucky hands, you said. Fine hands, you said, too. He deceived you, Moshe. He deceived everyone. Let me tell you a story.

Eichmann's hands, then. No words about Moshe and Moshe's father. Did Nagar listen to me? Did he understand who, what I am? Or had he been daydreaming, lost in thought during all my revelations, only snapping up the last few sentences on which to build his next story, unaffected like a machine? A narration machine, which can be fed with anything you like, out comes Eichmann. Nagar's Eichmann? I didn't care at that moment. I was even grateful that he had buried my story, Eichmann's Moshe, once more, covered it like a picture that didn't deserve a second or third glance.

When Eichmann came to Argentina, he met lots of old comrades again, you know. They had new names and new jobs now, but they were still Germans. Nazis. They had their own clubs, where they'd meet. If there was something important that needed to be discussed, they would meet at each other's homes. They were safer there, but it still wasn't secure. They could rely on their wives, but what about the children? If they said the wrong word to the neighbors, at school—

What do you mean, the wrong word?

Names, I mean names, Ben! When they were among themselves, they used their real names, of course. Eichmann was Eichmann, Mengele Mengele. And now think of Eichmann's sons running around telling everyone Mengele came to see us yesterday! That could never happen. There were secret agents lurking everywhere! So Eichmann took steps to protect himself. If a visitor was expected, he lined up his sons in a row. Pay attention, he said, we will be receiving visitors tonight, and you must not tell anyone about them, do you hear me? And then he boxed their ears. Whenever a Nazi came to visit, he slapped them in the face! Just so they knew what was going on.

And did that work?

What do you think? Eichmann's methods always worked.

During the trial, reporters sought out his eldest son and wanted to know who had visited them at home. The son said he couldn't remember any visitors, just his father hitting him. He could still feel that today, he said. Eichmann had—

Enough, Shalom. I think we should go now. Moshe looks tired.

No, wait, Ben. I want to finish the story.

Eichmann had tested this method of slapping people beforehand, in Austria, what is the name of the capital—

Vienna.

In Vienna, that's it. The Germans had disbanded the Jewish community and put the leaders in jail. Eichmann said that was all wrong. He needed the community, otherwise nothing would work. So the men were released. Eichmann talked to them and then he picked one of them, Dr. Löwenherz, a lawyer. You are in charge of the community now, he said. It is your responsibility. First of all, write down the names of all the Jews here in Vienna. But do not say a word to anyone. You understand? And then he slapped him in the face.

He was a real bastard.

He's evil, Ben. His hands are evil. Later on, at the trial, he told a different story. He said he'd asked Dr. Löwenherz a question and

Dr. Löwenherz had given him the wrong answer. Eichmann was so angry that he slapped him in what he called a moment of uncontrollable anger. Not a slap that would do any harm, he said, because I do not have the hands for that kind of work, just a tiny, little slap in the face. Though he regretted it later. He insists he apologized to Dr. Löwenherz officially, in uniform, in front of his men.

He deceived everyone. He hides his power. Anyone looking at his hands is supposed to think exactly what Moshe thought: What delicate hands, hands for files, not made for hitting. But he is so strong! On the inside of his arm, here, there was a code, numbers and letters. It started with IV B 4, Eichmann's department, followed by more letters and numbers and dashes. IV B 4a dash 2093 slash—I can't remember any more. That was his sign. The signal for the transport! Whenever a transport of Jews was ready anywhere, Eichmann arrived, rolled up his sleeve, and pressed his arm against the carriages. He branded them with his arm: IV B 4a dash 2093—

You mean he marked the carriages? With chalk?

With his arm! He doesn't need any chalk. He—it was a transmission.

Eichmann the conjurer.

It was the sign, Ben. He was the master. His arm had power. As soon as all the carriages were marked, the trains departed. No one could stop them! They never turned back a train, so Eichmann said. He's proud of that. Later, after the war, he used cigarettes to burn away the sign. I saw the scar; it runs down the whole of his lower arm. But no one at the prison noticed.

Noticed the scar?

How strong he was. Always gentle, always polite—please, if I could just ask, *gracias*, *gracias*—he never raised his voice, never raised a hand to any of us. We didn't have any weapons. None of the guards were allowed to carry weapons. What would have happened if Eichmann had attacked me in the cell? With his bare hands? The colleague on the other side of the door wouldn't have been able to help me. He had the keys, of course, but the doors could only be opened from the inside. Eichmann could have trapped me like a mouse. But he didn't do anything. Ever. I thought they must have caught a saint.

Late Shift

Once again, Nagar is to share the prisoner's night. A night without darkness; for
twenty-four hours, the light remains on in
the cell, which is still full of shadows,
although the prisoner sleeps like a baby,
silently, free of anxiety, free of guilt.
His sleep is a lie which Nagar must share.

He buttons up his uniform jacket with
a deep sigh. Ora watches him, revealing
through her smile and her small, encourag-
ing gestures that she does not know what is
troubling her husband. As far as he is concerned, that is for the best.

When Nagar enters the cell two hours later
the prisoner checks the time, lays down his
pencil, and takes off his watch. He stands
up, pushes the chair under the table, goes
over to the bed. The usual reaching under
the blanket, the few paces back to the
table. His movements are smooth, his posture perfect. He lays the pajamas, precisely
folded as always, on the table, next to the
pages he has written that day; as though
able to extend time he strokes the thin
cotton, the buttons, straightens the collar that was already straight, takes off
his glasses, turns to the wall, removes
his cardigan, his shirt, his vest. Nagar

closes his eyes to the naked back, presses
his eyelids shut, filters this pale white
through his eyelashes, this skin, no longer
touched by the sun, German skin, shimmering
so defenselessly, intangible.

Whose back is that? What does Nagar know?
He senses a person, a border, he thinks,
which needs to be secured.

The prisoner undoes his trousers. Nagar
fights the impulse to lower his head; he is
not allowed to look away, but he focuses on
the wall instead of the exposed body, out of
modesty, a forbidden solidarity between men.
Straightens his lower back with an exagger-
ated movement while the prisoner slips on
his pajamas, sits down on the hard chair,
restless, until the other has settled under
the woolen blanket, face turned toward the
wall, as always, as though leaving everything behind him, cell and prison and
Nagar, his guard. As though the man could
command himself to fall asleep in just a
moment. This man can. His consciousness
obeys.

Nagar turns his head, looks over at his
colleague behind the cell door, nods to
him, returns to his guard position. The
now-complete silence in the room penetrates
him, in a way that is so familiar to him.
A silence that is timeless, that transcends

time. Time for thoughts of things beyond
work, time for questions that no lawyer
asks.

The prisoner sleeps almost silently, his
square shoulders rise and fall almost
imperceptibly. Confused, Nagar notices that
he is breathing in time with the prisoner;
he adjusts his own rhythm to match this
man's sleep, his peace.

Can such a man find peace?

In sleep, it is said, people wear no
masks. In sleep, people cannot check themselves, expressions are removed like a pair
of glasses or a shirt. What would Nagar
see if he walked the three steps over to the
bed, bent over the prisoner, as quietly as
possible, as far as his stoutness allowed?

Nagar remains seated. He does not trust
sleep and does not want to believe that the
prisoner, that familiar person, is a mask,
he is afraid of looking into the face of a
mass murderer, contorted with anger and the
thirst for revenge, he is even more afraid
of seeing calm features, a face that reveals
nothing other than devotion and fatigue.

Nagar remains seated. What is Ora doing
now? Reading newspapers? The child will
long since be sleeping, dreaming. Sometimes
he calls out in his sleep, to whom they do
not know. Nagar thinks about the fact that

the prisoner has sons, too, the youngest
just a few years older than his own. Stops
thinking. Little by little, his breathing falls back in line with the prisoner's.
Hours pass.

At some point he starts, there is a disturbance in the other room. Changing of
the guards. Nagar hears murmurs, stifled
laughter, they will have exchanged jokes
in the corridor, obscenities perhaps, or
more unbelievable facts about the prisoner's
life. Over the last few weeks, the chicken
story had been spread around. The prisoner,
they said, tried to make it as a poultry
farmer after the war. At first he had no
success at all, the animals ran wild, laid
their eggs where he could not find them,
and ignored his attempts to lure them out
by calling "chick, chick, chick." So he
built a small pen, locked the chickens in,
and trained them until he could order them
around by whistling. If he whistled with
two fingers, the chickens lined up in rank
and file. And they only laid their eggs in
the place he had marked out specially.

The key is passed through the door hatch.
Nagar stands up, tries to stop the chair
from creaking, he succeeds in this but the
key jolts in the lock, the bolt scratches
over the metal, the heavy door crunches on

the hinges. Everything is too loud. Someone is sleeping here! When the door finally
opens the murmuring outside stops, his colleague enters, too loudly, nods to him, and
because Nagar does not react, his colleague
takes the key out of his hand, grips his
arm, pushes him gently but firmly out of
the room.

Nagar feels as though he has been repri-
manded, is ashamed of the closeness between
himself and the prisoner, is ashamed that
he should feel ashamed.

Behind Glass

At the same time, twelve thousand kilometers away, a woman is boarding a passenger plane. It is her first ever flight.
In the large handbag that she keeps pressed
to her side lie the documents that she has
been sent, passport and visa, in a false
name. Instructed to avoid contact with the
other passengers, the woman closes her eyes
and surrenders herself to her plummeting
thoughts. She is allowed to stay for one
afternoon, one night. By the next morning she will already have left this foreign
country. When the plane lands she has to
wait for all the other passengers to dis-
embark. She is alone in the plane for a few
minutes before two officials come down the
aisle, stand in front of her, and one of the
two quietly says her name. She stands up,
the men escort her to a car. She remembers
nothing of the journey, barely looks out
of the window; she is not interested in the
people out there, the landscape, the houses
that pass by.

Nagar sits in the cell, both hands resting on his thighs. The prisoner sits opposite him at the table and does what he has
spent the last few weeks doing. He writes.
Nagar hears the door in the hall, then

voices, someone gives an order that the colleague passes on through the barred hatch:
Aquarium.

That means they must go to the meeting room. Since the sentence was given the
guards have begun passing on the prison
director's orders to each other in a casual
way, as if form no longer matters. The meeting room is a separate area from the hall,
it measures two by three meters wide and is
divided into two bulletproof, soundproof
chambers by a piece of solid glass reaching all the way up to the ceiling. Microphones and headphones sit on the narrow
tables that have been fixed to both sides of
the wooden base. Unless the intercom system
is switched on, visitors and prisoners are
unable to communicate, silent as the grave.

As Nagar leads the prisoner into the room,
the afternoon light falls through the narrow ventilation shaft on the back wall, it
scatters over the glass and is reflected
as if by a mirror. Only a silhouette looms
behind the glass. The prisoner starts,
stands still, stares. Is he disobeying the
order? No—when he feels Nagar's hand on
his shoulder he walks the two steps to the
glass wall. Now it is clear: The visitor is
a woman, in a plain dark dress, small and
plump, a motherly type. Quickly, as though

trying to recover the lost moment, the
prisoner sits on his chair and places the
headphones on his head. As he moves closer
to the microphone and bends over it, words
fail him. For the first time since Nagar
has known him. Pity? Perhaps. Yes, indeed,
Nagar feels pity in this moment. Two years
of loneliness lie behind the prisoner, two
years under the scrutiny of official, at
most correct, often hostile eyes. Two years
without an unintentional, unthinking, tender touch. Two years without his wife, who
now sits opposite him, for who else could
this visitor be?

No one here knew she was coming, even the
prison director had only just heard about
her arrival. From Argentina. Two people,
two continents, oceans apart. Now she sits
opposite the prisoner, close enough to
touch. His desire for a handshake, a hug,
a kiss, even under the eyes of the guards,
must be overwhelming. But he cannot fulfill this desire. Her plane has crossed the
waters of the ocean, but here they sit up
straight as though before the pharaoh and
his chariot, become crystallized in the
middle of the glass that divides the room.
This time the glass hurts.

When the couple do eventually begin to
talk, Nagar studies the condemned man's

voice in order to try and follow the conversation. No officer tone like the one
he uses in the courtroom, just a regular
rise and fall—soft, calming, reassuring
sounds. The conditions are relatively good,
he seems to say, he is healthy and has not
given up hope for a change in his fate. If
he does say that then it must be for her,
thinks Nagar.

The woman nods and kneads the leather
strap of her handbag. After a while she
opens her bag, takes out a stack of photos.
A questioning glance over her shoulder, the
guards behind her have no objections. One
after the other, she holds the photos up to
the glass. Nagar bends down so he, too, can
see what she is showing him. A house with
a flat roof, half plastered, as if it is
still being built, a somewhat wild-looking
piece of land. Three young men, surely
the prisoner's sons. They look like their
father, Nagar thinks. Finally, a young boy.

He sits on a piece of wall sticking out
behind a wire mesh fence, which he is holding on to, looking through it at the pho-
tographer with wide eyes. In the background
is the house; the woman stands in front of
it, holds up a hand, perhaps as a greeting or to call the child back. Between the
fence and the house is a patch of deep ter-

rain filled with water, what looks like a
swamp, part of which has been drained. The
woman has to hold up the photo for a long
time. The prisoner studies it carefully.
He hardly recognizes his youngest son
anymore.

Toward the end of the visit the woman
turns around once again, asks something, gestures with her hands, points to
the trousers and the shoes of one of the
guards. It takes a while before the guard
understands, then he goes to the microphone, points at the prisoner's headphones,
at Nagar. The prisoner gets up, gives
Nagar the headphones, the guard repeats the
request: She wants to see her husband from
top to bottom, wants to be sure that his
trousers and his shoes are all right. For
a moment Nagar is not sure what to do, then
he pulls the chair back a bit, to the middle of the room. The prisoner has already
understood, he stands on the chair, laughing awkwardly. Lets her look at him from
head to toe. Sees the indignant look on his
wife's face when she notices the slippers
on his feet. Checked felt slippers, with a
zip. Of course, she had not expected boots,
the times of the Obersturmbannführer are
over, but slippers? Slippers are only worn
by men—if at all—in their own living room,

after work, not in public, where others can
see them. This is not his home, and this is
not the evening after work. Or perhaps it
is, thinks Nagar.

Perhaps his wife thinks the same. Nagar
sees she is crying now. She turns around
to hide her sobs. The prisoner has climbed
down from the chair and is standing in
front of the glass wall. His wife wipes
her eyes again, then she, too, stands up,
silently places her palm on the glass. She
must be hoping he would return the gesture,
must know that he will not do it.

See you soon, he says. He says it with
emphasis. Gives her the future she needs.

Ben says you're writing again, Moshe?

Yes.

What are you writing?

I've just written about the day Eichmann's wife came to the prison.

I saw her. The woman. I felt sorry for her.

Because her husband was going to die?

No, because Eichmann loved another woman.

One? You said he had lots of lovers, Shalom. The white lady, the young widow, the land owner, the cook.

I don't mean them, Ben. Not his mistresses. They meant nothing. I mean his true love. The desert princess.

Desert princess! True love! Are you telling fairy tales now? Have you heard about Eichmann's desert princess, Moshe? No? Moshe doesn't know the story either, Shalom. And he knows what Eichmann wrote.

Eichmann didn't write the story down, Ben. It was a personal affair. He only told me.

When?

I don't know. At some stage.

Where? In his cell?

No. Not in his cell.

Well, it can't have been when he was in the bathroom. He always turned on the tap. You wouldn't have heard a word.

Not in the prison. It was after that.

In your dreams, then?

This is a true story, Ben. It was after the war. Eichmann was living by himself, without his family—

In Argentina?

He calls it the district. It was in the desert. Eichmann lived alone, he had his horse with him, a white horse, but that was it. The district had been occupied, but when Eichmann got there, the soldiers were gone. He didn't meet anyone, no one alive, no one dead.

What about the princess?

If she was real.

What else could she be? A ghost?

I'm telling you. Eichmann rode through the desert from one fortress to the next. These were palaces the soldiers had built in a row like pearls on a string, each one a three-day ride from the next. Mighty houses, Eichmann says, forbidding and stately, with tall windows dulled by sand, and sand in the corridors and great halls, sand up to your ankles on every floor. I usually left the palaces—

You!

Eichmann!

Why did you say "I"?

Because I'm telling the story the way Eichmann did! These are his words. Usually, I left the palaces as soon as I had inspected them, he says, rode on again and slept out in the open, with all my senses attuned, the horse beside me and the cosmos above in perfect equilibrium like nothing on Earth.

But on that day, I got lost in the corridors, staircases, and wings of the building. It was a huge estate, hardly damaged, and in some of the rooms, I imagined I could still sense the breath of the occupiers, the officer taking off the coat and jacket I saw hanging on a hook, rubbing the sand out of his eyes as he sits down at the desk and stretches his legs out under the table. I had set up camp in the inner courtyard beside a well that had almost seemed to beckon to me. The deep, calm water mirrored a sky that I could not see above me, that was no longer there, that had never existed, perhaps. And as I undressed and washed, the woman came. All at once she stood there without making a sound, watching me with deep, dark eyes. She untied her hair and dried my body with her long dark tresses. She stayed with me all night. When the morning dawned, she disappeared.

She came back the next day, then failed to appear for several days, then she was there again, and so it continued. I never understood what rule she was following, or if there even was one. But I waited for her to return and stayed in the palace courtyard, which seemed to attract her, where she might have lived at one time, whether to serve or rule, I did not know.

The only thing for sure was that she would have an animal with her when she came. The animals followed her, as if carried on the wind and bound to her light quick step. Animals from the woods, a little owl with gray feathers and black wing tips flew silent circles around her, she had draped a weasel over her shoulders like a shawl, and a fox licked the heels of her feet and rubbed its tail across her slender legs.

That is how he tells the story? He's a poet, your Eichmann.

It's his most important story, Ben. He excels himself when he tells it.

And you know it off by heart?

Every word. I know every word. This really surprised me, he says. I could not fathom where the animals had come from or how the desert had created them, as there were no woods in the district, or even anything remotely resembling a wood. But when we lay together, the woman and I, when she slid into my arms and I buried my head in her hair, I discovered the answer. The scent of the forest wafted through her hair: Spruce and cedar needles, moss, the rooted earth, and rays of golden green shimmered across her body like sunbeams breaking through the branches of leafy trees and conifers. I realized then that the forest was within her and so were the animals, and not just them, I thought. She carries all landscapes within, coasts, lakes and plains, the deepest valleys and the stoniest peaks.

A poet, who'd ever have thought it? I don't believe a word you're saying, Shalom. I have no idea who told you that story, but it certainly wasn't Eichmann.

He did tell it to me! Again and again.

Eichmann was a Nazi, Shalom. Not a poet. He forced Jews into trains to be gassed.

During the war, yes. But he was in the district after that!

And he changed that much?

Change? He didn't change. He was German, he was evil. He was just as evil when he was in the district.

The way you're telling it, he was simply lonely, Shalom. So lonely that he imagined a woman who would dry him off with her hair and lie beside him. And whose body meant the whole world to him.

Not imagined! The woman is real.

The desert princess who loved him even though he is evil?

When Eichmann reaches the part I just told you, when he says that the woman had the woods within her and all the other landscapes, too, he pauses every time, Ben. He looks at me like this, from the side, and waits. I think he wants me to see the woman. He wants me to sense and smell her, to recognize that she is all women.

Eve?

I don't know. Maybe. Maybe someone else. One day, Eichmann

said, the woman arrived with a young wolf that stayed by her side
from then on. She carried it in her arms at first because it was
sick or injured, too weak to walk, and when it was able to stand
by itself, it swayed and limped whenever it tried to follow her.
She nursed it tenderly and allowed it to sleep beside her at night,
cuddled up close, while I had to stay away. And she talked to it,
gently and lovingly, kept repeating the same word: Habibi. Habibi,
Habibi, which sounded like bells tinkling. I was surprised and, I
must admit, I felt slightly jealous as she had never uttered a word
before. I had simply assumed that she was deaf and dumb, and had
been content because we would never have been able to understand each other, the language of the district was alien to me and
my own language was alien to her, too.

Habibi. I tried to work out what it might mean. Perhaps it was
just the word for wolf, but the soft intonation the woman used
when she pronounced the word suggested it might mean "little
wolf" or, and here was another thought, "darling." I did not want
the woman to talk to a wolf that could not understand her and
could not answer, I wanted her to caress me with her words, me,
the man she had chosen of her own accord.

Eichmann had whispered German words to her then, as they
lay together, but all she did was smile, he says, and put her finger
on his lips.

Eichmann was jealous? Of a wolf?

Not jealous. All living things must obey a certain order, he says.
There are higher and lower beings, humans and animals, there
are lines drawn that must not be breached. The wolf didn't stick
to them. It laid claim to the woman, Eichmann says, guarded her
and would not let me come near, not during the day and not at
night. The woman let it have its way, but this was too much for

me, Eichmann says. And then one day his anger got the better of him, he says, and he lost his temper. The wolf had followed him to an outer wing of the palace, had growled at the door and bared its teeth. So he kicked it with his boot, not a hard kick, he says, though it was aggressive. But the wolf fell to the ground and ceased to move, lying lifeless on the dark stone tiles, which were covered in a thin layer of sand. And suddenly the woman was in the room, Eichmann says, kneeling beside the animal, whispering "Habibi," covering its eyes with kisses. He says her lament sounded like a call, the cry of man to his fellow animals, a raw endless tone that grew and wavered. Maybe it was the lament of life, I thought, and that thought cut me to the quick, maybe life itself was lamenting within this woman, the lament for a lone wolf and thus for all living things that had failed to achieve their goals, or come into their own. I had become the tool of doom, he says. He left the woman with the wolf, saddled the gray, and rode away.

And that's the end of the story?

No, Ben. The story isn't over.

We've heard enough, Shalom.

Don't you want to know why Eichmann left the district in the end?

I don't, how about you, Moshe?

I didn't either. The pathos of the last sentences was clanging in my ears. Life's lament! Tools of doom! That sounded like Eichmann. Was it Eichmann? Who told Nagar that story?

No Tears

One month after the condemned man said
goodbye to his wife, the appeals court
announces its verdict. Among the small
audience in the Beit Ha'am is the Reverend
William Lovell Hull, a Canadian preacher
who is trying to save the condemned man's
soul. The preacher has already sat opposite him in the meeting room on twelve occasions, together with his wife Lillian, who
acts as the interpreter. The condemned man
speaks very little during these visits;
most of the talking is done by Hull, who
looks like a businessman and offers salva-
tion in exchange for remorse. The man opposite him smiles politely. After the preacher
and his wife have left, he writes; Hull
has already received several long letters
explaining what the condemned man thinks
of the Christian mission. Not much. To
him, the Christian God is too small. And
yet Hull does not give up; he wants this
soul, perhaps the darkest soul he knows.
Delivering this soul would be his greatest triumph. He wants to defy Satan himself, Satan, whose power he believes he can
feel through the glass in the meeting room
on each visit, oppressing, challenging, an
exterminating grip that must be disarmed

by the gentle spirit of evangelism. If only
there were enough time.

Today, too, Hull sees the man behind
glass, but here in the courtroom he does
not give anything away, he looks pale and
tired. The five judges enter, the chairman opens the session, then the verdict is
read. The judges take it in turns to read,
each one reading faster than his predeces-
sor, they race through the text, the final
word has already been read, the appeal
denied, the verdict of the District Court
is confirmed on all counts. The session is
closed, the judges leave the room.

The hastiness strikes Hull as indecent.
Such an abrupt ending, he writes in his
book "The Struggle for a Soul," cannot be
reconciled with the severity of the decision, and neither can the speed at which the
verdict was read. A situation such as this
one requires composure, he believes, a solemn rhythm, loaded pauses. He is equally
unimpressed by the behavior of the public;
when leaving the room, the people beam as
though they were coming out of the cinema.
They could not be expected to shed tears,
writes the preacher. But perhaps there could
have been even the slightest hint that the
matter was being taken seriously.

The people in this country do not want

such seriousness anymore, no burdens, no
grief. In the four months since the verdict and the telephone survey that followed,
the mood has shifted. People want an end, a
beginning. A death. As soon as possible.

The prison director is tasked with carrying out the necessary preparations for the
death. For a while now he has had an English manual on his desk: "British Judicial
Hanging." The director has studied the book
thoroughly and has made his initial plans.
He will have to improvise; this country is
not set up for executions. The walk to the
gallows must be short, it is inconceivable that they would lead the condemned man
through the nine doors, across the courtyard, from one floor to the next. The director decides to have a hole knocked through
the wall of the meeting room, leaving just
one landing and one corridor to cross. The
gallows, a simple wooden construction with
a hook in the middle, will be set up in the
unused room at the end of the corridor—the
wood has already been ordered. Beneath this
room is a storeroom, where they will be able
to take the body from the rope. They will
make a hole in the floor for the trapdoor, a
square iron plate.
    For the hundredth time the director

studies the book's Official Table of Drops,
which shows how far the condemned man must
fall in relation to his weight. He has done
a few provisional sums to calculate the
length of the rope. The Manila hemp rope
recommended by the manual is not available.
They will somehow have to strengthen the
rope they do have to hand. Or make a double
loop.

The director puts down his pen, massages
his temples, looks out of the window. Double barbed-wire fence, unnecessarily high,
with trestles every few meters on which
searchlights are mounted. Behind the fence
is a narrow access road with open land on
either side. Even this area is patrolled
by guards. The director wants to go to the
mountains when this is all over. He does
not want to see anyone, either alive or
dead. Vineyards, perhaps. Or perhaps simply
the sky.

At the same time, in another block of
the prison, the condemned man's guards are
called together, twenty-two seasoned men.
The commander stands at the door, hands
behind his back, rocking on the balls of
his feet. If he were not in uniform, he
would take off his jacket and roll up his
shirt sleeves. When the men have gathered
around he makes a short speech, ending

with the question of who would be willing
to carry out the death sentence. Twenty-one
hands shoot into the air. Only Nagar does
not want to. The commander draws lots. The
lot falls to Nagar.

An Eye for an Eye

After his appeal has been rejected once
and for all, the condemned man submits an
appeal for mercy to the president Yitzhak
Ben-Zvi. The wording is not known; it is
said to have consisted of four handwritten pages, composed by the condemned man
following strict instructions from the
defense.

What would he have written if he had not
been forced to follow legal guidelines?
Would he have begged for his life, appealed
to the power of forgiveness, talked about
his six-year-old son who needs a father?

That is not his style. He does not think
like that. Individual people do not interest him, they have nothing to do with
him. He talks only about what he calls
the matters, the affairs. Evacuation matters, transport affairs. For them he would
have asked for mercy, perhaps even demanded
mercy. I believe I have the right, Mr. President, he would have written, to suggest
that these matters have been sentenced to
death along with me. They will die without
having been resolved. Because, I must reit-
erate, a guilty verdict for me will not help
secure an understanding of these matters.

Perhaps he would also have used the word

truth, explained that without him, without
the statements he is yet to make, the truth
would remain unsaid, unheard. Had the three
judges at the District Court not called
the extermination a secret? He—and only
he—could reveal this secret and he would do
so if they let him. I ask you to give me the
chance, even after the confirmation of my
death sentence, to make a detailed statement
on the concrete matters with no yes or no,
otherwise this confusing mess will never
be explained, Mr. President, he would have
written.

Haunted, Ben-Zvi would have followed the
structure of this statement, at first gram-
matically confused, then semantically disturbed. With no yes or no, what does that
mean, he would have mused, how does he want
to make a statement without saying yes or
no? After all, making a statement means
to say what is and what is not, what happens and what does not. Do you not have to
accept or deny, agree, reject? I must, Ben-
Zvi would have thought. I, the president,
must give a yes or a no. Either, or.

What I say will define me; at the end of
the day I am the man who said no, the man
who said yes.

Perhaps the president would have taken a
deep breath at this thought, staring with

unseeing eyes at the pages in front of him,
on which the sentences had transformed into
waves seeking the shore. Bit by bit the
eyes of the president would have returned
to this country, this city, this building,
this room, bit by bit the waves would have
congealed into words, syllables, letters.
Ben-Zvi would have been haunted by this
handwriting, these wide, low arcs, brought
up high and taken down again, decisive and
solicitous, at once authoritative and sub-
servient. The writing of a man with no yes
or no.

Perhaps the president would have sensed
that this writing is an echo, a reverbera-
tion of the condemned man's existence during
the years of the Reich. Living and acting
in a swirling no-man's-land, a crack that
tore through reality and severed everything
to which binary logic could be applied.
Right, wrong, good, bad, these simple
options no longer represented anything
in this condemned man's no-man's-land.
Instead—orders, obedience, enforcement,
a language that only knows the imperative, the sheer will, that in the end wants
itself. A will devoid of humanity, in which
commands command and obedience obeys.

An appeal for mercy, in this language?
It is possible the meaning of these words

would have escaped the president. Mercy.
Perhaps he would have remained sitting at
his desk, still, silenced.

That is not what happened. Another
text lies in front of the president. His
thoughts go in a different direction, as he
withdraws into the silence of his office.
He stays there for hours, four pages in
front of him that weigh more heavily than a
life, more lightly than millions of deaths.
The president writes a single sentence during these hours, on the first sheet of the
appeal, a verse from the book of Samuel:

As the sword hath made women childless, so
shall thy mother be childless among women.

I gave this chapter to Ben to read. I knew he was interested in Yitzhak Ben-Zvi. More than in Eichmann. As usual, Ben took the pages to the window, as usual he read slowly, mumbling the sentences to himself, as if he physically needed to taste them. Finally, he shuffled the pages back together and put them on my desk. Then he dug around in his pockets, pulled out his wallet, fumbled in the section for paper money. I didn't understand until he held out a hundred-shekel bill so that I could look straight at the person portrayed on it. Ben-Zvi. A grainy photo against a background with small colored squares, showing strong features beneath a straight high forehead, despite the blur. I'd seen it so many times, but only now did I notice that Ben had the same chin, the same nose.

Why show me that bill? Because you look like him?

How could I ever look like him, Moshe! He was a great man. Do you know that he and his family lived in a shack? When he became president, they wanted him to move but he refused. He stayed living there. Anyone who wanted to see him had to enter the hut. He was a man of austerity.

Ben looked at the money again and then put it away.

He didn't speak on the way to the meeting place, something was bothering him. When we got there, he pushed me over to the wooden table, but instead of tending to the fire and making tea, he stayed standing beside me. You think Ben-Zvi didn't know about mercy?

Of course he did, Ben. But I can imagine Eichmann tested his definitions. He tests all definitions because he rejects yes and no. For himself. For others. It's catching.

Not for me, Moshe.

If you'd been in Ben-Zvi's position you'd have been infected by his way of thinking, too. Mercy is not a law. You must obey the law, you don't need to think about it, you don't have to decide. Mercy isn't like that. Either you grant it or you don't. Yes or no. When you grant it, you give someone something he is no longer entitled to by right. Freedom, for example. Or his life. Someone has forfeited his right to live, and now he comes to you and asks you to pardon him. Why should you? You need to think about it.

Don't you question your heart?

No, Ben. Your heart doesn't understand mercy. Mercy needs reasons.

What are you talking about?

Nagar had arrived, humming so quietly that we hadn't noticed him.

We're talking about mercy, Shalom.

Why?

Moshe wrote about the president. He was asked to waive the death sentence. Eichmann asked him to do it.

And what did he say?

Eichmann?

The president!

He wrote one sentence. As the sword hath made women child-less, so shall thy mother be childless among women.

You see, the president understood.

What?

That Eichmann is Amalek. You know the verses, Ben.

We all know them, Shalom. Isn't the story read aloud on each Shabbat before Purim?

Samuel said unto Saul: Thus saith the Lord of hosts, I remember that which Amalek did to Israel, how he laid wait for him in the way, when he came up from Egypt. Now go and smite Amalek, and utterly destroy all that they have, and spare them not; but slay both man and woman, infant and suckling, ox and sheep, camel and ass.

And Saul smote the Amalekites from Havilah until Shur that is over against Egypt. And he took Agag the king of the Amalekites alive and spared Agag. Then came the word of the Lord unto Samuel, saying it repenteth me that I have set up Saul to be king: For he is turned back from following me, and hath not performed my commandments. And it grieved Samuel; and he cried unto the Lord all night. Samuel rose early to meet Saul in the morning and Samuel said the Lord anointed thee king over Israel. And the Lord sent thee on a journey, and said: Go and utterly destroy the sinners, the Amalekites, and fight against them until they be consumed. Wherefore then didst thou not obey the voice of the Lord?

And Saul said unto Samuel, I have sinned: Now therefore, I pray thee, pardon my sin, and turn again with me, that I may worship the Lord. And Samuel said unto Saul: I will not return with thee. For thou hast rejected the word of the Lord, and the Lord hath rejected thee from being king over Israel.

Then said Samuel: Bring ye hither to me Agag the king of the Amalekites. And Agag came unto him delicately. And Agag said: Surely the bitterness of death is past. And Samuel said: As the sword hath made women childless, so shall thy mother be childless among women.

And Samuel hewed Agag in pieces before the Lord.

Ben and Nagar stand motionless, reciting the verses from the first book of Samuel in turn. An antiphony of verses that loosen Ben's tongue to make a declaration of faith, although he normally only ever asks questions. I must remain seated, however, paralyzed and bound next to their empty chairs, must remain silent, because these verses may only be spoken standing upright, tall and humble at the same time.

Now they call upon him, the deadly enemy of Israel, Amalek, son of Eliphaz, son of hapless Esau, who was denied the blessing, the precious promise that Yakov his brother had stolen from him through deceit. Esau wept, so it is written, but there is no record of his father's tears, only the bitter words that the father spoke to Esau as his legacy: Your dwelling will be far from the fatness of the earth, Esau, and away from the dew of heaven from above. You shall live by the sword. What could grow from this other than hatred? Esau hated Yakov his brother, so it is written, and the hatred was passed on from one son to the next, smoldering in each of them just as it had smoldered in Esau. Eliphaz. Amalek. The kings of Amalek. The Amalekites. Whenever they could, they defeated Israel. They were evil, Nagar will say, and we are ordered to conquer them. More pious Jews write Amalek's name on the soles of their shoes to drag it through the dust at every step: Destroy the memory of Amalek from beneath the heavens. That is what the mitzvah says and this is how Ben and Nagar fulfill their duty in their own way. They call Amalek by name, let him rise up in the landscapes and times that he haunted, watch his destruction and his return and the repeated destruction that follows his every appearance.

Remember what Amalek did to you when you went out of Egypt. Destroy the memory of Amalek from under the heavens, do not forget this!

Yes, don't forget to remember, Israel. Remember to forget. What sounds like a contradiction to me, is an endorsement for Ben and Nagar.

In the wilderness of Sinai, Shalom. Amalek against Moses.

Amalek came and sought to fight with Israel in Rephidim. Choose your men, Moses said to Yoshua, and go into battle against Amalek! I will stand at the top of the hill with the rod of God in my hand. Yoshua did as Moses commanded him and went out to fight against Amalek. Moses climbed with Aaron and Hur to the top of the hill. As long as Moses kept his hand held high, Israel was stronger, whenever he let his hand fall, Amalek was stronger.

Aaron and Hur held up his arms, one on the right, the other on the left, so that his hand remained high until the setting of the sun.

And Yoshua defeated Amalek by the sword, Shalom. Unlike Saul, who spared Agag. Samuel had to come, Samuel swung the sword. Then came David—

That was in Ziklag, Ben, in the south of Judah. When Amalek had razed the city to the ground and stolen all the women, David set upon him at dawn and felled him by dusk the next day. He took back from him everything that he had captured, and David freed the women.

And Haman, Shalom, don't forget Haman, the Agagiter.

Did you say Haman? His happiness was incomplete, as long as he saw Mordechai the Jew sitting at the gates of the palace. But they strung up Haman, Shalom. They hanged him on the gallows he had built for Mordechai. That was so.

Amalek's hatred against Israel will never wane, Ben. Other enemies took bribes or were willing to be reconciled. But not Amalek. He follows Israel's trail. For, lo, thine enemies make a tumult: And they that hate thee have lifted up their head. They have taken crafty counsel against thy people, and consulted against thy hidden ones. They have said: Come, and let us cut them off from being a nation; that the name of Israel may be no more in remembrance. We must be like Moses, Ben. When Yoshua defeated Amalek, the Lord said unto Moses: Write this for a memorial in a book, for I will utterly put out the remembrance of Amalek from under heaven. Moses built an altar and called it: The Lord is my throne. And he said: The hand on the throne of the Lord! The Lord is at war with the line of Amalek from one generation to the next! To this day, Ben. To this very day.

He is at war, Shalom, and he wins again and again. Go forth and defeat Amalek! Destroy everything that belongs to him, the Lord says to Saul. He doesn't do so, but Samuel—Samuel did. Joshua—Joshua did. David—David did. Mordechai—Mordechai did. Shalom Nagar—Nagar did.

Ben speaks his sentences as if he has only now truly understood the meaning of this list, he raises his voice, repeating the names of those who overcame Amalek to accentuate them. Nagar reaches for his chair, sits down, and stares at the floor.

You are Eichmann's executioner, Shalom, Eichmann is Amalek; you belong on the list.

Let me tell you a story. When I attended the Torah school back then, after I'd left the prison service, my teacher told me what the word meant: Amalek. He was a wise man. He had studied the Torah for thirty years before he turned blind. But he'd seen everything. The son of Eliphaz, the grandchild of Esau. He asked me: Do you know what he is called, Shalom?

Amalek, I said.

No one knows his true name, Shalom, he said, but he was called Amalek. And do you know why? I didn't know! Amalek is a people "Am," who lick blood, Shalom, he said. Our blood! He feeds on the blood that flows from our wounds, like flies. He comes when we are weak and wounded to lap our blood and so he survives. Then he stands, made strong by our weakness, and opens his mouth to shout the war cry, gushing blood. Then I understood, you know. I saw him in front of me again. Eichmann on the rope, as Merhavi ordered me to lift him up. His tongue hanging out, down to here, down below his chin, all covered in blood.

Samuel cut Agag to pieces, Ben—Amalek returned. Mordechai hanged Haman—Amalek returned. And me, don't I see Eichmann every day, every night? Doesn't he follow me wherever I go?

Eichmann is dead, Shalom.

Do you know the meaning of my name? It means something.

You told us there was a kingdom called Nagar.

Yes, but in another language, I don't know which, Nagar means to gnaw at something. And it means to eat, too. Shalom Nagar, do you see?

See what?

Peace, Ben, gets eaten away.

Ashes to Ashes

Even on that morning, the morning on which
the president adjudges the appeal for mercy,
a stack of lined paper sits on the prison
director's desk. Pages written by the condemned man, delivered by the night shift
guard as his orders command.

They wait, demand to be read and sorted,
if necessary passed on. A routine imposed
on his guards by the condemned man; stubbornly, unobtrusively, authoritatively.
Simply by writing. The papers include letters, notes for the defense, and records
that he has called "My being and doing," or
"Here, too, in the shadow of the gallows."
He has already produced a library, sometimes up to eighty pages per day, the writing on every page stretching to each edge,
certified by the author's long signature.
Line after line in effortlessly flowing
handwriting that bears witness to his thor-
oughness and certainty.

The first page on today's stack is different; the director's gaze is drawn to a
bar, printed diagonally across the page, a
barrier that is evidently supposed to pro-
hibit reading of the text. Heading: Will.
Above the heading is written: Invalid
draft. The text, however, is not obscured,

the director takes the sheet and scruti-
nizes the last will of the condemned man
with a feeling of tension and uneasiness
that he can scarcely admit to himself. A
draft, declared invalid, yet not torn up,
instead sent to him, the prison director;
after all, the condemned man knows on whose
desk his pages end up.

The writing is bigger than usual, the
spaces that the author has left like pedes-
tals underneath each short sentence demand
respect, perhaps representing a deep drawing of breath that shows the solemnity and
heaviness of the author's thoughts while
writing, and conveys this to the reader.

In the case of my death, the condemned man
writes, I ask the following:

I wish my body to be taken by my brothers out of this country and returned to my
homeland.

There, it is to be burned.

My ashes are to be divided into seven
parts.

One-seventh of the ashes should be placed
in my parents' grave.

One-seventh of the ashes should be scattered in the garden of my house in Buenos
Aires.

The remaining five-sevenths should be

given to my wife Vera and my four sons.
These parts should be placed in each of
their coffins once their earthly lives, too,
have come to an end.

In smaller letters, he adds:

This should serve as a reassurance and to
dissipate any fear of death.

This is followed by a justification written in extra-large letters:

Because: Death is no worse than birth, and
thousands upon thousands of other lives
await us.

The prison director closes his eyes, listens to the echo of these final sentences,
which ring hollow and dull inside him.
Sees someone walking, scattering ashes like
grain. Obscuring the light, multiplying
in the dust. Graves open and take in his
ashes, graves that do not even exist yet,
graves of the future.

The director opens his eyes again, his
gaze wanders to the side, compelled, he only
calms himself when he sees the words at the
top: Invalid draft. He turns the page, lays
it face down next to the stack and takes
the second page. This, too, has the heading: Will. The director reads, hesitates,

turns the first page back over, lays the
two pages next to one another, and compares
them.

> In the case of my death I ask . . . to
> divide into seven parts . . . thousands
> upon thousands of other lives.

Word for word the same gloomy liturgy,
sentences hewed as though in stone. And
again, the bar that crosses out the writing, again the note: Invalid draft.

Numbed by the sentences that have sunk
into him, and that he already knows by
heart, the director takes the third page.
For the third time, now. For the third time,
he reads the same words, this will, that
a body be transported to the homeland and
ashes divided for the past and future. The
same sentences, word for word. Only the bar
is missing this time, this time the accompanying remark is missing. This page is
valid. Final.

The director reads, sees the previous
day's date and, at the edge, the signature of the condemned man. The desire to
exterminate the page courses through him.
He wants to tear it, burn it, unwrite it.
But the sentences remain, engraved in his
consciousness. Once again power, again
dominion. Once again this man is making

a decree, giving instructions, he wants to
enforce something. The master of transport.
Transport of a body this time, his body.
Cremation. Further processing. The scrawny
fingers of the director hold on, they
clutch the paper like the scruff of a neck,
he could kill, can, will kill. Will kill
and cremate, scatter the ashes in the sea.
The director stands up, shuffles the papers
together, and places them all, together with
the unread pages, in the safe.

I read Eichmann's will to Ben without rolling the r's, without pausing after a conjunction, without turning periods into exclamation marks. I read softly, to allow the number seven to resonate. Divide the ashes into seven parts; the legacy is contained in seven sentences. He uses our number just the way he recited our prayer.

But why, Moshe?

Creation took seven days, the menorah has seven branches. Perhaps Eichmann wanted to turn his death into his own godless genesis. Perhaps he knew that the last owner of the menorah was a German, king of the Vandals. Perhaps he thought that the symbol of the holy light belongs to the Germans.

Did he hope to let his ashes glow the way Moses lit the seven lamps of the menorah?

I don't know, Ben. I don't know anything. These entanglements, it's as if they can never leave each other alone, Amalek and Israel, not during their lives and not after death. Yesterday the newspaper said: Heinrich Müller's grave has been found. He was Eichmann's superior. The head of the Gestapo.

So?

Müller is buried in the Jewish cemetery in Berlin Mitte. Where Moses Mendelsohn was buried. In the Jewish cemetery, Ben! The persecutor next to the victims. All alike in death, their bones pale together.

Who buried him there? The Germans?

I don't know. Müller died in the final days of the war. That's all we know. Maybe the Red Army shot him, maybe he was killed in an air raid. One of thousands of people killed in Berlin. Too many to bury in single graves. They dug mass graves. There are so many cemeteries in Berlin, but they put him in the old Jewish cemetery in his general's uniform. It's not an irony of history, it's something else.

What do you mean?

An invisible force. An awful necessity?

Or is it just coincidence, Moshe? They had to bury Müller somewhere.

But not there. Not in that place, Ben. Did it have to be one of Eichmann's victims who was offered Eichmann's apartment, as happened to Leo Hauser, one of the few Jews to survive Auschwitz? How many residential areas were there in Berlin at that time? Fifty? A hundred? Hauser ends up in the one that Eichmann had lived in with his family. Two thousand apartments in that area and Hauser is given Eichmann's apartment. He had to live somewhere? I'd prefer to believe in chance, Ben. But it's such a close-knit circle. Think about my father, the persecutor who became a victim and who wanted to be a persecutor again. Caught in a circle. And look at Eichmann. When he starts school, what do the other pupils think he is? A Jew. The little Jew, that's what they called him. Who becomes his best friend? A Jew. Which department is he transferred to when he arrives in Berlin? To the Jewish department. Which race did he admire? The Jewish race. Somewhere he writes he would have made a good Jew. He could imagine that! And he's alleged to have said that one of the Jews he met in Hungary would have made a good SS soldier.

Moshe, stop it. That's disgusting.

Do you know that Eichmann only had good things to say about Hausner, his relentless prosecutor? I have often looked the attorney general straight in the eye, he writes. He never detected any hatred: His eyes look sad, beautiful, deep to me. He must be a good man in private. He liked him! And he even admired one of the judges—Halevi—he goes on about the intelligent-looking shape of his head and his pleasant voice. Cool-headed Eichmann,

Ben, who sent a chill through the courtroom—when he studied his own heart, all he found was warmth.

He was a hypocrite! A hypocrite and a liar. Foul and two-faced, through and through.

He praises his guards, too. They always treat me correctly. Never utter an unkind word. I have never faced hatred, Eichmann writes, and no hint of physical violence. He had the utmost respect for the men's composure.

He cursed Shalom and spat his blood on him, Moshe!

Says Shalom.

You don't believe him?

I think he believes what he says.

You know him, Moshe. You watch him. That was fifty years ago but you know how Shalom lives, Moshe, he lives in fear! Every single day. That fear is called Eichmann.

He can't let Eichmann go, it's true. And somehow, Eichmann can't let him go, either. And Heinrich Müller can't leave the victims alone, while he rots beside them in Berlin. They share the same earth, they share the same worms—

Stop it, Moshe!

I can stop, Ben. But this will never stop! Müller in the Jewish cemetery, Eichmann's victims in his own apartment, Eichmann's executioner sitting at the table with someone who owes his life to Eichmann. You call it coincidence? I say: These are signs.

Signs of what?

Maybe there can be no division of men. People try hatred, persecution, killings, but they achieve the opposite: They create a never-ending bond. Don't you notice the person you hate more than the person you love? Can't you see the person you are hunting more clearly than the one living quietly next door? And you will never forget a person you have killed, although you can banish someone from memory whom you brought into being.

You mean your father?

I mean so many fathers. You are not my son. How many have said that? But no culprit has declared: You are no longer my victim. And no victim ever let his persecutor go.

There is deliverance, Moshe.

If there is such a thing, then only through others. No one can free themselves.

Did you say Kaddish for your father?

No.

Why not?

How could I answer Ben's question? The orphan's Kaddish, the prayer of the son for the dead father, which allows his soul to rise up to the Lord. I had become a Jew, I had to fulfill the obligations. Reciting Kaddish was a part of that. But could I do it? Stand in front of a congregation, allow them to answer "Amen" for a man who had first been a Jew without knowing it and then against his will? Who hoped to annihilate the Jew in him through his son and his son's sons? To recite the Jewish prayer of death for him had seemed absurd and outrageous at the same time. I took my dilemma to a rabbi, told him everything. The rabbi listened with his head bowed, and remained silent when I had finished. A silence that would be followed by damnation, or so I feared. Damnation of the father and of the son. Weren't they both fleeing? One from his roots, the other from his duty?

But the rabbi did not condemn us. *Bera mesake aba*, he said. The son delivers the father. The factual calm of his answer confused me.

My father was a renegade, Rabbi, I said. He disowned his Jewishness.

A guilty Jew is still a Jew, the rabbi answered.

He was a wrongdoer, Rabbi, a persecutor of the Jews!

The evil father can be redeemed by the good son.

But he doesn't deserve that! I cried. My father does not deserve to have a Jewish congregation pray for him.

The Kaddish is not earned by the father, the rabbi said. It is the son's duty. And with those words, he dismissed me.

Why not, Moshe? Ben had waited while I was lost in thought, but now he was getting impatient. Why not? Your father was a Jew, after all.

The son of a Jewish mother.

Then it was your duty, Moshe.

It was, Ben, but I couldn't do it. The rule says: For eleven months you must say Kaddish every day, starting on the day of burial. Two months had already passed before I heard about my father's death. One day I received a letter that had taken many detours before it got to me. It said that my father had died—the date of his death, the date of the funeral, nothing else. I have no idea how he died or where he's buried, whether he was cremated, or if he was put in the earth.

The Kaddish wouldn't have counted because you had missed two months? That wasn't your fault. You could have simply prayed for nine months, or added on a couple of months. Did you think someone was counting?

That's what I wanted to believe.

What saying Kaddish for your father would have achieved can be achieved by living a good life, too. If you live a good life, you can still redeem him.

A Thousand Degrees

The decision of what to do with the body
was made a long time ago. An hour's drive
away, in a city called Petah Tikva—gateway
to hope—a man is welding together iron and
steel. He does not mind working late into
the night or until early morning. He is
even happy to stay behind on his own, alone
with his oven that is slowly taking shape,
after the last shift of welders leaves the
factory. Then he works in silence in the
empty hall, undisturbed by questions from
his colleagues, who must not be told the
true identity of the client or the purpose
of the oven. He says it is for a company
in Eilat on the Red Sea that processes fish
bones. They want an incinerator for sharks,
he says, whale sharks, reef sharks, white
tip sharks; he describes the shape of these
predators, their skeletons, and he adjusts
their sizes, at which he can only guess, to
fit the size of his oven.

Pinchas Zeklikovsky is proud to have
been chosen for this secret mission. He is
an expert in his area, was recommended as
a reliable specialist. The fact that he
is the only survivor in his family, that
his father, mother, brother, and sister are
among the victims of the man whose sentence

is soon to be carried out, was not taken
into account. It is just a coincidence.
Zeklikovsky carries out his work for them,
too. His client's instructions are kept to
a minimum. The design and materials are
up to him; he has only two conditions to
fulfill. One: The oven must be big enough
to hold a man lying down. Two: The burning temperature must be able to reach 1,800
degrees Celsius.

At first, Zeklikovsky thinks there must
be a mistake; ovens normally burn up to
800 degrees. But the number is confirmed. A
thousand degrees more than necessary. Zeklikovsky had wanted to point out the problems associated with such temperatures—the
time it would take to light, the danger
for the men operating the oven, strain on
the materials—but he stopped himself. He
thought he understood that there was more
at play here than technical measurements.
A thousand pieces of silver, a thousand
generations, a thousand victims of Solo-
mon's fire. When something can no longer
be counted, when something moves beyond the
realm of human comprehension, the Ethics
of the Fathers says: a thousand. A number
that represents the uncountable, an oven
beyond comprehensible standards. Built by a
human to fit a human, and yet destined to

exterminate a human, finally, absolutely,
to burn flesh and bones to more than just
ashes. To dust, perhaps, which flies up
into the depths of the sky, to the furthest
edge of creation, where the cosmos is still
no different from chaos.

Zeklikovsky began by making the incinerator, a cylinder measuring two meters in
length and one and a half meters in height.
For the base, he welded together square panels and then riveted three metal ribs around
the whole structure. He attached the oven
door to the head of the incinerator—a heavy
iron door that can be opened and closed
using a lever on the side. To finish, Zeklikovsky built the chimney, three meters
high. He fitted it to the rear end of the
chamber and attached it in such a way that
it can be removed for transport.

Now Zeklikovsky stands in front of the
finished oven. He cannot deliver it with a
clear conscience. He should check that the
chamber can sustain the required temperature, if the seams hold, how close a person
can get to the oven while it is at its hot-
test. Can the door even be opened at that
point? Or should he lengthen the lever?
These are not really his concerns. The order
was clear, the order has been fulfilled. But
Zeklikovsky does not want to hand over the

oven. As long as he is working on the oven,
his dead are with him, the dead whose graves
he does not know, who probably do not have
graves, who have become ashes, blown away.
Zeklikovsky's oven is an extension of their
vengeance. It is justice.

Zeklikovsky takes off his hat and
wipes his brow. This man, who has been
condemned—what does he do in his cell?
Wait? Does he imagine what it will be like
to be hanged? Does he think about the oven,
does he know that his body will be burned?
If he does know, does he imagine the flames
beating at his body, cracking the skin, the
flesh ripping apart, sizzling?

Zeklikovsky puts his hat back on, walks
around the oven, lays his hand on the
curved surfaces, runs his fingers over the
ridges that he has smoothed, strokes the
door, the lever. Opens the door, peers into
the darkness, this night before the rising flames. Soon. Soon he will lie here. A
chain: Zeklikovsky touches the oven that
will touch the body of the man who sent
Zeklikovsky's family to their deaths. He
can forge this chain even more closely, can
feel the incinerator not just with his hand
but also with his arms, legs, body, he can
lie inside it, just as the dead body will
lie inside it. Zeklikovsky holds on to the

door, pushes first his right leg into the
chamber, then the left, forces his broad,
muscular body in afterward.

The opening is narrow, too narrow for
him. He cannot fit inside fully, cannot
get out, either, breathes all the air out of
his lungs, pulls his stomach in, looks for
something to hold on to—that could work,
surely that would enable him to get free—it
does not work. Zeklikovsky is trapped. He
has no choice but to wait.

An hour later he hears a big truck pull
up outside the factory. The driver doors are
opened, closed again, footsteps crunch over
the gravel in the yard, men enter the hall,
one walks over to the oven. Zeklikovsky
painfully turns his head to one side, sees
the prison director, whose eyes fill with
blatant disapproval when he realizes what
has happened. He waves his men over, four
soldiers, who pull the oven builder out of
the incinerator. The director turns around,
gives a few short instructions, and leaves
the hall.

Zeklikovsky understands. This oven should
be pure, untouched. It may be used only
once, be fired only once. This oven is
meant for one man, whose death is to leave
no traces, as though a shadow were disappearing. For him they have erected a set of

gallows in the prison, which will be taken down again once his body has been removed from the rope. For him they have created a hole in the floor of the execution room, which will be filled in again as soon as he has fallen through it. For him they have ordered a new oven, which will never again be used once he has been cremated. And no one else will ever sit inside the glass box that was made for him. Perhaps, thinks Zeklikovsky, they will even destroy the cell in which he sat, will break down the walls, build new ones.

The driver has now maneuvered the truck into the hall, the soldiers have laid thick harnesses over the oven, a crane will lift it onto the loading platform. Zeklikovsky stands next to the driver, who watches the proceedings with a critical eye. Where will you take it? he asks. The driver shrugs his shoulders. No instructions yet.

Somewhere, an Oven

The body of the condemned man will be
transported. The transport destination
will be Zeklikovsky's oven.

The oven will be transported, too; secured
with chains and covered in a gray tarpaulin, it sits on the loading platform of
the truck that has just left the factory
and will soon cross the boundary of Petah
Tikva.

The driver, a level-headed man called
Epstein, has not yet been told his
destination.

He heads southward toward Ramla, where
the prison is, where the final preparations
are under way, where the body of the condemned man will hang, where they will take
him down from the rope. The truck moves as
if it has no driver. Is it the oven that
is setting the course, is it searching
impatiently for its purpose, for the body
that is to come? Epstein, who accelerates,
brakes, changes gear, is just the means.

The sun is already setting. The trees
lining the road have sprouted tall shadows, which lie across the road like railway sleepers. When the truck rolls over the
sleepers, the shadows slide over the hood
and for a moment darken the windshield, the

driver's cab, the hidden cargo. They even
touch the face of the prison director, who
sits next to Epstein with his eyes closed.
Just a few kilometers from the prison the
vehicle slows down. There are posts on
either side of the prison entrance, heavily guarded, on the highest alert. None
of the soldiers stops the truck, the men
nod, simply salute and wave them through,
point them toward the main entrance, where
the heavy gate is opened. Searchlights are
directed at the yard on four sides; where
the beams that guide them through the dusk
intersect, the truck comes to a halt.

It almost glows in the blazing light,
the edges of the oven can be seen underneath the tarpaulin. As though the prison
has finally received its core, a heart that
is already beating but is not yet pumping
anything though the iron veins.

The condemned man's cell has no windows;
he cannot see the truck. Perhaps he raised
his head as the engine sound grew louder,
looked up from the page he is currently
writing, listened and understood. If it is
so, his last will pounds within him, written out three times in the same words. The
three pages lie in the prison director's
safe; the third, valid, sits on top. Whoever
opens the safe now will be hit with the full

force of his sentences: I wish my body to
be taken by my brothers out of this country
and returned to my homeland.

There, it is to be burned.

There, in that place, on the other side of
the Mediterranean Sea, the Alps, in the former Reich, in a town in which the condemned
man was not born, but which he calls home.
There. Not here.

The director has left the truck and gone
into the main prison building. No one
comes, there is no one in sight, just the
truck in the yard and the oven. Epstein
rolls down the window. Is the oven murmuring, tugging at its chains? Probably just
the wind trapped under the tarpaulin.

The prison director comes back, climbs
onto the passenger seat, exchanges a few
words with the driver. Epstein nods, turns
the engine back on, takes his foot off the
brake, accelerates. The wheels spin, the
truck is unable to move a meter.

The oven puts up a fight. It gains weight.
It weighs as heavily as the sentence to
be carried out. The proximity to the condemned man reflects images in the darkness of its chamber, wakes it from its iron
stiffness. Chains clatter to the ground,
tarpaulins fold away to the side, a crane
grasps it from above. The oven glows under

the searchlights, it is lifted up, swung
to one side, set down alongside the truck,
it almost feels the gravel and the chips of
asphalt underneath. But the last stretch
is insurmountable. The ground puts up a
fight. Like arrow splinters in a magnetic
field the flints and chippings line up and
reject the oven. The oven insists on its
gravity, on its determination: It should
stay here, the court sentence should be carried out here! A struggle begins, a battle
between two forces, real enough but not to
be contained by the laws of physics. The
oven as a representative of the sentence,
against the ground as an advocate of the
words in the safe. In-this-yard against
in-my-hometown. Epstein releases the clutch,
the tires grip at last, the engine roars,
chucks out black clouds from the exhaust
pipe, the truck passes the gate, circles the
site, stops again. There are searchlights
here, too, but no gravel, instead there is
roughly cut concrete, more suitable perhaps. Fine, the oven wants to stay here. The
other will does not allow it.

I wish my body to be taken by my brothers out of this country and returned to my
homeland.

There, it is to be burned.

The vehicle starts to move once more,

stops again, moves again, stops, starts
once again, and then once again comes to
a halt. The oven sees stone slabs come
together and move apart again, a seemingly
forgotten tool sitting on top. Small, light
cones on the sandy ground, terebinth and
cypress trees have scattered their fruits;
they remain there, the ground rejects the
oven. Next, the fragrances, green and gold
they blow against it, intoxicating, full
of promise, and yet no place for ovens,
for this oven. It is driven in a wide arc,
northward, eastward. From this country
to my home country. The oven braces itself
against it, all for nothing. There, my body
is to be burned.

The air tastes of salt and the cool-
ness of the night as the truck stops for
the seventh, for the final time. There are
wooden planks beneath the oven, it touches
them carefully, lowers itself down, rises
and falls with them like the rhythm of the
waves.

Each of the seven places has the oven in its
own way—they keep it, are awarded it. The
body of the hanged man was cremated in the
prison yard, says one source. In a building on the edge of the prison grounds, says
another. In an abandoned factory in Ramla.

In a warehouse in Ramla. In a small patch
of forest outside the city. The oven was in
an orange grove near the coast, say others.
A journalist, chosen as a witness for the
execution, writes that the cremation took
place onboard a police boat. Where the boat
was heading, he did not say.

The oven can be seen in each of these
places, on every piece of ground, seven
times over. My ashes are to be divided into
seven parts.

Seven parts, seven places, one oven
that sits in each place, the burning of a will against the force of a
sentence—constellations, how we imagine ourselves to be when we have the freedom to do so, when something happens that
cannot be seen in its entirety. Beginning and end are marked, assigned a unique
index—everything else, the details, remains
open, an empty field, in which people can
plow furrows of fate and resign themselves
to things as they do in fairy tales.

This is not how it was. So how was it?
Perhaps there were not any transports at
all, perhaps no Epstein driving the truck.
Perhaps even the oven is just an image, an
expression of desire, the circle of perpetrators and victims can close itself. In

any case, Haaretz, the daily newspaper,
whose straightforward, reliable reporting is respected, knows nothing of the oven
that was transported. Instead, it mentions
a cement factory where the incinerator runs
both day and night. The decision was made
to cremate the condemned man there. No one
is allowed to give the name of the factory.
But its night lighting is clearly visible
from the prison.

In Petah Tikva—gateway to hope—a man is
welding together iron and steel. Pinchas
Zeklikovsky is building an oven for a company in Eilat on the Red Sea that inciner-
ates fish bones. He imagines he is building
the oven in which the condemned man will be
burned.

Every part of the carcass is used. The meat is filleted, fried, boiled, steamed, eaten, and the rest is processed: The skins are used for fish leather, and the bones, the fish bones, are ground to meal like other bones or simply burned to ashes. Fish bone ash, which is used for something or other. I wonder what.

The question runs through my mind, although any answer would do. It was just that I didn't want to let Zeklikovsky go, the oven builder who had been central to the story for a moment would now disappear. My writing couldn't hold him any longer— my writing had to return to Ramla, to the prison. Back to the cell, back to Eichmann.

I pulled the piece of paper out of the typewriter and picked up a new one. As I was feeding it in, I heard a bang on the door of my apartment, a real thud. I wheeled over to the door, listened, thought I could hear murmuring; muffled, hushed sentences that soon turned into a hum. Nagar was holding his kippah when I opened the door, wiping sweat off his forehead and temples with a large handkerchief. He put the handkerchief back in his pocket, picked up the bag on the floor beside him. I've brought you some lamb, Moshe.

Now he's standing at my desk, he won't sit down. I wanted to ask you, Moshe, I want to ask you.

He repeats his words, he hums and sings them. I want to ask you, Moshe, I want to ask you. That's why he's risked coming to see me; to get an answer. He still wants to ask me something, but the question must have got lost on the way, maybe it was drowned out by his feeling of unease, or perhaps the effort it took him to get here left no room for anything else. He takes out the handkerchief again, removes his kippah, wipes over his head and the back of his neck. What, Shalom? What do you want to ask me? He puts the kippah back on his head and tucks his handkerchief away again. His eyes, which have been dancing about until now, find a focus. He looks at the pages I've written, the sheet sticking out of the typewriter. He looks at me.

I want to ask you . . . Moshe, I want to ask: Where are you writing me to?

Why isn't Ben here? He would interrupt. What do you mean, Shalom? Nagar would have to explain, make it clear what he meant. I can't take on Ben's role, I am supposed to provide answers, my hesitation is a disappointment in itself. But what should I say? His question surprises and upsets me. This is what he's thinking about? Shalom Nagar, the narration machine, immune to any other story, wrapped up in his Eichmann like he's in a cocoon? And now here he is, quivering with unease, feeling sensitive about the papers on my desk, sensitive to my voice, my Eichmann, concerned about my Nagar. No, he's worried about himself. He can't differentiate between the Nagar in my text and himself standing there.

Although he only knows the beginning and two or three fragments, Nagar can feel himself in my writing. Where are you writing me to?

I'm writing about you and Eichmann, Shalom, I answer quietly, but I'm following Eichmann's path, not yours. From the day before the judgment to the end. Nagar—my Nagar—follows Eichmann on his journey.

Nagar nods, but I don't know if he's been listening. His gaze has drifted away; he can't stop looking at the papers on my desk. He points at them. Where are we?

May 31, 1962, Shalom. The president has denied Eichmann's appeal. Preparations are under way. I've just written about the oven being transported.

Zeklikovsky built it, Moshe. In Petah Tikva.

Yes, I say. The reporter from *Haaretz* can write what he likes. I'd rather have Zeklikovsky's oven than a furnace in some cement factory, too.

It was my day off, you know.

I know, Shalom. The beginning of the chapter was already finished in my head, and even had a title:

The End of a Day Off

May 31, 1962, is Nagar's day off. He has
slept in, cleaned his tools, patched up the
wire mesh of the chicken coop. Now he goes
for a walk with Ora and their little boy.
They live in a cramped development with ter-
raced houses, white cubes beneath bright
red, gently inclined roofs, barely a dis-
tinguishing feature among them. The main
street is wide, the rest are all alleyways
squeezed between the buildings. The only
bit of space is behind the houses, room
for a small garden, a shed, a few doves or
chickens. It is enough for Nagar, but Ora
wants to get out of town, as she calls it,
although they barely leave the development
and walk toward the hills, along a winding
path lined with power masts. The path is
dusty, full of stones, here and there a low,
dry bush. Ora is holding the little boy's
hand, Nagar is walking alongside them,
arms folded across his chest, head bowed,
deep in thought. He could not say what he
is thinking about. Nothing is weighing
on his mind, he has no problems to try to
solve, no plans. It is more a kind of waiting, like his mind is on pause but his body
will not follow.

Suddenly Ora stopped, Moshe. She picked up our little boy and turned around. A car was coming up behind us, driving so fast all we could see was a cloud of dust. We moved out of the way to let the car pass. But when it reached us the driver stopped, the back door flew open, someone grabbed me, pulled me inside, slammed the door shut, the driver put his foot down. Out of the corner of my eye I saw Ora's face, her mouth wide open, that's how shocked she was. I was confused, too, but then I recognized the driver, it was one of my colleagues. And the man who pulled me into the car was Merhavi, my commander. Neither of them said a word. There was no need. I knew what this was about.

Nagar tells his story in a different way from usual, sounding flat, somehow distanced from the story. His stories at the meeting place always brim with life even after the third telling, but he just rattles this off as if it's a chore. He's missing his familiar surroundings, missing Ben who always jumps in, asking for explanations, who'd ask about Ora now. Didn't Ora call the police? She must have thought you'd been kidnapped, Shalom! And Nagar could elaborate then, explain, make up another version; he might say that the car had stopped and turned back so he could reassure Ora. A colleague is ill, I told her, they're a man short for the night shift. She wasn't allowed to know about Eichmann, Merhavi had forbidden us to talk about him.

Ben's not here, but that's not all. Something is bothering Nagar. Not the question he came to ask. Something else, something he can't or won't say at the meeting place, something that's hard for him to admit and that he needs to tell me on my own. So I wait. Nagar looks around the room, digs his hands into his trouser pockets, takes them out again, shuffles together the papers lying all over my desk, stacks them in a nice neat pile.

You know, Moshe—I tell you stories, you and Ben. You come, I tell them to you. I always say they are true stories, about events that really happened.

They did happen, Shalom. On May 31, 1962, you had the day off. They picked you up—

The path Ora and I walk along is too narrow, Moshe. Barely two feet wide with stones everywhere. You couldn't drive a car down it. How would they have found me in the foothills anyway . . . I'm describing Eichmann's kidnapping, Moshe. It was him they pulled into a car a few meters away from his wife. It was their wedding anniversary, you know. He'd bought flowers for her, that's why he came home on a later bus. The Mossad agents had been watching him for weeks; he always took the same bus, got out, smoothed down his coat, let the bus drive off before crossing the road to his house. But on the evening they planned to kidnap him the bus came, the doors opened, the doors closed again, the bus drove away. No Eichmann. They thought: He knows everything. He must have seen us, he's got away. They were frantic. Why had they waited so long! They sat there in their cars, discussing the situation, wondering what to do. Then the next bus came. The doors open, Eichmann gets out holding his briefcase in one hand and a bunch of flowers in the other. They realize they've got him. That's how it was, Moshe. He often tells me that story. He doesn't blame the Mossad agents. They did a good job, he says. He knows all about it; after all, he used to work for the secret service. They were called the secret police, the Gestapo.

Nagar fiddles with my typewriter while he talks, takes out the crooked sheet of paper and puts it back in properly.

He tells me so often, Moshe. He tells me, I tell you. Sometimes I don't know who's talking—sometimes Eichmann is Nagar, and Nagar is Eichmann. It shouldn't be like that. You have to write, Moshe. You have to write it the way it was.

You have to write it the way it was. With those words he leaves me alone. When I'm back in front of my typewriter, I can hardly believe he was really here. But the meat is still on the table. The way it was? It could have been like this:

May 31, 1962, is Nagar's day off. He has
slept in, cleaned his tools, patched up
the wire mesh of the chicken coop. Now he
goes for a walk with Ora and their little
boy, through the dusty alleys to the edge
of the development. Ora is busy with the
child; Nagar walks alongside them, arms
folded across his chest, head bowed, deep
in thought. When they get home, there is a
car outside the house with two men standing beside it, both of them smoking. Nagar
recognizes one of them as his commander.
Now the commander sees Nagar, too, drops
his cigarette on the ground, stamps it out,
straightens his uniform, approaches him.
It's time, Shalom, he says. Nagar nods, as
if shaking his head.

No Fear, No Hope

The condemned man does not know that his
executioner is on his way. He has had to
endure a tedious medical examination, the
results of which satisfied the doctor. The
condemned man is ready to be hanged. Ready
for death.

Now he is back in his cell, lying on the
prison bed. Opposite him stands a guard
whom he does not know and does not like,
because he is as stiff as a board. He misses
the small, stocky man. The one with the
trustworthy eyes and the incongruous womanizer's mustache. There are still stacks
of books on the table, essays that the condemned man has spent a great deal of time
working through. Scoundrels, cheats, and
liars, all of them. Reitlinger and Poliakov,
not to mention Brand. He could prove it, he
will prove it, if only they would give him
some more paper. The evening meal comes,
simple as always: bread, sausage, olives,
black tea. He eats everything, as always.

The crockery and cutlery are cleared away,
passed item by item through the door hatch,
which has been kept mostly closed since the
appeals court announced its decision. The
condemned man, who no longer has any hope
of appeal, is to be given the pretense of

privacy, the illusion of being alone. Some
time later the hatch is opened once again,
the guard gets up stiffly, stiffly takes
the key, unlocks the door, and salutes
as the prison director enters the cell. The
condemned man, too, has gotten up and is
standing to attention. The director nods to
him. It is a long time since he has looked
at him. His gaze was always lowered when he
entered the cell, as though the tiles were
the only thing of any interest to him. Now
he looks at him. At midnight, he says. Asks
two or three questions, then asks for paper
and pencils to be brought.

The condemned man starts writing again.
First, a letter to his wife and his sons.
My last wish was to compose this letter, he
writes, to be able to smoke freely, and to
have a bottle of red wine. They have promised to bring the red wine a bit later, he
adds in brackets.

Many people say he drank a bottle of Car-
mel wine, the wine made in the country of
the victims that has been loved by the Germans ever since it was served at the Berlin trade exhibition in 1896. Kosher wine
from the vineyards of Baron Rothschild.
To choose this wine as the execution drink
would have been a special gesture, it could
have been interpreted as a concession, per-

haps even as a desire for some sort of rec-
onciliation. Had the condemned man not
written: I would like to find peace with
my former enemies, too? A desire so absurd
that you might, absurdly enough, want to
believe him.

But it was not so. I have now been given a
bottle of wine as well, continues the condemned man in his letter. They gave me the
choice of sweet red wine or dry white wine.
After brief consideration, I picked the
latter.

So, dry white wine, while smoking one
cigarette after the other. Does he eat something, has he chosen a last meal? It seems
not. He is not hungry anyway, he has no
time, he must write, must describe the
events in detail, provide evidence that
will explain everything. He keeps writing
after the letter is finished; the director
has given him plenty of paper, the pencils
are well sharpened as always. The condemned
man writes and drinks the half liter of
wine—the whole bottle.

His work is interrupted by a final visit.
So once again into the meeting room, once
again talking through the glass. The condemned man is almost reluctant to put down
his pencil, but then he straightens himself, stands up, and follows the guard.

On the other side sit Reverend Hull and
his wife, who is wearing a black-and-white
suit and a small, fashionable hat decorated
with a dove feather. In preparation for
this final conversation, Hull has written
the condemned man a long letter in which he
discusses his vision of man, the history
of mankind, and the great philosophic order
into which everything is integrated.

You say, writes Hull, that man is still a
work in progress and is continually devel-
oping toward perfection. It is a shame that
in the last two years you have not been in
touch with this world. You only need to
look at the world to see the hopeless circumstances that mankind has created on
Earth. Development toward ever greater perfection? I fear mankind has reached the
utmost limit and is about to throw the
world into utter chaos. You say that God
does not get angry or inflict punishment.
In other words, you do not believe he is
the judge of the entire world. You say your
soul will be freed from your body when you
die; you are convinced of this, and you ask
who can prove it is not so? I ask: Where
is your proof that this is the case? Cast
your own ideas aside. Read God's words and
believe. Take Christ as your savior and

allow yourself to be saved. THAT IS YOUR ONLY HOPE.

Yours in devotion, (Rev.) William L. Hull

He is slightly embarrassed by the capital letters now. The sentence is like a faded poster. Useless. It is not about hope now. The man who sits before him does not know this passion. Someone, something has killed it inside him. This man fears and hopes for nothing. No virtue, no desire for virtue, and in this emptiness completely calm, as if legitimized by some higher power. Satan stands tall within him, holds him, drives him, but to where? Hull shivers, then pulls himself together. His headphones crackle. Good evening, says the condemned man. You look so distressed. Why are you sad? I am not sad at all.

We—we are sad because your end has come, Hull answers, annoyed with himself for stammering. He must stay strong! And he has already lost the thread. The peace in this face, this soft smile. Hull cannot bear it. Satan should spit, drool, roar!

If you repent we will no longer be sad, says his wife. Her voice, already high, clangs when she speaks. Are you sorry for what you have done? Are you ready to repent?

I have not changed my mind, answers the
condemned man, with a friendly calmness.
Nor have I lost my inner strength.

When did they tell you that your end is
upon you? asks Hull.

Just now, says the condemned man. They
barely gave me two hours to prepare. They
are rushing it, just like the appeal.

Think of the murderer on the cross, says
Hull. In the last minute, hanging on the
cross, he repented. Call Jesus' name.

Yes, call Jesus' name, repeats his wife.

The condemned man moves his gray-blue eyes
over her. He sees a tightly wound woman,
clad in the armor of her evangelical fervor, who sits as though she is already
standing again, and stands as though she
is already well on her way. But where to?
Not to his destination. Just knowing that
is enough for the condemned man.

Will your husband stay with me to the end?
he asks the preacher's wife quietly. The
woman seems, wholly unexpectedly, to drop
her armor. Her expression becomes almost
warm and she settles against the back of
her chair as though it were a protective
shoulder. Yes, she answers. Until the very
last moment.

The condemned man takes off his head-

phones, gets up, gives a hint of a bow. The
guards escort him back to his cell. The
moment the door is locked, he begins writing once more.

The Walk to the Gallows

He is still writing when the door hatch is
opened, the key passed through, the door
unlocked, and two guards and the prison
director enter the cell. They nod to their
colleague in the cell. It is time.

The condemned man looks up, rises from
his chair, hesitates, and rests one hand on
the table top. The other he raises, places
over his glasses, covering his eyes.

A sudden faintness, the director thinks.
Now the man is feeling the weight of his
guilt, for which he is about to pay with
his life. Now the end is in sight, he finds
he does not want to see it after all. This
faintness is a sign, for which the man has
waited long enough, thus far in vain. At
last there is a human being standing in
this cell, and the director feels for him,
he cannot change that. He surreptitiously
gives the guards a signal to keep back.
He expects correctness and steadiness from
them, but compassion, too.

Meanwhile, the condemned man has sat back
down on his chair, taken the pencil in his
hand and continued writing. Faintness? Not
at all. He simply wanted to concentrate in
order to bring to an end his thoughts, his
sentence, this thing that he is writing as

though driven by the furies! As he realizes
his mistake the director is overcome with
disgust, even hatred. This is no human!
This is a monster.

Again he gives the guards a signal but
this time with a grimmer expression. They
move to the table, one of them lays a hand,
hard and dry, on the condemned man's shoulder. Unperturbed, he continues writing. The
two guards are forced to grab his arms and
pull him away from the paper. Confused,
he looks at the guards; he seems genuinely
not to understand them. One of the guards
points to his glasses, which he no longer
needs. Obediently, the condemned man removes
them.

He stands there with exposed eyes, focuses
his now-swimming gaze on the director,
points questioningly at the prison clothing
that he is still wearing. Where is his blue
suit? Surely they do not want to hang him
in a brown shirt and baggy brown trousers,
and these felt slippers? After all, the
agreement was that whenever he appeared publicly he would be given the blue suit, the
white shirt, the blue striped tie. And what
is this if not a public appearance?

The director says no. He will not be wearing the blue suit.

The guards handcuff the condemned man,

stand either side of him, and enter the
hall, where Reverend Hull is already waiting, a copy of the New Testament, with a
black cover, in his hands. They go through
the hole that has been made in the wall
of the meeting room. The ground is scattered with pieces of stone and brick that
crunch underneath Hull's black loafers, the
guards' sturdy boots, the condemned man's
felt soles. The prison director brings up
the rear.

The five men begin marching, they cross
the landing and enter the long corridor.
Slowly! Slow down! The prison director's
call is aimed at Hull, who is leading the
procession and has picked up the pace. Is
the preacher shying away from the physical
proximity of the condemned man? No glass
wall separating them now, no conversation
distanced by microphones and headphones,
only the sound of footsteps behind him,
growing ever closer. Only the eerie feeling
of having soulless eyes trained directly
on his back, through his back and on his
heart. The condemned man sways slightly,
perhaps that is to do with the wine that he
drank too quickly, perhaps because he was
not allowed to finish his writing and his
final, incomplete sentence is playing on
his mind—the guards drive him forward, the

sentence pulls him back, he must add in the
final period, otherwise these things, these
matters will never be explained.

Halfway there he begins to sway more
severely, the guards brace themselves
against him, the condemned man stands
still. Reluctantly, the prison director
barks an order from behind, the guards grab
hold of him, the condemned man struggles
against their grip. Now Hull stops, too,
turns around, the New Testament raised like
a shield.

No attack to fear: It is only the condemned man's nose running. Without his
hands, which are secured behind his back,
he raises his shoulder as a gesture, points
with his chin at his left breast pocket.
Now one of the guards understands, too, he
takes the tissue from the pocket and holds
it to the condemned man's nose, in a surprisingly gentle way, as a father might do
for his son. As they start moving again a
guard appears at the end of the corridor
and holds his hands up as if to ward them
off. Stop! Not ready. What a ghastly situation, notes Hull later in his writings,
behind me, the condemned man stands swaying
between his guards, he is ready for death,
but the executioners are not ready for him.

Halting actions that seem to follow some

kind of pattern; first, braked from behind,
then from the middle, now from the front.
All that remains is for something to happen from below, or to stop them in the
very last few meters from above. As though
this train should not, must not, reach its
specified destination. Perhaps the prison
director is thinking something similar,
perhaps he, too, has noticed the strange
pattern in these interruptions to the timetable. He gives a word of command that is
intended to banish the ghosts, cut this
knot once and for all: This must be seen
through! An imperative used as a declaration. Forward!

They walk on. The guard at the end of the
corridor who tried to stop them opens the
door. The preacher stands still to allow
the director, the guards, and the condemned
man to walk ahead.

A part of the room about the size of a
cell has been separated off by a black sheet
hanging over a length of wire, a curtain
that swings slowly and then stops. The
sheet, Hull thinks, is hiding a long lever
that sticks up out of the ground. He can
see someone behind it—one man, or two?

There are four journalists huddling in
front of the curtain, here to act as eyewitnesses, as well as the prison doctor,

and some more guards. Fifteen people in
total. Some say ten. Another source says
four. The others apparently stood in the
adjacent room and watched the proceedings
through a pane of glass.

What is certain is that those waiting
tried to keep their distance. None of them
touches the condemned man; none of them
touches the square iron plate in the middle
of the room.

Penultimate Sentences

No one moves. The guards look at their commander, the commander watches the director,
the director stares up at the ceiling. One
of them must take control of the situation.

There are no guidelines for this procedure, but everyone knows how hanging works.
The director knows from his manual, and
the process is familiar to the guards from
novels. Or from the movies.

One of the guards seems to be staring
at the condemned man; a man of the same
age, medium height, with a round, bald
head, glasses with lenses like magnify-
ing glasses, a mustachio. It is not clear
whether the condemned man can see him at
all, he is missing his glasses but perhaps
he can distinguish enough to appreciate
the similarity; the man could be the twin
brother of the officer who spent so many
months interrogating him long before the
trial even began. The kidnapped man confided so much to this captain, who seemed
so gentle, so polite—he confided more than
he wanted to. He had to revise some statements, take them back when he was given
the interrogation reports to look through
the next day. He even spoke of the hanging in the interrogation, explained that

he was prepared to string himself up in
this country, publicly, as a deterrent. And
he spoke about courage, about his desire
not to shift the blame but to take responsibility for the things in which he had
been involved. It is of course a sad courage that I have to muster today, he had
said, but back then I had the courage and
said yes, so today, too, I have courage
and say: Here you are! My head is—lying on
the—there, where it belongs.

Where it belongs: The condemned man takes
two steps, stands on the square plate,
straightens himself up, feet together in
his checked slippers. Now that he is in
this room he is no longer swaying.

As though they had been waiting for this,
the others now start moving, too, they
scribble headlines for the next day's papers
on their notepads, fumble in their coats
for their stethoscopes and mirrors, wind
the crank that will lower the rope with the
noose down from the ceiling. Jesus, Jesus,
Lord Jesus, my savior! comes the voice of
the preacher, who has stepped in front of
the condemned man and calls the savior
with fervor, in the hope of a miracle, a
conversion, a confession beneath the gallows. It does not require many words, no
debate, no justification. The condemned man

must simply call the name of the Lord. Just
this one word. This one time. The condemned
man opens his mouth. But what he wants to
confess requires more than one word and a
larger audience than the deathly pale Hull,
whose message he probably has not even
heard. It is not a poor penitent who speaks
from the plate in the middle of this room,
not a remorseful soul. Instead, it is a
statesman who speaks into the vastness, who
goes into raptures with his own sentences,
which he presents like flags flown at full
mast:

Long live Germany. Long live Argentina. Long live Austria. These are the
three countries to which I was connected
most closely. I will never forget them.
My regards to my wife, my family, and my
friends. I had to obey the laws of war and
my oath. I am ready.

The guards tie his feet with a belt. I
cannot stand like this, says the condemned
man. They loosen the strap. The commander
loops the noose around his neck, a rope
measuring four centimeters in diameter. The
noose is coated in rubber and double knotted; the condemned man must strain his neck
as though in a choker to make it fit. The
commander shows him a black hood, others
say it was a black blindfold. Do you want

this? he asks. No, I do not need it, says
the condemned man. His tone is impatient,
it is clear he no longer wants to be bothered, prepared, interrupted. Because he is
not yet finished.

His eyes fixate on the guards standing
behind the commander, their backs to the
wall. In any case, gentlemen, he says, we
will see each other again soon. That is the
lot of all people.

The guards do not move; they do not
understand German. The commander understands, but he does not move either. Only
the preacher, gripped by a vague terror that
took hold when the condemned man began to
speak, shows any reaction. With his last
strength, which he takes from an unfailing
belief in the inviolability of his delivery, he responds to this lost man with the
New Testament: Jesus. He manages only these
two syllables, he lays them on the book like
a communion wafer, searches pleadingly for
the gaze of the condemned man. The condemned
man does not look at him. He no longer
looks at anyone.

Drop

Ready! calls the commander.

The tension in the room is palpable, solid
as something with its own length, width,
and height. The smell of sweat hangs in the
air; the reaction of the nervous system to
various stimuli.

The guards' sweat is caused by first-
night nerves. They have no experience of
this situation, and no one knows if the
director's manual can even be trusted.
Is the mechanism underneath the iron
plate reliable, will the rope run down as
planned, and as planned come to a stop?
Will the frame of the gallows hold? Should
the British experts have been brought here?
The name Albert Pierrepoint was mentioned
several times in the media; it was assumed
that he would carry out the sentence. But
those responsible had never considered using
an executioner from another country. We
must do this ourselves, was the feeling,
and we can do this ourselves. They had used
a sack for the practice run, guessing its
weight because they did not have any suitable scales. The sack fell neatly through
the hole, then hung serenely from the noose,
but what does that mean? Broken neck? Chok-

ing? A sack does not die. It just hangs
there.

The preacher's sweat is biological disbelief. No human body says: Death, where
is thy sting? Everyone struggles, fights,
rejects this dull denial that frightens
everyone to the core despite all the Good
News. An age-old reflex, the fear shared by
all living beings, which no one can take
from us.

The prison director's sweat is metaphysi-
cal. A consequence of the absurdity that
these two poles, the extremes of being and
nothing, could be short-circuited in a matter of seconds. Not to be borne. All pores
open up, the cold secretions numb the skin
that is warmed by the overburdened brain.

Ready!

The matter is now delegated to the man,
the men behind the curtain. The preacher
has seen a lever. Other eyewitnesses describe
a piece of equipment with two buttons, in
front of which two guards stand. Both of
these guards, so they said, pressed their
buttons at the same time, but only one
triggered the mechanism. Neither knew which
was the real trigger. No one should be able
to say: It was me, I killed this man.

Ready!

The condemned man raises his head, opens his mouth—for one last, his very last sentence?

A click. The iron plate beneath his feet gives way, the condemned man falls into the depths.

It is two minutes to midnight.

Then silence. The self-sufficient song of the dead, monosyllabic, interrupted only by the swinging of the rope and the regular, persistent dripping of some liquid onto the floor of the room into which the trapdoor has opened.

Him and Me

After some time, there is movement behind
the black curtain. Something is shifted,
someone coughs slightly, clears their
throat. The sheet is pushed to one side,
Nagar comes out, blinking, the sudden
brightness in the room confuses him. No one
is there now.

Empty stage. Spotlight. And here he
stands, the small Yemenite, guard, executioner, with shaking hands. What has
he done?

He remembers, recalls each of the day's
events in turn, bringing them back out into
the light, onto the stage.

They pulled him into a car, tore him away
from Ora and the boy on the stony path to
the hills, with the engine screeching they
drove him to the prison, gave him hurried
instructions, charged him with the weight
of his duty. Representative for millions of
victims. Ambassador of a people. Hand of
justice.

Then the walk through the building, the
stairs, the long corridor. The men whom he
passed. His colleagues among the guards,
the preacher, the doctor, journalists with
notepads under their arms, the director
came toward him, hurried into his office,

the three judges who had given the death
sentence sat on three chairs. In front of
the door to the execution room were two
guards whom Nagar did not know. Everyone looked at him, with deference, respect,
perhaps awe—he should have grown under
their gazes but instead he shrank. The door
grew before him, he could hardly reach the
handle.

The condemned man stands in the room on
the plate that seals the hole in the ground.
Nagar is alone with him. No others there?
No one. They were all in the corridor. Even
the commander waited outside.

Nagar is alone with the condemned man.
He looks him in the eye and the condemned
man returns his gaze, for the first time
in all these months. Blue eyes, blue-gray,
eyes that reveal nothing. The soul of the
condemned man is reflected somewhere else.
Nagar sees only himself in these pupils.
The guard, the executioner.

Nagar loops the noose around the neck of
the condemned man, who once again looks
past him, pulls the knot tight, takes half
a step back. The condemned man nods. And
now he says something, a long German sentence, gives a brief German speech, with
raised head, as though speaking before an
audience, his victims perhaps, who have

come together somewhere here, in innumerable
numbers, they need very little space, only
the air that the condemned man breathes. Or
is he talking to his old Führer, reporting
numbers transported, the concluding fig-
ures, the final balance sheet? Or perhaps
he is just speaking to the walls, wants
his last words to reverberate in this room,
wants to know they will be preserved here
for all eternity, these baying words that
sound like polished boots and the death's
head, incomprehensible to Nagar.

The sentence is uttered. But the condemned
man raises his head once more, looks at
Nagar, calm and sharp, holds him firmly
with his gaze. Captures him. You and me,
say his eyes. The shadow of a smile plays
around his thin lips. He opens his mouth—

The commander comes, pulls a white hood
over the condemned man's head, and leaves
the room once more.

Nagar stretches his back, goes behind the
black curtain. He feels the weight of the
condemned man on the iron plate, wears the
noose around his neck, twice, three times,
the shackles are heavy, everything weighs
him down, grows strangely heavier. He can
hardly raise his arm. He looks ill, too,
the light is fading, soon it will be night
behind the curtain. Nagar—

Nagar does not know what he is doing.
Later, he no longer knows what he has done.
He knows what he hears; a loud click, the
buzz of the rollers on which the rope runs,
the muffled lurch as it comes to a stop.

His memory samples images, shows here a
black button that his thumb presses, there
a long lever that he pulls, a stick that he
moves, a knot that he loosens.

Nagar hears the click of the catch on the
iron plate being released, and as the rope
is ripped from the rollers, he feels how the
Earth turns and casts off a person like a
horse his hated rider.

The fall has no end. Two, three, ten
meters, this man falls forever.

The Final Sentence

According to the prison director's manual, the heartbeat of a hanged person takes
around twenty minutes to stop. No heart has
ever beaten for more than forty minutes from
the moment of hanging. The manual recom-
mends leaving the hanged person on the rope
for one hour.

The director leaves his man hanging for
two hours. Some say it was three. Nagar
remembers it being ten hours.

In any case the condemned man hangs
for a long time, feared even as a corpse,
although he is just a dead man being pulled
down by gravity. Someone must brace themselves against this gravity so that the
body can be taken down from the rope. This
task, too, is assigned to Nagar. He goes
with the commander to the storeroom underneath the execution room, palely lit by a
single light bulb.

Nagar does not look; he has seen nothing until now. He hears the commander pick
up the ladder they put there for this very
moment, wood scrapes across concrete, the
commander leans the ladder against the
ceiling opening, now the steps are creaking, the commander is climbing upward.

It stinks in the room, a faint mixture of
feces and urine.

What's wrong, Shalom? Lift him up!

Nagar opens his eyes with his head bowed.
There is a puddle on the floor, he has
already stepped in it. He slowly raises his
head.

Checked felt slippers pointing downward. Dark brown cotton trousers, far too
wide—two men would fit inside them. Light
brown cotton shirt, a dark streak, dark
flecks on his chest. Dried blood. His neck:
elongated, deep grazes and cuts on both
sides, skin hanging in shreds over them.
The noose under his chin, as if it wanted
to take his head off his body, only it
would not give way. Even so, his mouth is
half open, his tongue hangs out, it glis-
tens with something dark, that, too, is
blood, still wet, even now still wet. His
head is tilted toward the left shoulder, his
face bloated, white as chalk. His eyes pop-
ping out. His eyes oozing from their sockets, large, round. Set free at the end, they
looked for the last image they had seen,
searched for it until the very last moment.
Now they find it again.

The commander does not notice this; he
has seen everything else and will note it
down later in his report, which he keeps

dispassionate and factual. The director,
who receives the report for signing, knows
from his manual what these symptoms mean:
The cause of death was not a broken neck,
but a slow, agonizing suffocation. Begin-
ner's mistake. The drop was too short; the
man did not fall far enough. Or was he too
light, did he lose weight rapidly in his
final hours? No excuse. With his hands and
feet tied, he could only fight with his neck
after the fall. How long for? This question
will haunt the director. Years later, on the
morning on which someone shoots him dead
in the middle of the street, he awakes with
a sore throat and, looking in the mirror,
sees that he has bitten his tongue.

Hold him by the stomach, Shalom, with
both arms!

Nagar takes hold, but nothing happens.

Hold him lower down! Lift him up!

Nagar grips him lower down, lifts him
up, the body folds together, face in his
face, almost touching—the lolling tongue,
still wet, even now still wet, the popped-
out eyes!—and now the dead man speaks,
spits a deluge of noises in Nagar's face, a
bloody vocal clump, words, pressed together
somewhere in his throat, cut down from the
rope, now, two, three, ten hours later they
unfurl—the end of the sentence he was not

allowed to finish in his cell? The sentence
he spoke on the roof the day before the sen-
tencing, over and over, because none of the
guards understood him? A sentence meant
just for him, Nagar, a legacy, to spit out
after my death? A curse, a curse on the
executioner?

Nagar lets the body fall, staggers back
two paces, the commander grabs at the air.
What are you doing, Shalom? he asks, irritated. Nagar wants to undo everything. No
dead body should spit at him, sully him
with his blood. Blood is the dwelling place
of the soul, leave it, do not touch it! It
has touched him, colored him, marked him,
on his chest, it covers his face, it is
even in his mouth, which is open from exer-
tion and horror, this blood is even in his
mouth. Who is he now? Still Shalom Nagar?
It is someone else who once again stands in
front of the corpse—grips him by the hips,
lifts the dead body with all his strength,
until the noose is loosened—who stands
there, alone, the body in his arms.

Transport of a Body

Time does not stand still. The commander
climbs back down the ladder, two colleagues
come and take hold as well, a gray blanket is laid out, then the body is lying on
it. His head hangs to one side. His tongue?
Someone has put it back inside his mouth.

The colleagues undress him. They undress
Eichmann. Nagar stands beside them. Shirt,
felt slippers, trousers, socks, undershirt,
underpants, they cover him with the blanket. Someone fetches a stretcher.

They lay the body, wrapped in the blanket,
on the stretcher. They move through the narrow corridor, to the yard, where a van is
waiting. Nagar follows them.

Nagar does not know where they travel to.
He knows only that wherever they end up it
is hot. Bright and hot. They get out, open
the back doors, pull the stretcher out. No,
he does that. Alone. His hands shake, he
cannot get a firm grip, Nagar pushes the
stretcher like a wheelbarrow.

He notices that the prison director is
there. The preacher, too. Here, now he is
here, too. The body falls off the right-
hand side of the stretcher, without the
blanket. The naked Eichmann is on the
ground, it smells like a forest, is that

the smoke? Two men leap over, Nagar does
not recognize them, the director and the
preacher? No, not him, he turns away, holds
a book over his eyes. Eichmann is back on
the stretcher, Nagar pushes him onward. The
heat hits him like a blow, every step is a
struggle, the air becomes resistance. The
body falls off the left-hand side.

The oven, now he sees the oven, behind a
shimmering curtain. It sits on a small
hill; Nagar must push uphill. He knows the
man stoking the fire, his name is Kols. The
heat becomes a giant hand, Nagar swerves,
the stretcher sways. They have laid down
tracks, sees Nagar, rusty iron bars, along
the last few meters to the oven door. But he
is still too far away. How does Kols stand
the heat? He is made of something else. Or
he has already been burned by life.

Nagar pushes, lifts, trembles. Step by
step, his stretcher on the rails, up to the
oven, now Kols grabs the lever, opens the
door—a fiery gullet. The other men who were
here, the ten, twenty men Nagar saw along
the way, have disappeared. Only the gullet,
the rails, the body, and Nagar.

Flames shoot out, slide over the body,
which they do not want to touch at all,
the man lies still, head tilted, the flames
grip Nagar, tap him on the chest, in the

face, lick at him from all sides, a thousand arms, thousands upon thousands.

   Then the door is shut. A hum, as if the
oven might burst, a groaning, a sigh—smoke
billows out from the chimney. Nagar sits on
the ground, the commander stands in front
of him. It's all right, Shalom, he says.
Epstein will drive you home now.

Three

I hadn't seen Nagar again since his visit. Ben hadn't been to see me either, I didn't know why. I spent the days sitting at my typewriter, and the nights in flickering dreams full of elongated necks severed by a noose, and a face that melted in the flames. Sometimes it was the face of my father.

One day, Ben stood at my door again. I had been trying to write the beginning of the next chapter since early that morning but had only managed to type the title:

`Ashes in a Glass`

Are you writing, Moshe?

A question, of course. My friend, Ben. He'll never tell anyone anything. Like why he hasn't been over to see me recently. Or what he actually does on the days he isn't with me and Nagar at the meeting place. He points to the sheet of paper stuck in my typewriter: The final chapter?

What do I know? Is there such a thing as a final chapter? The hero is filed away, his life forced into a circle, it's just repetition from now on, so die: You put a period at the end of a sentence, and turn the following white, empty pages into the kind of nothingness that is often mistaken for eternity, even by the most critical readers. Or the hero finds water in a desert of woe that had seemed infinite, each hope just a mirage until suddenly, a spring appears and turns the white, empty pages into a future full of hope for readers who long for happiness and find harmony everywhere. What do I know?

Shalom was here, Ben.

He came to visit you?

He brought me some lamb, but that wasn't why he came.

Why then?

He had doubts. For the first time, he was doubting the stories he tells. He wanted me to help him. You have to write it the way it was, Moshe, he said.

And did you?

There is no real "way it was," Ben. If there were, you could never write it down. And if it could be written, then no one would be able to understand it. Not even the person writing.

What happens happens, Moshe. When something has happened, that's the way it was. And you can't write that?

No, because that isn't what happens. What really happens shatters. You're watching in a mirror that breaks at exactly that moment.

So you aren't going to help Shalom?

I had no answer to that. Let's go to the meeting place, I said.

We could hear the sheep bleating before we reached the compound. They stood there, nervously banging their heads against the chicken-wire fence. Ben gave them some water, fetched some food. Nagar's apron was dangling from its nail in the shed, his smock was gone. There were tools scattered all over the floor along with several shoes. The whole area looked as if it had been abandoned. The chickens are gone, Ben said. So are the geese. He pushed me past the coops—nothing there apart from a few feathers. He pushed me to the meeting place. There was a brown pool of water on our table and a few nibbled bones beside it. Do you think Shalom will come? He wasn't going to come, Ben knew that. Nagar hadn't been here for a long time. Shall we go and see if he's at home?

Singing interrupted by blows of a hammer. But this wasn't the little song of praise we were used to hearing. It sounded as if Nagar were singing all sorts of songs without finishing any of them. Ben opened the iron gate and pushed me around the house to Nagar's little garden. Chickens strutted through the long grass with geese standing next to them. There were doves sitting on the clothesline. Nagar stood with his back to us. He was wearing the blue smock, singing and working away at something big and square-shaped that he was making out of plywood. Two even bigger structures were already finished. They were obviously going to be used as coops for the chickens and geese. The one he was working on would be the dovecote. Nagar had painted the plywood red and paint had run and dripped everywhere. It looked as if it had been thrown or splashed onto the wood. The sides of the structures had also been painted with a checked white pattern of thin shaky lines. There was no door, just a few holes at different heights that looked as if someone had knocked them out with their fist. These weren't coops, really. They were cages, and there was more wood waiting along with a large roll of barbed wire.

Nagar didn't seem to have noticed us yet, he sang and hammered away, banging in long nails here and there, which didn't necessarily seem to be fixing anything but were being driven into the wood because there had to be hammering. Shalom! Ben called. He had given up the attempt to maneuver my wheelchair through the chaos of wood, wire, and tools. Shalom!

Nagar turned around at last, waved his hammer, banged in another nail, and then came over to us.

What are you doing here? Shalom?

The compound isn't safe anymore, you see. I had to bring them here—the chickens and the geese. I'm going to fetch the sheep later, as well.

What do you mean, not safe?

IV B 4!

What?

Eichmann's department, Ben. His number!

What about it?

It was written on the post where I hang my smock and my apron. In the shed beside the sheep pen.

The post is cracked, Shalom. The paint is beginning to peel. There's no number there.

Yes, there is. Scratched into the wood. His nails are sharp, you know. The compound is going to be his new department. IV B 4!

Nonsense, Shalom! What are you talking about?

He's taking over the meeting place, too, Ben. He's looking for staff. Has he asked you, Moshe?

What are you saying, Shalom? Why would he ask Moshe?

Nagar shrugged his shoulders. Then he started to sing again, left us where we were and went back to his work, to his blood-red cages. Fortresses for his chickens, geese, and doves.

Ben drew in his breath, but he didn't say anything. He grabbed the handles of my wheelchair without a word. Even at the end of the road, we could still hear the hammering and singing getting louder and shriller like a battle cry.

Although these days I think about Nagar more than ever, I don't talk about him when Ben is here. I don't mention his name. Neither does Ben, but I know he's thinking about him, too. Shalom runs riot in our heads, but he is dead in our mouths, extinguished. He greeted us with a raised hammer, he's knocking nails into wood for no good reason, the birdcages are going to spread everywhere, my mind tells me, swamp his house, the whole street, driven by the singing, hammering Nagar; they are going to spread to the edge of the compound, devour everything, the boundaries, the pens, even the meeting place, everything will be daubed in bloody red, decorated with shaky white squares, everything wrapped in barbed wire, until there is no outside left, until everything is cover, fortress, defense.

Aren't you writing anymore, Moshe?

Ben has started visiting me regularly again, always on the same day, at the same time. He's at the door, he unbuttons his coat, comes in, stands by the window, looks out. Has he noticed that the satellite dishes on the neighboring houses are no longer pointing toward my apartment? If he has, it is no surprise to him. He stares out, as if he needs this view, this monotony, the barricaded sky. Sometimes I think that is the only reason why he comes. He stares, turns around. Goes to my desk, leans on it, supporting himself with his large hands. Investigates.

Nothing to check today. No papers, no typed pages, no blank ones. The typewriter has its cover on. Everything I have written has been tied up with string and put on the shelf beside the folders full of newspaper clippings and the books on Eichmann.

Aren't you going to carry on writing, Moshe?

No, I'm not going to carry on writing. He can see that, can't he?

Are you finished?
Finished? With what?

Ashes in a Glass

Those were the last words I had written. Is that an ending?

Are you finished, Moshe?

No.

Why don't you carry on writing, then?

How can I explain this to him? He will ask questions, cut in, object, and I'll say too much.

I'm scared that what I'm writing is actually happening, Ben.

What do you mean?

One of the chapters I wrote before we went to see Shalom was about a Nagar who loses himself:

```
It is someone else who once again stands in
front of the corpse—grips him by the hips,
lifts the dead body with all his strength,
until the noose is loosened—who stands
there, alone, the body in his arms.
```

And what happens? Nagar's no longer himself. He's changed. He stands there by himself, holding the body of Eichmann in his arms. He guides his fingers. Makes him scratch his sign on the post.

You told me what happens shatters, Moshe. It can't be written down. If you can't write what actually happened, then how can anything you write happen?

I tell myself the same thing. They are just words written on paper, lying on a shelf. No breathing, no metabolism, no heart pumping blood between the lines. No matter how my words and sentences connect—they will never be anything but text. Reality feels different. And yet Nagar's question lingers: Where are you writing me to, Moshe?

You're right, Ben. But still I can't get over the idea.

Are you feeling guilty about what is happening to Shalom?

I know I'm talking nonsense. I talk nonsense, I think nonsense. Everything is slipping through my fingers. I don't even believe in Eichmann's death anymore.

Moshe!

Nonsense, you see? Lunacy, even. Eichmann was born in 1906. More than one hundred years have passed since then. Even if he had managed to escape everyone, he would still have been the victim of what people like him called natural reduction, a long time ago. But what can I do? I don't see him as a dead person anymore. I see him alive, growing younger, wearing his black boots again, with a whip in his hand, striding through the halls of the Palais Rothschild, which is full of victims who shy away from him. Jews who can't keep hold of their Judaism, it's escaping them, they let it be taken away. They no longer trust in their God, the covenant with him, Jews who falter, who stand with their backs against the wall. And I see myself standing beside them, but not as one of them. As a traitor. The man Eichmann ordered to be brought to life.

Ben has been to see Nagar. And this time he didn't come back with questions. Instead, he told me about it in a few short sentences. Ben, actually telling me something! For the first time. The world is turning upside down.

Nagar hasn't stopped building those pens, Ben says. He has made more. They take up all the space in his garden now. One cage even sticks out past the house and you can see it from the road, it's painted black. But he has also dismantled some of the pens. Ora doesn't know what to do, Moshe. Shalom has started going to the compound again. To see the sheep.

Ben pushes me to the meeting place. Nagar is nowhere to be seen. Ben makes tea. Takes three pears from his coat pocket. Cuts them in two and puts the pieces beside our cups. We don't talk much. Just a few words about the weather. It's been too dry, it would be good to have a few days of rain. We notice that someone has wiped the table and swept the floor. We look up suddenly at the same time and see him.

Nagar is standing a few feet away from the sheep pen. He's got his suitcase with him. He wipes the sweat from his brow with his sleeve. He turns around once more. His eyes scour the hill lined with cypresses and palm trees and the dilapidated shed in front of it, the corrugated iron fences.

Everything is as it should be. Nagar goes to the shed beside the pen. He swaps his black coat for the blue smock hanging on a nail. Then he puts on his blue apron, opens the suitcase, and takes out a pair of thick rubber soles, a towel, and a wooden box. He ties the soles to the bottom of his shoes.

He opens the latch of the gate, talks to the animals, holds one back, pushes the others away. He forces the chosen sheep to the ground, binds its legs together with two ties. Then he heaves it into the wheelbarrow. Its body hangs over the side, the bound legs stick out. The animal is calm. It stares at him as if it has been stunned. Nagar opens his wooden box. Undoes the catch, lifts the lid, looks inside. He doesn't take anything out, he closes the lid again, fastens the catch. He sits down on a stool next to the wheelbarrow, puts his hand on the sheep's head. He stays sitting like this for a long time. Then he gets up, undoes the ties on the animal's fetlocks, gently tilts the wheelbarrow until the sheep stands shakily on its four legs. Nagar pats the animal and it goes back into the pen, where the others welcome it back. Nagar glances across the compound, sees us, raises an arm, and then comes over. He walks across the square. He walks slowly, putting one foot in front of the other, as if he is walking a tightrope.

My knife is broken, Nagar says. He broke my knife.

Eichmann?

Yes.

That's enough, Shalom! I've had enough. Can you see Eichmann anywhere here? Is he running around, does he have hands and feet? Do you see Eichmann anywhere, Moshe? No? I can't see him either. Perhaps he's hiding? Shall we call him? Eichmann! Eichmann! Adolf Eichmann! No answer. Or can you hear him calling? No? So he doesn't have ears either. Maybe—

Ben—

Leave me alone, Moshe. Does he have a nose then? Shall we fry a piece of meat for him? Maybe Eichmann's nose will appear then. Followed by his mouth. And then the rest of him!

You don't know anything! You know nothing. You don't know him. He deludes us all. Who is Eichmann? Where is Eichmann? Nobody knows.

You know very well who he is, Shalom.

Adolf Karl Barth.

What?

He's him! He's Otto Henninger, too. Adolf Eckmann, Leo Ehrenreich, Alfred Veres, Ricardo Klement, Ernst Radinger. One was a prisoner of war, one was a lumberjack, one poisoned himself, one got shot in the woods. But he was the wrong Eichmann.

Just codenames he used after the war so no one could find him, Shalom. So what? Lots of Nazis did that.

Not codenames, Ben. He is always Eichmann. And he's someone else. But who is he? Sometimes he plays a game with me; he asks me what he's called. I'm allowed to say all the names I can think of except for Eichmann. Eichmann is not allowed! If I say the right one, he smiles, like this, with really thin lips. And then he disappears. If I say the wrong name, he heats up. He burns me, my skin starts to blister. And then I disappear. If you don't know who he is, you'll never know where he is. Before the trial started, they dug out some of Eichmann's old colleagues they wanted to question about him. One of them, I don't know his name, it was something double-barreled, couldn't understand what they wanted. Eichmann? He said it was just a codename, an alias for an undercover operation. They showed him photos; here, they said, this is him. He's in prison in Israel; we are going to put him on trial. The man with the double-barreled name just laughed. I don't know who you've caught there, gentlemen, he said, but I can assure you there is no such person as Eichmann. Eichmann is a codename.

So you were guarding a codename then, Shalom? A codename was sitting at the table? A codename lay on the bed? You tasted food for a codename?

No.

You see? It's all nonsense.

The codename isn't Eichmann.

Well, what is it?

Let me tell you a story. When Eichmann was on trial, the attorney general blamed him for the marches. They happened in the final months of the war. In some country or other. I can't remember which one. But the Jews were to be taken out of that country. But how to do it? There were no more trains running, the lines were broken. So they called for the master. If they cannot be transported, they will just have to walk, he said. Thousands of Jews were rounded up, old people, young ones, men, women, and set marching, back to the Reich to work and be shot.

And the codename?

Wait, Ben. You'll see. Many of the Jews didn't survive the march; it was two hundred kilometers, it was raining, it was cold, they had nothing to eat, they didn't know where to sleep. Many of them died on the side of the road. Eichmann did it, said Hausner, the attorney general. Eichmann ordered the marches, he is responsible. No, Mr. Attorney General, Eichmann said. I did not do that. Hausner lost his temper; he pulled out a piece of paper from the pile on his desk, held it up for everyone to see, and slapped it with the back of his hand. Here, what is this? What does this say, this is your name! he shouted. Eichmann didn't know what he meant, so I was told to fetch the document from the attorney general and take it over to the glass box. Eichmann changed his glasses, lowered his head, and studied the paper. It was very quiet in the courtroom. Everyone was watching Eichmann. Eichmann stared at the document. He removed his glasses, brought the paper up to his face, and read it again. From top to bottom, from left to right. He even turned it over, but there was nothing on the other side. Read it! the attorney general shouted. What am I supposed to read, sir? Eichmann asked. Your signature! The line where you've signed your name. Eichmann looked confused, he turned the page this way and that. The chairman called him to order and told him he must obey the attorney general. So Eichmann started to read, slowly, hesitantly, he took off his glasses, put them back on again, read a few words, commented on them, read a few more, and so on:

A brief recap of the day . . . what is this?

Then I can tell you, I know very well all and sundry were opposed to it.

I know, though I cannot remember who told me. Not int. either . . . no idea, it is absurd.

Not int. at all. Weeks . . . I worked on it for weeks.

The Reichsführer was never . . . what? He never said I was responsible, he never reproached me, the Reich's emissary actually congratulated me . . . on my elegant procedure.

What about Dr. E . . . no idea. E? Dr. E congratulated me for the elegant procedure as well.

Afterward I drank to that with E., schnapps, it was schnapps made from fermented horse milk, mare's milk, I remember because I had never drunk it before.

Great . . . what is this?

Great pleasures . . .

The attorney general had been growing more and more agitated while Eichmann read, he threw his arms into the air, as if he couldn't stand it a moment longer, and then he interrupted him: Just your signature! he shouted. The signature! Your name!

My name is not on this document, Mr. Attorney General, Eichmann said. Hausner caught his breath and the judge looked at Eichmann without a word. I think he was angry, too. Above all, though, he was disappointed. Eichmann noticed and gave an explanation. I am prepared to admit everything I was responsible for, Mr. Chairman, as I have no choice, but in this case, the marches, I must deny any form of participation. It wasn't me. This was no concern of mine, Mr. Chairman. I could not give any orders in this case, I could not stop anything. I had absolutely nothing to do with it, Mr. Chairman, in any manner whatsoever. I must be clear on this. The documents prove it.

The attorney general asks for the paper Eichmann had read to be returned. I fetch it from Eichmann and take it to the prosecutor's table.

Hausner takes the document, looks at it—the page falls to the floor. He picks up the other pages on his desk, stares at them, turns pale, drops them on the floor, one by one. He's as white as a sheet and collapses onto his chair.

The council for the defense, a large, heavy man called Servatius, stands up. Mr. Chairman, I see that the name of the accused doesn't appear on a single one of the documents presented. My client is the victim of a fallacy.

There's disturbance in the courtroom. Judge Landau calls the spectators to order. When things have quieted down, one of the judges intervenes. He is called Raveh. He asks the council for the defense to state the name on each document. What was the name the witnesses had repeated, again and again, with fear and loathing?

I think the attorney general should answer, Servatius says.

But Hausner can't say anything. He is folded up in his chair and shakes his head.

The audience gets more restless. Landau threatens to have the courtroom cleared. Then he asks a guard to collect the papers strewn across the floor. The man comes over, picks them up, and takes them to the judges' table. Landau proceeds to study the documents one by one.

It takes a long time. Occasionally, Landau examines a page several times, while he skims over others or reads every single word, comma, and period.

Finally, Landau puts the documents in order and looks up. Everyone is watching him, he looks back at everyone. All the documents are signed with one and the same name, he says. It isn't the name the witnesses repeated, again and again, with fear and loathing. It isn't the defendant's name.

The audience gasps in horror. People wearing coats wrap them around more tightly, it has suddenly gone cold. Freezing cold. Servatius stands. Would you kindly tell us the name, Mr. Chairman?

Landau leans over and whispers something to the judge called Halevi, sitting on his right. Then he whispers something to Raveh, who is sitting to his left. They both nod. Landau stands.

Nagar, he says. The name is Shalom Nagar.

You see—I was the codename. Just my luck!

Shalom—

No, wait, Moshe. Let me tell you a story. Eichmann used to have a banker, what was he called—

Storfer?

That's right, Storfer, who organized the money for—for his affairs, and later on he bought the ships that were supposed to sail to Palestine. Old ships with broken rudders. They never went anywhere. Eichmann liked Storfer. He looked after him. Then one day, Eichmann comes back from a business trip and hears that Storfer has been deported to Auschwitz. Eichmann gets back into the car and drives to Auschwitz. It's a long journey, it takes him all night, but he doesn't mind. When he arrives the next morning, he walks through the gate and sits down on the first bench he can find. I always stayed by the entrance at Auschwitz, he said. I could go no further. I could not stand all the oven business. The camp commander is informed that he has arrived. His name is Höss: Obersturmbannführer Eichmann is sitting on a bench at the entrance to the camp. Höss has no idea what this is supposed to mean. He goes over, welcomes Eichmann, and then sits down on the bench beside him. They have a chat, talk about German Shepherds and Christmas. Then Eichmann tells Höss that he has come to see Storfer. Höss doesn't know who he means.

Eichmann explains. Storfer is sent for.

Well, well, dear old Storfer, Eichmann says, when the old man is standing before him. This is a bit of a turn for the worse, is it not? Storfer admits that he made a mistake. He hopes everything is going to be all right now. Eichmann shakes his head. I am sorry to say there is nothing I can do, dear Storfer. This is not an official visit, you must understand. It is strictly personal. But even if it were official, I could not do anything for you. I cannot get you out of here.

Storfer complains that he has to sleep on uneven bales of straw. That's hard for me, Herr Obersturmbannführer, he says. I'm an old man, I can only sleep on bales that are flat. Eichmann tells Höss that Storfer needs a decent mattress. Höss sends for the person responsible and orders him to find a mattress.

Storfer complains that he is forced to work too hard in the camp. He can't manage it at his age. Eichmann says to Höss: Listen, I do not want Storfer doing any hard work. Höss calls for a broom. Storfer takes the broom and starts sweeping around Eichmann and Höss.

Höss sends for tea and cake, they drink their tea and eat the cake. Storfer sweeps. When they've finished, Eichmann gets up and says goodbye to Höss. He pats Storfer on the shoulder. And then gets into his Mercedes.

The car drives off. Storfer stands at the fence with his broom in his hand and watches it leave. As soon as he is out of sight, Storfer is shot in the back of the neck. Just his luck.

Twenty-two guards, and one has to go into Eichmann's cell: Shalom Nagar. Just his luck!

Twenty-two guards, and one has to be Eichmann's executioner: Shalom Nagar. Just his luck!

Nagar pushes the button! Nagar is told to take the body down from the gallows! Nagar gets covered in spewed blood. That last sentence written in blood went all over the little Yemenite.

Just his luck!

Eichmann had targets to meet, you know. A number! He was giv-
en a number: ten point three million. That was how many Jews
there were, that's how many he was supposed to dispose of. He
does his sums: How much time does he have, how many trains
will it take, how many carriages? How many Jews can he fit in one
carriage? They started off with passenger trains, third-class carriages, but they couldn't fit enough in, it took too long, he needs
different material, Eichmann said, the Jews need to roll faster! Not
passenger trains, he said, Jews are cargo! He needs freight trains,
cattle trucks, that's what he wanted. They were used to transport
troops to the front, forty-eight men per car. But that still wasn't
enough for him. He reasoned that soldiers carry luggage and weapons, which take up space. Jews don't need luggage. He could put
seventy, eighty, a hundred in one cattle truck. That's what he
did. He was at every station, pressed his arm against the trucks,
and then the trains set off, no one could stop them, and he kept
his lists. Fanatically! He told me himself. My fanaticism, my zeal!
he said, and he is proud of it. The master demonstrated what he
was capable of. I am not interested in the individual Jew, he said!
I am not concerned with small fry, I only register ten thousand
Jews or more. I have to deliver numbers. Huge numbers. And I did
deliver, he says. I operated ruthlessly with exacting elegance, the
transports rolled, it was magnificent. And if anyone tried to put a
wrench in the works, I stepped in. I turned up everywhere. They
had to reckon with me at any time, I was there, even when I was
not there. Eichmann! Was that a name or an order? They could
never tell.

Then the war was over. Eichmann said: I am not interested, it
is nothing to do with me. I have my number. And he carried on
working. On and on. But he didn't ever finish. Then the people

from Mossad caught him, brought him here, and put him in prison. He still couldn't stop. He carried on making plans, writing lists. If he disappeared—then that was part of the plan. He had his quota, the quota had to be fulfilled. He's done his duty now! He is almost finished. There is just one Jew left on the list. He saved him for last. His special Jew, his guard, his keeper. He marked him while he was hanging from the gallows. Blood is the dwelling place of the soul, you know. I could wash his blood from my face, I could do away with the uniform covered in his blood. But his soul. Can you wash away a soul? He has been biding his time. He has stayed with me, never lost sight of me, day and night. He talked! I know everything. And now he is coming. He broke my knife; he is taking over the compound. The meeting place, too. IV B 4, his department. He is looking for workers. Has he asked you yet?

Shalom, he's not asking anyone anything. He can't break anything, he won't do anything. Eichmann is dead!

What do you mean?

Dead, he died, I mean. Fifty years ago!

He doesn't know the difference, Ben.

Who?

Eichmann! Let me tell you a story. After the verdict had been announced, when Eichmann was sentenced to death, a preacher went to see the prison director. His name was Hull and his wife never left his side; she was a slight little woman, dressed elegantly with high heels and a hat and scarf. He had come to save Eichmann's soul, he said. The prison director didn't want to see him. Eichmann will have to look after his own soul, he said. Hull went to someone else, a minister, perhaps, someone who didn't have any objections. Then they asked Eichmann. He didn't want to see a preacher, he didn't have time, he needed to write. Then suddenly he changed his mind. So Hull was allowed to see him after all, twice a week. We took Eichmann to the visiting room and they talked. At first, only Hull spoke, Eichmann listened and shook his head. At some point he ran out of patience and cut off Hull's words. Are you finished? I have had enough, he said, I will not listen to any more. Now I want to have my say. I do not believe the things you preach, he said. You keep coming at me with the Bible and God and Jesus Christ, but I am not interested in what is written in the Bible. It has nothing to do with me. I have my own beliefs. And then he had his say.

I do not believe that God created man, he said. I do not believe that God has a son, and I also do not believe that there is such a thing as hell. I have studied science, I have read many books by mathematicians and physicists. I have gazed at the stars through a telescope, and I have seen the endless realms of heaven mirrored in a well at night. Everything I have seen and read corresponds with my beliefs.

Everything is energy, he said. Us included. We are energy. Energy gets transformed. Something moves, it stands still, it moves again, it stands still. Something heats up, it cools down, it heats up again, it cools down. Back and forth, to and fro. And it is the same with me, he said. Energy is transformed into Eichmann, Eichmann is transformed into energy, energy is transformed into Eichmann again, Eichmann is transformed back into energy. I get posted from one state to the other, he said. Sometimes I have to be energy and then I have to be Eichmann, I cannot control it. It is to do with the greater order of things, the will and the power. This transformation has nothing to do with life or death, Eichmann says. Those are just human concepts. He can be energy and alive, or Eichmann and dead. But there is a secret, he said.

The preacher didn't want to listen to this. He didn't understand what Eichmann was going on about. He kept going back to the Bible, he even brought him one, with passages underlined and lots of handwritten notes. We had to give it to Eichmann when he sat opposite Hull in the visiting room. Eichmann always swiped it away to the edge of the table immediately. It fell to the floor once and he left it lying there. He actually tore up his wife's copy. She often read the Bible and he wasn't happy about that, so he took it away from her and tore it apart in the middle. From then on, his wife either read one half of her torn Bible or the other.

Eichmann wanted to tell his secret, do you understand? But the preacher wouldn't listen. Repent! Repent! he cried, and his wife folded her hands. She had to translate everything. Eichmann and Hull couldn't understand each other, the preacher only spoke English and Hebrew; Eichmann could only speak German and Spanish. Repent! Repent! Eichmann just stared at the two of them blankly. He's trying to tell them his secret, and they won't listen. He couldn't understand that.

And what was his secret? Or don't you know?

I do know.

But you won't tell?

I will tell you, Ben. There is something that stops the transformation.

What?

Ashes. If you transform the human state into ashes, all the energy disappears. It goes into the fire. The flames devour it. There is nothing left to be transformed. The person is gone. He can no longer exist! Like—like a square circle. It was meant to happen to the Jews, do you see? It's what Amalek wants. He gave Eichmann the order. The other leader, what's his name?

Hitler?

He's just a stand-in. The highest German officials talk to Amalek directly. Flammenführer. That's what they call him. Eichmann is Flammenführer's favorite. His Habibi. He whispers in his ear.

Where did you get all this, Shalom?

Habibi? That's what the woman called the wolf in the district. You remember, where the sky is mirrored in the well? That's when Eichmann started to believe.

No, I mean Flammenführer. Where did that come from?

From Eichmann! Sometimes he looks away and talks into the air, you see, when he thinks I'm not listening. He speaks and then he listens for ages. When he's done, he clicks his heels and stands to attention. *Jawohl*, Herr Flammenführer! At your command!

Nagar nudges Ben in the ribs with his elbow. He seems relaxed, almost buoyant. At your command! Herr Flammenführer! *Jawohl!* They're nuts, the Germans. Mad, that's it. He stuffs his two halves of pear into his mouth, then mine and then the ones lying beside Ben's cup. He is beaming happily, with gleaming eyes.

Ben is quiet. He's grinding his jaws as if he were chewing something. Not pears, something tougher. Nagar gets up, Ben grabs him by the arm and pulls him back down onto the chair.

What is it, Ben? I was going to fry us some meat. I've still got some left.

Wait, Shalom. You can fry your meat later. First, you've got to listen. Eichmann isn't here, Shalom. He won't set up a department; he's not going to do anything. He was destroyed! You just said so yourself: If the human state is transformed to ashes, the energy disappears. It goes into the fire, is devoured by the flames. There's nothing left to be transformed. The person is gone. He can no longer exist! Eichmann is ashes, Shalom. You pushed his body into the oven. He is ashes!

Shalom looks at his friend Ben. There is warmth in his gaze, gratefulness and the gentle despair reserved for those we love who cannot and will not understand.

Eichmann is Amalek, Ben. One of Amalek's people. You can't defeat them. Samuel cut Agag to pieces, but the pieces remain—transformation! Mordechai hanged Haman, but the body remains—transformation!

Nagar pushed Eichmann's body into the oven—ashes! Remember the ashes, Shalom! You destroyed him. You are the last in the line.

Let me tell you a story. Us guards were ordered to keep the light on in Eichmann's cell at all times. We had to watch what he was doing every minute. But sometimes we did turn it off. It was very bright and enough light from the hall fell through the door hatch. A small square of shimmering light—like the first streak of dawn. Eichmann always avoided the square, he never stepped on it, not once. He squeezed past it to get to his bed, arranged his slippers in such a way that they could never touch the shining tiles. Then it was the night before—before he was hanged. None of us knew it was his last evening, but he—he could tell. At some point, we turned off the light. The square of light shone on the floor. Eichmann sat at his desk, he was still writing although he could hardly see a thing. When it was time for him to go to bed, he got up and stepped onto the lit-up tiles. It was the only time he didn't skirt around them. Suddenly it was his light; on this last night, it belonged to him. There he stood, illuminated. That was a sign, do you see? He knows he's going to die. Death is on its way. It's the same for all people, darkness, the end. But he, he stands in the light.

Eichmann is nothing but ashes, Shalom. Hanged, burned, scattered in the sea, hounded across the world, dissolved in the oceans, no trace of him anywhere. It's over.

No, Ben. He is here. He is coming to get me. It's always me they're after, you see. I am Saul.

Who are you?

The people spoke to Samuel: Give us a king. We want to be like all the other nations. Samuel turned to the Lord and the Lord said: Follow their will. There is one among them and his name is Saul, which means the requested one. Samuel did as the Lord commanded. He anointed Saul and said to him: You will be king. Only the people knew nothing about this. Samuel didn't want to set a king before them. He wanted him to come from among them. He let them cast lots. They had all come. All the tribes of Israel, each and every one. So they cast lots and the lot fell on Saul. But Saul was not there. He refused to take on his role. They searched for him and couldn't find him. At last they pulled him out from behind some crates and bundles and he stood among them. Long live the king! But Saul, the requested one, didn't want this. So many men, but the lot fell on the one who didn't want it.

You aren't Saul, Shalom. You didn't hide. They didn't have to search for you behind any crates or bundles.

They did. They searched for me. It was my day off. I went for a walk with Ora and our boy. They found me by the hills and dragged me into the car. And afterward, when Eichmann was hanging on the gallows—I hid behind my colleagues. But Merhavi called for me. Come over here, Shalom, he said. This isn't a game. I was dragged out from behind crates and bundles. I've been hiding ever since. Every day. Every night. But he always finds me.

He's dead, Shalom. You're his executioner.

Executioner? The only one this country ever had? I come from Yemen, you know. I was thirteen, fourteen years old when I came to Israel. They'd told us about the war, but not about the other things. Eichmann? Who is he? I knew nothing about him. I'm Salaam Nagar from Sanaa. What did I have to do with Eichmann? They mistook me for someone else—there was someone who looked like me. He was called Yoram, I didn't know him. It's a play. Nagar was played by Yoram. Who was Eichmann? He was somebody else, too. A stand-in on behalf of someone else. The gallows, the noose. Those were just—what do you call that in the theater?

Props?

Props, that's right. The same goes for the body. And the blood! Nothing is real.

The oven, Shalom! The oven was real. He was cremated.

Oven? Nagar blinks and squints, as if he has only just now noticed the evening sun standing low in the sky, shining on us for real.

The oven was made of iron, Shalom. They don't make props out of iron.

Zeklikovsky built it. In Petah Tikva.

You see. So it does exist!

Nagar doesn't say anything to that. He studies his hands, wipes them on his clean blue apron. Not a drop of blood to be seen.

The oven exists, Shalom. Built for Eichmann. Eichmann's body was burnt in it.

Where?

I don't know where the oven stood. Surely you must know?

I wasn't there, Ben.

Of course you were there! You pushed Eichmann into the oven!

I felt ill. Merhavi said: It's all right, Shalom. Epstein will take you home.

Eichmann was burnt in that oven!

They hid it afterward.

Eichmann's remains?

The oven. No one was ever meant to find it.

So it is still there somewhere!

In the prison. They took it to the prison, Ben.

It was below the stairs, they'd taken off the chimney.

Maybe it's still there, Shalom! It must be there. We'll go tomorrow, the three of us. To Ramla. And if you stand in front of the oven, you will know that Eichmann has been reduced to ashes. No more transformations!

Where are you asking us to, Ben? Where are you talking us to? If we stand in front of the oven, you will know that Eichmann has been reduced to ashes. A conditional sentence. Does he understand the implications of this grammatical form? If—then. If not—then not. White or black. That's Ben. He doesn't question the two forms of logic, the basic equation of reality. The world and its telling must surely comply. That is why he asks questions, jogs memories, corrects. And if something can't be explained with words, then it needs to be checked.

So tomorrow we will go to Ramla, to the prison. Will they even let us in? They probably will. They'll do a favor for their old colleague Nagar.

The evening came. The morning came. That wise alteration praised by the priests on the rivers of Babylon in their hymn to creation. No night should last forever, not even for Shalom Nagar, the first and last unwilling executioner, the brave adversary of Amalek. I am still sitting at the table, feeling uneasy, when Ben arrives to pick me up. It is time to go, Moshe, he says.

Ben has borrowed a car for my sake. Nagar wants to go on the bus, by himself. I imagine him walking round his old haunts in the prison before we arrive. He climbs up the stairs past Eichmann's apartment, his knees turn to jelly, he opens the door that leads to the prison roof. Up there everything is just how it was fifty years ago. The barriers are still there, railings lined with sacks to hide Eichmann from view, the path past the railings leading to the square the guards called the sports ground is still there. So is the chair. I imagine Nagar crossing his arms in front of his chest, bowing his head, and pacing around the square, down the side, then turning around, walking halfway back, then across the

square, turning around again, walking back to the start. A pattern
that doesn't make sense. I imagine him sitting down on the chair,
waiting for someone to come and give him his cigarette. Then he
remembers that he doesn't smoke.

Ben parks the car at the prison gate, walks around to the trunk to
fetch my wheelchair, which he took apart for the journey, and puts
it back together. We show our papers, the guard nods, lets us into
the yard, and points us in the right direction. The main entrance
is over there, he says. They are expecting you. Step by step, Ben
pushes the wheelchair across the yard. The ground puts up a fight.
Either the wheels sink in or they get jammed by stones and Ben
has to pick another route. Soft like flowing sand or hard as a rock.
We don't leave any tracks as we make our way, no tire prints left
by the wheelchair, no footprints from Ben's shoes even though he
puts all his weight into the ground with every step forward. We
crunch on, inch by inch, concentrating on the next move.

We don't see Nagar until his shadow falls over us. Ben pauses,
I look up. And I am struck by a thought so sharp and clear, that I
can almost feel my legs again:

You're the wrong victim, Shalom. Eichmann is only following
you as a stand-in. In place of another. It's me, Adolf Schneider, I'm
the one he's after. The traitor.

We reach the main building. Ben is breathing hard, worn out
by his battle with the gravel. My hands are shaking. I can't keep
my head still. A guard meets us at the entrance. He has been
ordered to take us to the oven. Your description on the telephone
helped, he says to Nagar, we found it on the ground floor of the
office building, behind the stairs. Over there, just across the yard
on the left. Then he looks at me and at Ben, who is covered in

sweat. We can go through the main building, he says. This way, gentlemen.

One corridor after the other, light from the barred windows crisscrosses on the floor. As Ben pushes me through it, we slice up the shadows. There is hardly a sound. Just the echo of footsteps. Out of sync at first but then they fall into step. At the end of each corridor the guard unlocks the door, lets us pass, locks it again, and then walks ahead of us into the next corridor. Eventually he slows down. Just one more door to go, he says. Nagar starts to hum, but the creaking hinges drown out the sound as the door opens. I'll leave you here, the guard says.

Behind us, the heavy door bangs shut. We listen to the key being turned in the lock.

In front of us, fitted into the triangular space beneath the stairs, we can see the outline of a bulky object partly visible beneath a gray tarpaulin. Ben hesitates before he nods at Nagar. They lift off the tarpaulin together, carefully folding it to one side. As it slides to the floor, dust whirls through the air and settles on the exposed oven standing there all black and solid. I recognize it, although I have never seen it before, compare measurements in my head, stare at the incinerator, the metal ribs, the heavy door at the far end. Everything fits. But seeing is not enough if I'm going to banish my doubts. Ben can tell what I'm thinking and moves me closer. I stretch out my hand. Touch the metal with the tips of my fingers, notice the gritty texture and a long straight welding line. Ben is next to me. He makes a fist and raps the cylindrical frame once, twice. And Nagar? Nagar is standing beside the oven door, resting his hand on the side of the oven. He strokes it, cautiously, gently. Then he pauses and looks at us, tears in his eyes.

The Lord is my throne, Ben. And Moses said: The hand on the throne of the Lord!

When the guard returns, Ben and Nagar have just finished covering the oven up again. He lets us out through the door to the yard. The oven was pushed and dragged through this door fifty years ago. Outside, the sun has stopped shining. Nagar embraces Ben, then he bends down to me and takes hold of my shoulders, winks at me. For the first time since we've known each other, he grips the handles of my wheelchair.

The guard comes with us. Is the gravel beneath the wheels more even now, or is it thanks to Shalom that we are gliding?

When we get to the middle of the yard, the guard stops. We shake hands, say thank you. The guard pushes back his cap, wipes his brow. Something wasn't right with that oven, he says. The incinerator didn't get hot enough, all the heat escaped. Maybe they didn't know how to operate it, or maybe it had a defect. At any rate, Eichmann didn't burn properly. Only part of his body was burnt to cinders, the rest—I don't know. They scattered the ashes into the sea and buried what was left.

I feel giddy; I can sense Nagar stiffening behind me. I cling to the sides of my wheelchair and try to start humming. Nagar joins in. Ben doesn't join in. Instead, he asks a question.

Buried? Where?

Somewhere nearby, the guard says, and makes a vague sweeping gesture. Perhaps here, where we are standing.

About the Authors

Astrid Dehe is a journalist, translator, and teacher. She lives in Varel, Germany.

Achim Engstler is a university and adult education lecturer and writer. He lives in Varel, Germany.

Dehe and Engstler have worked as a writing duo since 2008 and are the authors of six books in German.

About the Translators

Helen MacCormac has been a freelance translator since 1998 and lives in Kassel, Germany.

Alyson Coombes is an editor and translator and lives in London.

Celebrating 25 Years of Independent Publishing

Thank you for reading this book published by The New Press. The New Press is a nonprofit, public interest publisher celebrating its twenty-fifth anniversary in 2017. New Press books and authors play a crucial role in sparking conversations about the key political and social issues of our day.

We hope you enjoyed this book and that you will stay in touch with The New Press. Here are a few ways to stay up to date with our books, events, and the issues we cover:

- Sign up at www.thenewpress.com/subscribe to receive updates on New Press authors and issues and to be notified about local events
- Like us on Facebook: www.facebook.com/newpress books
- Follow us on Twitter: www.twitter.com/thenewpress

Please consider buying New Press books for yourself; for friends and family; or to donate to schools, libraries, community centers, prison libraries, and other organizations involved with the issues our authors write about.

The New Press is a 501(c)(3) nonprofit organization. You can also support our work with a tax-deductible gift by visiting www.thenewpress.com/donate.